A killer on the loose . . .

An oversized showerhead, like a lime-stained metal-lic sunflower, centered over the wide porcelain tub.

From it hung the nude remains of Katya.

Her hands were fastened high, wrists bound to the fixture with what looked like industrial-strength fila-ment shipping tape; her knees were half-bent and her torso hung in a shockingly stiff posture.

It was a ghastly scene.

But worst of all, I decided, were Katya's eyes: open wide, and fixed forever on something distant but none-theless horrifying.

Praise for *Final Epidemic*

"A NOVEL OF LETHAL INTENSITY . . . Chillingly timely. . . . A tense, roller-coaster ride that readers will find impossible to put down, *Final Epidemic* comes very highly recommended."
—WorldWeaving.com

"AN UNRESTRAINED ROLLER-COASTER RIDE. . . . Merkel just doesn't let go. His writing is sharp and crisp, the action doesn't stop, ever. . . . I can't recom-mend this book highly enough." —*Rendezvous*

DIRTY
FIRE

Earl Merkel

A SIGNET BOOK

SIGNET
Published by New American Library, a division of
Penguin Group (USA) Inc., 375 Hudson Street,
New York, New York 10014, U.S.A.
Penguin Books Ltd, 80 Strand,
London WC2R 0RL, England
Penguin Books Australia Ltd, 250 Camberwell Road,
Camberwell, Victoria 3124, Australia
Penguin Books Canada Ltd, 10 Alcorn Avenue,
Toronto, Ontario, Canada M4V 3B2
Penguin Books (N.Z.) Ltd, Cnr Rosedale and Airborne Roads,
Albany, Auckland 1310, New Zealand

Penguin Books Ltd, Registered Offices:
80 Strand, London WC2R 0RL, England

First published by Signet, an imprint of New American Library,
a division of Penguin Group (USA) Inc.

First Printing, October 2003
10 9 8 7 6 5 4 3 2 1

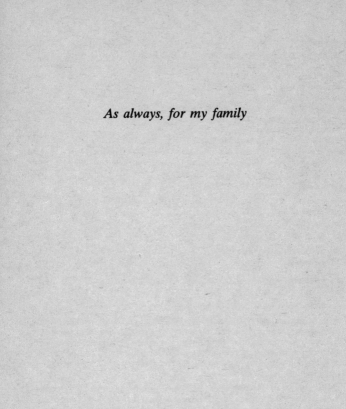

As always, for my family

ACKNOWLEDGMENTS

Bringing a book to market is a dark art that few understand, and that even fewer can accomplish. Certainly, even in this, my second novel, it remains a complete mystery to me. For that reason, I want to thank—no, strike that: I *need* to thank, with all my heart—the following people:

Kimberley Cameron, superagent and superlady, who is one of the few who can navigate the trackless and illogical jungle that is publishing; Laura Anne Gilman, whose talent as an editor is reflected in all the passages that work and none of those that don't; Albert and John and Mike and Julie and all the other working writers whose creativity and energy have helped fuel what I hope is my own; and all of you who read my first novel, *Final Epidemic*, and asked me what other books I had for you to read next.

But as grateful as I am for the help of these people, none of this writing stuff happens, or ever would have, without the support and assistance of my wife, Linda, and my sons, Jeffrey and Steven; moreover, none of it would be worthwhile without them.

—Earl Merkel
February 2003

January 20

Prologue

The truck flashed its lights once and swung out to her left. The slush thrown up in its passing beat against the side of the car in heavy, soggy thuds, and Rebecca Hunt's hands tightened even harder on the steering wheel. The windshield went suddenly opaque, as if a gray blanket had been tossed over it. Then the truck was past, a partially obscured pattern of red-and-yellow taillights and reflectors through the muddy smear left by her wipers. In a moment, even those pinpricks of light were lost in the relentless volley of wet snowflakes—each the size of a half-dollar—that flew at her from the darkness.

"Shit, shit, shit!" she said aloud, and heard the near-hysteria in her voice. She took a deep breath and willed her heart to stop hammering. Once again, she clicked on her high beams; once again, the amplified glare from the millions of flakes only made it harder to see outside the windshield. She switched back to her driving lights and unconsciously leaned forward in the seat, intent on the road ahead.

Winter weather is a fact of life for Chicago-area drivers, and Rebecca had learned to accept the often hellish conditions it entailed. Being sound of mind, she had never learned to enjoy it.

Not even her choice of car allayed the concerns she always felt driving on the expressway. It was an almost new BMW convertible, less than a month from the showroom floor and a surprisingly extravagant vehicle *for one so young. Rebecca had selected it more for the sinful leather luxury of its interior than for any bad-weather handling capabilities it might have offered.*

When she had made the purchase, Rebecca had envisioned herself as she would look in the springtime, speeding top-down along Lake Shore Drive: a carefree beauty—heiress to some vast old-money fortune, no doubt—envied by every woman and admired by every male she left in her rearview mirror.

She had not envisioned herself crawling along a snow-slick expressway, an undersized and insignificant piece of prospective roadkill for the massive trucks that buffeted her in passing. She had not envisioned herself on the expressway at all. Still, it was the only practical route from the trendy Lincoln Park neighborhood where she now lived to the sprawling north-suburban campus of TransNational Mutual Insurance Company.

But here she was, in the inky black of a late January predawn, the object of scorn from faceless Teamsters who rocketed past in a spray of impatience and dirty slush. In less nerve-wracking weather conditions, Rebecca would have felt humiliated. She would have preferred to be in bed at her apartment, even though she well appreciated the secret benefits that an unusual work schedule had provided.

Suddenly visible through the snow, a green sign announced her exit. She almost sighed in relief; the campus was only a half mile away now. In fifteen minutes, she would be at work—a mixed blessing, given the often stultifying nature of her job. In her experience, insurance companies offered little stimulation, and less excitement.

But there was money. Insurance companies deal in great sums of money. Everywhere, it seemed, lots of it coming and going—buckets of money, rivers of money, vast torrents of money. In the three years she had worked at TransNational, Rebecca had seen no small amount of it flowing around her, in quantities that were so large that it first seemed to her unreal, and then unfair.

Despite the plowing by the night maintenance staff, the snowfall overwhelmed their efforts. A two-inch layer of slush covered the driveway that ran a quarter mile to the multilevel company parking garage. As she turned onto the entry road, Rebecca's car fishtailed slightly.

She snapped back to attention and wrenched at the steering wheel. It only made matters worse. She over-corrected, jabbed inexpertly at her brakes and barely avoided a skid off the pavement. The car slid to a stop, angled crosswise to the roadway.

Rebecca Hunt took a deep breath, straightened the wheels and stepped on the gas pedal as if it could shatter under her foot.

Aside from the foreshortened tunnel of light her headlights carved before her, the snowy darkness dominated. Rebecca picked her way along tentatively, grateful for the faint pathway that another early riser had blazed toward the garage. She followed the parallel indentations, trying to match her wheels to the rapidly filling tire tracks.

At the ramp, she rolled down her window, her right hand fumbling in her purse for the digital ID card that raised the garage entrance gate. There was no need. On this godawful snowy morning, some maintenance staffer had taken pity on his coworkers and ignored what Rebecca had always believed was a silly company policy. The gate was already up, and Rebecca barely slowed as she rolled up the slipppery incline. She turned right, toward the lower level of the garage.

One of the advantages of being among the first to arrive each day was the selection of parking spaces. Senior managers and executives claimed the very best slots: those in the basement level, the only level completely protected from the elements and, extravagantly, the only one that was heated. But some oversight of *bureaucratic planning had left a handful of basement spaces unassigned. Whenever possible—and with her early hours, it was almost always possible—Rebecca descended the sloping ramp to park in one of them. They were located on the far side of the garage from the elevator. It was an inconvenience counterbalanced by the secret satisfaction it always gave her to park among the executives. It had the added advantage of providing her with a car that would start at the end of the day.*

The basement level was still empty, the only evidence of early morning human activity a single pair of wet tire tracks that rounded the corner toward the executive parking spaces.

She motored through the concrete parking expanse and turned toward the stairway.

He pressed back against the rough concrete and waited. His hands, clumsy in the lined leather gloves he had pulled on before leaving the car, flexed noiselessly.

The gloves were expensive. The long coat he had donned was not, an off-the-rack brand he had bought especially for this occasion. The tight twill weave was more than adequate protection against fingernails, should that problem arise. Just as important, it would leave little fiber evidence. He had bought it several sizes larger than what he normally wore, and the sleeves reached almost to his fingertips. According to the label, the coat been factory-treated with ScotchGuard, though he did not anticipate an excess of bodily fluids.

He had been confident that his preparations covered every contingency, but the heated garage had been a surprise. Under the coat, beneath the suit jacket he wore, a trickle of sweat itched along his spine. As he waited, he shifted slightly in discomfort.

Finally, he heard the wet tires sing on the concrete floor, noted how the efficient Germanic hum of the engine rose slightly as the transmission shifted into park before it shut down. A car door opened, and there was the slight squeaking noise leather makes when fabric slides over it.

Then the door closed, and light footsteps approached the stairwell.

For a moment, Rebecca had been tempted to park near the elevator. She still had not recovered from the anxiety of her drive, and the relief of having arrived safely rapidly transformed itself into irritation. It found a focus as she passed the empty executive parking slots: the last time it snowed like this, almost none of them came to work.

With difficulty, she fought down the urge to pull into the space adjacent to the elevator doors, the one usually occupied by an immaculate Jaguar.

My luck, she thought, *I'd get towed as well as fired.*

She parked in her customary location, and walked toward the stairwell. Her footfalls echoed in the vast, empty room.

The woman passed his hiding place, so close that he could smell the slight floral scent she wore. It seemed to flood his senses, to become almost a physical presence around him. He looked down at his hands; they shook as if with an intense chill. At the same time, he found his heart pounding madly. All his senses felt magnified, intensified. He saw everything with a clarity unprecedented in his experience.

It was, he discovered to his surprise, not an unpleasant sensation.

He stepped around the door, moving quickly but feeling as if it were slow motion. She was three steps above him now, and he lifted his hands high, as if they were joined in prayer. As he did, his sleeve brushed against the wall. It sounded unnaturally loud to his ears.

And to hers.

He saw her stiffen in surprise, but it was too late. He was already upon her.

January 23

Chapter 1

Gil Cieloczki moved gingerly over the ground, trying to avoid the worst of the ice-coated rubble. He glanced back at me, his expression wordlessly repeating the warning he had given in the car.

It was an unnecessary caution. A slip, I knew, would mean more than just a painful fall: everywhere I looked, a wide assortment of impalements awaited the unwary, the impatient.

It was a surreal landscape, painted in stark tones of blacks and grays and dirty white.

Razor-edged shards of plate glass; steel reinforcing rods broken and contorted by intense heat; shattered brick and concrete: all jutted from mounded-up ice that in places rose almost knee-high. Spray from the fire hoses had frozen on the tangle of pipes that had burst from the heat, their ends jagged and menacing. What once was, by all accounts, a showcase of North Shore architecture was now reduced to just so many scorched and sharpened mantraps. Even the steel-shanked boots I had borrowed from Gil were scant protection.

And, of course, making everything geometrically more difficult was the wind—a hard, flat and relentless rush of frigid mid-January air TV weather reporters like to call an "Alberta Clipper." Firefighters and other unfortunates forced to work outside in the Chicago winter call it "The Hawk," a term of wary bravado that includes no allowance for contempt. The Hawk dared us to keep our heads up, and slapped tears from our eyes when we tried.

Alongside Cieloczki, a short and stocky figure whose firefighter's helmet bore a lieutenant's shield also picked his way, hunch-shouldered against the icy gale, toward the burned mansion.

"We lost this one bigtime, Cappie," said Jesús Martinez, his heavy turnout coat crackling with sooty ice. "We lost it before we even *got* here."

"Yeah," Cieloczki said flatly. "All we did was make a lot of steam. Somebody wanted to build a vacant lot here." He eyed the ruins and shook his head. "And did a damn good job of it."

At the one remaining wall, a thin figure watched us approach. His face was owl-eyed where goggles had shielded him from grit and soot, and he stood with the overly stiff posture that signals extreme exhaustion. A cigarette hung on his lip as if forgotten. He nodded as we stopped, sharing the windbreak of the wall.

"Chief Cieloczki. Lieutenant. I see you brought the cops with you. How's it going, Mr. Davey?"

He did not offer to shake hands. Instead, he took the cigarette from his mouth and waved it vaguely in the direction of a half dozen men, one of whom was holding the leash of a black dog. "Not much yet. It's a mess, naturally. We had to wait for things to cool down, and our prelim search didn't turn up anything. The dog got here an hour ago, just after sunrise. They're still looking."

"Any thoughts, Roy?" Cieloczki asked. "What's your guess on cause and origin?"

"Careless smoking," the firefighter replied automatically, and grimaced at the callousness of his own reply. "Sorry. Bad joke, Gil. When my guys got here, the ground floor was already completely enveloped, and before we even got off the truck we had breakthrough flames on the roof. This one went fast. The house had one of those systems that ring through to Emergency Services automatically when the smoke alarm goes off."

"Arson?"

Roy nodded grimly. "If the log is right—and we got no reason to doubt it—I'd bet there was one helluva load of accelerant in there. We'll know soon. You can't put that much stuff in a house without leaving a lot of evidence around."

Martinez had been watching the dog and its handler. "Directory says this place belonged to a couple named Stanley and Kathleen Levinstein. Any sign of them? Anything to indicate somebody was still in there when the fire started?"

Roy shook his head. "Lieutenant, all I can tell you is that by the time we arrived, anybody who was inside wasn't coming out alive—for sure, not on the ground floor. We got a ladder team up to the second floor as soon as we could, but there was no way to get access."

He stopped, and written on his smoke-smudged face was every firefighter's recurring nightmare: the horror of having done something wrong that cost a life—or worse, the lingering self-accusation that he had *not* done everything possible to have saved one.

"I don't know—maybe somebody could've been in a bedroom on the second or third floor . . ."

Cieloczki reached out and grasped the firefighter's arm.

"Roy," he said, with a gruffness meant to mask the compassion. "Don't go there, son."

"They've found something," said Martinez.

As one, we turned.

On the far side of the gutted structure, the black dog was sitting on his haunches. His tail wagged as his handler squatted beside him. The rest of the search team had gathered around the pair, and even at a distance I recognized the peculiar attitude they struck. It was a not-quite-embarrassed, not-quite-awestruck, fascinated-yet-repelled posture that even experienced firefighters assume when they see what flames do to human flesh.

Suddenly the air seemed even colder. Without a word, we began walking through the rubble.

It was the last case I would work as a police officer. Later that day, I was handcuffed and placed under arrest.

April 10

Chapter 2

There is a perverse psychology to the penal system that to me had always seemed both deviously subtle and crushingly blunt. The placement of what is perhaps its most notorious penitentiary, as I neared its grounds, appeared to cover both extremes.

A few miles outside Joliet, as you approach from the north over the rural roads that wind past sprawling car auction markets and the staked fields of undeveloped subdivisions, you come upon a sight that seems puzzlingly out of place. Dozens of white-and-gold squad cars are lined up in front of a modest-sized yellow brick building. A sign identifies it as District Five Headquarters of the Illinois State Police, whose primary responsibility is patrolling the vast miles of expressways and interstate highways that crisscross the Land of Lincoln. Here, miles from the nearest interstate exchange, so much law enforcement so prominently displayed seems incongruous, a mistake.

And then, almost before you know you are upon it, the massive complex that is Stateville Penitentiary rises up from the prairie as if to pounce. Always faceless, always menacing, the mismatched collection of 1930s-style masonry and 1960s-style concrete construction stands as coldly impassive as a street tough in a stare-down on his own turf.

Civilians driving past unconsciously ease off the pedal and shoot a guilty glance at their speedometers;

parents instinctively use it to quiet children unruly in
the backseat, transferring the sudden tightness in their
own stomachs to a new generation. A few irate tax-
payers might, a moment earlier, have expressed outrage over the apparent excess of armed police support
so readily available; now, on a far more elemental
basis, they suddenly worry if there is nearly enough.

I turned my aging Pontiac onto the long driveway
that runs past the guard booths and checkpoints in an
unbending line. Before me was the main administration building, built of brick the color of dried blood,
constructed back when there was no debate over
whether incarceration was meant to rehabilitate or
to punish.

People come to Stateville for a litany of reasons and
motivations. Most have no choice. Some, a few, come
on their own volition out of some sense of duty or
charity or personal obligation. But once inside Stateville, the effect it has on each of them is uniformly
similar. It is a malevolent shadow, a silent chorus of
violence and fear and hopelessness.

I felt it, considered how close I had come to a sentence here or somewhere much like it. It was not a
pleasant thought.

My lawyer had shaken my hand, though his enthusiasm was blunted by a confusion he was unable to completely conceal.

"Lucky break, that," he said, a little too genially.
"One doesn't often have videotape evidence ruled
inadmissible."

I had nodded, staring through the rain-spotted
courtroom window at a raw day in early March; I was
trying hard not to look like a man either surprised by
an unusual legal decision, or relieved by it.

Everyone involved had played their assigned roles
to perfection. For example, there was the prosecution's primary witness, a veteran Cook County detective. The assistant state's attorney led the man through

a recitation of his background and expertise. But despite years of undercover experience on his resumé, the detective had been surprisingly inexact in his recollection of the bribery solicitation I had made to him only months before.

The transaction had been dutifully recorded by a hidden surveillance camera. Video evidence usually made for a powerful case.

But at that point my lawyer had moved to suppress the recording, on a technicality that had sounded weak even to me. There had been only a cursory objection by the prosecution; as the judge ruled in his favor, my defense counsel was unable to hide his own surprise.

The state had called one other witness, a county deputy who testified that he had known me for years. Now, responding to curiously lackluster questioning from the prosecutor, he testified he could not positively identify the defendant as the man he had observed accept the bribe money.

There was no cross-examination of the county deputy. There was none needed. Without the tape itself in evidence to bolster his testimony, the judge had acted quickly upon my attorney's motion to dismiss all charges.

"*Without* prejudice, Mr. Davey," she had emphasized. "Should the state's attorney decide to refile these charges at a later date—on the basis of *admissible* evidence—that option is open to them."

She waved in the direction of the court stenographer. "Off the court record, and as a personal observation—sir, you are a very fortunate man. Crooked cops have a very hard time in prison, which is where I certainly would have sent you. We're back on the record. This case is dismissed." And she rapped the gavel once, hard enough to signal her displeasure with the outcome.

From the corner of my eye, I noted the figure who had risen in the back of the courtroom, a well-dressed man with hair that showed careful attention by an expert barber. He slipped out the frosted glass door without a backward glance.

I walked down the black-and-white tiled corridor, marching in unintentional lockstep with the uniformed corrections officer who had introduced himself as Orval Kellogg. Kellogg had dispassionately watched me sign the fanned-out forms that absolved the State of Illinois of responsibility should any mishap occur inside the facility. One of the various papers that now bore my name had assured me that, in the event I was taken hostage, there would be no attempt to negotiate my release.

Kellogg was gray-haired and middle-aged, built strong, with a thickness throughout his body that displayed no hint of softness. Corded muscles in his forearms pushed against the starched white twill of his uniform shirt. A set of green sergeant's chevrons on each sleeve had the muted look of many washings since they had first been stitched on. Kellogg's skin was the color of lightly creamed coffee, his cheeks pocked with purplish nodes of ingrown beard.

He also had a look not uncommon here, one I had seen in people on both sides of the bars. Orval Kellogg had witnessed everything imaginable in this place; in some bleak moment of his soul, he had granted it permission to forever fester in the darker corners of his mind.

"The man says he's ready to cop'erate, and the li'l taste he gave up was good enough for your people to want the rest," Kellogg said, in a voice that carried undertones of red clay and kudzu.

"They're not my people anymore," I replied. "Does he know I'm not a cop now?"

Kellogg shrugged. "He knows. Tol' the guy they sent here first he don't care if you was law or king of the fuckin' gypsies—he was going to talk to you or nobody. Says the rest of us could kiss his sweet white ass. His words, exac'ly."

I nodded. It sounded like vintage Sam Lichtman: he had always believed that he had a gift for expressing his every thought or desire. And why not? So many people had always appeared so anxious to comply. Often, it had taken nothing more than a pointed glance to have people stumbling over themselves on his behalf.

Sam Lichtman had convinced himself that he had a lyrical streak, the soul of a poet. But during a long and increasingly violent career, a series of prosecutors, judges and juries had decided that any poetry in Lichtman's soul could not be detected with then current technology. Even if it had existed, it would have been the sole characteristic of his personality that was remotely more than reptilian.

"I never knew we were all that close," I said. "The last time I talked to him was four, five years ago. He skated—a theft ring we couldn't tie him to. He didn't give up word-one back then. What makes him so talkative now?"

Kellogg snorted. "They didn't tell you? He's dyin'." He walked on a step or two before realizing I had stopped dead in my tracks.

"Yeah, ain't *that* a kick? Man's on death row for three years, fin'ly gets his sentence turned over. Lawyer convinced some judge they fucked up on evidence in th' first trial, lets him cop to manslaughter two. He was maybe lookin' at parole in another year, tops. Then, whaddaya know? Man finds out he's got a brain cancer. They give 'im a month or two. Me, I figure he's mean enough to last three."

Kellogg passed the paperwork through the grillwork to a guard, and nodded in the direction of an interview room on the secure side of the steel grate.

"Kinda makes you b'lieve there really is a God, y'know?" he said, with a cold thin smile in which his eyes played no part.

As a species, Sam Lichtman was not unique. Mutant varieties have spawned themselves on the streets of every major city, individuals who used a native cunning and instinctive viciousness to find their own definition of success outside the pale of civilized society. Lichtman was freelance, operating on the periphery of what newspapers tend to call "organized" crime. He had carefully threaded his way through the often complex boundaries, rules and fiefdoms of the criminal underworld. He was considered a solid citizen of his particular universe, paying without complaint the street taxes levied by bosses. In turn, they granted him permission for the incidental warehouse theft, extortion or robbery he engineered in their territories.

Word was that he was available as the occasional button man when an outside enforcer was needed. The fact that he played no favorites on such assignments gave him a measure of immunity among the various families and factions who utilized his services.

In the quid pro quo of the street, this also earned him entrée to many otherwise unadvertised opportunities in his selected field. By the time he went down for killing a Jamaican whose ambitions had included part of Sam's action, there was no doubt that he was one of the more active freelancers in the very active Chicago area.

In the outside world, he had been a sharp dresser, favoring dark, expensive suits and custom-made shirts. When it suited him, Lichtman could display a rough-edged charm that belied whatever prowled the subterranean levels of his mind.

But the people he did business with, even the ones with their own reputation for violence, tended to avoid working a second time with Sam. Many of them, in fact, would cross a busy street if they saw him on the sidewalk ahead. They knew Lichtman as one of their own: a street-smart tough with a reputation for muscling his way into a wide variety of "deals" that had as their common denominator a tendency to turn nasty.

But they also knew him for more, for what he really

was. Few men—at least sane ones—were not, on some very personal level, afraid of Lichtman.

There was still some of the old Sam Lichtman in the convict who sat behind a steel table in the interview room. He still had the full head of black hair, though the temples were now fringed with silver just above each ear. The set of his mouth, lips twisted in a vague, superior smirk, was unchanged. The eyes were still a chilling blue, and they still never seemed to blink when he pointed them at you.

But there were new lines on his face, and an unhealthy pallor to his skin that was somewhere between gray and yellow. It came from something even darker than confinement in a sun-starved cellblock.

Sam Lichtman looked up into my eyes, and raised both his hands in an awkward gesture.

I took it to be a greeting, until the convict twisted his head to put the cigarette into a corner of his mouth. The wrist manacles, attached to a chrome chain that led to a ring-eye solidly bolted to the table, glinted in the room's hard institutional light.

Lichtman fumbled with a book of paper matches until I took it from his hand and lit the cigarette.

"Been a while, Sam. I'm sorry to hear about your problem."

He took a long, pensive drag, and blew out the smoke in a sharp exhalation. "Yeah—well. You know, shit happens. This time it happened to me. Maybe I was overdue, you think?"

It wasn't a conversation I wanted to have.

"C'mon, Davey—now's your chance. Don't you want to know if I've found Jesus? You wonder if I wake up screaming a couple times a night, maybe? You want a little payback for the old days, go for it. Take your best shot."

I looked over Lichtman's shoulder at the raw concrete wall, and pretended to look bored.

The convict laughed, a single harsh bark. "Yeah, I

know. Life's tough all over, right? 'Sides, you got your own troubles, don't you?''

"You know I'm not a cop anymore, Sam. I'm also not a priest, or a shrink, or a social worker. If I had anything better to do, I wouldn't be here now.''

"But here you are.''

"Give me a reason to stay, Sam. What do you want from me?''

Lichtman's mouth twisted in derision. "I want to see a cop, all I got to do is look around,'' he said. "I want to talk about my goddam immortal soul or my bad upbringin', I got people for that, too. You're here 'cause maybe I want to do you a favor, okay?''

"Same question, Sam. Why me?''

He was silent for a moment, in a way that I sensed was uncharacteristic for the convict.

"Remember Hugo Castile?'' he asked, almost noncommittally. "Made man, ran a crew for the Morelli family up by Waukegan?''

"I remember how he looked stuffed in the trunk of his Chevy,'' I said.

Lichtman nodded. "Then maybe you remember there were a lot of people who wanted to see me tagged for it. Bullshit. You whack a made man, you either got a death wish or a license from the top guys. Way I heard it, some people on both sides of the fence had a real hard-on to tie me into it. Word was, you kept it off my head. That the way it went?''

"The way it went, Sam, is that we arrested the guy who did it. That time, it didn't happen to be you.'' I glanced pointedly at the manacles Lichtman wore. "Next time, it was.''

"Uh-huh. They tell you that I got the murder rap reduced? Six months, maybe less, and I'd have been out on time served.'' He shook his head. "This fucking thing I got growing in my brain. It's called a glioblastoma. After the doctor told me what I had, I had her write it down. Looked it up myself in the prison library.''

He took a deep pull on his cigarette.

"Bad shit, Davey. Real bad. There's no cure. Where it is, they can't cut it out without killing me straight up. It's too far along for radiation, and the smart money says not to count on no chemotherapy." He sounded perversely proud of his scholarship. "Can't get the chemicals through what they call the 'blood-brain barrier.' Least, not enough of 'em. So I'm completely fucked, man."

He stared at me, his chained hands holding the cigarette so that it pointed at my face. "I heard about you, Davey—even in here, 'specially in here, you hear when a fine, upstanding guy like yourself steps in shit. You're in the joint, a cop you know gets caught with his hand in the kitty, it's like Christmas, right?

"But you know something? I didn't believe it for a minute. I said to myself, nah. Not my man Davey. He may be wound a little too tight sometimes—now, I'm just repeating what some people say, okay?—but he's stand-up all the way. Even when you were—what? locked up in County a month, right?—hey, I figured it was a cooked deal." He nodded judiciously. "And then your trial. You walk—on a technicality."

His cold blue eyes fixed on me, unblinking. "You used to raise some *serious* hell with the semi-tough guys, Davey. It got to be a contest for some of 'em, how fast they could get you to smack 'em upside the head when they mouthed off.

"But this bribery business, Davey. Must be hard to get *any* kinda job, much less as a cop, when you're carrying that kind of shit on your sheet. Even when it's thrown out, people remember, don't they? Figure there's gotta be *something* there, at least a *little* fire for all that smoke."

His voice became oily, insinuating. "After all, lotta people remember your old man. Acorns falling near the tree, know what I'm saying?"

He waited for me to respond. We stared across the table, holding each other's eyes for several beats longer than what would have, in different circumstances, ended in blood and broken teeth and perhaps a resolution that no judiciary could overturn. Then Sam Lichtman bent forward, took a final deep drag and dropped the still-burning butt on the concrete floor.

"So what are the chances that we'd both be here, two old buddies who both get busted, both get taken outta the game—and then both get overturned? It strike you as unusual that somebody fucks up both our cases so bad that the evidence gets thrown out? Or you just like to call that pure dumb luck?"

"What do *you* call it, Sammy?"

"If you got the balls, I call it your ticket back, Davey boy."

Lichtman prodded a new cigarette out of the pack before him and popped it into his mouth. Handcuffs clinking on the steel tabletop, he pushed the matches to me.

"Light me up, Davey. Hey, how much you know about collecting art?"

Chapter 3

It was after sundown when I drove back to Lake Tower from my meeting with Sam Lichtman. The darkness was soothing, a companion of sorts. In recent months, I had found it to be a presence I could talk with, or at least to. On the long drive back north, it let me ponder Lichtman's story, and his determination to give it to me, and me alone.

I dismissed Lichtman's implied reason out of hand. Gratitude? I shook my head doubtfully; my recent experiences had soured me on the milk of human kindness—at least, the kind of milk that came without cost. It did not compute: try as I would, I had no success at making Sam Lichtman fit the role of grateful benefactor. With the Lichtmans of the world, there would always be something else—or at the very least, something more.

But I didn't have the luxury of waiting for Mother Teresa to summon me in dreams. Whatever game Lichtman was playing, it was the only one I had.

I pulled my Pontiac into an empty slot next to a rust-dappled Ford Mustang, and cut the ignition. In the sudden silence, the darkness felt larger—unnaturally loud, in its own way. It might have been laughing, though whether in sympathy or scorn I could not decide.

Not for the first time, I wondered if I was losing my mind.

Near my building's doorway, a pinpoint of light

moved like a red-orange firefly. It glowed brightly for
an instant before fading, and the smell of tobacco
merged with the other scents of the city night. As I
neared the entrance, a black man of medium height
watched me approach. He was wearing an expensive
sports jacket under an authentic Burberry coat. He
pitched a thin cheroot into the crabgrass and pushed
himself away from the cement block wall.

"You must be the last person on earth who hasn't
bought an answering machine," the man said, the irritation obvious in his voice. "No cell phone, not even
a pager. How the hell is anybody supposed to get in
touch with you?"

"*Mister* Washburn," I said, and my voice was tight
in my throat.

"Come on, man—I only make the assholes call me
that. You and me, it's Len and Davey. See? I know
you don't let anybody call you 'John.' "

I let it pass. "How's the book coming?"

Washburn grunted. "Huh. Ain't no book—not
much of one, that is—as long as you keep pretending
you weren't tossed in the middle of some *deep* dog-
shit."

I shook my head. "Sorry," I said flatly. "No comment."

"That's what I mean," Washburn said, a disgusted
look on his face. "C'mon, Davey—bribery charge, my
ass. I know, and you know that I know, that you were
set up. You just have to tell me how."

His voice dropped. "Look, Nederlander and his little rat pack can't go on like this forever. There are
too many stories about the . . . uh, extracurricular
activities your little police department is involved in.
And I know the Feds are looking at what's going on
in Lake Tower."

I half turned to walk away, but the writer grabbed
my arm.

"Man, I'm on *your* side!" Washburn said, and there
was frustration in his tone. "This town isn't the

squeaky-clean little burb it wants everybody to think. I've talked to your so-called mayor, and some of the other rubber-stamping gentlemen on your city council. They just refer me to Evans, and your city manager acts as if he's never heard of police corruption."

He looked into my face, seeking a response that could not come.

"Help me with this, Davey," he said. It did not sound like a request. "I guarantee you'll come out looking like one of the good guys. Hell, I'll make you the hero if you want. We can end all this, man. I just need the facts, and you can give them to me."

I stood motionless, trying to pretend I wasn't tempted by the writer's words. Then my eyes fell deliberately to the hand that still held my upper arm. Slowly, they rose to Washburn's face. Whatever the black man saw in them was enough to make him release his grip.

As I closed the door to the unlighted foyer, I heard the parting comment from the writer. It was pitched softly, almost gently, and I was not sure it was meant for me to hear.

"Start using your head, Davey," Len Washburn advised, not without compassion, "for something more than a target."

The night walked me to my door, and accepted my invitation to come inside. I did not bother to turn on any lights in the small apartment I had called home for the past five months. I had long since discovered that the dark was a courteous guest; it obscured the shortcomings, large and small alike, of my present situation.

In my previous incarnation as a cop, I had known this building as one of the faceless cement-block motels that rented by the hour. It was the kind of place where fresh sheets cost extra; the clientele, with other priorities in mind, had seldom considered the expense necessary. A series of high-profile vice raids had shut-

tered the building for a time. More recently, a new
owner had seen the profit potential in the near hope-
less and started charging by the week.

The apartment itself reflected the same fiscal philosophy. Concrete-block walls, inexpertly painted in institutional grays; a refrigerator, randomly dappled with
brown rust spots; flimsy chipboard sets of drawers
scarred with the char marks of old cigarettes. A television, its unplugged cord trailing on the floor like a
thin black tail.

I had added little to the ambiance, or lack thereof.
Near the bath lay several large cardboard boxes, one
of them ripped open at the top to reveal a jumble of
socks and other carelessly packed clothes.

Books—mainly hardcover, a conceit my finances
had already forced me to reconsider—littered the
room, dog-eared or butterfly-spread. The latest was a
James Lee Burke novel, untouched since I had lost
the ability to focus on anything but my own problems.
A crumpled wrapper from a fast-food outlet gave a
splash of garish color to a Formica countertop, nonde-
script except for the chips and scratches.

The only real order I had brought to the room was
in the stacks of newspaper clippings and photocopied
documents, arranged by subject and each marked in
red. A pile of minicassette tapes, each of them also
carefully labeled, teetered precariously next to a
pocket-sized tape recorder and spare batteries.

Such was my contribution to the room's feng shui—
that, and the bottle of vodka on the low coffee table.
The bottle was neatly aligned with the single glass
tumbler and precisely an arm's reach from the *sitz*-
pocked sofa.

It wasn't much of a home, but neither was I the
kind of tenant landlords care to seek out.

Aside from a few odd jobs and the infrequent wager
based on insider tips, I had spent the past three
months existing on an oversight. Shortly after my arrest, when the government had moved to seize my

assets, my bank had, immediately and automatically, frozen my modest checking account and canceled the Visa card it had issued. I had been shocked almost to paralysis, and then outraged. What saved me was that rage, a modicum of luck, and the cop-knowledge of how the system can be worked.

It had taken an additional day for the government's notice to reach Atlanta, home of the megabank that carried a MasterCard I had seldom used. Their bad timing was my salvation, at least temporarily. By the time that card could be canceled, I had already maxed it out with a last-minute cash advance. It had come to barely three thousand dollars, but it was better than broke.

The crisp new hundred-dollar bills had fit awkwardly into my wallet, providing a comforting bulk. Now, despite a concerted effort at fiscal conservation, not many remained.

I tried not to think about a future that was, at best, uncertain. Four or five drinks helped, were sufficient to coax a kind of sleep; it was not quite enough to choke off the dreams. I had not yet encountered the volume of alcohol that did that.

The Cubs were playing an early-season game in San Diego, and I half listened to the game on the radio. They were, of course, already struggling. As a kid, I had bought into the perennial optimism of wait-until-next-year; but next year had been a long time coming, and I was wondering if I should rethink yet another of my allegiances. I was pouring my second vodka of the evening when the telephone on the wall rang, discordant as a brick through glass. I let it ring a half dozen times.

"You're late with the money order," Ellen said. "It wasn't in the mail."

Amid the emotions that rose in me at that moment, I was relieved to find, I still had enough residual decency to include shame.

"Davey?" her voice said in my ear. She no longer

pretended tears, as she had so often, back when all this had begun; she was not even angry anymore. Her voice sounded only annoyed, peevish at an undeserved inconvenience.

"I'm sorry, Ellen," I said finally.

"Don't be sorry," she said. "Mail one. *Fix* this." Her voice hung for an instant, and in the silence I knew she was struggling to keep from saying something else. "I'll wait until the end of the week. But then I'll have to talk to Don."

Don was the lawyer who had represented her during the divorce. He had done well by his client, all things considered.

"I'll work something out."

"You've been found innocent. Why are you still broke?"

"The charges were dismissed," I corrected her stiffly. "The IRS doesn't think it's the same thing."

"They sent a letter to my manager," she said. "He called me in and wanted to know why I am being investigated. It was embarrassing, Davey. Really, I didn't know what to tell him."

"Then tell him the truth," I said. "Tell him your ex-cop ex-husband was accused of taking a bribe, and the government is afraid he didn't pay taxes on all that illegal income. Tell him they're looking at every dime to see how I hid all my payoffs over the years. Or how's this—you can tell him they seem to be doing it just because they *can*."

"I'm barely getting by on my salary, week to week," she said, as if she had not heard my words. "Davey, I'm sorry for you—really, I am. But all this has to end, Davey. Whatever you're involved in, whatever you've done. Stop. Give it up, now."

"I didn't do anything either, Ellen. Not what they said I did."

"Then why?" she asked. "Our bank accounts are still frozen. Why? You can't get a decent job. Why? Tell me, Davey. What is it, exactly, that you want?"

"I want my life back, Ellen. I even want *us* back."

"Face the facts, Davey; your life was never really that great. *We* weren't, either. So what is it you really want?"

I had no answer that either of us could accept. So I stayed silent. For a long moment, I stood with my forehead pressed against the cool wall—listening to the sound of my own breathing and hearing hers over the line.

When she finally spoke, the anger was gone from her voice. What replaced it was thoughtful, almost calculated; she had come to a decision, and I had no illusions that my own welfare factored highly in her choice. But as they always did at times like that, her words sounded tender.

"Davey, Davey," she said. "Why did you let this happen to us?"

Before I could think of a reply, she had hung up.

April 16

Chapter 4

As I watched, Terry Posson spread her fingers wide over the sheet of paper laying flat on the desk. Abruptly, she closed her hand, crumpling the paper into a loose ball. With a single gesture that may have been frustration, the policewoman launched it at the brimming wastebasket across the conference room.

That I was in the flight path seemed irrelevant, an oversight. But there was no apology offered, either. Officially, I was the Invisible Man here.

The balled paper flew past my head, rimmed off a paper cup—one of a dozen stained with the dregs of the morning's coffee—and fell to the floor.

Gil Cieloczki leaned to the side and picked it up. Without turning in his chair, he caught my eye and arched his eyebrows minutely. It was the act of a co-conspirator. I closed an eye, the one out of view of the others at the table, in a slow wink.

I wondered if I somehow had been transported back to the third grade.

"Take it easy, Posson," a voice growled, and it was not the classroom monitor. "Let's try to get through this in a professional manner."

The owner of the voice was Robert Johns Nederlander, whose official title was director of public safety for the municipality of Lake Tower. He tapped a gold pen against his own legal-sized pad. I was familiar with the make of pen, but only from a respectful distance.

When I had been a detective here, with a desk less
than twenty feet from this very conference room, it
would have taken the better part of my weekly paycheck to buy one like it.

In my current circumstances, it exceeded my net
worth by an uncomfortable margin. Like so much else
in Lake Tower, it was beyond my reach. And maybe
even my grasp.

It appeared likely to remain so, if my former supervisor had any say in the matter. When Cieloczki had
arrived with me in tow, Nederlander had glared at me
with an expression that combined equal measures of
disbelief and outrage. Before he could speak, Gil had
waved me to a chair at the far corner of the table.
The firefighter had then moved to Nederlander, and
the two men spoke in low voices: Cieloczki's, reasonable but firm; Nederlander's, tight-lipped and cold.

For a tense moment, it was by no means certain
that Nederlander would remain in the room. His eyes
flickered between Cieloczki and me; he appeared to
be weighing options, all of them unsatisfactory. Then
he made his decision, and settled pointedly in the conference room chair. He did not acknowledge my presence. The two plainclothes cops flanking Nederlander
followed his lead: in the previous twenty minutes, they
had addressed every comment to Cieloczki alone.

"So, in a nutshell, here's what two months of arson
investigation has bought the fine citizens of Lake
Tower," said Posson, frustration heavy in her voice. "We
have two dead people, Stanley Avron Levinstein, sixty-
six, and Kathleen Morris Levinstein, fifty-nine. Married
thirty-one years, no children. Upstanding citizens; nothing in the incident files except for a couple of ten-
fourteen calls—that's a possible prowler report, Gil—
and the most recent of *those* was three years ago.
Members of B'nai Abraham Temple; that's the big
one over in Highland Park."

"Place got written up in the *Beacon* last year," Mel
Bird offered. "Sends more cash to Israel than any

other synagogue in the country." Bird was junior to
Posson on the investigation. Like his partner, he was
physically short, but he had the body of an offensive
guard and an underlying impatient energy.

"Levinstein probably could have financed a kibbutz
or two on his own—I guess the construction supplies
business did okay for him," Terry continued. "Semire-
tired, which his brother—he's running the business
now, has been for a couple of years—his brother said
that meant he could show up at the office or not.
Usually didn't, at least not in the past year or so."

Nederlander shook his head and looked at Gil.
"You have copies of the interviews we did. We talked
with people from the temple, the business, the
neighbors—"

Bird interrupted. "And *that* was a waste of time,
doing a door-to-door with people in that tax bracket.
Most of the time, you can't even *see* the house next
door through the trees and stone walls. Nobody exactly drops by to borrow a cup of sugar."

He fell silent as Nederlander fixed him with a
stony eye.

"We have worked this investigation by the book,"
the police chief said, and his tone did not invite comment. "The case files are extensive. They *have* to be,
or we'd be derelict. Every lead that we've developed
has been followed."

"What it all adds up to is that Levinstein was just
an ordinary citizen, if your ordinary citizen happens
to have a house the insurance company says was worth
about four and a half million bucks," Posson said.
"That's about par for the area, of course."

"So no leads," I broke in. "Nothing to follow up
on."

"Nothing I can put a finger on," Posson agreed,
before remembering that I was unofficially a nonper-
son. She slid another sheaf of papers, clipped together
with a heavy metal clasp, from the thick folder.

"Okay, physical evidence—based on the state police

forensic report, Stanley was shot in the head with a
.38-caliber weapon," Posson said. "No casing recovered at the scene. But that could mean the gun was a
revolver, or it was an automatic but the shooter took
the brass away with him."

"Or we just couldn't find the damn thing in the
ashes." Nederlander frowned. He held up a hand,
waving off the objections of the two detectives. "Not
likely, but possible. We all know what the crime scene
looked like."

Cieloczki thumbed through several pages, and
tapped on one of the neatly typed items. "You have
the bullet, though. Ballistics?"

"Got the slug. Need a weapon to match it to,"
Bird replied.

"Anyway, Levinstein's body was charred pretty
badly," Terry Posson said. "But at least we have a
body for him. There's luck for you—seems that when
an outside wall collapsed, the body was close enough
to get a partial coverage. The ME was able to get
blood gas. Negative on carbon monoxide. That, and
no soot in the lungs or airway, lead to the conclusion
that he was dead before the fire started."

"Of course," Bird interjected, "that conclusion may
have been influenced a little by the fact that Levinstein had taken a bullet to his brains."

Terry Posson sat back in her chair and looked
around the room. "Yeah. Well, that's a wealth of information compared to what we know about the wife.
Listen to what the ME wrote here."

She flipped to the photocopied medical examiner's
report and recited in a singsong voice. " 'Determining
the exact cause and time of death for Mrs. Levinstein
is somewhat more difficult. The body was reduced to
a portion of skull, a long tooth and a long bone. These
artifacts'—that's what he calls them, artifacts—'are insufficient for determination of proper forensic conclu-
sions.' Helpful, isn't it?"

"So here's our best scenario," Nederlander said to

Gil. "Person or persons unknown enter the Levinstein house—could have broken in, could have been a home-invasion kind of thing. Hell, maybe all they had to do was knock on the door. Once in, they confront either Mr. or Mrs. Levinstein, or both of 'em. They make demands, probably rough them up. Somewhere along the line they shoot Levinstein. My guess is they shoot the woman, too. They take whatever they were after, or whatever they found. And then they torch the house to destroy any evidence."

Nederlander blew out a long breath. "It's a nice theory. The problem, Gil, is that it doesn't give us anyplace to go. That's the same problem every other theory has right now. As a murder investigation, we're at a standstill. We're catching hell in the newspapers— worse, I've got the city manager climbing all over my backside. The biggest murder case this city has ever had. And we don't even have a decent motive, let alone a suspect."

Nederlander locked eyes with Cieloczki.

"But this is an *arson* murder, Gil. Look, I won't kid you. You probably saw more arson cases in a month with the Chicago Fire Department than anyone on our police force sees in an entire career. You have the expertise, and Evans wants us to use it. And when the city manager talks, I damn well listen."

He took a deep breath. "So. The reason we set up this meeting today is to see if you can give us a direction—*anything*, to break us out of this goddam logjam." Nederlander looked at the policewoman seated alongside him, and made an impatient motion with his hands.

Posson cleared her throat; as lead investigator, listening to her boss ask for help from outside the department had to be sour medicine to swallow. "Gil, you've had a chance to review our case files as well as your people's reports. If you, uh, would, can you give us some of your insights?"

"Sure," Gil said, as if she had asked him to pass the

salt. "Let me start by saying that I'm limiting myself to my own field of expertise. That means the fire itself, and what it tells us.

"Okay. First of all, this was a big job somebody took on. The burn patterns we've reconstructed, the speed of progression we've documented—three floors were systematically drenched in gasoline, room to room. It's a big house, and it burned hot. We know what it did to Mrs. Levinstein."

He glanced at Nederlander, whose face wore a mask of polite interest.

"A conservative guess is that the arsonist used as much as thirty gallons of gas, maybe more," Cieloczki replied. "And that alone tells us the fire was almost certainly premeditated. He already had the gasoline— enough to not just burn it down, but to burn it down thoroughly and quickly. Our guy went in knowing what he was going to do to that house. You don't just go to the corner Mobil station on an impulse and fill up a half dozen gas cans."

"Could've gone out after the fact and bought it at different gas stations," Bird objected. "Five gallons each stop, it takes him six stops."

"Uh-uh," Posson told her partner. "The math's right, but I don't buy the logic. Guy pops two people, then rides all over town buying gas? Even if people don't notice, it's going to *feel* like somebody does."

"He goes to self-serve pumps, what's to notice?" Bird argued.

"Can't buy a gas *can* at a self-service pump," Posson retorted. "You gotta talk to a clerk for that." She made a note on her pad. "In fact, unless you figure he went back to empty it in the house each time, he had to buy *six* cans. You don't do that in any one gas station, either. So we got a guy who dealt with six clerks, maybe."

"It gives you something to look for." Nederlander nodded. "You go back, canvass gas stations. Ask

about people who bought one or more gas containers.
Maybe we'll pry something loose."

"Check it out," Cieloczki agreed, and turned to Posson. "But don't limit yourself to the day of the fire. If
he had this planned out in advance, it makes sense that
he would have had everything ready before he went
in—a couple of days, possibly as much as a week."

"What makes you think he bought the stuff around
here?" Bird's voice was stubborn. "Why couldn't he
have brought it with him from—I dunno, someplace
down in the city?"

"That's possible," Gil conceded. "I just don't think
our arsonist would want to drive too far with all that
gasoline. Plus, there's the question of the containers.
In almost every arson case I've seen where gasoline
was involved, you find an empty container nearby. Not
a lot of people want to get caught walking away from
a fire carrying even *one* empty gas can. How many
cans did you find at the arson scene?"

Neither Posson nor Bird spoke. Nederlander
watched Cieloczki with the air of a man who has been
asked a trick question.

"None," he said finally.

"Exactly. Our man went to the trouble of taking
them with him. He didn't want us to find them there.
Why? Why risk it?" Gil shook his head. "There has
to be something about them that we might find
significant—something that might give us a lead."

Posson was chewing her pencil, her eyes unfocused.
"Okay, here's a thought. All those cans—yeah, that's
a lot of stuff to put in a car trunk. And I don't think
our guy would want to drive around with 'em in his
backseat, empty or full."

"So we're looking for a van, or more likely a panel
truck," Nederlander interjected. "Something with a lot
of space and a minimum of windows."

"That's probably a good supposition," Cieloczki replied. "I think it bears looking into."

There was a moment of silence while the two plain-clothes officers scribbled on their notepads. Nederlander's fingers, I noted, tapped on the tabletop.

"The question of premeditation bothers me," Nederlander said finally. "I see the point about the quantity of gasoline. But frankly, that's a damn weak basis to build a whole theory around." He raised an eyebrow, inviting the firefighter's response.

Cieloczki looked at me, briefly, and made a decision. "Well, Bob—we do have more than that to go on here, as a matter of fact. For one thing, I think we've found an indication in your case files that whoever set this fire either had experience, or had some coaching from someone who did."

He tugged a single typed sheet from the file. "Every fire alarm that comes in triggers a set of automatic actions from my people. The firefighters are dispatched, sure. But it's also standard procedure to notify the police in case we need traffic- or crowd-control assistance. We'll alert the hospital or trauma center closest to the fire in case we require medical support. And we contact the utility companies for an emergency shutoff of electricity and gas service."

Gil tapped on the report. "ComEd and the gas company arrived a minute or two after our first truck—that's confirmed. ComEd cut electrical power from the main transformer serving the entire block. That's standard procedure for them. But it's different with the natural gas. Whenever possible, NI Gas tries to shut off the natural gas service from the outside valve that serves the individual house. At the Levinstein house, the valve is under an access cover about thirty feet from the house—but according to the report, he couldn't shut it off this time. When he arrived, it was already turned off.

"We've talked to the guy," Gil said. "He said he figured one of the firefighters did it. Technically, that's against procedures, but nobody wanted to make an issue out of it. Except we polled the firefighters who were on the scene first, and they were still pulling hoses when the gas company arrived."

Cieloczki paused, to emphasize the significance. "Our arsonist took his time inside, soaking everything with gasoline. Gasoline fumes are heavier than air, so they flow down to the lowest point in the structure. The last thing this person wanted was to have a pilot light—for a stove, the furnace or water heater, whatever—touch off the fumes before he was done and out of there."

"So what?" said Bird. "I mean, how does that make our guy special? If I smell gasoline, I'm going to want to avoid open flames. Turning off the gas is the easiest way to make sure you get all the pilot lights turned off."

"That thought might occur to a lot of people," Gil agreed. "But what most people forget are the electrical ignition sources. For instance, it was a cold day outside. Have you ever been around at night when your thermostat clicks on? In a dark room, when the mercury switch makes contact, you see a little flash. That's more than enough to touch off gasoline fumes, once they reach the right level. You've also got refrigerators, blowers, sump pumps. Anything that has an electric motor is a potential ignition source. So what do you do?"

"Our guy also cut the power to the house, right?" Posson said.

Gil nodded. "And that's not too surprising, either," he added, anticipating Bird's response. "At least, it wouldn't be if there wasn't a question about the timing."

Nederlander frowned. "What question?"

"The Levinstein house had a pretty sophisticated alarm system," Gil said. "When the heat triggered it, a signal was sent simultaneously to the fire department and to the alarm service's central monitoring system. Our signal is pretty basic. Location and time, essentially. But the alarm company gets much more information—including the status of the alarm system

itself. I had them send us a copy of their printout for
the incident."

Gil pushed two sheets of tractor-feed computer
paper to Nederlander; Posson and Bird leaned over
to look.

Lines of type, tapped out by a dot matrix printer,
marched down the fanfold sheet. The top line read

SYSTEM STATUS: ** OK ** 1215 1/23

"Routinely, the alarm system does a diagnostic self-
check every fifteen minutes, and automatically dow-
nloads to the alarm company's computers," Gil said.
"That way, the company can monitor minor problems
that might require maintenance."

Most of the other lines were identical except for the
first set of numbers, which in each line increased by
fifteen-minute intervals.

But midway down the page, Cieloczki had used a
red pen to circle a line that was printed in capital
letters:

SYSTEM STATUS: ** AUX POWER SUPPLY ON** 1723 1/23

"That's when the system went over to a battery
backup," Gil said. "A power failure isn't considered
a major breakdown. The system simply records when
it happens. From 5:23 on, the system was working off
the battery."

Finally, on the last page of the fanfold paper, Cieloczki had circled two lines several times:

!! ALARM ** 10-73 ** 2119 1/23
!! ALARM ** 10-70 ** 2119 1/23

"The alarm service computer uses police ten-codes
in its system. Ten seventy-three is code for smoke detected in the residence," Gil said to me.

"The initial alarm came at 9:19 P.M. Almost immediately—with gasoline as the initiator, probably only a few seconds later—the system reported a ten-seventy, flames detected," Cieloczki said.

"We assume that whoever cut gas and electric to the house also set the fire," Gil continued. "We know the system went on its standby battery power at 17:23 hours. But that's 5:23 P.M., almost four hours before the fire set off the alarm." He looked around the room. "So what happened during those four hours?"

As Cieloczki spoke, I studied the faces of the three police officers. Nederlander was outwardly calm, though his eyes had narrowed noticeably throughout the presentation. Bird was frankly enthralled, his head bobbing as his eyes moved between Gil's face and the papers on the conference table. Posson's neck between the white turtleneck and the fringe of her close-cut black hair was already a deep crimson. I sat quietly, waiting for what would come next.

It was not a long wait.

"As you know, under Lake Tower ordinances arson investigations are formally the responsibility of the fire department," Cieloczki said, his voice almost gentle. "The police department has been actively pursuing a murder investigation. As a matter of professional courtesy we've limited our official involvement. But with your investigation stalled—at a standstill, to use your term, Bob—I feel that I have no choice. I have to exercise my prerogative to assume the lead role here."

"*Lead* role?" Nederlander's voice was tight with barely suppressed emotions I could guess did not include mirth. "Forget it, Gil. This is still a murder investigation. That's *police* work, not . . . something for a fireman."

"I'm sorry, Bob," Gil replied, his voice level. He reached down to his briefcase, which was leaning against the legs of his chair, and removed a folded letter. The paper was high-quality bond, so heavy and crisp that it cracked slightly at the creases.

"This is a memorandum from the city manager's office," Gil said. "Talmadge Evans has decided to create a joint task force to continue the investigation into the case. Police and fire departments, and any outside support we require. The memo directs me to review the case files. At my discretion, I am instructed to assume the supervisory responsibility as it relates to the Levinstein investigation."

Cieloczki handed the memorandum to Nederlander as if it were a loaded weapon—which, from the police chief's point of view, it was. Even from across the table, the precise, distinctive signature of the man who was both Nederlander's and Cieloczki's boss was unmistakable.

"As public safety director, of course, you remain my direct supervisor, Bob. You're definitely in the loop on all reports, and I'll brief you regularly. This is just an administrative action to streamline the investigation."

It was anything but, and Nederlander's impassivity signaled that he knew it. But he was an experienced veteran of turf warfare, and he knew when to attack, when to dig in and when to pull back. He chose the latter.

"I see," he said, leaning back from the table. His voice was now almost casual, as if he had suggested the new arrangement. "Well, Gil—you're the one with the training and experience in all of this." He spread his hands. "Just tell me how we can support you. You want to keep Terry and Mel on the case, I assume."

"Definitely, if that's all right with you," Gil said. "They're important members of the joint task force. But I'm also bringing in a consultant to work the investigation—someone with police experience who can help me understand the procedures involved. Davey, here, was working the case when he was . . . when he left the police force. He will be an acting fire marshal and report to me."

No one in the room had seen Nederlander speechless before. It did not last nearly long enough.

"Are you serious?" he demanded. He looked at me fully for the first time since the meeting began. "This . . . *person* was dismissed from the police force—"

"I resigned," I interrupted. "Voluntarily."

"After you were led out of here by three county deputies, in cuffs," Nederlander retorted, with heat. "You quit before I had the pleasure of firing you."

"I'll be working this case," I snapped. "Get used to it."

I realized that I was on my feet with no memory of having risen, leaning over the table, nose-to-nose with my former employer. Nederlander was standing, too, and I doubted that anyone in the room could tell which of us had risen first.

Cieloczki also stood. "Let's keep it together here," he said, in a voice accustomed to commanding people in tense situations. "Bob, I have to say that Davey is uniquely suited for this job. I won't go into specifics right now. But it's my decision to make, and I've made it."

Nederlander straightened; in an act of sheer will, he forced his voice to become calm and level.

"Yes," he said to Cieloczki, though he was looking into my face. "You certainly have."

He pivoted and stalked out the door. Posson and Bird watched him leave, both their faces impassive masks. Only then did I realize I was breathing hard, and that my fists were balled white-knuckle tight at my sides.

Cieloczki sat down, unruffled at the scene he had orchestrated.

"Davey," Gil Cieloczki said, looking down at the file on the table before him, "welcome to the team."

Chapter 5

"Well, *that* went well, don't you think?" Gil said, a little more than a half hour later. To me, walking with Cieloczki across the hall to the offices of Lake Tower's fire department, the humor in his voice sounded unforced. It might have been facetiousness, or extreme relief.

The meeting with Nederlander and his investigators had indeed gone well, in that it had followed a script Cieloczki had outlined barely two hours before. That earlier meeting had been very private indeed, with attendance limited to Cieloczki and three other people. One was me; another, a well-dressed man with hair that showed careful attention by an expert barber.

The final member of our cabal was a tall, almost painfully thin man named Talmadge Evans.

His eyes had studied me with extreme skepticism as he listened to a story that came from a dying convict. He had asked an occasional question, raised the expected objections. His disbelief had been obvious. Nonetheless, in the end he had signed the memorandum that effectively removed his own police chief from the investigation.

Then he had turned baleful eyes on me.

"I'm not naive, Mr. Davey," Evans had said. "I know your history here. I also know that you have not held a steady job since you left our police department. I will be honest: I believe you have come to us with this . . . story, for several reasons. But mainly because you need the money."

He held up his hand before I could speak.

"Very well. You have a job, temporary as it may be. Gil feels strongly that you are needed to resolve this matter." He nodded toward the other visitor in the room. "His view has the support of the FBI, it appears. That is correct, Agent Santori, is it not?"

Then his voice grew steely, and I knew it for a warning.

"But hear this, clearly: I will not stand for a vendetta of any kind. If there is to be an investigation, it will be handled fairly and professionally. You *will* toe that line, sir; any behavior that does not meet that standard will cost you dearly. I will see to it personally."

Evans had folded the crisp, heavy paper and handed the memorandum to Cieloczki. He nodded in dismissal.

As we started to leave the room—through the seldom used side door, not the one that opened on the main administrative section of the city manager's office—Evans spoke again.

"Gil."

He paused, as if the act of framing his words would give Cieloczki a last chance to reconsider.

"You are taking a chance—a *serious* chance—on the basis of this man's credibility, Gil," Evans told the firefighter. "And, I might add, on his stability. You are about to burn your bridges here, personally as well as professionally. I only hope you understand: if this turns out badly, I cannot protect you."

Cieloczki nodded. The message was clear and unequivocal.

Evans had given him his support, grudging as it might have been. With it came more than enough rope to hang himself, and the rest of us, too.

April 17

Chapter 6

Much of what I knew about Gil Cieloczki was ancedotal, the blend of rumor and outright fiction that passes for conversation in most organizations. After I found myself on what Cieloczki euphemistically called his team, it seemed very important to find out a lot more.

The basics I had gleaned from watercooler gossip back when he first arrived in Lake Tower; for instance, I knew that he made it a practice to get to work early and leave late. That alone made him an oddity among his fellow municipal executives, whose personal preferences tended toward late arrivals, early departures and occasional over-long lunches.

To such tidbits I now added what data I could pick up. Some I eased from the cadre of firefighters who had worked with him in Chicago and subsequently had been recruited to form the nucleus of the professional organization he envisioned for Lake Tower. I dug through clippings and microfilm in the Lake Tower library. I even coaxed some information from Cieloczki himself, items I suspected he thought it was important for me to know.

But nobody knows you like your spouse, for good or for ill.

And so it was, when I was invited to Gil's house for a briefing session preceded by my first sit-down dinner in months, I made it a point to arrive early—even before Gil arrived home from the office. Rather than leave an early-arriving guest sitting alone with a cup of coffee in her husband's den, Kay Cieloczki stayed and was easily coaxed to talk about him and his achievements.

From all of these sources—supplemented by a few private favors called in from Len Washburn and other select members of the news media—I constructed a detailed profile of my new boss.

In Chicago, where he had been promoted from ladder company to battalion and subsequently to deputy chief, Gil Cieloczki's life revolved around the almost constant clamor of the fire bell. A talent for the strategic aspects of firefighting—quickly recognized by his superiors—was tempered by his affinity for the hands-on tactical. At home behind either a desk or a three-inch line at a fire, Cieloczki became a fixture both at fire department headquarters and at virtually every major blaze in the city.

Veterans from the line companies nodded approvingly when Gil's name came up during bitch sessions in the beer-and-a-shot taverns favored by off-duty firefighters. Cieloczki was not your typical cotton-top, they'd tell the rookies at the table, referring to the unscarred, pristine, white firefighter helmets worn by the department's upper echelon; Cieloczki had the "bell in his blood"—he was a firefighter's firefighter who had never forgotten what the job was all about.

Which had made it all the more shocking when Cieloczki quit.

By then, Cieloczki was in his late thirties—relatively young for a deputy chief, especially one with a reputation for having risen on merit rather than politics. He had been at the tail end of an eighteen-month stint supervising the Department's Investigative and Forensic Services. The nuances of arson methodology, ignition source identification and accelerant trace analysis filled all of his waking hours and many of his nights.

Late one Saturday afternoon, he was working alone in the renovated firehouse that served as the offices for Investigative and Forensic Services. The door opened, and Gil looked up from the memoranda and reports covering most of his desk.

"My name is Talmadge Evans," a man said. "And I need your help."

He sat in the visitor's chair at Gil's desk and set down a file folder, aligning it carefully with the edge of the desktop.

Evans was a tall man in a suit that had been carefully tailored to a frame that was thin, almost emaciated. Then in his late fifties, Talmadge Evans had the air of a precise man—one who would have been quite comfortable running a major corporation. As it was, he ran the municipality of Lake Tower. Evans had spent the past dozen years in that role, serving a long line of elected officials.

All of them, upon taking office, quickly recognized the value of a city manager who knew his place. Evans took care not to interfere in matters of simple patronage, nepotism or other occasional political featherbedding. That is, unless and until such practices intruded on the areas Evans categorized under the phrase "efficient municipal management." If something kept the trains from running on schedule, Evans could be uncharacteristically blunt.

Still, accommodation was always possible. After all, as several past mayors and aldermen had assured each other, Evans was an employee, and a mere bureaucrat at that. As Evans himself was the first to admit, he possessed statutory powers limited largely to what they granted.

Yet over the years, as their own political fortunes waxed and waned while Evans remained, a few of the more perceptive came to realize something profound. Inevitably, the accommodations they had reached with Evans had ultimately evolved to follow the course he had championed in the first place.

Evans thumbed through the folder and selected a neatly cut newspaper clipping. He pushed it toward Cieloczki without a word. The headline type was large and black, the size usually reserved for major tragedies.

NINE DEAD, FORTY INJURED
IN LAKE TOWER APARTMENT FIRE
By A. STEVEN MELSHENKER
Beacon Staff Writer

LAKE TOWER, Ill.— A fire of questionable origin roared through a three-story apartment complex yesterday in Lake Tower, a community of 25,000 north of Chicago. In its wake, seven children and two pregnant women are dead and dozens more being treated in several area hospitals. The fire, which broke out at approximately 2:30 a.m., also left five other children in extremely critical condition.

Fire Chief Carl Devroux said that the fire began on the second floor of a forty-unit apartment building in the Westlake section of the city. Devroux declined to comment on reports that residents had repeatedly complained to the city that the building lacked working smoke detectors and that fire doors—used to prevent the spread of flames and smoke from one section of the building to another—were habitually propped open. The open fire doors allowed the smoke and super-heated gases to move rapidly through the hallway and may have contributed to the high death toll.

According to residents interviewed outside the scene of the blaze, repeated complaints to the owner of the building, listed in county tax records as Monmouth Development Corp. of Lake Tower, were disregarded. Three complaints filed with the Lake Tower Building Department—the most recent less than four weeks ago—were also ignored, the residents charged.

The cause of the fire is still under investigation,

City Manager Talmadge Evans said this morning. Evans said that a total of sixteen apartments were destroyed by the fire, and that there was no evidence of working smoke detectors. He said that the fire was declared under control within an hour of its inception, but not before the smoke and flames took their toll.

Evans declined comment on the reports of the alleged complaints. In responding to a question from the media, he acknowledged that safety inspections of existing buildings were the responsibility of the city's Building and Zoning Department. However, Evans added, in practice such inspections were routinely assigned to the Lake Tower Fire Department.

Cieloczki had known about the fire. Even in a city as accustomed to tragedy as Chicago, this one had stood out. It was remarkable for the age and number of the victims, and for the senseless, preventable way they had died. Smoke detectors were inoperative, or missing entirely; fire doors had been latched open, and in some cases removed. Worse, inspections required by a litany of state law and local ordinance had been cursory at best. As a result, tragedy had been inevitable.

"We weren't—*aren't*—prepared," Evans said. "It's just that simple. The same thing could happen tomorrow. At this moment, Lake Tower has a fire department that has become too comfortable with meeting minimal standards. That includes, I'm afraid, our personnel standards. Starting with our fire chief."

He locked eyes with Cieloczki.

"Carl Devroux is symptomatic of a problem I have faced since I accepted my present position," Evans said. "You are no doubt aware that Lake Tower has a tradition of . . . let us say, *opportunism* among its public officials."

"I've lived in Chicago all my life," Gil said evenly. "And I read the newspapers."

"Then you know we have had more than our share of such men. For them, public service was little more than a license to enrich themselves. When I was hired as city manager, it was on the heels of a scandal not unlike this one"—he tapped the clipping with his finger—"and part of my task was to keep it from happening again."

His face was grim. "I won't lie to you, Mr. Cieloczki. I am still far from succeeding in that task."

The firefighter frowned. "Mr. Evans, I don't quite understand what you want here. What does this have to do with me?"

"Chief Devroux became head of our fire department the year before I was appointed city manager," Evans said. "As the city grew, the job grew. He did not grow with it. My failing was not making this issue a priority; I settled for what I thought was an adequate firefighting system. That's why we need somebody like you."

Gil shook his head. "I'm afraid I'm not—"

"Please hear me out," Evans interrupted. He pulled a sheaf of papers from the file. The photocopied top sheet, which carried the Chicago Fire Department logo, was the first page of Gil's own personnel file.

"I didn't just pull your name from the telephone book," Evans said, with a smile. "I know a number of people who know you. In the past few days, I've talked about you to people both inside and outside your department. Let me speak frankly, if I may. You are a valuable member of the Chicago fire department, but you are not *valued*, if you understand the difference."

"I don't," Gil said, wondering if he had just been insulted. "Enlighten me."

"From a career standpoint, you have risen as far as you will go," Evans said flatly. "We both understand that your department is part of your city's political environment. You are not a political animal by nature; you have no clout outside the department itself. For the next twenty years, the most you can hope for is to do what you are doing now—an increasing amount of administrative assignments, each taking you further away from the ability to make a real difference. Oh, I'm certain they are important—but may I ask you this: are they what you became a firefighter to do?"

"And that would be?" Gil asked, leaning back in his chair.

"Saving lives," Evans replied. "Building the kind of fire department that operates on a professional basis. One with the resources, the training and the personnel a city like mine needs to be fully protected. A department that knows what it must do, and does it fully and without favoritism."

Cieloczki's eyes locked on those of Evans. Evans looked back from behind the steel-rimmed frame of his glasses. The silence held for several moments, as each of the two men took the measure of the other.

Gil spoke first. "You know of an opening, I assume?"

"Chief Devroux will resign before the end of the week," Evans said. "Very likely, before the end of the day tomorrow. I know this, because I know that in tomorrow's edition of this newspaper"—Evans tapped the clipping, still on the desk in front of Cieloczki—"it will be reported that Carl Devroux is one of the owners of the Monmouth Development Corporation. The story will be quite explicit in showing that Monmouth, through a series of shell companies, owns a number of substandard, rent-subsidized apartment buildings—among them, the building where this tragedy occurred. The article will also carry a quote from me expressing surprise over Devroux's previously undisclosed relationship to the property."

Gil nodded. "Let me be frank with you, Mr. Evans. I appreciate the situation you're facing, and I under-

stand the . . . ethical problems involved. So even if I
were looking for a new job, I'm not sure this would
be the time to—"

"The time will never be better," Evans said. "I, too,
want to be candid with you. First, the publicity this
has received has damaged our image. Every member
of our board has been embarrassed. Despite what
some may see as a checkered past, Lake Tower does
not like to be embarrassed. We require an immediate
solution to the problem Devroux has created.

"Second, there is a purely practical matter. Our
board has been advised to expect a number of lawsuits
alleging that Lake Tower was corporately negligent.
As a result, the tragedy was compounded. We anticipate some very large claims against us. And justifiably
so, of course."

Evans shrugged. "Fortunately, we have been assured that our insurance will assume the cost of the
settlements we will make. However, our carrier has
notified the board that it is withdrawing future coverage. They are canceling us out. Worse, we are told
that without an immediate, substantive correction of
our public safety situation, Lake Tower will not be
able to obtain insurance from any other carrier."

He smiled, thinly. "Very honestly, a new fire chief—
a professional, someone with the knowledge of what
a topflight fire department should be—would have the
ability to write his own ticket. That is an advantage
not to be wasted."

Evans had paused. Without appearing to, he studied
Cieloczki. The firefighter was still silent, but there was
something in his eyes that had not been there before.
It was the right moment, and Evans had made his
voice harsh and accusatory, with just the proper touch
of personal regret.

"But finally, and most important, we had nine
human beings die in my city—*and it didn't have to
happen!* I am going to have to live with that fact every
day for the rest of my life. I will do what it takes—

whatever it takes—to keep something like this from happening in Lake Tower again. I'm looking for a person who shares that commitment to help me. And I need him now."

Gil Cieloczki and Talmadge Evans spoke for two hours that evening. They talked of budgets and personnel and the requirements needed to build a professional system. Somewhere in the midst of this initial meeting, Evans realized that Cieloczki had begun interviewing him. It was, he thought with satisfaction, a good sign.

Evans left with a substantial volume of notes, written in his precise hand in a leather-covered notebook. He did not leave with what he came for, but he also did not leave disappointed. Evans had a keen ability to read other people, and he was a man who knew the value of patience.

Cieloczki had taken Kay to a late dinner that night. "Not Eli's or the Fishmarket tonight," Gil had proposed. "Someplace quiet where we can talk." They had settled on Dannaher's, a Near North restaurant where the decor favored dark walnut booths and the menu was printed in green. There, nursing a Bushmills to Kay's single glass of burgundy, Cieloczki recounted every detail of Evans' visit.

"You *want* the job," Kay said, studying her husband over the rim of her wineglass and marveling at how, after eighteen years of marriage, he could still surprise her.

Cieloczki leaned back and lifted his hands, palms up. "I honestly don't know," he said, tacitly acknowledging Kay's reaction. "And Kay, that surprises me. I've never been anything but a Chicago fireman— never wanted to be anything else." His eyebrows knit together in deep concentration. "Before today, I never considered doing anything else."

Kay reached across the table and took his hand. Even then, she told me, she had known they were about to move to Lake Tower.

* * *

Later that night, after they had fallen asleep in the warmth of each other, Kay had awakened alone in their bed. Outside the room, light spilled from the stairwell that led down to the living room. Soundlessly, she walked to the head of the stairs.

There, in a circle of light cast by the reading lamp at Gil's favorite chair, her husband sat. His eyes looked into some unseen distance, and his forehead was furrowed in deep thought.

He held something between the fingers of his left hand. From her vantage above and behind him, it looked like a story clipped from a newspaper. But the headline type was large and black, the size usually reserved for major tragedies.

Chapter 7

Many of those who knew about my father automatically assumed that they had uncovered the motive behind my own actions, even if they were convinced I had long since buried it in my own mind.

They were perhaps right, though my own opinion is that the grave they had excavated was not as shallow as they thought. But certainly, the fate that Gerald Davey had brought down upon himself—and by extension, on my mother and myself—was the genesis for what had turned into my own sort of Children's Crusade.

I understood that. But I also understood something else, all too well. There is a self-knowledge that all zealots possess despite our denials: that buried deep inside each of us is not a revulsion, but a secret fascination. The sins we profess to hate the most, we crave to commit ourselves.

"But I saw the story in the newspaper," Father Frank Bomarito repeated. The priest frowned, his face no longer the nonjudgmental mask it had been as he listened to the recitation of my sins. "You were acquitted."

We were sitting in the rear pews, near the sacristy. It was dark here, lighted only by votive candles that flickered red and blue beneath statues of saints and virgins. At the front of the church near the altar, a single taper burned white over the tabernacle, signaling to the faithful that the Host was present inside.

"Yes," I said. "Otherwise, I would be in prison right now."

"I haven't asked if you were guilty," the priest said carefully.

"No," I said. "You haven't."

He waited.

"I didn't go in there intending to keep any money," I said finally. "I know that for certain. But when I walked out, I had five thousand dollars in my pocket. And I remember thinking that nobody knew, except for people who didn't particularly care."

I shook my head. "I don't know, Father. Was I tempted? Yes. Definitely. Is that why I didn't immediately turn it over to . . . to the people I was working with? I tell myself no; I tell myself I wanted to come up with better evidence. Maybe mark the bills myself, use them for bait."

"But you suspect that you might have kept this money."

"I'm the son of a cop, Father," I said. "He worked in Chicago, back when even a traffic stop involved a shakedown, likely as not. My dad sold his share of ten-dollar pencils to drivers who ran a stop sign; the scores just got bigger after he made detective lieutenant. He used to tell me that on the job, nobody gave you points for being stupid." I chuckled softly. "I know *he* would have kept it. He always did."

"Davey, had you ever taken money before?"

"No."

"Then perhaps you're trying too hard," Father Frank said. "Sometimes we try to assign ourselves guilt where there is none. Usually we do it because we feel we have sinned in other ways, ways that we cannot admit to ourselves."

"I don't understand."

"I mean your divorce, Davey."

"Ellen and I were a mistake, Father. We always

were. In less than five years of marriage, we were separated half a dozen times."

"And you always came back together again."

"I always came back to her. It was never the other way around."

"Because she is the woman you married. Because you love her."

It was not a question, but I chose to answer it as one.

"I don't know that, either," I said. "I think that Ellen and I are both difficult people to love. What we felt—all right, what I *still* feel—may be more of an addiction."

"You know the Church doesn't recognize divorce, Davey."

"You can't divorce an addiction, Father," I said. "In that way, at least, the union is still intact."

He shook his head, though whether in regret or impatience I could not tell.

"About the money—merely to experience temptation is not a sin," the priest reminded me. "I can only absolve you of what you do, not for what you may have been thinking about doing. And I can't 'absolve' you for agreeing to a divorce; it's not a sin, per se—it just doesn't exist, under Church law. You're still a married man."

"I'm not asking to be forgiven for the divorce," I said.

"Maybe not," Father Frank said. "But don't be too sure."

Chapter 8

At the time I was arrested for soliciting a bribe, Chaz Trombetta had been my partner for almost four years. It was a record, of sorts: almost three years longer than any of the others had lasted.

On our first day together, Chaz had laid out the ground rules.

"You're supposed to an asshole, but good at detective work," he had told me, without pretext. "Me, too. Do your job, let me do mine." He had waved off the response his new partner was about to make. "I don't figure we'll ever whisper sweet nothings in each other's ear—but I'll try real hard to live with the disappointment. We understand each other?"

Within a month, we were fast friends. By the end of the year, our record of clearing cases was among the best in the detective bureau.

It helped that Chaz was smart, and a savvy investigator. Where I might have been impulsive, Trombetta was reflective. People kept making the mistake of underestimating him. Chaz took it as a compliment, and kept putting them in jail.

I pulled to a stop outside a two-story house. The yard was meticulously groomed, and shrubbery artfully placed provided an accent to the pale gray of the brickwork. I was midway up the stone pathway to the porch when the front door opened. A man of moder-

ate height and with a permanent five o'clock shadow
stepped outside, his hair dark and curly and his arms
knotted with thick muscle. He carried a half-filled
green bottle in one hand.

"Hey, J. D!" Chaz Trombetta yelled. He lunged
forward and engulfed me in a bearlike embrace, wrap-
ping both arms around me. He slapped an enthusiastic
tattoo across my back and side with the hand not occupied with his bottle, and mock punched me lightly
in the stomach. Then he stepped back, his face smelling of Old Spice and his breath of Rolling Rock.

"Junie! Look what the cat dragged in!"

Junie Trombetta appeared at the doorway. Had I
been thinking clearly, I might have been puzzled at
the mix of emotions that crossed her face.

"Hey, Davey," she said softly. "Chaz, let him
breathe." She started to step outside, but her husband
waved her back.

"I want to show him the roses, baby," he said to
her. "How about you bring us a couple of Rocks,
okay?"

He led me around the side of the house, through an
arched gateway in the cast-iron fencing. The backyard
looked like a spread in *House Beautiful,* with flagstone
pathways winding around shade trees just starting to
fill with leaves. Beds of early-blooming perennials bordered an inlaid-brick patio, and a small, screened ga-
zebo stood guard near the rear property line. It all
looked very beautiful, and very expensive.

"You've done some work since the last time I was
over," I said, nodding.

"Well, you know," Chaz said, with studied nonchalance in his voice. "With Terese off at Notre Dame,
we got more time than we know what to do with. So
Junie and I, we decided to finally fix up the place the
way we always wanted."

He stopped at a carefully constructed trellis as tall
as a man, a support for the fan of stems that waved

gracefully in the light air. It was still early in the season, but already tight knobs of rosebuds formed blood-red drops against the deep green of the thorned tendrils.

"Remember these beauties?" he asked, cupping one branch with a surprisingly gentle touch. "They're going to have a good summer this year."

He looked toward the house, and cupped his hands around his mouth.

"Hey, *Junie!*" he shouted, and his voice was unexpectedly harsh. "J. D. needs his drink!"

It was out of character, and surprised me. Then Trombetta turned back, and I realized my old partner had been avoiding my eyes.

Chaz finished his Rolling Rock with an almost greedy passion, tilting the bottle farther and farther back, his Adam's apple bobbing. It was an impressive display; I had forgotten Trombetta's startling ability to consume, and the speed at which he did so.

Chaz lowered the now-empty bottle, and noticed the expression on my face.

"Had half a bottle spill, once," he said gruffly. "Swore I'd never take that chance again."

As if the act had steeled him in some way, he studied my face for several moments. His own was expressionless, his eyes wary. Then, in a soft underhand motion, he lobbed the drained longneck onto the neatly trimmed grass near the patio.

"So—haven't seen you around all that much, old buddy," Chaz said finally. "Come to think of it, haven't seen you at all for—what, three months? This is the first time you've looked me up." He shook his head, mock sadly. "I'm hurt, Davey. Deeply hurt. Anything new with you?"

"Ellen and I are still divorced," I said. "Looks like we may make it a success this time."

He nodded, suddenly serious. "Junie ran into her a while back. You two still talk?"

"Hard not to. Mainly about money."

"Government still on your back?" He glanced at me, sidelong, read the expression there and nodded. "If you need some cash, Junie and I could probably—"

"Thanks," I interrupted, "but no thanks."

We walked in silence for several paces.

"I've missed you, J. D.," he said. Almost against his will, his face lit up in memory. "Hey, remember the time you tried to shut down Bobby Calderon's action? Ballsy move, man, walking in to bust the guy right in the middle of the United Way awards luncheon." He grinned at me. "Refresh my memory. What'd the judge call it when he threw out the arrest?"

"Poor judgment," I said, and smiled. "He might have also said something about grandstanding. Didn't mean he was right to let Calderon go."

Chaz was looking away when he replied.

"Well, what the hell anyway." he said. "Calderon skated, sure. Screw 'im. He wasn't laughing for long."

A week after the arrest was tossed, and before we had the chance to convince the state's attorney to re-file, a pair of Chicago cops found Bobby Calderon. He was in a soiled burgundy Dumpster behind a North Halsted Street restaurant, and had been there long enough to attract the local rats.

His obituary had described him as a "prominent, well-connected and successful Lake Tower contractor." Whether out of deference to the deceased's family or for less noble reasons, the newspaper had not detailed the extent of Calderon's connections or the reasons behind his success.

"Big difference," I observed, "between going to jail and having somebody park a half dozen .22 slugs in the back of your head."

Again, the silence fell heavily. After what felt like an eternity, Chaz spoke.

"So, what's up? What do you want? I heard you were back on the city payroll, J. D. I hear from now on maybe all our big cases are gonna get assigned to

firemen and shady ex-cops. No offense, of course—
I'm just quoting. Hell, *I* know you're the cleanest thing
since Spic 'n Span."

He waved his hand, a dismissive gesture.

"Hey, everybody's talking about how you and Cieloczki jerked the Levinstein murder right out from
under the department. Can't say us cops are all that
happy about it—kind of makes us look like we're too
stupid to run the case, you know? Except even us
dumb cops know it means that all of a sudden you
are tight as a tick with Evans. That's the big leagues,
at least in this town. So what could you possibly want
from me, ol' buddy?"

His voice had risen, and at any moment I expected
to see Junie's face at the window.

"Chaz, right now it's me, Gil Cieloczki and Evans,"
I said. "I need somebody who knows the score . . .
somebody I *know* is on my side."

Trombetta snorted. "On your side, hell," he said.
"You mean on the inside, don't you?" He thought for
a minute. "Santori in on all this?"

I nodded, and Trombetta's face darkened.

"Damn it, J. D! You never learn! You just have to
screw with Nederlander, don't you?"

"Everybody's got their little hangup," I said. "Nederlander's mine."

"You know something, J. D.? It's time you stopped
trying to make up for your old man. It's twenty years,
partner; get over it."

My partner's tone took me aback, and I decided to
treat it as a jest.

"Gosh, thanks for the insightful analysis, *Doctor* Trombetta. When'd you get so deep into pop psychology?"

"I think the reason you're so pissed at Nederlander
doesn't have anything to do with whether he's bent.
It's because they can't catch him at it, like they caught
your dad. Tell me I'm wrong."

"I don't even think about it anymore. Everybody
took something under the table in those days."

Chaz's face did not change its expression, and I frowned.

"Ease up, buddy. Look, I need to know: can I count on you, or what?"

Trombetta looked hard at me.

"You're an idiot," he said flatly. "Look, you don't have any friends in the department. You screw with Nederlander, you're screwing with their money, man—with their goddam lives. They got bills to pay, families to feed, you know?"

"Chaz," I said. "They're dirty. They're cops and they're dirty."

"Exactly who's getting hurt, J. D?"

"Where does it end? They're past merely scamming phony insurance claims. I hear the stories; shake-downs, 'private' vice raids where nobody seems to file a report. So what's on the menu for tomorrow? At the very least, they've got to keep it covered up. And I know, man—*I* know."

"Yeah, you know. Then you better know that I got no reason to help you, Davey." He looked at me from under his thick eyebrows. In his voice was something not quite defiant and not quite ashamed. "Look—you want to go hunting with Santori, I guess I can't talk you out of it. But I'm not going to get dragged into it, either."

I shook my head. "You don't get it, Chaz—this time, there's no wiggle room left for Nederlander and his people. The Feds are behind this all the way—wiretaps, financial records, immunity offers, even wit-ness protection if it's needed. It's everything we wanted—*needed*—the last time."

Trombetta's face was stony. But the harder I had pressed, the more trapped Chaz Trombetta's eyes had looked.

"Chaz, what the hell's wrong with you? I'm giving it to you straight. It's going to be the endgame. I want you in on this, man. I need you in with me."

He took a deep breath, and blew it out hard.

"You've been among the missing for a while, ol' buddy," he said, and his voice was hard and low. "You want it straight, here it is: these days, I got just as much to lose as any of the others in there." His voice dropped. "You understand? Is it crystal clear now?"

It came too quickly, too unexpectedly for me to have hidden my reaction and Chaz reacted as if he had been struck. He took a step forward, as if he was ready to swing back.

"Here's a thought: why don't you just get the fuck off my property?" he said, pushing forward until his nose was an inch from my face. His hands balled into fists at his side. "You heard me! Get out!"

From behind us, Junie's voice was barely audible.

"Stop it, Chaz," she said. "Davey is a friend." Two green glass bottles, condensation dripping onto the grass, dangled from her hands. Chaz Trombetta looked at his wife, then back to me. Our eyes locked for a long moment, and the scarlet of his anger dissolved in an inverse proportion to the rage that rose inside me.

I was breathing hard, my face twisted, filled with the force of my emotion.

"How deep, Chaz?" I asked, my voice tight and distant in my throat. "How deep are you in this now?"

Trombetta turned away and walked to his wife.

"Just go, Davey," Junie said. "Please."

I stared at the two of them for a moment, as if I did not recognize either. When I spoke, it was to Chaz.

"This time, I'm not stopping," I said. "I can't. You have to understand that, Chaz. It's going all the way, and you'll get hurt. You'll go down with the rest of them."

"You're not wearing a wire—I checked," he said, and I remembered the bear hug with which he had greeted me. "Keep trusting the wrong people, ol' buddy, *you're* the one who's going down. And you won't get up again, not this time."

I looked at Junie, as if in appeal. There was hopelessness written in her posture, along with a loyalty that was unequivocal but not blind. Still, she stood silent with her husband.

I tried one last time.

"It's not too late," I said, probably to both of them.

"I'm not going to do anything to stop you, J. D.," Chaz said. "But I can't stop anybody else from doing what they have to, either."

"Then God help you," I said.

"God help all of us," Chaz Trombetta corrected me. "But you're going to need Him most of all."

Chapter 9

I could not remember the last time I had slept well, or easily. Over the past year, even before my arrest, I had found untroubled sleep increasingly elusive. Since then, most nights had been spent like this one: alone in a rented room intentionally kept dark, a tumbler of vodka held loosely in my hand.

Usually, the vodka worked sufficiently well. It would drug me into a rough approximation of sleep. But in treating the insomnia with alcohol, I found myself plagued with dreams—most of them terrifying, all of them vivid. In the ones I remembered, I was usually alone.

I reclined on the sofa, occasionally taking a long pull on the drink. The rest of the time I stared wide-eyed at the ceiling, listing to the restless sounds of nocturnal traffic. My father had been an insomniac, too, even before he was dismissed from his job as a Chicago police detective. For most of his adult life he had also been a borderline alcoholic, though sufficiently functional to operate the tavern he had inherited from my grandfather in Bucktown, just off Armitage Avenue.

He had been wildly popular with the clientele, largely policemen and firemen—in those days, there were few policewomen and virtually no women firefighters—from around the neighborhood.

At least until his trial, if someone alluded to the

circumstances of his dismissal, his reaction would be a devilish, if rueful, grin. As often as not, he would then launch into an unrelated story that soon had everyone within earshot convulsing in laughter. My father had accumulated a wealth of stories, most of them involving his experiences as a cop—cases that, in his tales if not in his life, never went unsolved.

Gerald Davey was lively and entertaining and a devastatingly attractive man; that is, between the weekly binge blackouts, when his world turned into a dark and frightening place for those of us who inhabited it with him. It was during these periods that my father revisited those other cases—the ones where he had slipped the unmarked envelopes into his pocket, where he had bartered away whatever honor he had accrued along with his badge. He would relive every detail, his eyes burning with the intensity of a man trying to justify, or at least expiate, his past sins. He never could, not even at his most drunken moments; instead, he railed, lost in a helpless rage at his own weakness and guilt.

By the next afternoon—occasionally a little longer— he would again be the Gerald Davey his friends and customers knew.

He never fully remembered what he called his "episodes," and neither my mother nor I ever told him the truth about what he had done or said. As a result, he thought it a trip he had taken alone, though nothing could have been further from the truth.

Tonight, as in so many nights over the past year, I lay in the dark and pondered both heredity and the definition of irony.

Talking with Chaz Trombetta had done nothing to lull the demons that walked night sentinel in my mind. I had hoped for Trombetta's assistance, expected it as a matter of course. But even more, I had needed someone to trust. I was on a dark road, and I had counted on Chaz to walk it with me. Now that was gone, too.

"Maybe," I said aloud to the dark room, "I ought to have another drink."

As if to answer, there was a quiet tapping at the door.

I frowned. It was too late for a call by Jehovah's Witnesses, and none of my neighbors had the appearance of people who socialized easily or well. I had half decided to ignore it when a voice, low and tentative, spoke my name.

I opened the door. Even in the dim light, I recognized the figure who stood there.

"All the lights were off," said a voice that had once been familiar to me. "I wasn't sure you were here. I'm glad you're still awake. Or have you started sleeping in your clothes?"

"Hello, Ellen," I said. "Come in."

Ellen was dressed in a blue oxford shirt that was too large for her slight form. I wondered if it was one of mine, though a darker corner of my mind suspected it was not. She had rolled the sleeves to just below her elbows. The shirttail was tucked into a pair of soft khaki trousers that emphasized her trim figure. Many women might have pulled their hair into a ponytail to match the gamine look of the outfit. Not Ellen; hers fell in a fine ashen cascade that emphasized the compact beauty of her face. It made me remember how soft her hair had felt beneath my hands.

She walked directly to the sofa and sat in a way that invited me to sit beside her. Instead, I drew a chair from the dinette set. I settled across from her at what I hoped was a safe distance for both of us.

We sat in silence for a long moment as Ellen surveyed my lodgings. Before she could speak, I did.

"It used to be a motel," I said. "A long time ago. Now they rent rooms by the week."

She nodded. I wondered if she had noticed the vodka on my breath.

"I found a job," I said, in the tone used by two acquaintances catching up on each other. "Temporary, but it pays the rent. I'm back on the city payroll—as a fire marshal."

Ellen looked at me. "A fire marshal," she said, as if I had told a joke with a punch line she could not understand.

"It's an arson investigation," I said. "More or less. A couple of people died in the fire."

She frowned. "So you're working with the police again. With Bob Nederlander's people. Davey, why? I know the way you feel about them. About *him*."

I felt my anger rise.

"A job is a job," I said, "and I needed one. But let's talk about *you*, shall we? You look well—or is it 'you look good'?"

I leaned back, and pretended to ponder.

"Doesn't matter. You've always looked great, as I remember. Of course, I haven't seen you in months—not since the divorce hearing. That's right, isn't it? You even missed my trial. Then, last week, you call me about a late check—"

"And you fixed it," she interrupted. "Thank you for that."

"Thank Gil Cieloczki," I snapped. "He gave me the job." I drew in a breath. "For months, we've only communicated through lawyers. Suddenly, I hear from you twice in one week. Why is that, Ellen?"

She flushed, and was silent for a moment.

"I've been approached by the government," Ellen said finally. "Yesterday, two people from the IRS were waiting for me when I came home. They wanted to talk about the bribes they say you took. They offered me a deal."

I frowned.

"What deal? What is there *to* deal? I never took a payoff. You know that. How could they give you—" I stopped short, and looked closely at my former wife. "Ellen, what do they want from you?"

"Almost nothing," she said, too quickly. "They just want me to sign a statement that you handled all our finances. That I wouldn't have known about anything you . . . may have been doing."

She looked up at me, and a familiar petulance was in her voice.

"And really, isn't that the truth, Davey? Okay—not about money, maybe. But everything else. I didn't know what you were doing, or who you were doing it with. Now you're back to playing policeman, and I *still* don't know."

Ellen's voice broke, and her hands flew to cover her face.

"If I cooperate, they promise to remove my name from their case," she said from behind her hands. "They'll take the liens off. They'll even unfreeze our bank account—at least, partly. The part of it that belongs to me."

Ellen's hands dropped. I saw her lovely eyes glitter, even though they were curiously dry of tears.

"Maybe I won't have people looking at me as if I was some kind of criminal. Or was married to one." She bent her head. "That didn't come out the way I meant. All I'm saying is—"

"If that's what you came to tell me," I said, "I understand. Go ahead, Ellen. Do the deal."

When she looked up, she had stopped crying, or perhaps pretending to. But now there was something new in her expression.

"I wanted to come here tonight," Ellen said, "to tell you I would. And to be with you."

She rose from the sofa, and stood over me. The scent of her was a memory—earthy, compelling, full of hungers and delights only partially recalled. But mesmerizing, nonetheless.

"We were in love, once," she whispered. "Remember?"

My voice was hoarse. "Ellen," I said. "That's over. We're over."

"I know," she said. "I know."

She took me by my hand and led me toward the bedroom. I followed, as if in a dream.

There, Ellen bent to remove the coverlet. Her legs were slightly spread, stretching the khaki trousers tight over her hard, rounded bottom. It was, intentionally or not, an exquisitely provocative stance.

In that instant, I knew how badly I wanted her, wanted the connection to my past life that she represented to me. Even more, I wanted to rip the clothes from her body, to move inside her like a wild animal in heat. I wanted to hear her voice, pitched high in passion, cry in my ear when she came. My pulse pounded in my temples, and I felt myself rise.

I moved close behind her, put my hands on her shoulders. For a moment, Ellen was still, almost pensive. Then she slowly arched back into my embrace, and my body responded to the feel of her pressed against me. She turned her head over her shoulder, eyes already closed and lips slightly parted. We kissed deeply. I felt the blood rush to her face, burning beneath my hands.

When her weight shifted, I sensed rather than felt her right leg bend at the knee. She pulled one of my hands downward.

My flattened palm cupped, teased her breast in passing, not stopping; slipped lower, across the toned flatness of her stomach, not stopping; brushed the edge of a hip, still not stopping. She moved into my touch, and I heard her breath catch in her throat as she pressed back against me even harder.

We were like that for what seemed an eternity, our lips and tongues lightly probing, seeking; our bodies responding to featherlight touches and caresses. Then she broke away, violence in the movement. She stared at me, neither of us moving, while thoughts I could not decipher swirled apace behind her eyes. Finally, her expression slipped into one that looked as if it had confirmed a questioned fact, verified a secret knowledge.

I heard the rasp of a zipper, the rustle of cloth being pulled free. Then she stood before me, a naked and sensuous silhouette.

She came again into my arms, kissing me hard while her fingers tore at my buttons. When I stepped out of the last of my own clothes, we clutched and fumbled in a frenzied need for each other. My hand slid along the smoothness of Ellen's back, tracing a contour lower and lower into her dark, secret places. This time she did gasp, a high-pitched inhalation quickly cut off. Her breathing became fevered, so loud it was almost a low, keening moan, feverish against the side of my face.

We slipped to the floor, ignoring the narrow bed. Her arms reached up for me, hot and passionate, her hips pumping involuntarily, grinding against me. I felt an impatient hand reach between them, guiding me. We both shuddered in a pleasure so tight, so deep.

I could feel every gyration, every intake of breath, every hoarsely whispered exhortation that escaped her swollen lips. Again and again we moved against each other, a mounting syncopation of physical heat. Her face grew crimson with lust, her eyes squeezed shut, her mouth wide in the need to cry out her passion. I could feel her thighs clenched tight against my hips, her ankles crossed at the small of my back. Her fingernails raked hard along my sides, dug deeply into my shoulders.

The pleasure was incredible, indescribable.

Now she was grunting with each stroke, a wordless and hungry sound that was both demand and plea. It spurred me, pushed me closer to my own release. I thrust again and again and again. Her cries were louder now, joined by a second, deeper voice that I dimly realized was my own.

I took her hands and forced them down to the floor over her head and held them there. Suddenly she arched up, her little cries loud in my ears as she came, once and once again. I exploded along with her, and violent shudders tore through both our bodies.

For a long time afterward we lay together as the sweat cooled, chill on our bodies. Our breathing slowly returned to a regular rhythm. My arm was around Ellen's shoulder. I moved to stroke her arm, and felt her shrug away my touch. Her body, I realized in alarm, had turned stiff, angry.

"What are we doing, Davey?" she asked, and her voice was cold. "Is there a point to all this?"

"I don't know."

Silence.

Then:

"You don't know," she said, mockingly. "Once again, you get to be the nice guy, and I get to be the slut?"

"You came here, Ellen."

"Yes, throw that at me, Davey; you've been standing on my doorstep enough times. Do you think it's going to be like this from now on? I drop by your place, we'll fuck, and then go our separate ways? Until the next time?"

Her voice had risen, and she pulled away from me.

"Ellen," I began, hearing the confusion in my voice, "I don't understand why you're angry. I thought that we—"

"We? There is no 'we,' Davey. If you think hard enough about it, maybe there never really was."

In stony silence, Ellen dressed with her back to me. The door slammed behind her as she left.

I don't know how long I sat there, the air around me still pungent in the shadow of our lovemaking. My mind was adrift, numbed by the lash of Ellen's rage. I stared into the darkness of my room, aware once again of my own inadequacy and failure, particularly in regard to the enigma that was Ellen.

In my self-pity, I replayed the evening over and over. At first, I thought I did so merely to pick at a

still fresh wound, but gradually I realized that there
was something more. Whatever part of me that made
me a cop stood to the side, watching the movie loop
again and again and coolly analyzing tonight's
performance.

And finding it wanting, somehow lacking in
conviction.

Ellen's anger had been real enough, though I remained baffled at what I had done to trigger it. Certainly, the sex had felt real, too; still, I had never
known Ellen to possess a need to counterfeit her actions in that area.

Our marriage had been episodic at best, but during
it I knew of only one emotion that invariably ignited
a firestorm in her: during her not-infrequent transgres-
sions, Ellen would soothe her own sense of guilt
through a wrath that was never directed toward
herself.

She had told me of the deal she had made—but had
she told me the full story? For reasons I could not
fathom, various enforcement agencies of the United
States had targeted me, personally. In addition to what
she had told me, what other arrangements had Ellen
made? Was it part of a larger campaign, and if so,
why? I had been party to no systematic corruption,
participated in no crime that would merit the kind of
full-court legal press that was descending on Ellen—
and through her, on me.

That is, unless my guilt or innocence was
irrelevant—and the enormity of what that might mean
momentarily left me breathless.

It was a physical sensation: I could clearly feel the
bulls-eye that, I had no doubt, was painted on my
back. For the rest of the night, the weight of it—and
perhaps of the suspicion of who had put it there—
crushed down on me.

April 20

Chapter 10

As a young Catholic sent to the parish school, I had
been taught by the nuns that the original sin commit-
ted by Adam and Eve was their discovery of the sex
act. Once this had been communicated as unassailable
fact, the teaching sisters brooked no additional analysis or discussion of the subject.

For the most part, we were too young or too innocent to question our teachers further; still, the lesson
stuck, adding an element of dark and delicious taboo
to much of our adolescent courtships and ex-
perimentations.

It was only later in life, when I started to relate the
events in my personal and professional life with the
dogma I had absorbed, that I began seriously to question the nuns' interpretation.

For God to have expelled from Eden those He created in His own image was a horrendous chastisement—
one that must have required an act of defiance equal
to the punishment. Banishing man for an act He had
made compelling—not to mention essential—seemed
far too frivolous for an otherwise all-merciful deity.

As a police officer, I had come to believe that the
sin of Adam and Eve had nothing to do with either
orgasm or procreation, though it clearly involved the
loss of their innocence. I am convinced that original
sin, and perhaps all sin, involves the loss of faith—a
wholesale abandonment of belief in God's capacity for

mercy. It is a collective guilt, born of acts that, whether performed or only witnessed in the deeds of other humans, are so black and so evil that they drive us to deny His very existence.

This was a truth that my father, whose sins I seemed determined to have visited on me, would certainly have embraced.

Gerald Davey had been a detective on a police force that was institutionally corrupt from bottom to top. The price of services rendered rose exponentially and by rank, so that lieutenants and captains and commanders routinely calculated their pay grades on an unofficial scale far more generous than the civil service schedules.

Not all Chicago officers were dirty, of course; but at the very least, most were complicit through their silence. They accepted the corruption as readily as one accepts the occasional sour whiff from a down-alley Dumpster.

But Gerald Davey was an active participant, and had been so his entire career.

"He once described the system to me as a crooked-cop Amway pyramid. An organizational structure that ensured graduated, orderly profits up and down the line, but mostly up."

"Your father certainly had a way with words," Father Frank said, jabbing his garden trowel at a particularly stubborn dandelion root. On the portable radio near his knees, it was the bottom of the third inning at Wrigley; Sosa had just stroked one onto Waveland Avenue, cutting the Mets' lead to six. Both the priest and I were trying, unsuccessfully, not to think about it.

"By the time he made detective, Gerald was pretty well established as a player on the force," I said. "When he was assigned to the Vice and Morals Squad, it was like becoming a vice president at IBM."

The priest looked puzzled.

"He'd bring home bonuses that were four or five

times his city paycheck. Except that the bonuses were always in cash."

Father Frank stood up, and brushed the dirt from his hands. He studied the plot critically, bending once to realign one of the stakes.

"So what happened to him?" he said, trying to sound casual.

"He got caught," I said. "He started to skim too much off for himself. So the cops higher up the ladder decided to make him an example of what happens when you stiff the brass. One day, he went to work and the Internal Affairs Divison was waiting for him."

"He went to jail?"

"No," I said. "It took about a year for the case to go to trial. He was found guilty, but sentencing was set for a week later. Somebody in IAD had the bright idea of trying to flip him, get him to turn on the people who had turned on him. But he had been a cop all his life, you see."

Father Frank nodded. "He was too loyal to implicate other policemen. I've heard that happens."

"Not too loyal, too proud," I corrected the priest. "Three days after he was convicted, I came home and found him upstairs, in bed. He had put on his dress uniform. Then he ate his gun."

Chapter 11

Lake Tower is a diverse community—or at least it had
become one, sharing in the explosive growth fueled
by the exodus from city to suburb that marked every
American metropolitan area since the 1950s. The difference was that it had started rich, an enclave of the
affluent founded by and for the beneficiaries of late-
nineteenth-century industrialism.

Unlike many of the instant cities that evolved from
small town roots, Lake Tower had both the fore-
thought and the resources to plan much of its own
destiny.

To maintain a solid tax base without overly taxing
the residents themselves, Lake Tower nurtured
growth, courting corporations with various incentives
to construct new headquarters campuses on what was
then greenfield outskirts of town. Later, when developers began scouting sites for sprawling shopping centers, Lake Tower readily expanded the incentives to
embrace the malls and collect the hefty sales tax reve-
nues they provided.

This served as a beacon to both ends of the economic spectrum. The ranks of the well-off were
swelled by newcomers who sought both the status traditionally associated with the enclave of older money
and the surprisingly low property taxes on their substantial homes; housing developments, many of them
as tasteful as they were distant from the more affluent

neighborhoods, drew middle- and upper-middle-class homeowners.

A tradition of Waspishness gradually moderated as growth pushed the city borders closer to Jewish and Catholic areas and an inevitable cross-fertilization. In the mid-1980s, the profits available in lower-income, multi-family housing further democratized Lake Tower, though it was carefully controlled through zoning and construction permits.

In sum, all this contributed to a proven equation for success, though one with inverse properties. In Lake Tower, wealth begat prosperity, which in turn begat more wealth.

I was in the passenger seat and Terry Posson was driving, heading east on a busy thoroughfare that was alive with the kind of shops and shoppers that were the logical extension of the mathematics of wealth. Trees in the parkway were already green with foliage; it reminded me of Chaz Trombetta's painstakingly landscaped yard. We had seen each other several times since that day—rather, I had seen Chaz, who had looked straight through me without a word or sign of recognition. It was a warm-hearted enthusiasm compared to the looks and occasional muttered comments I was receiving from other former colleagues on the Lake Tower police force.

I shook off the memory, and tried to concentrate on the early afternoon April sunlight, warm on my right arm where it rested on the open window frame.

It was time to get to work.

"So, Terry," I said, conversationally, "how long have you been on the job here?"

She drove with both hands on the wheel at two and ten o'clock, just like they taught in high school driver's ed. "Year, come June," she said. "I was on the force in Seattle before I moved to Illinois."

"You and Bird work together before this case?"

She nodded. "We've been partnered up since I came on board. Mel's an okay guy."

I checked the sign at the next corner. It was as good a place as any.

"What *is* it with this case? I mean, you two actually have been working it, right? Full-time, since January?"

"We were assigned to the case right after you were arrested," she said, her voice level. "About a week after the fire. So it was February, if you want to be accurate."

"Sure, yeah—February. I want to be accurate, all right. So tell me: how'd you two pick your interview subjects? Did you look in a phone book, or just stop people at random on the street?"

Posson shot a glance at me. I smiled politely, showing more teeth than usual.

"We talked to a couple of dozen people who had a connection to the victims in one way or another," she said, in a tone so without emotion that it signaled something radically different. "We followed the leads we had, and took them to where they led. You know how some cases are—you drill a lot of dry holes along the way."

"A *lot* of dry holes," I agreed. "Everything just seems to have turned into a dead end, hasn't it?"

"You got something on your mind, just say it." She drove like somebody who had a lot of experience on the street. I watched her eyes tracking regularly between the road ahead, both sets of mirrors and the activity on the sidewalks we passed. Only the fixed set of her lips and the knuckle-tight, two-handed grip she had on the steering wheel signaled just how furious she was.

"How long were you on the force in Seattle?"

"Five years," she said. "Two in uniform, a year on a tac unit, and the rest in plainclothes investigations. Vice and narcotics, mainly."

"You run many investigations out there?" I kept my voice neutral. "Head them up, I mean."

"A few," she said, and I noted her struggle not to sound defensive. "What's your point?"

"So you come to Lake Tower, you're on the force less than a year—and you're assigned lead investigator on a double homicide."

I waited a second or two for a response. "C'mon, Terry—I read your jacket. It's your first homicide case here. Tell me if I'm wrong; this is your first homicide investigation, period. Didn't you wonder why you caught this case? Didn't it occur to you that there must have been a half dozen guys with gold shields— *real* detectives, with tons more experience—that should have gotten a case as high profile as this?"

She shrugged, eyes locked on the road. "And we used some of 'em. Look, a lot of people have logged hours on this case. Even Nederlander put in time on it, particularly the first couple of weeks. If you want to know why I'm still on it, ask him. Maybe he liked the work Bird and I did."

I laughed, intentionally making it harsh and ugly.

"Yeah," I said, "Well, a girl's got to start somewhere—but *you*, Terry, you started right at the top. They didn't even partner you up with somebody a little more . . . seasoned. Somebody who could, say, show you the ropes." I grinned, wide and insinuatingly. "Lead investigator. You find it hard to sell that one? Probably not, eh? Not with a randy old boy like Nederlander."

Posson's lower lip curled, and she nodded. "Uh-huh. Now we get down to it, right? 'Who's she sleeping with?' That's original as hell."

She turned to face me directly, and her eyes burned into mine. "Well, fuck *you*." She returned to her driving. "Get this straight. I didn't ask for this case: I was assigned to it. Yeah, I was glad to get on it. Yeah, I got lead—but that was assigned to me, too. I didn't ask anybody for any favors on this."

"Oh, I see," I said lightly. "This is one of those

affirmative action things. This is where we make up for years of oppression, in the name of all those women blocked out of police work by sexist pigs. Strike a blow for sisterhood united."

I made a show of looking out the window. "Of course, it also meant three wasted months of investigation, didn't it? That's a hell of an on-the-job training program. Cheap at the price, don't you think? I'll bet Kathleen Levinstein would have been proud to be part of your personal campaign to break through the glass ceiling."

I felt Posson's eyes burning into the back of my head, and turned to take them head-on. Her lips were a tight thin line and the muscles on one side of her jaw twitched furiously.

"I don't know you," she said evenly. "But it's a cold day in hell that I have to put up with crap from somebody who sold his ass and that gold shield you're so proud of, just for a few bucks from a couple of low-life car thieves."

She pulled to the curb and stopped.

"It's your goddam interview, and you don't need any help from me. Find a taxi, or just start walking," Posson said. Her tone was the one taught by the better police training academies for use in explosive situations. "But you want to get out—right *now*!"

I stepped out and closed the door, then started to lean in to deliver what would have been a final stinging exit line. Instead, the car surged forward from under the hand I still had on the door handle. I concentrated on delivering my toes away from the spinning wheels.

I stood on the curb, and watched her turn the corner. Above the other traffic noises, I heard her tires squeal in protest.

I flagged down the second of two empty cabs that passed in the next few minutes. The first had slowed at my gesture. Then it had continued on, the driver studiously avoiding my eye.

The second cab pulled up for the red light, and I climbed in. In the mirror, I saw the driver look at me with a flash of irritation, and I realized that I had slammed the door much too hard.

Years ago in Chicago, long before I had met Ellen, I dated an actress from the Goodman Theater. Like most performers, she enjoyed talking about her profession almost as much as she enjoyed talking about herself. The secret of being persuading in any role, she had told me, is simple: you just convince yourself that you're not acting.

I looked at my reflection in the mirror, and saw a man whose face was still flushed an angry red. My former girlfriend would have been proud.

I had been convincing enough to keep Terry Posson from coming along to our appointment at B'nai Abraham, and accomplished it in a way she would think was her own choice.

All by being, for lack of a better term, a flaming asshole.

It's easy, I told myself, though my smile was grim. *I haven't done it for a while, but it's good to know I still remember how.*

Chapter 12

Temple B'nai Abraham was a large white-brick complex located well back from the busy thoroughfare it bordered in Highland Park. The white-striped parking lot would have done justice to a medium-sized shopping mall. But on this midweek midafternoon, only a half dozen cars were parked randomly near the main entrance.

Rabbi Bernard Jerome was a surprise. He was younger than I had expected, a trim man in his early thirties whose black hair had probably started to recede when he was in high school. He was dressed casually, a Clan Stuart plaid wool sports jacket and dark slacks, and his shirt was open at the collar.

On the wood-paneled wall behind his walnut desk hung framed photographs, many of them featuring politicians or celebrities I recognized from newspapers and magazines. Jerome was the common denominator in all of them, the varying degrees of formality or intimacy gauged by the handshakes or the arms draped over shoulders.

We were sipping very good coffee. It had been served in surprisingly delicate china cups by a white-haired secretary whose elongated glasses gave her the eyes of a startled cat.

For the past half hour, we had examined the Levinsteins from every angle I could conceive. The results were scarcely worth the effort. I knew nothing more

than what I had at the start, and was nearing the end
of my list.

I leaned over the desk, checking the remaining tape
supply on my recorder. It was a Sony, voice-activated
and miniaturized to the size of a cigarette pack.

Sensing the interview was nearing its end, Jerome
offered to have the cat-lady call a cab.

"We were all devastated when we heard about Stan
and Kathleen," the rabbi continued. "It was a
tragedy—in addition to being members of our congregation, they were my friends."

"Did Stanley Levinstein have any hobbies, any interests you know about?" I pressed. "For instance,
I've heard some talk about an art collection. Did he
ever discuss it with you?"

The rabbi looked puzzled. "I didn't even know he
had one."

"What about Mrs. Levinstein? Do you know if she
had an interest in art? Did she ever mention pieces
she might have bought—the artist, or where she
bought them?"

"No, not that I recall." He paused, considering.
"No . . . but that doesn't mean she didn't collect. I
mean, they clearly could have afforded to buy anything they wanted. Stan was a very successful business-
man, and she had money of her own. I understand
she came from people who were quite well-off."

"Really?"

"So I understand. I'm afraid I don't know a lot
about her background. Kathleen was very quiet. But
I know that she was Stan's source of strength," Jerome
said. "Really, I think it was the same for Stan; the
two of them were dedicated to each other. They were
childless, you know."

"Were the Levinsteins active? In your temple, I
mean."

"Stan was very active," Jerome replied. "Kathleen
less so—she had converted to Judaism when they married, and I think she attended temple only because of

Stan. But Stan—he took his religion very seriously, like many of our members, and he actively supported a lot of our initiatives. The thing about Stan, he did more than just contribute money."

Jerome turned to the wall, and carefully lifted one of the framed photos off its attachment. He handed it to me.

It showed a very young Jerome wearing an M-65 field jacket, one shoulder bearing the yellow-and-black crest of the First Cavalry Division. He was leaning, aggressively, over a blue police barricade. Though the photo was cropped to focus on the young man, a discerning eye could also see that he was surrounded by mostly older men dressed in an eclectic variety of military attire. In the photo, their faces were tight and their eyes hard.

Jerome's own face was contorted, his hands cupped around his open mouth. Passing closely in the foreground, in blurry focus, I could make out a figure wearing a white cowl and pointed hood that covered the face.

"You probably remember back—oh, years and years ago? The Klan and the American Nazi Party got a permit to march over in Skokie. Stan worked around the clock to try to get that parade permit canceled. When that didn't happen, he organized a group of veterans from the synagogue to show up for a counter-demonstration. He told everybody to wear their old military uniforms."

Jerome chuckled. "Truth be told, Stan was one of the few who could still fit in his. He had been a combat infantryman in Korea, you know."

"He sounds like a man who liked to get involved."

The rabbi nodded vigorously. "Very much so. As they say, Stanley Levinstein didn't just talk the talk—he walked the walk, all the way."

I handed the photo across the desk, and Jerome carefully returned it to its place. The rabbi took exceptional care, I noticed, to align the frame perfectly level.

"Did a lot of your people show up in Skokie?" I asked, wondering how he would react. The glance he shot me was thoughtful and penetrating, in equal measure. But his tone, when he spoke, was mild.

"Oh, sure. You have to remember, a lot of people at B'nai Abraham lost family members in the Holocaust," Jerome explained. "We have almost a dozen actual survivors of the camps in our congregation. For some of our older members especially, what happened to the Jews in the thirties and forties isn't a part of history—it's what they and their families lived through. Stan Levinstein just didn't want to let the world forget the horror. Or the injustice."

He tented his fingers and frowned in concentration.

"Let me give you an idea what kind of guy Stan was," he said. "This was before I took the appointment here, back in the bad old days of the Soviet Union. B'nai Abraham sponsored the emigration of a pretty substantial number of Russian Jews. The temple formed a lot of committees, raised funds and put together a letter-writing campaign to urge the Soviets to let their Jews go to Israel.

"Well, Stan didn't believe in committee work or writing letters." Jerome smiled. "So the son of a gun packed his bags and went over there himself. He spent weeks at a time in Moscow, working and making deals with the Russians to let those people leave for Israel. Then he'd go to Israel to help arrange for their resettlement. The infrastructure he set up is still operating, I understand."

Jerome leaned forward, in the manner of someone passing along a confidence.

"Just between you and me, I've heard he found some unofficial channels that he used, too."

He gave me a significant look, and pressed a forefinger against the side of his nose. It was a gesture I

had seen only in movies, and I choked back my smile
when I saw the rabbi was serious.

"Russian gangsters, I mean." Jerome nodded solemnly. "For every Jew who he got out with a passport
stamped by the Russians, he smuggled another half
dozen out in the back of some unmarked truck, probably." The rabbi sat back in his chair, a satisfied smile
on his face.

"So you see, Stan liked the, uh . . . direct approach,"
Jerome said. "For him, it worked. And let me tell you,
a lot of people have good reason to be grateful. You
know the old Hebrew saying? 'Whoever saves one life
saves the entire world.' That's what 'never again'
meant to Stan. I miss his fire and dedication. He was
always . . . oh, 'creative' is a good word for it. The
man could always surprise you."

Unexpectedly, the young rabbi grinned. "I have to
wonder what he'd be doing today, with all the furor
over the Swiss gold."

I raised my eyebrows politely. "I thought all that
had been resolved. Didn't the Swiss banks agree to
pay some kind of reimbursement?"

"You're talking about the fund the Swiss banks set
up," Jerome said, with a dismissive movement of his
hands. "A little more than a billion dollars to reim-
burse Holocaust survivors who held accounts that pre-
dated 1939. Rather, in most cases, pay off their heirs.
Of course, you know this story?"

His lips twisted in derision, and he did not wait for
a response. "The majority of the 'missing' depositors
died in the extermination camps. Then the Swiss
would declare the accounts 'dormant.' Effectively,
they confiscated the funds. So what else is new? With
the Swiss, it's always about money. They laundered
gold for the Nazis throughout the war—gold stolen
from treasuries of countries they occupied, melted
down from looted art objects and jewelry—even
pulled from the mouths of Jews they murdered. Many
historians believe the war would have ended before

1943 had the Nazis not had the financial resources of the Swiss to fuel their war machine."

Jerome threw up his hands in disgust.

"So, for decades they stonewalled any attempt by the heirs to claim the accounts—denying they had any records, usually. But a couple of years ago in Zurich, some bank employee with a conscience looked in a bag full of paper just before it went to the shredder. What do you know? It was full of documentation on Jewish property."

The rabbi shook his head in outraged disbelief. "Still, the Swiss resisted. It took class-action lawsuits, sanctions against them by cities and states, even the threat of action against them by the Senate Banking Committee before they finally agreed to the billion-dollar settlement in 1998."

"So you won," I said. Without being obvious, I glanced at the wall clock behind the rabbi's head.

Jerome shrugged.

"One battle in a much larger war," the rabbi replied. "Important as they were, these private accounts are only the tip of the iceberg. The real issue is much, much bigger. It's about all the property—some of it Jewish, much of it not—that's still 'missing' from World War II. One of our members—she's a professor of art history at Northwestern University—spoke to the congregation on this a year ago. I tell you, sir, it's staggering!"

He aimed a finger at me as if addressing a reluctant student in his history class.

"The fact is that confiscated property, worth tens of billions in today's dollars, never went to the proper owners or heirs. After the war, the Allied powers appropriated a lot of this stuff for themselves. Especially the Soviet Union. The Russians took all the Nazi loot they could get their hands on—gold, statues, paintings, even the drapes from German houses. They carried it back home and called it 'war reparations.'"

"Kind of hard to blame them," I ventured, this time

openly looking at my wristwatch. "As I recall my history classes, the Germans killed millions of Russians. Devastated their country."

"What does it make you when you steal from a thief?" Jerome asked, his tone making the question anything but rhetorical. "You're still a thief if you don't return it to the rightful owners. And the scale of this particular theft is enormous, Mr. Davey. You are interested in collections of artwork? The Russians won't even admit to all the works of art they're still hiding—famous pieces, some of them, lost to the world."

"And quite valuable, I guess."

"You want a conservative estimate? The artwork alone is worth perhaps ten times, perhaps *twenty* times all the gold that was stolen. Perhaps even more. I've seen estimates of $140 billion."

"In artwork," I repeated, and my attention was no longer on the clock.

Jerome's voice turned scornful. "Of course, all this was addressed in 1998—oh, so fully and completely. There was an international conference in Washington, D.C., a very impressive gathering of more than forty nations hosted by our government. During this meeting, our former secretary of state—a very sincere lady, I am certain—announced a 'breakthrough.' The Russians, she said, had agreed to return all art that could be proven to belong to Holocaust victims."

Jerome looked at me expectantly for several seconds, his expression that of a man waiting for someone else to supply the punch line.

"*Proven,* Mr. Davey—as it turned out, that was the key word," he said. "The Russians made a great show of pledging cooperation, and all the conference delegates were very excited. So excited that they failed to listen to the rest of what Moscow's representative was saying. The gentleman cautioned the conference that it would be quite difficult to separate 'victim art' from the rest of the so-called 'reparation art' that the Soviets had taken from the Nazis. As I recall, the Russian delegate asked for what he termed 'international research assistance' as a first step. Of course, nothing substantive could be done in the interim."

He snorted, loudly and derisively.

"It turned out to be typical Russian stonewalling," Jerome said. "Purely for the purpose of manipulating public opinion. It was no coincidence. The same day their pledge was made to the art conference—*the very same day, sir!*—the head of the International Monetary Fund was in Moscow. Russia wanted immediate aid. Remember? They were in their worst economic crisis since Communist rule ended."

The rabbi smiled coldly. "Modern Russia has become quite adept at public relations. If the looted artwork is a barricade to getting IMF cash, defuse the issue! Promises are cheap. Much cheaper than surrendering billions in real assets. "

"And it worked?" I asked.

"It worked," Jerome said. "It's working today. Look at the headlines. The Russians still lurch from one financial crisis to the next; the West is still holding the purse strings. The Russians hold perhaps a hundred billion dollars in stolen art, like a kidnapper demanding a ransom. At the same time, the conservatives in the Russian Duma have passed a law that officially claims the 'confiscated' art as Russian national treasure. And aside from a few minor art pieces turned over to the heirs of Holocaust survivors, the 'research' is still unfinished. My guess—it won't be finished in my lifetime. Failing something dramatic, that is."

The intercom buzzed. "That'll be your taxi," Jerome said. "I'll walk you out."

I snapped off the tape recorder and dropped it in my pocket.

We passed the white-haired secretary's sentry post in silence. I was about to break the silence when Jerome seized me by the arm, startling me with the strength of his grip.

"So there you have the real outrage, sir," Jerome said. "The Russians are still hiding many billions of dollars' worth of stolen art, a lot of it taken from Jews. Everybody knows it, but nobody has ever been able to present any legal proof. And for political purposes, no Western government has ever had the courage to demand a real accounting. Even the United States prefers to maintain the fiction. To say that this artwork was destroyed in the war, or is simply 'missing'—it's moral cowardice, on an international scale."

He again fell silent, almost abruptly. In the sudden stillness, I could think of nothing to say.

"Well, just listen to me," he said, suddenly. A carefully jovial tone had replaced the previous heat. "See what happens when you get a rabbi talking?" He laughed, not quite apologetically.

At the temple entrance, we shook hands.

"If I can be of any further help, don't hesitate."

"I appreciate it. I'll watch the newspapers to see how you're doing with the Swiss, and the rest of them."

"Temple B'nai Abraham has formed a committee," he said solemnly. "I suspect we'll organize a letter-writing campaign."

Then he winked.

"Oh, yeah," the rabbi said, "I *really* miss Stan."

Chapter 13

About the time I was leaving Rabbi Jerome's office, a conversation was taking place in the Winery, a tavern located conveniently close to the Lake Tower Municipal Center. It was late in the afternoon, and the darkened room was populated mainly by off-duty cops and other city employees making a decompression stop before heading to their homes.

Concealed in the majority of the booths along the wall are small microphones. This is not generally known, except to the agency that installed them and the establishment's owner, who allowed the installation in exchange for an agreement involving interstate gambling charges.

I would not know any of this until later that day, when I listened to the recording. It was played for me by an FBI agent who had been sitting in a booth with a view that commanded the barroom.

"The guy is a real asshole," Terry Posson was saying.

She stared stonily into the smoky depths of a drink she held in a loose two-handed grip on the table. "He thinks I got lead on this case by screwing Nederlander."

Across from her, slouched on his side of the booth, Mel Bird grunted sympathetically.

"Prick," he agreed.

"He sits there, tells me to my face that I'm the reason the case turned into a flameout."

Bird nodded. "Dickhead." He sprinkled a few grains of salt into his beer glass, and watched the trails of tiny bubbles rise through the amber liquid in unerringly straight lines.

"Hell, he practically accused me of torpedoing the investigation!"

"Dumbshit."

There was a silence from the other side of the table. It amplified the background sounds of the room. Bird again reached for the salt shaker, and looked up to see his partner glaring at him.

"What?" Bird said, defensively.

"What?" she mocked. "I'm telling you how this bent son of a bitch we've got to work with says we're morons. Thinks we fucked up the biggest case the city's ever had. And do you have anything to add? Hell, no! You can't even look me in the eye! What the hell's the matter with you?"

"Look, Ter—there's a simple answer here," Bird said. "Why don't you just *tell* him? Or better still, tell Cieloczki."

"I can't—not without clearing it through Nederlander first," she said. "Mel, I don't know what the hell is going on with this thing. We're cops, right? So all of a sudden, we're working for the fire chief . . . on a homicide. And he decides to bring in a crooked ex-cop—a guy who dodged a bribery beef by *this* much. I mean, what the hell?" She raised her glass and drank.

"Yeah, well," Bird said, "I've been asking around about Davey. You know something? There's a lot of people in the shop who aren't too sure that bust was on the up-and-up. Nobody wants to come right out and say it. But, dammit, I get the feeling that they think maybe the guy was set up to take a fall."

Posson looked at him, incredulous. "What do you mean, 'set up'? Set up by who? For what?"

"Right," Bird said. "Like I got any answers for that.

I tell you, nobody wants to talk about it. Even his old partner—Trombetta—blew me off. It's like they're all relieved that his case fell apart when it did. As in, it could have led to some deep shit in the department."

"Like what?"

Bird looked at his partner with irritation. "C'mon, Terry—you can't tell me you haven't felt something is a little . . . *off* around here. Jeez, you've got to have noticed it. There's two kinds of cops on the job around this place—the guys who have been around forever, like Nederlander, and the people who have been hired in the last year or so. You. Me."

He took a deep swallow from his glass.

"Hell, I know you've felt it. That's why you jumped at that little arrangement when Nederlander gave you the chance to get on the Levinstein case."

"All I did—"

"I know what you did. I went along with it, too, remember? I want a gold shield just as much as you do—explaining I'm 'just' a plainclothes cop is getting real old, okay? But when Cieloczki took over the case, everything changed. And this Davey thing—everybody knows it wouldn't have happened without Evans' go-ahead."

Bird shook his head vehemently.

"Anyway, the guy's right and you know it. Hell, we advanced the investigation more in that one meeting with Cieloczki than we did in the past two and a half months. We had the same information available as he did—we just ignored it and spent all our time shaking the wrong bushes."

Bird drained his glass and looked around to signal the woman behind the bar. She held up two fingers and raised her eyebrows. Bird glanced at Posson, and nodded.

"Morons?" he muttered. "Hell, he's being kind."

"Jesus, what a mess this is turning into," Posson said. "I even threw the bastard out of my car today, on the way over to reinterview that rabbi. I was so

ticked off I was ready to go to Cieloczki and quit the
case right then."

"Whoa!" said Bird. "This case is the biggest game
in town. I want to stay in, even if we have to eat
humble pie for a while."

"Yeah. Me, too, I guess."

"So?"

"So I guess I apologize and kiss his ass tomorrow,"
she said. "Not that I have much of a choice. Nederlander wants to be filled in on everything Cieloczki's
got us doing. Especially, he wants to know what that
shit Davey is up to. I am to, quote, report in detail
who, what, when, where and why. So now I'm undercover on my own investigation, for God's sake."

"Well," Bird said, "you know I'm with you. Any
way you want to play it, okay? But I gotta tell you, I
think Gil's got the right ideas. Don't forget it was
Nederlander who was telling you what doorknobs to
try the past couple of months. And we were going
exactly nowhere with it."

"Yeah, but now it's a question of who I want to piss
off the most," Posson said. "The guy who's heading up
the investigation? When you get down to it, he only
runs the fire department. Or I can get in the crapper
with the police chief—*our* boss, a guy who's been
around so long he's also director of public safety.
Which, by the way, makes him the fire chief's boss,
too. Sweet suffering Christ!"

The barmaid brought over the two fresh drinks, and
picked the correct change from the bills and coins on
the table. Terry waited until she was gone before
speaking again.

"And when this is all over, we'll still be working
for Nederlander."

Bird looked into the foamy head of his beer, as if
he could, with just a little more effort, read the future
in its opaque depths.

"Glad to hear you think so," he said. "Me, I'm not
so sure about anything anymore."

Chapter 14

The Lake Tower Health and Racquet Club caters to the bottled water and designer sweatsuit crowd. In addition to indoor tennis and racquetball courts, it features exercise machines in gleaming chrome. The club can accommodate the radically different needs of the aspiring triathlete or the poseur, here more to socialize than to risk salt-staining his Spandex.

Like most such facilities, it is frequented throughout the day by several distinct groups. There are the early-morning crowds who time their workouts to the schedules of trains that take them to their downtown jobs. There are the young mothers, the senior retirees and the assorted work-at-home types who make up the bulk of the banking-hours crowd. And there are the evening exercise habitués of both sexes, many of them optimists on the prowl who see one type of sweat and heavy breathing as foreplay to another.

At six-fifteen p.m., I pulled into a space marked GUEST in the parking lot. The club was at that slack-water period between tides, one cycle having ended and the next not yet begun. I hoisted the gym bag I had collected from my apartment, and walked inside. There, a smiling woman barely out of her teens checked my name against a list on a clipboard and buzzed me through.

"Men's locker room to the right," she said, handing me a thick white towel embroidered with LTHRC in discreet blue script. "Our juice bar is upstairs on your left, just past the meeting rooms."

I waited until the door closed behind me before turning to the left. At the top of the stairway, I opened a conference room door and stepped inside.

Talmadge Evans and Gil Cieloczki sat talking at the oak-veneered table that filled most of the available space. At the back of the small room, looking through a window at a hardwood court below, stood a well-dressed man with carefully combed dark hair. He turned when I entered, and gestured a welcome with a glass of a pale liquid stringy with pulp.

"Hi, Davey," said FBI Special Agent Ron Santori. "Good to see you again. So, you have a chance to talk to"—he looked at a pad on the table—"this Rabbi Jerome? Did we finally find a person who knows something relevant to this case?"

I shook hands with Cieloczki, and nodded to Evans. Gil pointed to one of the bottles of mineral water and raised his eyebrows. I nodded, and Gil passed it to me.

"No coffee," the firefighter said with an apologetic smile. "The health club fellow almost fainted when I asked for a cup."

Santori sipped at his glass and grimaced. "I got this from him. He said it was a very healthy drink. Good for my energy level." He placed the glass carefully on the table and pushed it far away from his reach.

"The rabbi said he didn't know anything about an art collection," I said, without preamble. "He's the kind of guy who likes to talk; he enjoys letting you in on all the inside details he's picked up. If he knew anything about a Levinstein collection, he'd have made sure to mention all the times he'd seen it."

"There you have it," Evans said. "It's just like the other interviews our officers did when all this happened in the first place."

He looked at Santori, then around the table. "I suppose it's not conclusive, but doesn't it indicate that there is no police cover-up? After all, we're basing all of this on the credibility of a convict—a known criminal, for God's sake. Am I the only one here who thinks that this may all be simply the fantasies of a man in prison? Or a hoax he's pulling for revenge, or because he's bored?"

Nobody responded. I looked at the ceiling, working at keeping my face impassive.

Finally Santori broke the silence.

"If there is any possibility that Lake Tower police are involved in murder, arson and felony theft," the FBI man said, "then certainly, we can't afford *not* to investigate. Don't you agree, Mr. Evans?"

"That's the only reason I agreed to participate in this," Evans said flatly. "That's why I let you talk me into taking Bob Nederlander out of the investigation. I'm cooperating, Agent Santori. But I also want to protect the reputation of my people and my city, as far as I can. To date, I see no evidence that this purported artwork ever existed, let alone was stolen. How do we resolve that question?"

Again, there was a moment of silence around the table.

"Maybe it's time to bring the artwork issue out into the open," Gil said finally. "I think it looks like the most likely trail to follow."

"Why not?" Evans responded. "After all, who are we keeping it from? Whoever killed the Levinsteins knows what was in there. Or, for that matter, what was not there."

"Lichtman told Davey that the house was burned to the ground to make sure nobody could be certain what had been in there, or had been taken out of there," Santori objected. "The killer may not know that we believe paintings are missing. And that gives us an advantage—the only one we have."

I shook my head. "I'm with Cieloczki. Look, you don't have to buy all of Lichtman's story—but he has too many details right for it to be complete fiction."

"He's full of details," Evans said. "The question is whether any of them are true."

"We had to check out what we could," I said doggedly. "I agree—this would all be a lot easier if we could confirm that the Lake Tower cops knew about the missing artwork and tried to cover it up."

"And you can't."

"No, Mr. Evans, I can't. The rabbi was the last name on the list of original interviews Posson and Bird did. I've reinterviewed every one of them. Not one knew about Levinstein's alleged art collection. It wasn't pursued as a lead simply because it never came up in the original interviews. Without the Lichtman story, *we* wouldn't know to ask about it."

Gil spoke up again. "Let's assume there is some kind of cover-up of the theft aspect going on. Is there any reason to think whoever's behind it is going to make the mistake of being impatient? I doubt it. He can sit back and wait. If no one even knows he stole the art, that works for him. Clearly, if nobody's looking for it, nobody's looking for him."

"We're the ones making a mistake if we tip our hand." Santori's voice was stubborn. "This is the best opportunity we've had in two years. We have a real shot at breaking up the official corruption mess out here!" He turned his appeal to me. "Davey, I'd think you, especially, would understand that we can't afford to waste the opportunity—not by moving before it's time."

I stiffened. "Let me tell you what I understand, Ronnie. I remember when your people came to me with something called 'Operation Centurion.' Classy name. As I recall, the Justice Department was going to focus on public malfeasance and clean out the bad cops and corrupt officials out here in the burbs. Just like Operation Greylord targeted the federal judiciary in Chicago. Just like Operation Silver Shovel caught all those city aldermen lining their pockets. A real big-time investigation by the Feds."

I stood and walked to a window that looked out at one of the indoor racquetball courts. "I understand a lot of things, Ronnie. I remember listening to an assistant attorney general you guys flew out from Washington. What was it he said? Something about how it just wasn't the right time to act on what I brought you? Something about how 'we' were going to hold off, try to get more? Maybe even make a deal so 'we' could go after the bad guys higher up on the food chain."

"Davey, be fair," Santori said, and even with my back turned I could hear the admonitory tone in his voice. "What happened to you had nothing to do with our probe. *You* freelanced, on your own. And you took the money from those dealers."

"You tried to squeeze Nederlander with the information I gave you," I said. On the court below, two T-shirted women weaved back and forth, caught up in the rhythm of their own game; I turned back to mine.

"I'll give the FBI the benefit of the doubt. I don't really think you gave Nederlander my name, just to put a little extra twist to the screws. But I think your people drew him a picture that was just complete enough. He knew it had to come from somebody in the department. And I was his leading candidate, wasn't I?"

I turned back to face the group. Evans had the look of a man impatient with the bickering of two strangers. Cieloczki looked uncomfortable, and tried hard to look impartial. Santori was trying hard to look both unfairly accused and magnanimous.

But I was not finished.

"Fair enough; I know the rules. Still, it might have been . . . *polite* to let me know about that conversation," I said, and heard my voice become hoarse and tight. "It might have influenced my decisions. I might have thought twice about a few things. Like meeting with a couple of lowlifes who were supposed to have half the squad on their payoff list. Certainly I might have reconsidered going in alone, right? Or putting five thousand dollars in marked bills in my pocket, for evidence."

"Or stashing it in your house," Santori retorted, "until the county sheriff's police went in with a search warrant. Three *days* later, Davey. Okay, you think we screwed you? Gil may not have heard all the bloody details yet, Davey. Let's let him decide, okay?"

He kept his eyes fixed on me as he addressed the firefighter.

"Gil, a Cook County task force had been running a sting operation for six months, targeting stolen cars being cut up for parts to resell. Part of the setup was they spread the word it was a 'protected' operation—paid off the local law on a regular basis, right? Davey gets wind of this right after we tell him Centurion isn't ripe enough yet. He's feeling impatient, and figures he'll speed things up for us.

"They had a nice little chop-shop deal going—a front counter where they'd do business, with video surveillance out the wazoo. They had enough hidden cameras to broadcast a football game. In back, just in case somebody got suspicious, they had a couple of deputies in overalls with cutting torches, making sparks like they were stripping a couple of confiscated cars.

"Really, it was a beautiful setup. They had creeps from the city, all over the suburbs, you name it—all of 'em lining up to bring in parts cut from cars they had boosted. It looked like the automotive department at K-Mart on a Saturday afternoon. Now, all of this is happening with marked money, okay? Then our boy here shows up, flashes his badge, and goes into a back room with the head guy. All this is being recorded on videotape, remember.

"Well, lo and behold, Davey tells our guy he's the new Lake Tower bagman—asks for five grand, and puts the money in his pocket." Santori shook his head, as if he hadn't heard this story before. "Marked bills, of course. Plus, one of the county cops in the back was watching the video monitor and recognized Davey right off. Well, you combine that with the surveillance tape, and you can see how it looked. Especially when Davey neglected to turn in the cash. Or even report the meeting to his supervisor."

"Just who was I supposed to report it to?" I spat through gritted teeth. "Who was I supposed to trust?"

Santori shrugged, and put on a placating face. "Okay—you know *I* believe you. You were trying to get us a better case and you stepped into the toilet. And you know how much we appreciate the way you kept Centurion out of it all. Hellfire, Davey—we're the reason you're not in jail right now. Didn't we get you out when we got the chance?"

Gil interrupted before I could respond.

"This isn't helping resolve the question we're dealing with now," he said. "If we take the Lichtman story at face value, the missing artwork is the key. And when we find this—what was the name Lichtman gave you?—this Sonnenberg person, I don't see how we can compartmentalize it anyway."

"Exactly," Evans said. "Agent Santori, we appreciate your situation. No one shares your concerns about corruption in government more than I. But you are working on a much larger canvas than we can afford to do. We have two murdered persons whose killer is at large." Evans' voice rose for a moment. "My God, I had met Stan Levinstein once or twice. He struck me as a decent man. He—they—didn't deserve to die like that."

The city manager shook his head sharply. "No." And his voice was firm. "We must move ahead on whatever basis is necessary to protect the lives of our citizens. Can you convince me that we can do that without following what appears to be a critical lead? No? Then I'm afraid that your Operation Centurion must take a subordinate position here."

Santori looked around the table and found no allies: he raised his hands in a sign of reluctant acquiescence. "All right. The artwork is no longer off-limits, okay? We'll provide whatever assistance we can—with the provision that you will protect our investigation in every possible way."

He turned to Gil. "How do you intend to proceed?"

Gil looked at me. *Are you ready to handle this like an adult?* his eyes asked.

I took a deep breath. The desire to commit a felonious act on a federal officer had been strong, and the memory of it had not completely faded. But the intent was gone, at least for the moment. It was a sign, I hoped, of my late-developing maturity.

Still, when I twisted my head slightly, my neck popped audibly as the taut muscle flexed. I drew a deep breath before I spoke.

"To quote the late, lamented President Nixon, we'll go the 'limited hang-out route,'" I said, and was relieved to hear my voice sound normal.

"Gil and I will brief Bird and Posson. We'll tell 'em that stolen artwork may be the motive. But we keep it sketchy; one of several theories. I think maybe it's best to keep Lichtman out of it." I considered for a moment. "For now, at least. Let's play it by ear. Until then, the information is attributed to an 'unconfirmed but reliable' source."

"I don't know much about art, let alone stolen artwork," Gil said.

"Maybe we can help there," Santori said. "Again, without tipping our interest in the Levinstein case itself."

"You may have to help with a lot of the background information we need," Gil replied. "The files I ask for from our esteemed police department seem to take a hell of a long time just to make it across the hall. And there's been a few gaps in them that even *I* have picked up."

"I can talk with Bob Nederlander," Evans volunteered. "Perhaps a direct order to—"

"Frankly, I don't know how productive that would be, Talmadge," Cieloczki interrupted. "I don't know how much I could trust the information he or his people might supply. Not while all this is unresolved."

"What we have in federal files is yours, as far as I can make it available," Santori said. "And there are some sources I can call and set you up with interviews. Tell me what you need, and I'll see what we can do."

Gil nodded. "What's your program, Davey?"

"Finding Sonnenberg is a priority," I answered. "From what Lichtman says, he's most likely to have been involved with the Levinsteins at some level. I've looked at his file. There's no record of violence, but he looks awfully good for the theft. It's up his alley. He has a couple of priors involving possession of stolen goods, including a collection of old icons he lifted from an Orthodox church a couple of years ago."

"Know where to start looking?" Santori asked.

"We have an address for Sonnenberg that might still be good," I said. "It's down in the city, on Devon Avenue. We'll have to coordinate with the Chicago PD, but that shouldn't be a problem. We'll use Posson and Bird for any heavy lifting we need."

"That's a good idea," said Evans, dryly. "As a fire chief and an acting fire marshal, you two might find it handy to have an armed police officer along."

"Even if he or she might be working against you," Santori added cheerfully. I looked at him, but said nothing.

The meeting was over, and we started to file out. But Santori put a hand on my arm, motioning Evans and Gil ahead. He waited until the door had closed behind them.

"Got a minute, Davey?" he asked, and pulled a small tape player from his side pocket. "There's something I think you should hear."

Outside, the air tasted of ozone and flashes of light danced on the far horizon. Spring was once more demonstrating its volatility, and fat drops of rain began to fall heavily from the darkness overhead. Shoulders hunched, I dashed to where I had left my car.

On the windshield, where raindrops were spotting the dust on the glass, a piece of paper folded to the size of a matchbook was tucked under the wiper blade on the driver's side. I placed my gym bag on the hood near the windshield, and made a show of patting my pockets as if looking for misplaced keys. As unobtrusively as possible, I put my other hand on the car and palmed the note.

As I drove away, I smoothed the note on my lap. In the dim glow of the lighted dashboard, I could barely make out an address, written in pencil and with a distinctive backward slant. There was no signature, but even in the near darkness I had no trouble recognizing the penmanship.

The rains fell as they fall only in the springtime, flung from young clouds that boiled black and furious. They fired indiscriminate volleys of huge blue-white forked bolts as if to punish the earth for some imagined slight. The world was alive with the noise of it all, the thunder so close I could feel it rock the car.

The downpour beat a tattoo on the car's roof as I waited in the far corner of the strip mall's lot. I was at the right address, parked in the shadows cast by a tall picket-frame enclosure. I could smell the sour tang of the Dumpsters behind it, even with the windows closed.

Then I jumped, startled at movement outside the glass, and suddenly Chaz Trombetta was standing beside the car. As I moved to open the door, Trombetta stopped me with an abrupt negative movement of his head. Instead, he motioned for me to roll down the window.

"You never got it from me," Chaz said, his voice low and tight. "Hell, you never *saw* me—understand?"

He reached under his raincoat, and my heart raced for an instant. Then, instead of the pistol I had half

expected, Chaz drew from under his raincoat an envelope. Its sides bulged against a thick red rubber band.

The rain pelted down, spotting the paper like a
maiden's tears.

Trombetta contemplated the envelope for a moment, a man taking a final look before touching flame
to his last remaining bridge. Then he pushed it quickly
through the window, as if mailing a check written on
a defunct account.

The envelope dropped heavily into my lap. Chaz
Trombetta walked away in the dark without looking
back.

I rolled the rubber band off and riffled through the
papers inside the envelope. They were photocopies of
computerized receipts, each detailing what appeared
to be a transaction. I pulled one from the stack and
studied it under the dim light.

There was a line of eight numbers, followed by a
three-letter suffix. Below, another line of sans-serif
type read 27.6 GAL, followed by a time and date. I
scanned through several more of the half sheets in
the envelope. All were similarly marked, though the
numbers differed.

I had seen similar receipts before, though not for
almost a quarter of a year. It had been that long since
I had fueled the car assigned to me by the Lake Tower
Police Department, keying the codes to activate the
automated gasoline pumps behind the municipal
center.

April 21

Chapter 15

The Everett McKinley Dirkson Building is part of
Chicago's Federal Plaza, located in the heart of the
south Loop. The steel-and-glass edifice is an imposing
structure. It was meant to be.

The early-morning crowd of federal employees had
already entered by the time Gil Cieloczki, Mel Bird
and I walked across the open-air expanse past *Flamingo,* Alexander Calder's storklike welded-steel
sculpture. It is painted a hideous red-orange, only a
shade or two away from the color used to warn sailors
of hazards and obstructions.

Among the alphabet soup of helpful federal bureau-
cracies that call Federal Plaza home is the Chicago
Field Office of the FBI.

As befits a major metropolis, in Chicago the Federal
Bureau of Investigation maintains a substantial presence. In the Dirkson Building, the FBI occupies all of
the ninth and tenth floors, and grudgingly shares the
eleventh with the Federal Communications Com-
mission.

The Special Agent in Charge—SAC, in Bureau jar-
gon, pronounced "sack"—is an august personage.
Currently, she presides over more than four hundred
agents, technicians and other specialists here and in
satellite offices scattered throughout the metropolitan area.

Of the fifty-six FBI field offices across the country,

Chicago is considered one of the more active areas for the FBI and the Justice Department attorneys with whom they work. Everything from political corruption cases to bank robberies—the Windy City is a perennial national leader in both categories—can be found among the active case files here.

As a result, the Chicago office tends to take pains to maintain good relationships with local law enforcement departments, also recognizing that local officials usually have direct lines of communication to their congressperson—who in turn usually has the home telephone number of the attorney general on his or her speed-dialer.

We were met at the eighth floor reception area by a neatly dressed, clean-shaven man who was polite. He smiled at us politely, the way one smiles at strangers. Clipped to his pocket was the laminated ID card issued to FBI agents; affixed to it was a separate card that read LIAISON OFFICER, COP/COMMUNITY OUTREACH PROGRAM.

"Is one of you Chief Cieloczki?" he asked, and Gil nodded. "Good to meet you, Chief. My name is Santori, Ron Santori. I'll be your guide today."

Gil spoke my name, and I shook Santori's hand as if I had not spent much of the previous night reviewing my not inconsiderable history with him. Santori turned to Bird.

"You must be Detective Bird."

"I'm plainclothes, not a detective," Bird said, but Santori had already returned his attention to Cieloczki.

"Chief, we do a lot of work with fire departments, but its mainly consulting and providing lab backup on arsons." He smiled. "This is the first time I've had a firefighter ask to speak to an FBI art expert."

Cieloczki smiled back. "I'll be honest with you," Gil said. "I was more than a little surprised to find out you guys had one."

We walked down a hallway chaotic with activity,

Santori leading past closed office doors marked only with room numbers.

"Hey, Uncle Sammy has everything," Santori said. "You've seen *The X-Files*."

He turned a corner, dodging a mail cart being pushed by a woman in dark pants and a blazer that did not quite conceal her holstered Glock. "But not only do we have *an* art expert, we have *the* art expert.

"Gentlemen—you're going to meet with Charlie Herndon, and there's *nobody* who knows more about the criminal side of the art world. He lectures to police departments around the country, and places like the Art Institute here in Chicago ask *him* to consult with their experts. I heard Charlie talk at Quantico a few years back. He had a standing-room-only crowd—a lot of them were senior agents, and it takes a lot to impress those people."

Santori stopped outside a door, and lowered his voice. "A word of advice, okay? The man is a genius when it comes to his specialty. He's been with the bureau since the Hoover days, and he's like an encyclopedia. But"—the agent gave us a significant look—"one thing he is not, and that's a politician. Okay?"

Santori knocked on the door without waiting for a response, and ushered us through.

The room looked smaller than it probably was, which I initially attributed to the bookshelves that lined every available inch of wall space. Then I realized I was mistaken. What made the room feel cramped was the man sitting behind the polished wooden desk of a senior civil servant. It looked undersized, because Charles Herndon was a big man.

Herndon remained seated. From the corner of my eye, I could see Gil—whose firefighter's eye still measured people in terms of carry-weight and rescue difficulty—studying the oversized agent as well.

I estimated Herndon as only two or three inches shy of seven feet tall. His hands, poised over the keyboard of a desktop computer, were the size of catcher's mitts. He was dressed in a navy blue suit jacket, a white shirt and a striped blue-over-green silk tie. His silver hair was trimmed unfashionably short; the eyes of a drill instructor broadcast a confident challenge from behind black-framed glasses.

"Oh, yeah," the man muttered in a voice so deep it rattled windows, "the fireman." An index finger like a broomstick pointed to three visitors' chairs, arrayed plumb before the desk. "Sit." To Santori: "Ronnie, why don't you leave these people with me for a few minutes?"

Santori left—a little too willingly, I thought. My own bottom was still an inch from the seat of the chair when Herndon began.

"Okay—I'll talk, you listen. You can ask questions later," Herndon said. He held up a thin sheaf of papers, which I recognized as the fax Gil had sent the afternoon before.

"Chief Cieloczki, I appreciate you sending me your case notes. When you called yesterday, you told my SAC that you wanted the *Reader's Digest* version of art crimes. From what you told her, you're assuming your case may involve the theft of valuable, possibly museum-quality, artwork. Maybe, maybe not. Let's look at that."

"First off, I'm going to oversimplify. While there's a lot of art and cultural artifacts being stolen these days, stealing art is not exactly the easiest way to make an illegal living. It happens, because it's been my experience people will steal damn near anything. But with artwork, you buy into a hell of a lot of headaches. I'll get to some of them in a minute, but right now you should just know that it's a pretty specialized crime. Most thieves avoid it. Fact one for you: there aren't that many places you can go to with a really valuable painting and sell it."

The FBI agent leaned back in his chair and locked his fingers behind his head. The movement pulled his suit jacket apart. I could see the big .40-caliber Glock riding high on Herndon's belt, butt angled forward in the approved FBI position.

Herndon held his fingers up in a V for Victory.

"Fact two," Herndon continued, "the value of this stuff is its authenticity. Say you have a painting you're convinced is by one of the old Dutch masters. Or something by Matisse, or a Pissarro, whatever. You've got to be able to prove it's the real McCoy. The key word is 'prove.' I'm talking authentication by reputable authorities, as well as an ironclad, documented chain of ownership."

"But people still get burned, right?" Bird asked, his tone carrying a hint of challenge.

"Oh, sure," Herndon said. "Fake documentation and fake art go hand in hand. And believe me, there are enough fraudulent pieces out there—damn good fakes, the kind that even the experts get into arguments over—to fill up every museum in Europe. And there'd still be enough left over for a new wing on every museum east of the Mississippi. You ever hear of Elmyr de Hory?"

"Back in the fifties and sixties," I said, "he pumped out hundreds, maybe thousands, of fake Impressionists."

Herndon eyed me closely, as if seeing me for the first time.

"I was starting to wonder if you spoke English," he said, not smiling. "You know about art?"

"A little. I took a couple of classes back in college."

Herndon looked at me, his skepticism apparent. "Please don't tell me you were an art student."

"English major. But I can still write a coherent sentence, if the need comes up for one." I expected a reaction but perhaps he had never heard of Raymond Chandler. "Whoever drew up the curriculum believed in a well-rounded education. That included two semesters of art appreciation. De Hory's name was mentioned."

"Yeah, it would have been. Elmyr did 'em all—Gauguins, Chagalls, Cézannes, you name it. A lot of them are still hanging in museums, and the curators swear they're genuine. Don't get me wrong; what I'm saying is that in art, it's a buyer-beware world."

Herndon smiled wickedly.

"And that brings us to fact number three. It's also 'seller beware,' because there are people like me under every other bush," he said. "You remember, back a few years, some guys climbed a ladder into a museum in Norway and left with a painting called *The Scream?* Every schoolkid in the world knows that painting. Sure, maybe they think the idea came from that *Home Alone* movie, when the kid puts on aftershave lotion. But they know what the painting looks like, right?"

He seemed to expect a response, and waited until Gil nodded.

"So one day it up and disappears," Herndon said. "Well, just about right away stories started going around about how it was being shopped to rich Arabs and software billionaires and even Colombian drug lords.

"That was a load of bullshit, and we knew it. The same kind of stories made the rounds thirty years ago when some goofs walked out of the Louvre with the *Mona Lisa.* Both times, the thieves didn't even try to sell the paintings to anybody. They'd have been arrested in a minute, and they knew it.

"All in all, there's almost nothing trickier to sell than a stolen work of art. And I don't mean just the famous ones, either. We live in the information age. Just about every piece of art you'd want to steal has been photographed and catalogued and cross-indexed. Hell's bells, that's the basis for the National Stolen Art File. If anything substantial goes on the market, the art newsgroups on the Internet go crazy. People talk about it; if it's a piece that's gone missing from somewhere, a lot of people know about it. It's a thief's nightmare!" He didn't sound displeased at the thought.

"What about private collectors?" Bird asked.

"What about 'em?" Herndon retorted. "Most of the stolen art that's missing isn't in a private collection— it's at the bottom of some damn trunk or storage locker the thief's hiding 'em in. Look, there really aren't all that many buyers out there. You need a customer who is rich enough to have a private art collection. He also has to be bent, and stupid enough to buy something hot. *Really* hot. So hot that anytime they show it to somebody, they run the risk of having a cop with a warrant knock on the front door.

"But okay—let's say you could find somebody crooked enough *and* dumb enough to buy on that basis," he conceded. "You can bet what they're being offered are fakes. Pretty good fakes, maybe, but al- most never the real article. See, it's a better setup for a swindle than a sale. Who does the buyer get to authenticate the piece? Where can he go to get a sec- ond opinion? All the usual safeguards are off, which makes it all pretty dicey."

"The chances of getting burned or busted are just too high for most of the lowlifes." He smiled. "Partic- ularly when, as you seem to be saying in your notes, there's a number of art pieces involved."

He held his hands palm up, and moved them up and down as if weighing small trucks. "What I'm trying to tell you is that an art theft is a complicated thing to pull off successfully. It's not like knocking off a conve- nience store, or stealing a car. Even a really good car."

Gil frowned. "But it happens," he persisted.

Herndon nodded, in what for him must have been a magnanimous show of patience. "Sure," he said. "A few years back, a couple of goofs dressed like cops bluffed their way into a Boston museum and walked out with maybe three hundred million in Rembrandts, Degas and Vermeers. Disappeared without a trace. But you can't sell stuff like this out of the back of a truck. Okay, there are crooked dealers out there who broker stolen art—but the vast majority of it was stolen a long time ago. Long enough for the dealer to put together a convincing chain of ownership.

"If you put together a decent provenance—one that is at least plausible—maybe you have a chance at some money. There are ways—a year ago, we caught a guy who was doctoring old museum catalogues and archival files. He was trying to establish fakes as 'rediscovered' authentics, but the concept is the same. Compile a really convincing provenance, and even places like Christie's and Sotheby's will give you a pedigree that can translate into big money."

"Both those places have been stung with a tricked-up history on a painting," I added.

"Yeah, but your case is different," Herndon countered. "It's more like somebody walking into the Treasury Building with a whole sack of counterfeit bills and asking for each one of them to be certified as genuine. That could happen, in theory. But I doubt it."

Bird had been sitting deep in his chair, his legs crossed widely and his foot twitching like the tail of an irritated cat. Now he slapped his ankle and interrupted the agent.

"C'mon," Bird said. "You keep telling us how hard it is. Are we just wasting everybody's time here?"

Herndon looked at Bird with the expression of a man who suffered fools only occasionally, and never gladly.

"No, friend," he said, after a long moment of studying the plainclothes policeman. "I'm saying there's only one real market for this kind of stolen artwork. Here's the fourth and final fact about stolen artwork in the *real* world. You try to sell it back to the owner or the insurance company, which usually comes to about the same thing."

He turned to Gil.

"Look, try to think of it more as a kidnapping than a theft; the art thief's leverage is that you either pay a ransom or he destroys the stuff. And he prices the ransom so that a buyback is reasonable. It's simple and more or less straightforward, and everybody wins but the cops.

"But in your case, if anything was stolen, there's no owner left alive to buy it back. Even worse for the thief, a dead owner turns this into a murder—hell, *two* murders, right? That kicks everything up into another league altogether. No insurance company is going to make a deal in a murder case."

Herndon paused, and picked up the fax of Cieloczki's case notes. "But that's all kind of academic, isn't it? See, from what it says here, there was no insurance taken out on any artwork."

He selected one of the sheets and held it out for us to see. It was gray with neatly balanced lines of type that nearly filled the page. I recognized the letterhead of TransNational Mutual. The firefighter had pored over the lengthy breakdown the insurance company had provided on the coverages Levinstein carried on his home, business, cars, personal property.

Gil looked up at the FBI agent. Herndon's own eyes looked back from under arched eyebrows, an expression that both mocked and encouraged.

"Am I speaking too fast here? We're talking possibly millions of dollars of art, stolen from a guy that *this* says damn well knew to insure everything else he owned," Herndon said. "Is it just me? Doesn't that say something to the three of you?"

"You don't think there was any artwork to begin with," Bird said.

"Oh, no," Herndon protested, in a patronizing tone that made Bird's teeth grind. "We have to assume there was artwork, or this remains a motiveless crime—so I think there *was* artwork. I just don't think there was any insurance issued on it.

"And that leads me to one of two possibilities. One, the guy didn't take out any coverage, for whatever reason—say, he had bought it hot, and knew it. But given the man's lack of previous criminal record, I consider that a long shot. Two, *there is no insurance*— but your dead collector *thought* there was. That's the only way a careful, apparently honest guy like this"— again, Herndon tapped on the sheet listing Levinstein's coverages—"could sleep at night."

He paused to let the implications sink in.

"And if that's the case," Herndon added, mildly for him, "don't you people want to go home and look into exactly why he would think so?"

Chapter 16

"Welcome to our own little United Nations," said Phil Sozcka. "Mother Russia is just a few blocks ahead."

He was sitting in the middle of the backseat, leaning forward with an arm draped over either edge of the front bucket seats where Terry Posson and I sat. On the car radio, the Cubs were dropping the second game of a doubleheader to St. Louis; it seemed an apt metaphor for the day so far.

Sozcka was somewhere between his late thirties and mid-forties, with an unlined open face and pale blue eyes. High on each cheek, a bloom of broken capillaries gave him a look of perpetual embarrassment. His hands were broad and blunt. If I looked hard enough, I could see a faint indentation around the third finger of his left hand. He had taken off the curiously comical checkerboard-banded hat issued by the Chicago Police Department, and his razor-cut blond head was on a swivel from side to side as he cheerfully surveyed the bustle of unruly commerce and sidewalk diplomacy through which we were passing.

I had linked up with Terry after the session at FBI headquarters in the South Loop. On our ride north along Lake Shore Drive she had been polite but terse, responding in monosyllables when I tried to make conversation. But she had not attempted to throw me out of her car, either; it was what I considered a distinct improvement in the relationship.

Inside the aged brownstone that served as the district police center, Phil Sozcka had been volunteered to us by his shift commander. The commander had accepted without comment that a material witness in an arson investigation was believed to be living in his district at an address on Devon Avenue.

He glanced briefly at the warrant, and examined Terry's ID with only slightly more interest. But when he looked at my newly issued card, his brow furrowed.

"Davey. Davey." He studied my face, then looked at the card again. "You have any relatives on the job? Here in the city, I mean."

"No," I said. "Not for a long time."

He started to shrug. Then I saw a light come on behind his eyes, and his expression flattened. He checked his duty roster, suddenly all business. When he spoke, his voice was frosty and distant.

"There are no detectives available at the moment, *Mister* Davey," he said, punching hard on the title. "But if your witness is hanging out up there with Russians, you'll want somebody who's a Russian speaker." Then he had waved over the uniformed officer sitting at a desk on the far side of the squad room, and spoken to him in low tones.

Phil Sozcka was the kind of cop Chicago had always bred. He was built solid, though wider at the bottom than at the top, and exquisitely schooled in the lore of the neighborhoods he patrolled. As we motored along the busy avenue, Sozcka talked and Terry and I listened.

Chicago has always been a city of neighborhoods, making the metropolis a patchwork quilt of ethnicity. We were driving east down Devon, one of the places where, Sozcka noted, the seams of this quilt traditionally overlapped.

In the section immediately east of the Chicago River's north branch, the street has long featured a population that boasts the single largest concentration of Jews in the city.

But as you continue east, the influence of its more recent arrivals also makes Devon Avenue the place to purchase a sari or rent a videotape of New Delhi's latest cinematic triumph. Around the corner from a Pakistani grocery are the offices of the Assyrian National Council. The Croatian Cultural Center draws strong participation from its share of the area's residents, and what was until a few years ago the historic 1920s-era Temple Mizpah is now well-attended as the Korean Presbyterian Church.

The latest addition to this multicultural mix is displayed in the windows of the groceries and doctors' offices on Devon: the offerings for both supermarket specials and medical specialties advertise in English, Yiddish, Hebrew, Hindi, Korean—and, most recently, in Cyrillic script, disorienting in its dyslexic mix of recognizable and backward-facing letters.

For the Russians who live here, migration had mirrored the state of diplomacy as it had evolved between the two countries. A trickle that began in the late 1970s as part of the Cold War's earliest thaw swelled into a steady stream during the détente of the eighties. The Soviet government, seeking to limit the potential embarrassment this modern exodus posed, issued passports listing their nationality as "Jewish" rather than "Russian," regardless of their actual religious affiliations. By the time the Berlin Wall became just another pile of rubble celebrating failed Soviet imperial aspirations, the rivulet had swollen to become a torrent of Russians.

Throughout the nineties, newly arriving Russians of all beliefs—or lack thereof—followed the linguistic and cultural path of least resistance that led to Devon. Each successive influx had brought along its own unique blend of hopes and paranoia, optimism and anxieties, expectation and experience. But Russia is an ancient country, a culture that has left certain indelible imprints in generations of its sons and daughters. Among the more pervasive of these, reinforced under

both czar and commissar, was a certain mistrust of
anyone who carried a badge. It was a skepticism born
of often bitter experience, as deep-seated as it was
well-deserved.

Sozcka, pleased at the opportunity to simultaneously escape his desk in the Eighth District records
room and to display his knowledge of local lore, kept
up his running commentary as Terry inched around
various traffic hazards. Cars and trucks—many of
them dappled with rusty reminders of the recent winter's road salt—lined the curbs like the levies of a
river. Occasionally she edged around a truck, double-
parked as strong-looking men in work clothes pulled
boxes from open tailgates.

"In the last census, they counted like fifty thousand
plus native Russians living inside a quarter-mile radius
of where we are right now," Sozcka said. "There's
more now. Some of them are doctors, lawyers,
engineers—or they were, in the old country."

He thrust a thick finger at the windshield. "There's
a guy who works in that tearoom, over on the corner,
who was a professor of Slavic literature at the University of Kiev. Now he's serving seed cakes and petit
fours to other émigrés while he learns English. You
also have a lot of your first-generation, hardworking,
babushka-wearing, green-card-carrying immigrants,
straight out of Minsk. Then you have kids who came
here to avoid getting drafted into the Russian Army."

"So you got all kinds," Terry said, concentrating on
the traffic.

"Good folk, most of 'em," Sozcka said. "But I'd be
willing to bet a few of our new arrivals know what
the inside of a Russian jail looks like. Not because
they were political prisoners, either."

"No kidding," I said, over my shoulder. "What kind
of calls do you catch here?"

"You know how it is—the commander said your
father used to be a Chicago cop." I twisted in my seat

to look at Sozcka, hard; but his face was open and guileless, and looked genuinely puzzled at the expression on my own.

After a moment, he resumed speaking.

"You have your better-off individuals living around the corner from people who are not too far off the poverty line," Sozcka replied. "Nothing new about that in Chicago. We get our share of burglaries, purse snatching, the occasional mugging—the usual stuff, though the area tends more toward property crimes than violent ones. Weekends, we field some interesting drunk-and-disorderly beefs, the occasional domestic. Nothing all that out of the usual, really. The big concern these days is coming out of OCU."

This time it was Terry who turned, her interest obvious. Chicago's Organized Crime Unit was considered one of the best-informed in the nation, and its concerns were seldom unfounded.

"They're seeing signs that the Russian Mafiya is establishing itself pretty strongly among the émigré population," Sozcka said. "That's 'M-A-F-I-Y-A,' no relation to our Sicilian friends. Except these Russians are following the same pattern the old Mustache Petes did when they were getting started way back when."

His hand waved at the storefronts outside. "Past few years, they've been hitting up local businesses for protection, extorting money from illegal immigrants, all your garden-variety strong-arm stuff. But OCU says that now they're moving heavy into the traditional big-ticket stuff—drugs, hookers, games—and even some pretty sophisticated computer fraud and shit." Sozcka blushed, surprisingly. "Pardon *me*, miss."

Terry winked at him in the mirror; the gesture only deepened the spots of color on Sozcka's cheeks.

I rescued him. "We appreciate your help, Sozcka. How is it you speak the language?"

"My mother. Her people were ethnic Russians who lived in the western part of Estonia," he said. "Most of the folks there spoke either Russian or German. Usually both—I guess so they could understand the words 'hands up' whenever they got invaded."

Sozcka had a healthy laugh.

"She was a DP after the war, talked her way into a job with the U.S. Army as a translator. Then she married a Polish-American sergeant from Chicago—hey, where else?—and came back with him. He died when I was a kid, so it was just the two of us. When I was growing up, Ma was the only person on our block who spoke Rooski. I think she made me speak it at home just so she'd have somebody to talk to."

He leaned forward and peered up through the windshield at a street sign. "It's just up on the next block," he said. "Now there's seven Russian-language newspapers in the city and a radio station that broadcasts full-time in Russian. All the schools in the neighborhood have to have teacher's aides who know Russian and the YMCA over on Pielmar Street has night classes that teach ESL—that's 'English as a Second Language'—for the new arrivals."

Sozcka tapped Posson on the shoulder and pointed to a space being vacated by a rusting Buick. Terry pulled the car in expertly.

"I guess these days, Ma would have felt right at home," said Sozcka, "except she didn't particularly like Russians. Or Germans, for that matter. She never told me any of the details, but she had her reasons. Your address is just a little ways up—we can walk from here."

The entryway was next to the Interbook, a Russian-language bookstore. Its expansive window displayed stacks of what looked like Russian paperback mysteries, computer textbooks in Russian and a wide range of Russian-English dictionaries.

A wooden door, with peeling strips of gray paint fringing the old brass of the doorknob, opened to a stairway leading upward. There were six mailboxes on the right wall, four of them with names printed in ink or pencil in the small recesses. None of them were the name of the man we sought.

"We'll try a few doors and see if anybody's home," Sozcka said. He squinted up into the half-light at the top of the stairs. "Sonnenberg, you said?"

"Sonnenberg," Terry repeated. "First name Paul. Nickname of Sonny."

The first door was on the left-hand side of a corridor lit by a naked bulb. Traffic sounds rose muted up the stairway and the air smelled of scorched onions and the tang of hot metal. Somewhere on the floor, a television was on, tuned to what sounded like a child's cartoon program. Automatically, Sozcka stepped out of the direct line in front of the doorway, and Posson moved to the right of it. The Chicago officer reached around and rapped loudly, shaking the door in its frame.

The door opened to a two-inch slit, and a balding man with a gray-flecked mustache looked out. His eyes flickered between Terry and Sozcka.

"Shto eta?"

"Dobriy dyen. Ya Chicago police," Sozcka growled in a low voice, holding up the photo Terry had collected along with Sonnenberg's rap sheet. *"Kto etat 'Sonnenberg'? O doma?"*

"Nyet." The voice had a petulance tinged with suspicion that was evident despite the abruptness of the answer. *"A chyom vi gavareetye?* Chicago *balshoy gorat."*

Sozcka gestured down the corridor, and said something in a tone between a question and a demand. It brought a swift reply.

"Nyet, eeh soo'kin sin nyet doma!" What they could see of the man's lip curled in annoyance. *"Ya nye ochyen lyooblyoo."* The door slammed in the policeman's face.

"Balshoye spaseeba," Sozcka said to the closed door, and despite the language barrier Davey could hear the sarcasm heavy in the policeman's voice.

Sozcka turned to Terry.

"He says he doesn't know any son of a—anybody by that name," Sozcka said, his voice a stage whisper. "And he doesn't know if his neighbors—who, incidentally, he, uh, doesn't seem to think highly of—are home."

I said, "Let's keep trying. Our guy may have moved on, but let's make sure."

"Right," said Sozcka. He stepped to the next door and lifted his hand to knock. But before he could, from inside the apartment we heard the sounds of a sudden scuffle, of a woman's voice rising and cut short, punctuated with the sound of what might have been a hard slap against flesh. Then there was a crash, like a table loaded with glassware had collapsed.

Sozcka looked at me.

"Kick it," I said. "Let's go!"

Sozcka pulled his side arm and sucked in a deep breath. On the far side of the door, Terry had her pistol out—a 9 mm Beretta that looked too large for her hand—and I could see her tense in preparation.

"Police!" Sozcka bellowed, and the flat of his heavy shoe hit the door just below the knob. The jamb splintered and the door slammed against the wall, bouncing back on its hinges.

Before it could swing closed, the Chicago cop had shouldered past it, his chromed .357 revolver at arm's length sweeping the room right to left. Terry was right behind him in a similar stance, her pistol moving in a left to right arc. "Everybody fuckin' *freeze*!" Sozcka screamed. "Freeze, goddamit!"

From where I stood in the hallway, I could just see between them, marking the drapes of a window blowing in the draft from a broken, empty frame; on the floor, a woman in tight black jeans and a loose sweater held both hands to her mouth, blood dripping between her fingers. Her eyes were squeezed tight, either in pain or in terror at the violent maelstrom of which she suddenly found herself the center.

"Room's clear! Window!" Terry shouted to Sozcka. He jumped to the open frame, flattened himself against the wall next to it, and in a smooth, rapid movement shot a fast look down the grated fire stairs outside. "Asshole's heading east!" he yelled to her, and thumbed the radio microphone that was clipped to a loop on his left shoulder.

And then I was running down the stairs to the street, bursting into the dazzling sunlight.

I hit the pavement at a dead run, turning left and sprinting, weaving, jostling, brushing through the astounded pedestrians. I hurdled a two-wheeled shopping basket being pulled by a tiny woman with white hair and a long black coat, and bumped hard against a man in a denim jacket. The collision spun him into a storefront's wall. I could hear his curses follow me as my legs pumped hard. I ran for all I was worth—swerving now to avoid a startled man holding his young daughter's hand, and then tightroping along the curb to find an open pathway through the crowd.

At the corner, I grabbed the upright pole of a street sign with my left hand, spinning half around it to maintain my momentum as I changed direction ninety degrees. Ahead of me was the alley that ran behind the buildings and bisected the block. I had almost reached it when a man skidded out, flat-footed, as he prepared to change his own direction of escape. He was facing me, still skidding sideways. His eyes only had time to open wide before I lowered my shoulder and ran through his chest at full speed. All the anger and frustration I had stored for so many months exploded in the force I threw behind the collision. There was an impact that I felt all the way into my heels; a confused cacophony of sound that was loud but distant filled my ears.

I must have closed my eyes at the instant of collision, because when I opened them I was half lying on top of the man. Both of us were jammed against the base of a parking meter where we had skidded. My arms were wrapped around him, hard under his armpits and locked behind his back. The man's body had taken the brunt of the force when we smashed into the cement of the sidewalk. He was twisting in pain, his mouth open wide as he tried to replace air that had been slammed from his lungs.

I unwrapped my arms and was pushing myself to my knees just as Terry Posson slid to a halt above me. Her gun was out, and it was pointed in a two-handed grip at the man writhing on the ground. I looked down at my hands, where blood was beginning to well. Grit was imbedded in the abrasions on several fingers.

"Son of a bitch was listening at the door when we talked to the first guy," she said to me, breathless from her own sprint. "He must have heard Sozcka mention his name. When the woman tried to come to the door, he slugged her and went through the glass."

I sat back on the sidewalk as Terry began to pat down the man beside me. His eyelids had opened to slits now, and he watched her pull out her handcuffs while she held the pistol steady at his forehead. His eyes swiveled to where I sat, rasping hard to deal with an oxygen debt that was, like most of what I owed, far beyond my present ability to pay.

I felt happier than I had in months.

"Hey," I said between breaths, addressing the man whose mug shot I had handed Sozcka just a little while ago. "So—how're you doing, Mr. Sonnenberg?"

We were in the interview room at the same district station where we had picked up Phil Sozcka earlier in the day. Two ambulances had been dispatched along with three tactical units. Despite my protestations, I had been taken to Riverside Memorial's emergency room along with Sonnenberg and the woman who lived in the Devon Avenue apartment.

Katya Butenkova, a native of what was once again

being called St. Petersburg by the time she had left it
to immigrate here, was not seriously injured. It was
neither the swollen lip nor the chipped tooth that kept
her responses to Terry's questions short and unin-
formative.

When told she had the option, she had declined to
press assault charges.

Sonnenberg's condition was even less serious. I had
held high hopes that I had broken at least one of his
ribs, or even caused moderate internal injuries.

"You're getting old and infirm, officer," the emergency room resident had chided me. He cleaned and
bandaged the two abraded fingers on my left hand.
"The guy you tackled is in better condition than you
are."

The injured had all been treated and released;
Katya declined a trip back to either the station house
or her apartment in a CPD squad car, and left in a
cab. With the Lake Tower material witness warrant
now formally, if somewhat spectacularly, served on
him, that option was not open for Sonnenberg.

It did not start cordially. He had had his rights read
to him when he was lying on his back around the
corner from Devon Avenue. I now placed my Sony
tape recorder on the table between us, set to voice
activation, and leaned back. Then, out of habit, I repeated the Miranda warning while Terry paced back
and forth behind Sonnenberg.

He leaned back insolently, balancing on the rear
legs of a hard aluminum chair. I was sitting across
from him at the table, and informed Sonnenberg that
he was being held as a material witness in a police
investigation.

"So, you get up to Lake Tower much, Paul?" I
asked. "Or do you prefer 'Sonny'?"

Paul "Sonny" Sonnenberg shrugged, and my leg
lashed out under the table in a hard, vicious movement. It swept Sonnenberg's chair hard sideways, and

only his wildly windmilling arms kept him from tumbling out of it. The front legs hit the floor with a loud metallic crash.

From behind Sonnenberg, Terry's eyes had snapped open at the unexpected maneuver. She glared, and for an instant I thought she would explode at me. Instead, she turned her anger at Sonnenberg.

"You want to pay attention," she suggested, leaning forward so that her face and his were inches apart. "We're talking about your future."

"Jesus, what's your damn problem?" Sonnenberg rubbed his elbow where it had smashed against the tabletop as his arms flailed. He looked warily at me. "What is this? If you're the 'bad cop,' what the fuck does that make her?"

"I'm not bad, Sonny," I said. "I'm just the one picking gravel out of my hand because some turd wanted to play rabbit. Puts me in a bit of a mood, Sonny. So if I was you, I'd listen to her."

"Look," he said, "I'm sorry I took off like that. I didn't know you were cops. And I'm sorry I hit Katya—I'm going to make it up to her. You know. People in love, they get into little tiffs sometimes."

"Katya says you hit her when she started to go to the door. How come?"

Sonnenberg tried to look embarrassed. "Look, she's a Russki, okay? Maybe she knew what you guys were saying out in the hall, I dunno. All I heard was a bunch of Russian monkey talk with my name attached. Maybe I've got some Russki friends who think I owe 'em a few rubles, okay? Whatever. I just didn't want her to open the door, so I tried to stop her. Then you busted in with guns, and I bugged out."

Terry was looking at him like she might have looked at a particularly nasty clump of bathroom mold.

"Uh-huh. Here's the way it reads," Posson said. "We have you on a domestic assault with injuries. Obstruction of justice. Flight to avoid arrest—"

"All bullshit," Sonnenberg said, "pissant stuff."

"—and felonious assault on a public official during the aforementioned flight." She smiled chillingly. "That one can put you away for five years, minimum. No early-out, either."

Sonnenberg had a look of outraged incredulity on his face. "No way! What the hell 'public official' am I supposed to have assaulted?"

I raised my hand close to the man's face, and involuntarily Sonnenberg flinched. Without guile, I smiled and waggled the fingers the emergency room had wrapped in gauze. "That would be me. And I *am* inclined to press charges."

Sonnenberg shook his head in disgust. "Bullshit," he muttered.

"So let's you work hard to make friends here, okay?" Terry said, leaning next to his face again. "Let's have a little conversation. I'll go first. We're interested in art. Some nice paintings—I dunno, maybe a statue or two. Now you tell me where we can find some really nice items along those lines, okay?"

Sonnenberg stared at her for a long moment, then shook his head, hard. "Nope. You're so wrong on this, we ain't even in the same time zone. I handle contracting, roofing work, general repair. And you haven't heard anything else, because there's nothing else to hear. Am I being clear here?"

I doodled on the notepad. Without looking up, I asked "What do you hear from Sam Lichtman, Sonny?"

Sonnenberg looked startled, then alarmed. "That shithead? Nothing. Why would I?"

"He's heard about *you,* Sonny," I said. "He says to tell you hello. He mentioned you just the other day. He was just thinking back on some business you two did together once. You know, memory lane stuff. What was it, Terry? Elgin or Aurora?"

She picked up the ball without missing a beat, though she must have been as puzzled as Sonnenberg.

"Elgin," she said, challenging Sonnenberg with a hard, steady stare.

"Right, Elgin." I nodded solemnly. "Well, Sam heard I was going to look you up, and said I should say hi for him. He says he hears you're doing real good these days."

Sonnenberg had regained some of his composure.

"Elgin," he said, making it sound like a dirty word. "Sam Lichtman never told you anything about Elgin, or anything else. Whatever else the guy is, he's stand-up."

"One of his best qualities," I agreed. "Still, you know how it is when a guy is dying—oh, you knew that, right? That Lichtman's got a tumor in his brain, and that he knows he's only got a few weeks to live? Anyway, you know how some people get, times like that."

I looked him dead in the eyes. "*I* don't care about Elgin, Sonny. Whatever happened there is between you and . . . refresh my memory, Sonny. Was it the Garcias' warehouse you helped rip off? No? Maybe it was the Tripetti family, right?" I put admiration in my voice. "Man, you must have *big* brass ones, Sonny. I don't know many people who would skank either one of those crews. Me, I'd be scared to death—even if by some mistake my name ended up getting mentioned in the same sentence with the Elgin gig."

I looked benevolently at Sonny Sonnenberg, who was now staring at me with something akin to hatred.

"Well, I guess you're safe," I said. "You don't know anything about Elgin. But are you sure you didn't hear something about an art collection up in Lake Tower? Just a rumor? A hint, maybe?"

"I ain't talking to you," he said flatly. "I remember you now. You're the guy who got caught in that sting op. Yeah, and you ain't a cop no more, neither."

He shot a hard look at Terry, then turned back to me.

"Pull any hard-guy shit with me and I'll swear out a complaint against the both of you. Now I want a lawyer, and he's going to take your bullshit material

witness warrant and use it for Kleenex. And you and
your bull-dyke girlfriend here are in for some fun
times ahead. Remember where you heard it first."

Terry put a hand in his collar and pulled him to his
feet. "Okay, you'll get your lawyer. But you'll get to
call one from a cell up in Lake Tower, because that's
where you're going, right now. Let's take a little
ride, asshole."

Sonnenberg straightened himself and leered at the
police officer.

"Yeah, let's go to Lake Tower," he said, smirking.
"You poor dumb cow."

He sounded like a man who knew a secret. I hoped
I was right.

We waited near the front desk while the Chicago police processed the paperwork that would release Sonnenberg to our custody. From behind us, a voice
called. It was Phil Sozcka, and he approached with a
troubled look on his face.

"Officer Posson, I just want to tell you I'm sorry,"
he said. "I was *way* outta line."

"Call me Terry, Phil," she said, "and, I'm sorry, but
I don't know what you're talking about."

He looked abashed.

"Back at the perp's apartment. I want you to know
I wasn't trying to be harassing, or set up a hostile
environment or anything."

Posson looked blank. "I still don't get it."

Phil sighed. "I've been written up two times, and
the captain sent me to sensitivity training after both
of 'em," he said. "That's why they've had me in Records for the past month. I've been trying to do better,
I swear to God—and I don't do it hardly at all anymore. Except when, you know, things get all stressful.
Like today."

Terry just looked at him, determined to wait him
out.

"My language," he said, looking contrite. "All the

'assholes' and 'shits' and the rest when we busted in the door. It's just a bad habit I got into because I've been out on the streets so long. The CPD's got a policy against it. They take it real seriously, 'cause it creates such a potentially damaging climate on the job. Particularly when officers are of different, uh, genders. So like I said, I'm real sorry."

They give medals for conduct above and beyond the call of duty, and for what Terry Posson did next, I was ready to sign the recommendation for her.

"Phil." Terry smiled, and clapped him on the shoulder. "Don't give it a fucking second thought."

Chapter 17

The way Gil Cieloczki described it to me later, when we met in his office to compare notes, he thought the interview at the Cook County Sheriff's Police office was going to be over before it began. All he did was say Nederlander's name; he was unprepared for the reaction it evoked.

"I beg your pardon?" Gil Cieloczki said, looking across the desk at the county officer and wondering what he had done to piss him off so quickly and so thoroughly. "Lieutenant Erlich, I just thought you may have worked with the, uh . . . Chief Nederlander at one time or another."

"I'm sorry if I've offended you," Virgil Erlich said, not looking sorry at all. "And I apologize for that 'son of a bitch' comment. I've only met the man once."

He reached for a packet of chewing gum, one of several which rested beside a desk plaque that identified Erlich as head of the Major Crimes Division, Cook County Sheriff's Police.

"I've never had any extended contact with your Mr. Nederlander, and as far as I personally know, he's as pure as the driven snow." He stared, with no small measure of irritation, at the firefighter seated across from him. "I don't know what you want me to say, Mr. Cieloczki."

"I was given the impression that you would be candid with me, Lieutenant. Off the record, of course."

"Mind if I ask why you want to know all the dirt about your town's police chief?"

"Call it a public-spirited concern."

"Uh-huh. Your ID says you're a fireman. But just because a person isn't *entirely* a civilian doesn't make him—specifically, you, who I also don't know from Adam—my soul brother and trusted confidant, you catch my drift?"

He picked up the pack of gum, put it into his pocket and carefully straightened the brightly patterned tie he wore. It was primarily scarlet, flecked with small yellow and green diamonds. Then Erlich sighed theatrically.

"Okay, Mr. Cieloczki—I don't seem to have the patience I used to have, so let's cut through the crap, right? Without all the goddam dancing around the issue, you're trying to find out if we—that is, if *I*—have any direct information to indicate your police department may be a little . . . tainted."

He chewed furiously for a moment.

"First of all, that's a hell of a thing to ask. But given the nature of the phone call I got from our mutual friend at the Dirkson Center, you're not just trying to come up with a little juicy gossip."

Erlich shot a look at Gil that spoke volumes. "And by the way, the FBI is chock-full of sons of bitches, and my advice to you is to watch your own tail feathers if you're dealing with that bunch. Give my regards to Santori, that jerkoff, when you see him."

Erlich plucked a tissue from the box on top of his desk. He delicately spat the gum into it, wrapped it almost reverently, and dropped it in the wastebasket near his feet. Almost immediately, his hand went back to his shirt pocket for another stick.

"My second comment is, 'Direct knowledge, no.' I have no direct knowledge that might lead me to believe your department might not be operating in an honorable and ethical manner."

He looked hard at the fire chief. "But maybe you

want to reword the question." He waited for Cieloczki to respond, then again sighed loudly.

"Let me tell you a little story," he said, peeling the foil back and popping the gum in his mouth. "Two or three years ago, right before Christmas, my predecessor in this office got passed a tip from the Drug Enforcement Agency boys downtown. They had word a guy we were both looking for—a small-time coke wholesaler name of Ravanza Ben El—had taken up what you might call permanent residence out in the burbs."

Erlich smiled, a cold thin line. "Mr. El, you see, had been accepting a small stipend from the DEA for finking out his competitors. He was also on *our* pad; as it turns out, ol' Ravanza was dropping the dime on homies who made a habit of paying late or never. And to finish icing the cake, he had started stepping a little too hard on product that he was selling as uncut.

"Everybody's all-American boy, right? So when he dropped out of sight all of a sudden, we didn't exactly figure he was off at church camp. Well, according to the *federales,* their snitch said we could find our boy in the trunk of a white LeBaron at the bottom of the Northside Sanitary Canal. That runs up by you, right? Anyway, he even gave up a pretty good idea of where to look. The feds wanted to keep everything at arm's length from their office, and they figured since we were interested, too, we could front for them and maybe take a quiet look.

"So, my guy said what the hell, why not, and got permission to use the County Search and Recovery dive team. The scuba boys were really thrilled, as you might imagine, because the 'sanitary' canal isn't—it just sounds better than calling it a big, deep ditch full of Chicago's shit. This being a beef where the DEA had expressed an interest, there wasn't anything they could do about it, but that doesn't keep them from wasting a couple of hours bitching about diving for dead dope dealers."

Erlich took a moment, repeating the ritual with the tissue and the new stick of gum. "By the time all of this gets done, it's past quitting time," he continued. "My predecessor, having those great family values you want in a civil servant, is in a hurry to get home for dinner. So he tells his secretary to send a fax to the police chief over there as a courtesy, just to let him know we're going to be poaching on his turf, and heads home for his meatloaf and mashed. And bright and early the next morning all us grunts troop out to see if we can find the missing Mr. El.

"I had a case where my man Ravanza was down as informant, so I got invited to the party. It was a nice sunny morning—a little cold, but the divers had those big rubber suits and anyway, there's so much crap dissolved in that water I don't think it ever freezes over. But even with the sun out, that damn canal was so dark and thick it looked like chocolate syrup flowing past.

"So the S and R guys put on their tanks, rope up and go in. Not more than a minute later, bingo! There's the vehicle. We had this big wrecker truck along—the kind they use when the big rigs tip over on the interstate, you know?—and they winch the car up.

"Except even covered in weeds and shit, you can see it's not white and it's not a LeBaron. And there's no body in the trunk. So back in the divers go. Another minute or so, they're waving for the winch cable. Wrong car again; it was like a Jeep Cherokee or something.

"This goes on all morning. It's like we discovered the damn Legendary Graveyard of Lost Cars. We got maybe two dozen of 'em lined up on the shore—and none of them, not one, has a license plate or a VIN plaque under the windshield. A couple of the cars, you could still make out the gouge marks where somebody had pried the vehicle ID number plate right off the dash.

"So now it's after noon, and all of a sudden we

hear these sirens and they're getting closer and closer. Everybody's looking up the embankment, even the divers in the water, wondering what the fuck is happening. Then half a dozen Lake Tower squad cars—Mars lights flashing, sirens wailing—come tearing over the hill and lurch to a stop in, like, a semicircle around where we're fishing for wrecks. Out jumps the local police chief— your Mr. Nederlander—and he's yelling about jurisdiction and waving a piece of paper that turns out to be the fax my guy's secretary sent the night before."

He arched his eyebrows and smiled.

"Except, see, she didn't send it the night before. It was late and she wanted to get home, too—so she decided, all on her own, that it wouldn't do any harm to wait until the next morning to type up the fax to your chief. *Late* the next morning, as it turned out. By the time Nederlander read it, we had been hauling cars out of that damn canal for hours. But the son of a bitch sure burned rubber getting down to the canal."

"Then what happened?" Gil asked.

"Well, the long and the short of it is, " Erlich said, "he threw our sorry asses out of there. He gets on his cell phone to my sheriff, who—as luck would have it—knows your man pretty good. Seems your police chief made a habit of dropping some serious pocket change into my man's campaign kitty over the past decade or so. Anyway, they kidded each other about their golf scores, threw a little shit about who's doing what with whose wife. In general, yucked it up like all get-out. Then Nederlander mentioned his department had been investigating a stolen car ring and asked why the sheriff's police was in his town screwing up the case.

"Your guy's a pretty cool customer, I'll give him that. I happen to be standing closest, so he's looking right into my eyes the whole time he's talking to my boss."

The investigator shook his head in what Gil was fairly certain was not admiration.

"Nederlander cited 'probable cause' on the basis of the 'evidence' we had spent all morning gathering; then he claimed jurisdiction. Next thing I know, we're all driving home with our peckers in our hands."

Erlich chuckled. " 'Probable cause'—well, he had that one right. It didn't take a genius to figure there was a stolen vehicle report on file somewhere for every damn one of those cars. But that's not the crime we fell into out there."

"I remember reading about this," Gil said, cautiously. "Something about a car theft ring operating in the area."

"Car theft ring, my ass," Erlich snorted. "When somebody steals a car, it's almost always because they can make some cash on it. They strip it for parts, carve it up in a chop shop. They smuggle it out of the country to sell to some new-rich shithead in Prague who wants to impress the local coke whores. What they don't do is take a little joyride and dump it in a canal. Not often, and for sure not in the numbers we found out there."

He shook his head.

"Nope. The probable cause at that goddam ditch wasn't car theft. It was your basic, low-level insurance fraud. Hell, somebody gets behind on their car payments, or maybe they're just bored with it but they're in the bucket and owe more than they can sell it for—they dump the damn thing and report it stolen."

"Sounds like a lot of trouble," Gil said doubtfully. "I wouldn't have thought it'd be worth the risks."

"There's more money than you'd think in it, and long as nobody looks too close, everything's dandy. The bank gets paid, the mope collects the difference and gets out from under. Everybody's happy but the insurance company, and they just jack up everybody else's premiums to cover their margins."

"What happened with all the cars you pulled out?" Cieloczki asked. "They find out who was dumping them in there?"

"You may have missed my subtle message about my predecessor," Erlich said, picking up another pack of gum and putting it down gently. "At times he took a kind of . . . uh, low-intensity approach, particularly when something looked like it might make him late for dinner. The 'car theft ring'? Still an open investigation, as far as I know. I guess I could call there and ask the chief—it's his case. But officially, I have no interest."

"I guess it makes it tough to trace a car if the plates and ID numbers are gone," Gil said noncommittally.

Erlich gave him a disgusted look. "There are traceable serial numbers stamped all over every car. They put some of 'em in hard-to-reach places like the frame or under the engine block, but they're there." Erlich waved his hand dismissively. "Pulling off license plates and the dashboard VIN plaque—that's what you do when you just want to discourage your casual observer. It won't stop somebody who really wants to trace the vehicle."

Cieloczki held up his hands, palms toward Erlich. "Hey, I'm a fireman." He smiled. "I'm just curious as to your guess on this thing. Do you think finding the cars stopped what was happening?"

"My guess," Erlich repeated, amused. "Okay, why not? My *guess* is that all we did was to screw up the lazy man's technique for dumping cars. Most likely they stopped pushing 'em into the canal. We may even have done somebody a favor and made 'em more efficient. It just takes a little organizing. See, taking a cut of the insurance settlement on just one or two stolen cars is pretty chump change. The only way to make it worthwhile is to deal in a lotta volume, and over the long run that's asking to get caught.

"So, if they decided to get serious about it, they probably linked up with a chopper to sell the parts and started making real money on both ends of the deal. Plus, once they've made that connection, they probably start dealing out the stripped-out hulks as scrap to a junkyard or two where nobody asks for titles before the heap goes to the crusher. No fuss, no muss and no embarrassing questions get asked."

He grinned, showing Gil teeth like a wolf smiling. "Least, that's the way I'd go about it."

Gil smiled back. "Still, I get the impression you have . . . a *feeling* about this incident," he said. "Am I right?"

Erlich pursed his lips and raised his eyes to a point above Gil's head.

"Being charitable of nature," he said, as intentionally toneless as if he were giving testimony, "I interpreted everything that happened as the legitimate concern of local law enforcement to maintain control over their own jurisdiction and to preserve a potential crime scene for subsequent investigation."

Erlich paused, and looked Gil directly in the eye. "Were I a less trusting person, I might question why a police chief comes running out with half his police force to stop a routine search and recovery. I might wonder where all those cars came from, who owned 'em, and how much the insurance company paid out on them. Hell, I might even want to look at whether any of the payments got made to people who wear a badge, or maybe are real good friends with somebody who does."

Erlich gestured significantly at the file folders stacked on his desk. "But, like my boss tells me, I have my own open cases to worry about. Hey, crime never takes a holiday, right?"

Gil stood to leave. "Thanks for taking the time for me." He held out his hand to Erlich, then said as if it were an afterthought, "Did you ever find your drug dealer?"

Erlich reached for a tissue, then stopped, his hand in midair.

"The missing Mr. El? How nice of you to ask. As a matter of fact, we did. A few weeks later, a couple of kids found ol' Ravanza under a piece of dirty cardboard in a vacant building. He was smelling up the neighborhood about a block from where he used to live."

"Natural death?"

"Natural as hell, given what got done to him," Erlich retorted. "Best the pathologist could tell, what with the rat bites and everything else, somebody used a big-ass framing hammer on just about every joint in his body. Then they cut his throat right under the jawline and pulled his tongue through the slit."

Erlich put one hand on his brightly patterned tie and held it against his Adam's apple. "They used to call it a Colombian necktie before everybody started doing it."

"So the tip you got was completely wrong," Gil mused. "That seems funny, your source being so specific on where to look and all."

"Like I said, it was a tip the feds passed along to us from one of their snitches. They didn't tell us who." Erlich shrugged carelessly. "If they don't offer, it's not considered polite to ask. You know—it's like a gift horse. You don't look in its mouth."

"Sure," the firefighter agreed. "But even gift horses can bite if you get too close."

Erlich raised his eyebrows. "Meaning?" he asked.

"Oh, nothing really," Cieloczki said. "I have a pretty charitable nature, too. It just crossed my mind that if I didn't, I might start to think somebody maybe wanted to jerk the chain on that police chief—you know, just do something to let him know something bad could happen if he didn't want to get, as you said, more efficient. I might even wonder if maybe you guys were used to send somebody a message. Crazy idea, huh?"

Erlich laughed, as if the firefighter had made a joke. "Nice talkin' to you, chief," he said, turning back to reach for a folder on his desk.

As Gil left, he glanced back. Erlich was watching him leave, a thoughtful look on his face. For the moment, fleeting as it was, the stick of chewing gum in the policeman's hand was forgotten.

Instead, Erlich looked like a man who had just had a sudden, and troubling, revelation.

April 22

Chapter 18

"Well, that didn't take long," Terry Posson said. Her voice was that of a woman who expected little satisfaction, and had not been surprised when none arrived.

Two dozen feet away from us, Sonny Sonnenberg was shaking the hand of a prosperous-looking man who was carrying an expensive leather briefcase. It was the kind of case purposefully made thin to signal that the owner had subordinates to carry the heavyweight loads.

Sonnenberg had proven himself a prophet of note: a judge had taken only a few minutes' deliberation before vacating the material witness order, and even less time to rule invalid the litany of charges Posson had convinced an assistant state's attorney to file.

"Assault on a public official," the judge had said, with only a hint of amusement in his otherwise impartial tone, "does not include two scraped fingers on a fire marshal—an *acting* fire marshal—who tackles a citizen on a public street. In the absence of a signed complaint from the alleged victim in this domestic assault—has Ms. Butenkova filed a formal complaint, counselor? No? In that event, I am dismissing all charges against Mr. Sonnenberg. He is ordered released immediately."

At that moment, Sonny had turned toward the courtroom gallery where Terry and I sat; in his look was everything he had not said during the long ride from Chicago the evening before.

Today, his attorney had done what little talking was required. And now, standing on the steps outside the courthouse in the sunlight of an April morning, we watched him leave in a cab and head south toward the city.

We walked across the street to the Lake Tower Municipal Center.

"He knows it's not over," I replied to Posson.

I worked at the fresh gauze I had wrapped around my "injuries" this morning, replacing the hospital dressings with what I had hoped, unsuccessfully, was a convincing bulkiness. Now I tossed the handful of bandage into a sidewalk container. "But right now, we still don't have the juice we need to make it serious. Even for a material witness warrant."

"We *have* stuff," she argued. "Damn it, we tied Sonnenberg to Levinstein's business. Four years— that's how long this guy's had an account with 'em. Levinstein's brother they found receipts for building supplies—roofing felt, fixtures, light construction stuff. So it's mainly cash-and-carry shit. So what? That's a documented link, for God's sake!"

I nodded. "It's a start," I said. "But we need to establish more of a direct connection."

I thought for a moment.

"Let's take a look at building permits. It might be interesting to see if Sonnenberg did any work for Stanley and Kathleen. Even better, get Building and Inspections to pull anything with Sonnenberg's name on it—he could've been casing the Levinstein house from a job next door, or down the street. Let's at least try to put him in the neighborhood. While you're at it, ask Levinstein's brother to fax over all the records they have. I'll go through them, name by name. Maybe there's a third-party invoice, or a delivery address that can give us something to cross-check against the permit list."

We walked on for a few steps in silence.

"It just doesn't fit that he would take off like he did," I said.

"It's been bothering me, too," Posson admitted. "Guy goes through a window, he's anxious about something. And I didn't exactly get the feeling that we were all that much of a concern to him. I keep remembering when I was putting the cuffs on him, when he was laying in the street sucking air. It's like, when he knew I had a badge, he got relaxed."

"Okay. So?"

"So how about we take what he said at face value?" Terry said. "He hears Sozcka talking in Russian, hears his name mentioned, takes off. That tells me he's worried about being found by somebody who's Russian. Make sense to you?"

I nodded slowly. "It adds a whole new element to all this—maybe. Or hell, maybe not. A guy like Sonnenberg, even he probably can't remember all the reasons somebody might have for wanting to take him off."

Terry pondered for a moment.

"Tell you what," she said. "How about we try talking to the woman? Call it a follow-up, see how she's doing after being slugged. Maybe one of us can get her to open up a little, talk to us about the jerk."

"Yeah, maybe," I said. "Let me try first. I'll see if Sozcka wants to go along; maybe showing the uniform will loosen her up. One way or the other, maybe it'll just be good to keep up the pressure on Sonnenberg." I grunted in irritation. "Lot of 'maybe's' in this case."

"Here's another one," she said. "Maybe I need to know a little more about a few things. Like, who's this Lichtman guy you threw at him? If he's locked up in Joliet, how does he figure in any of it?"

I walked a few steps without replying. When I spoke, it was with a studied nonchalance.

"Lichtman's a source," I told her. "Even in Stateville, he's connected. He thinks he owes me, so he gave up some information that linked Sonnenberg to a planned theft in Lake Tower. Word was it involved artwork, high-priced stuff. Then Lichtman heard it all went sour, people got killed and everything got torched to cover up the mess. I brought it to Cieloczki, and he let me in."

"Why not take it to Nederlander?" Posson asked.

I laughed, and even I could hear the bitterness that gave it a saw-toothed edge.

"In case you haven't noticed, Bob Nederlander and I don't exactly exchange Christmas cards," I said. "Besides, he had . . . *his* people already working the case." I pretended to ignore the face Posson pulled.

"More to the point, I needed a job. I haven't had one—not a steady job, anyway—since I left the force. I have legal bills that I still owe on, big-time. I've got the Internal Revenue Service putting the screws on me and my wife—excuse me, make that my former wife—because they got a tip that I've been stashing dirty money. The odds are good your boss is behind that, too. It's the kind of thing he'd do, just to enjoy the show."

Posson looked at me in a manner both dubious and wary.

"Don't take this the wrong way," she said, "but you sound like a whacko paranoid head-case."

I stared at her for a moment, then threw back my head and laughed. It felt as genuine as it was unanticipated. After a few beats, Posson started to smile herself, then joined my laughter.

"Ever consider taking up grief counseling?" I grinned. "You'd clear your caseload in a week—though the suicide rate might go right off the chart."

We had walked on a few more steps when I twisted my head to look at her.

"You want to know where I was headed? I was drinking myself to sleep and waking up with the night sweats after a couple of hours. I'd stare at the ceiling

until dawn, wondering if there was a reason, even a
bad one, to get out of bed. Then I hear there's this
convict who wants to see me."

I paused.

"Maybe he's full of cow flop, maybe not. But he
seemed to have some solid information on the Levinstein murders. So I took what I got from Sam Lichtman to Gil Cieloczki, and he went to Evans. And
that's where we are today."

"Still drinking?"

I shrugged. "Some. Maybe not as much."

We entered the municipal center, and the uniformed
old man at the reception podium glowered at us like
we were trespassing. We walked down the hallway to
the wing occupied by the Department of Public Safety.
The departments of police and fire squared off against
each other, separated these days by more than a
hallway.

As we each split off to our own side, Terry Posson
stopped and spoke.

"I just want to say you showed me something yesterday, when you ran down Sonnenberg," she said,
almost as if she had to force the words past her lips.
"It wasn't exactly by-the-book procedure, and I don't
know how smart it was, either. But you did okay."

I was more pleased than I should have been, a discovery that startled me as much as the embarrassment
I realized we both felt.

"You coming on to me, Posson?" I asked, to cover
the moment.

"In your dreams," she snorted, and went into the
offices of the Lake Tower police without looking back.

Had I followed Terry Posson into her office a few
minutes later, I would have seen her tapping a finger
on the desk, in obvious agitation.

Around her, the din and semiorganized chaos of the
squad room rose and fell unnoticed by the police-

woman. On her face was the look of someone who had just touched a glass of milk to her lips before realizing it had spoiled.

Her eyes flickered around the room. Finally, she picked up the telephone on the desk, and dialed one of the four-digit numbers assigned to the private-line extensions that were not listed in the municipal center directory.

She heard the line ring, once.

"Nederlander," a familiar voice growled, and Terry Posson began to speak.

In a darkened van parked three blocks away, a recording device blinked into life and began to whir, softly.

Chapter 19

A clerk walked past, and dropped several heavy folders into my in-box, like coals to Newcastle. Before me, on every available surface, buff-colored file folders already were stacked in uneven piles. A few of them were the case files I had compiled personally; most were the archived results of the multitudes who had, at one time or another, touched the investigation.

After the initial meeting with Nederlander when Gil had assumed command of the investigation, we had moved quickly to secure all the materials that Terry and Mel had held. Leaving them in a police department that was at best hostile seemed highly inadvisable, the way the investigation was moving.

We had organized the materials into manageable sections, and I had laboriously keyed a master index into Gil's computer. The electronic index was protected by a password system; for the reams of paper files, Gil had commandeered a safe in which all files were locked when we were out of the office.

I reached for the topmost of the folders. It was one of the thicker ones, and I recognized the contents immediately. It was the thick fanfold printout of permits Terry had requested from the Building and Inspections Department.

"Our friend Sonny was a busy man," I said, leaning forward to drop the sheaf of printouts on Gil's desk.

"I've been looking at a list of building permits for work Sonnenberg did in Lake Tower."

"Any new links between Sonnenberg and Levinstein?" Gil asked.

"Not quite," I answered. "It doesn't appear Sonny did any contracting work for Levinstein. But there is something interesting. Eight months ago, the Lake Tower Building Department issued a permit to him for roofing renovation at 2759 Terrace Pointe. That's less than two blocks from the Levinstein place. According to the city directory, the house is owned by one M. Travers."

He frowned, thinking.

"That sounds familiar," he said finally.

"Yeah," I replied. "It ought to. You've probably been in the Nathan Travers Public Library, or driven past Clarence Travers Junior High School. Nathan was one of the few guys who *made* money in the twenty-nine crash. Clarence was his son, and a two-term Lake Tower mayor back in the eighties."

"Old money," Gil observed.

"Among the oldest in Lake Tower," I said. "I imagine there is a genteel layer of dust on it, down in the family's subterranean vaults."

"Who's M. Travers?" Gil asked. "Anything there for us?"

"Ms. Marita Travers," I said, "is Nathan's granddaughter. Father died in 1989, the mother four years ago. Cancer—lung and ovarian, respectively. I walked across the hall and ran Ms. Travers through the police department computer. She had a steady string of tickets—moving violations as well as parking—and an impressive list of misdemeanor arrests. Disorderly conduct, carrying open containers of booze, one public indecency complaint—basically, the kind of kid stuff you'd expect from somebody with a chip on her shoulder. Then, nothing. There's been no new entries for the past three years."

"That's interesting, isn't it?" Gil asked.

"Interesting, yes," I said. "Relevant—well, I'm not so sure. Maybe she finally decided to grow up. The cases were all dismissed—not even a probation among 'em—which leads me to believe she has more than enough money to hire good legal representation."

"At least we've placed Sonnenberg in the right neighborhood," Gil said. "Are you feeling up to a visit to Terrace Pointe?"

"I believe our Ms. Travers might be worth an interview," I agreed. "It'd be nice to find out that she referred our pal Sonny to our late pal Stanley. It would be even nicer if she happened to see something suspicious. Like Sonny—or anybody else—carrying paintings down the street."

"While wearing a mask," Gil said, deadpanning, "and carrying a bag labeled loot. We could use a break like that. But I won't hold my breath."

Chapter 20

"I don't know what more I can tell you, Mr. Davey," Marita Travers said to me, her expression showing a precisely correct polite impatience. "We had some roofing damage during the winter while I was in Palm Beach. It was already repaired when I returned last month."

She was an attractive woman in her late thirties, dressed in a pair of cutoffs and a man's blue dress shirt knotted at her midriff; in the breast pocket were two brushes that could have come from a long forgotten child's watercolor set. Marita Travers wore no rings or other jewelry, not even a wristwatch. I did not imagine she worried overmuch about the time, or anything else; but that may have been my own class bias showing.

"Do you recall who referred you to the contractor you hired?"

She looked startled for an instant, as if I had suddenly started speaking Esperanto. Then she spread hands that were well cared for by an expert manicurist. "I couldn't even tell you who did the work. It was handled under our insurance, I believe."

I nodded, thinking of F. Scott Fitzgerald's comment to Ernest Hemingway that the very rich are different from the rest of us. Hemingway's famous rejoinder— "Yes, they have more money"—seemed woefully insufficient to cover the situation I had found upon my arrival.

I had pulled my Pontiac next to a new Mercedes that was parked in the circular drive, though "parked" was a generous misuse of the word. It sat near the front entrance, miraculously unmarked but angled crookedly. I had closed the driver's side door, which had been ajar, and removed the keys that still hung from the ignition.

Marita Travers had met me at the door, inviting me inside only after I told her that I was investigating an arson homicide. As she led me to the rear of the house, I noticed phones that had been taken off their hooks or disconnected from their outlets. In the spacious dining room, a man's green silk shirt hung carelessly over a chair; I saw a black dress shoe, its laces still tied, carelessly discarded in a corner of the kitchen.

We sat at a butcher's block table in the well-appointed kitchen. On it were tubes of oil paint of varying vintage—some almost new, others rolled and crimped and squeezed almost empty long before—as well as a handful of charcoal sticks and a half bottle of spirit thinner. Occasionally—in fact, frequently—her eyes would drift away from my face to look over my shoulder.

"I'm sorry," she said. "You were saying?"

"I said, perhaps I could talk with someone from your insurance company," I repeated.

"I suppose," she said, and her eyes did their drifting act again. We sat in peaceful silence for several seconds.

"What is your insurance company?" I asked finally.

"I'm sure I don't know," Marita Travers said, still occupied with other sights.

I followed her gaze.

A few feet away, an arched doorway opened onto the garden patio. Here, an impromptu studio had ap-

parently been set up for the benefit of a tall man who
looked to be in his late twenties. He was barefoot and
bare-chested; paint of varying hues and colors spat-
tered the expensive-looking soft wool trousers he
wore, as well as much of his exposed skin. His "easel"
was a high-backed tall stool, apparently privateered
from a counter in the ultramodern kitchen.

"Is that your husband?" I asked. "Might he know?"

"That is Peter Comstock," Marita said, in a manner
that suggested I should recognize the name. "He's
staying here temporarily, as a guest. I'd introduce you,
but I don't want to disturb his concentration. Peter is
just coming out of a period where his creativity was
almost completely blocked, you see."

I nodded.

As I watched, the artist carefully lifted what looked
like a blunt-edged, thin-bladed paté knife. Almost delicately, he tapped the tip on the edge of what I suspected was a very expensive serving platter that had
been pressed into emergency service as a palette.
Thick daubs of pigmented oils, some partially dried
and others shining fresh and wet, ran riot like a poly-
chromatic explosion across its surface.

Then, with an explosive, violent movement of his
arm, Comstock slashed the knife in a diagonal arc that
angled sharply downward. It left in its wake a path of
bright wet crimson, startling and jarring beneath its
blade. He was in three-quarters profile to us; the expression on his face was primitive, almost indecent in
an excitement that I suspected was neither entirely
physical nor completely mystical. Still, it appeared to
have definite undertones of both—a complex mix of
raw, elemental emotions.

The artist let his arm fall to the side and stepped
backward. As if wanting to prolong the sensation, he
turned away, deliberately averting his eyes from his
handiwork. As I watched, he pressed one large hand
into the small of his back and arched into it, stretching
in an audible volley of pops and snaps. Only then did

he lift his view to the canvas, eyeing it with an expression that was in equal measures critical, skeptical and pleased.

Marita watched, the expression on her face one of unabashed delight.

"Peter! News bulletin: I found some brushes, too!" Marita Travers's voice was giddy in its self-satisfaction at her discovery. The artist turned and smiled broadly at her; she waited before he turned back to his canvas before addressing me.

"He hasn't left the house—not even for supplies," she said, her eyes still locked on the artist. "Yesterday morning, he said that the urge to begin painting took complete possession of him."

She smiled, and looked as if she were enjoying a private joke.

"I've been scrounging here. I used to dabble in oils myself, and we have crates full of old canvases from the last time this place was redecorated. I told Peter he can use as many as he wishes." Again she smiled at secrets unsaid. "They are, after all, not mine."

"Oh?"

"They belong to my husband," she said, almost sweetly. "We are—how should I say this?—estranged."

She turned to me with an air of finality.

"If there's nothing else, Mr. Davey?"

We rose as if in drill.

"Thank you for your time, Ms. Travers," I said. "I can show myself out. I apologize for the intrusion."

We shook hands as if we were members of the same club, and I waited for her to go through the arched doorway to the artist.

But I didn't leave, not yet.

As I watched, Marita Travers pushed up against Comstock's back, and playfully punched between his shoulder blades.

"Peter—I want to *see!*" Marita tried to look over his shoulder, changed her mind and slipped under. She leaned back against him, pulling his bare and surprisingly muscular arm around her waist. She stopped short and stared at the painting, her lips parting slightly. "Oh, my God—Peter, that's . . . that's *marvelous!*"

With his free arm, Comstock picked up the makeshift palette knife and scooped a tiny pinpoint of brilliant blue from the platter onto its tip. He carefully touched it to the canvas immediately below the diagonal red he had just added. Then, pressing the blade so it flexed lightly against the fabric, with a firm stroke he spread the blue pigment.

Before my eyes, I saw the immediate result: in contrast, the crimson streak seemed suddenly to become three-dimensional, dramatically levitating itself so it appeared to float weightlessly above the surface. I felt goosebumps rise on my neck, awed at the effect in spite of myself.

Marita evidently felt the same impact, if in a somewhat more elemental place.

"You're not done, are you?" she breathed, delighted. "Don't stop, Peter—I want to watch!"

The artist pulled her even closer, and rested his chin on the soft ringlets of her hair.

"I feel like the guy in that movie," he complained happily. "The one who gets chained to the bed by a crazed fan."

"Please don't tell me you enjoy bondage films?" Marita murmured, her eyes still on the painting.

"No, no . . . the guy who was Sonny in *The Godfather*," Comstock said. "The woman won't let him go until he writes a book for her. It was in . . . *Misery*. I feel like I'm in *Misery*."

"Poor dear." Marita tilted her head up at him, and tried to look sympathetic. "He's in misery. There, there now." She smiled into his eyes, and the imp suddenly supplanted the muse. "Perhaps there's some . . . comfort I can offer, sir?"

Comstock scooped her up and did a slow half twirl that made both of them laugh.

I took it as my cue to leave, and slipped away toward the front of the house. But I could not avoid hearing the next words they spoke, oblivious to anything but each other.

"Work, work, work," Comstock grumbled joyously, as he carried her into the house. "I think I need a union."

"What an interesting idea," I heard Marita Travers say, and her voice was anything but distracted. "Let's, shall we?"

Chapter 21

I was not present when Mel Bird made the discovery that gave us our first big break in the investigation; what follows is a compilation that I reconstructed later from interviews and reports, as well as assumptions that I consider logical. It may not be completely accurate, but in a larger sense I believe it to be true.

It was early afternoon when Mel slowed to a halt at a small glass and precast concrete structure. It stood astride the driveway leading onto a spacious campus, the world headquarters of TransNational Mutual Insurance. The uniformed guard, a carefully courteous, painstakingly trained smile of welcome on his face, slid back the green-tinted glass. The edge was thick and laminated, and Bird guessed it would stop a bullet from a hunting rifle with little difficulty.

He flashed the leather holder that contained both his badge and the photo identification issued by the Lake Tower Police Department, and was surprised when the guard examined it closely, even comparing the picture with its bearer.

"Who are you meeting with, sir?" the guard asked.

"Miss Melton," Bird said. "Corporate Relations, I think. I may be a little early."

"It'll be just a minute, sir." The guard slid the bulletproof window closed, and his fingers tapped on a computer keyboard while Bird's tapped impatiently on the steering wheel.

Around him, the suburban setting was a picture of verdant greens and the white blossoms of hybrid cherry trees that lined the driveway. A crew of landscape workers was laying thick sod around the edges of the asphalt drive, but Bird could still see the signs of recent paving work where fresh blacktop had been laid. The guard station, too, looked clean and new. His interest piqued, the police officer peered through his windshield, right and left. He knew what he was looking for, but even so he almost missed it in the artful placement and screening: three, possibly four, surveillance cameras.

The heavy window slid open again, and the guard leaned out to press a bright orange sticker on Bird's windshield.

"Please drive ahead on this road, sir. There's a visitors' parking area immediately in front of the main building, across from the parking garage. Somebody will be waiting for you there. When you leave, please make sure to leave your visitor's car pass with me here."

Bird looked at the guard. "Just between the two of us," he said, "is this a good gig?"

The guard studied him a moment, then leaned closer in a confidential manner.

"Eighteen bucks an hour, plus fringes, just to check in visitors and out-of-town salesmen," the uniformed man said, grinning. "And no heavy lifting, unless you count when I stand up to go to lunch. So far, friend, best job I ever had."

"The most simple explanation is usually the best one," Dane Tornell said politely, while wondering where in the world this policeman got off with this kind of nonsense. "There's no record of insurance because no insurance was issued."

Bird twisted his lips and inhaled deeply. *You stuck-up little*—a voice inside him said. He let the air out slowly, and took a moment to look around the large, well-appointed office. A corner window looked out over rolling acreage dotted with blossoming trees and shrubs.

"Yeah," he said. "You already told me that, Mr. Tornell. Like, a half hour ago. Now, just humor me, okay? If—remember, I'm saying 'if'—I came to you for coverage of my art collection, what are the places where somebody could've dropped the ball? You know—mislaid the paperwork or something, so that it turned out you didn't actually issue a policy."

Tornell nodded, as if considering Bird's hypothesis seriously. Long ago, well before he became a vice president for one of the world's largest insurers, Tornell had started his career as an agent for another, albeit smaller, insurance company. His early training in sales techniques and what the facilitators called "people-oriented" selling skills had ingrained in Tornell an almost fanatical belief in two precepts he still followed in his present position.

The first: always wear a tie and a white, short-sleeved shirt; it made you seem friendly, but in an avuncularly professional way. Second, never tell a prospect he was full of crap, even if he was. *Especially* if he was—and Bird, in Tornell's considered opinion, definitely fit that description.

Karen Melton, who sat in a chair at the corner of Tornell's large desk in a way that gave Bird a clear view of her exceptionally nice legs, spoke up. "Dane, perhaps we could review the procedure for a moment. Is that what you need, Detective Bird?"

"I'm a plainclothes officer, not a detective," Bird said, mentally sighing. "Yeah, that might help a lot."

"For one thing, Officer Bird, there is no paperwork," she said. "At least, not on an existing policy to which we are adding coverage. In Mr. Levinstein's case, he would have called us directly and an underwriter would have input the new information directly into his computerized account. It's a very efficient system. It immediately updates the account information

and coverage specifications, generates a confirmation
letter to the customer, and automatically becomes part
of the billing database. It also serves as a binder,
which provides the customer with insurance protection
immediately—or, if an expert appraisal was needed,
as it certainly would have been here, on an interim,
provisional basis."

"What about backup?" Bird asked. "You know—
duplicate records in case something goes wrong with
the computer?"

It was Tornell's turn. "There's no one computer,
Officer—we have a network of CPUs and data storage
banks in a number of locations around the country.
Information that is input here, or by any of our sales
agencies in the field, is automatically recorded in several secure locations simultaneously. In addition, our
underwriting staff is divided into teams targeted at
specific geographical areas in any given region. Each
team is supported by a senior coding specialist who
also receives and stores the incoming account data as
it is entered, and confirms that all of the computers
on the network have received, processed and recorded
the transaction. This means that at minimum, two people are involved with each account activity as it occurs.
In addition, the coding specialist's data records are
compared to the activity files of all the underwriters
on a daily basis, and computer-matched with each
other."

Bird pondered for a moment. "So that tells you
what goes in. What do you have that tells you if something goes out? I mean, why couldn't somebody just
erase, or change, whatever is in an account?"

Tornell shook his head. "Once it's in, it's in the
system permanently. If coverage is changed, canceled
or expires, that information is added to the account
record. But nobody can delete or alter any files—the
system isn't set up that way." Tornell smiled to take
the sting from his words. "We're not exactly amateurs
in all this, Officer."

Bird was stumped. He had run out of questions. While he would have liked to sit longer, particularly when Karen Melton periodically crossed and recrossed her legs at him, he was very tired of hearing about "foolproof" computerized systems. Computers screwed with people every day, Bird knew; worse, *people* screwed with people every day, and some of them used a computer to do it. Okay, so maybe Charlie Herndon had a point about Levinstein and his insure-every-goddam-thing hangup.

And maybe not, Bird thought, *but I'm getting nowhere fast, here.*

He stood up. "Well, thanks anyway," Bird said. "Looks like I took a little drive for nothing." Tornell gave him a handshake as practiced as the smile that went along with it. Karen Melton walked with Bird back along the corridors, alive with potted plants and adorned with eclectic artwork, through which she had led him when he arrived.

He walked alongside and slightly behind her, the better to sneak the occasional sidelong glance. She was dressed in a long-sleeved, high-necked, all-business outfit, black with two rows of brass buttons that led from the collar almost to the midknee hem of her skirt. It accented a figure Bird would have described as "voluptuous," had it been a word that featured in his day-to-day vocabulary.

Bird hated small talk with the passion of someone convinced of a personal ineptitude in a particular area. But the main entrance was not far away—and Karen Melton did have very nice legs. He tried to think of something with which to engage her conversation, and with luck, her interest. They turned at a corner, and he noticed the camera mounted high on the wall.

"You've got better security here than the CIA," Bird said. "Cameras all tied into the guard station monitors, huh?" He watched the camera pan to follow their progression down the hallway. "Looks like state-of-the-art stuff."

Karen Melton nodded grimly.

"Cost the company a bundle, too," she agreed. "But it's the kind of investment that makes everybody feel a lot better, especially after the incident."

Bird looked at the woman, puzzled.

"Incident?" he asked. "What incident?"

Melton looked mildly embarrassed. "I'm sorry," she said. "I just assumed you knew. I guess we've all gotten used to not talking about it around here. Three months ago, one of our people was attacked and killed on campus. Right in the parking garage. That's when the company got very concerned about security. Up until then, things were a bit more informal around here."

Bird felt his scalp tighten. It was a tingling sensation he recognized from other moments of impending excitement, and he was reasonably certain it had nothing to do with the proximity of Karen Melton.

"The victim, what did she do here?" he asked, and at that exact instant realized he already knew part of the answer.

"Ms. Hunt?" Melton asked, puzzled at the sudden intensity of the policeman's tone. "She was just one of our coding technicians."

Chapter 22

"I appreciate you coming up here again," I said, braking to avoid an elderly man with a walker who haltingly inched across the street at my bumper. "But I feel bad that you're taking your lunch hour to do it."

"Nah," said Phil Sozcka, and I could see the color rise on his cheeks again. "I don't mind."

He looked out the window of my LeMans at the noontime throng on Devon Avenue. Without turning his head, and trying to make it sound as casual as possible, he added, "I was thinking, maybe . . . you know Officer Posson pretty good, right?"

I glanced over at the Chicago policeman. A blush was spreading up the back of his neck, and I could not fight down the urge to tease him, just a bit.

"Oh, yeah; good cop, and a great dancer to boot. Too bad she couldn't come along this time."

Sozcka made a noise that might have been assent, and was silent for the next few blocks.

"Heard the man walked," Sozcka said, and the commiseration in his voice was only partly professional. "I'd have been glad to come up and go on the stand, you know."

I shrugged. "Would have been a waste of time anyway," I said. "All we really had was him hitting the woman, and she declined to press. And because he was out the window before we entered and announced, the judge tossed the flight charge. All we had left was a material witness warrant that was shaky in the first place, and Sonnenberg could have had a lot cheaper lawyer get that vacated."

"If it was all that loose, how come you busted the guy?"

"If he hadn't forced our hand by taking off, we probably wouldn't have," I admitted. "As it was, we were lucky. At least the judge didn't charge us with false arrest."

"Way you knocked Sonnenberg on his butt," Sozcka said, and the wistful tone of his voice made me regret having teased him about Terry Posson, "the judge might've been afraid to try."

The door Sozcka had kicked open the previous day was closed, and an unpainted strip of hardwood trim had been inexpertly attached as reinforcement near the lockset. Sozcka studied it briefly with a critical eye.

"Not locked—looks like it's propped shut from the inside," Sozcka said, "Lady needs a new door as well as a new boyfriend."

Once again, he automatically stepped to the side, out of the direct line of fire, and nodded to me to do the same. He raised his large fist and knocked, hard. The door rattled, loose in its frame.

He listened for a response; there was none.

"I should have called first, made sure she was here," I said. "Saved us both the trip."

"Nah, you did the right thing," Sozcka shrugged. "Usually it's better to catch 'em cold, when you want to talk and they—"

He stopped at the sound of footsteps climbing the stairway.

In a moment, a thin-faced man, the gray of his mustache matching that of the hair that fringed his balding pate, stepped onto the landing.

The man looked at us without apparent surprise.

"You have now come to arrest the other one?" he said, his words clear despite the pronounced accent.

His hand fished in his side pocket and emerged with a keyring. "Good. Perhaps *this* night I will sleep."

Sozcka looked at him through narrowed eyelids.

"Learned to speak English," the policeman asked, "since yesterday?"

The man smiled, though there was nothing of humor in it.

"You spoke in Russian. I spoke in Russian." He unlocked the door across from Katya Butenkova's apartment, and held it open, slightly. "She is shameless whore," the man said. "You remove her man, yes—so all night then, she has party. New man she can fuck, and fight with."

I frowned.

"Is she home?" I asked.

"O doma, he's saying," Sozcka said, still looking at the man with unblinking eyes. *"Da* or *nyet?"*

"Until long after midnight, she plays her loud music and throws things at her guest. Perhaps she is home. Whores sleep late, do they not?" With a single movement, he stepped inside and closed his door behind him.

Sozcka and I looked at each other. Then I leaned down and pressed my ear against Katya's battered door.

"No music now," I said, my eyes closed in concentration. "No sound at—"

My nose wrinkled, and I twisted my head to squint up at Sozcka.

"How's your sense of smell, Phil?"

Sozcka arched his eyebrows. "Okay, I guess. Why?"

I sniffed again before straightening.

"Take a whiff. I smell something in there. Like a gas leak, maybe. You smell it, too?"

Dutifully, he bent close to the door jamb.

"Not really."

"Try again." I looked at him, significantly. "You smoke, don't you? Sometimes that affects the sense of smell."

"There could be something, I guess."

"Enough to give us reasonable cause to check it out, you think?"

This time, there was hardly a beat before his reply.

"Absolutely. It's a question of public safety."

Inside, whatever sense of reckless conspiracy had fueled our action ended abruptly. The apartment was silent in a way that raised the hairs along the back of my neck, and I thought of the weapon I had not brought.

I fought down the sudden heart-pumping rush that accompanies any form of trespass; irrationally, I found that my next impulse was to go to the range and crack open a burner valve for a few seconds.

Instead, I raised my voice and said, loudly, "This is the police, Ms. Butenkova. We're inside now. Are you all right?"

"I guess we were wrong about the gas leak," Sozcka said, in a voice so low it was almost inaudible. "Honest mistake, just doing our job."

His posture was tense, and his hand rested on the butt of his service revolver.

The room looked much as it had the day before, with two notable exceptions.

The window Sonny Sonenberg had broken through was covered with a piece of plywood, wedged roughly into the wooden frame. Sunlight streamed in parallel beams through two finger holes the size of quarters someone had bored through the panel. The broken crockery had been swept up; parts of the floor were cleaner than the surrounding hardwood, indicating where the blood from Katya's split lip had been carelessly mopped.

Also on the floor near the doorway was a kitchen clock radio, its short cord plugged into the closest outlet.

"Funny place to put that," Sozcka said, echoing my thoughts.

I walked around the apartment, taking in the dirty utensils in the kitchenette's sink and the undisturbed layer of dust on the top of the rust-spotted refrigerator. I was, I noticed, being careful to touch nothing, and wondered if it was for hygienic or evidentiary reasons.

"Katya's not much for housecleaning," I said, and with my foot gingerly opened the door to what I assumed was the bathroom. It too was a mess, with towels carelessly tossed on a floor that had seen far better days.

But I did not notice, because something else had now caught my full and undivided attention. I sensed Sozcka come up behind me, and heard his sharp intake of breath.

"We need backup, Phil," I said, and heard the hiss of static as he pressed the button on his shoulder microphone.

It was an old-fashioned bathroom, the kind that still had a claw foot bathtub dominating the ancient tile of the floor. It had been converted, inexpertly, to include a shower; the black iron shepherd's crook of pipe was affixed solidly to the wall alongside. An oversized showerhead, like a lime-stained metallic sunflower, centered over the wide porcelain tub.

From it hung the nude remains of Katya Butenkova, her torn and mottled flesh a curious mix of rust streaks against a hideously blanched pearl gray. At intervals that appeared oddly regular in placement, I could see the clean white of exposed bone. Katya's head was thrust back, and her hair hung in damp black tendrils, spiky and tangled. What may once have been a yellow sponge bulged from her mouth.

Katya's hands were fastened high, wrists bound to the fixture with what looked like industrial-strength filament shipping tape; her knees were half bent and her torso hung in a shockingly stiff posture. It appeared, in the eerie calm of my initial shock, like some obscene supplication.

It was a ghastly scene.

But worst of all, I decided, were Katya's eyes: open wide, and fixed forever on something distant but nonetheless horrifying.

"The Chicago medical examiner doesn't want to do much guessing over the phone." Terry Posson's voice was unnaturally tight; I was willing to attribute it to the quality of the speakerphone in Gil's office, though I knew better. "But, unofficially, he's willing to say it looks like she died sometime after midnight and before five this morning."

"That fits," I said. "A neighbor says Katya was 'partying' until well after twelve."

"She was tortured?" Gil asked unnecessarily, and for a long moment I fought back the impulse to react with sarcasm, even black humor.

"Yeah, she was tortured," I repeated instead. "The killer had music on, loud, to cover the noise of the struggle. He took Katya into the bathroom and taped her wrists to the shower pipe. Then he used a damn kitchen sponge to gag her; she could talk when he wanted her to, but not loud enough for the neighbors to hear."

I took a deep breath. "He slashed the hell out of her, Gil, all over her body. But not like he was in a frenzy; it was definitely methodical, organized. This guy knew what he was doing. After she was dead, he knew to run the shower—to wash away whatever random evidence he might have left. Then he went out the window and pulled the plywood back into place. Probably took a fond look around before he went down the fire ladder."

Cieloczki was silent for a moment.

"There's no sign of Paul Sonnenberg?"

"Nothing. Even being generous with the time, he was still in lockup when all this went down," I said. "There's no indication he came back here after leaving Lake Tower."

We were silent for a moment, weighing how little we knew. Terry spoke first.

"Okay—this guy wanted information from Katya," she said. "My guess is he wanted to know where Sonnenberg was."

"If she knew anything," I said, "she told him."

"What do you want to do next?" Gil asked.

"I'm on my way out to Joliet," I said. "My source knows Sonnenberg and his habits. Maybe he can help us find Sonnenberg before somebody else does."

There was a curious silence on the line; I had no doubt all of us were once again picturing a horrific image that had been seared into our individual minds.

"Well, for Christ's sake drive fast," Terry said finally. "Our guy has a couple of hours' head start. And we already have three dead people in this case."

"Mel Bird just called in, too," Gil said. "He thinks he's found number four."

Chapter 23

There was a cat. It had jumped up and walked across Mel Bird's lap, raising its tail and sniffing delicately at the notebook he held. Then it had looked at him with its unblinking predator's eyes.

Sizing me up like I was a goddam canary, Bird told me later, and I could still hear the near shudder in his voice.

Mel Bird did not like cats. Even if he had not been allergic, he told me, he would not have liked cats. He also had strong opinions about people who did, particularly people who lived in a house with a nice-sized yard and could easily have had a dog instead. Or any kind of pet that neither clawed, nor hissed, nor made a man break out in hives.

But here, facing him like an anaphylactic nightmare, was undeniably a cat.

"Pepper likes you," the woman said, smiling indulgently at the beast perched on Bird's thigh.

He could feel his eyes beginning to itch, and knew in a minute he would have to sneeze. Instead of drawing his gun and shooting the animal, Bird smiled back at its owner, covertly twitching his leg in an attempt to dislodge the feline.

In retaliation, Pepper steadied him- or herself—Bird's expertise did not include the gender characteristics of house cats—by flexing his or her toes. Bird felt the needlelike tips of Pepper's claws through his trousers, and took it as a warning.

"Nice cat," Bird observed as a man who appeared to be in his early fifties entered from the kitchen. He was carrying a china cup filled with an opaque fluid that smelled somewhat like coffee. Carefully, almost fussily, he placed it on a cork coaster on the lamp table next to Bird.

"It's Taster's Choice," the man said, a nervous smile on his face. "We don't drink much coffee, I'm afraid. We prefer tea."

"It's fine, thanks." Bird reached for the cup, using the opportunity to push an elbow against Pepper, hard. The cat hit the floor, and stared daggers at Bird for a moment. Then, as Bird pretended to sip at the cup, the cat leaped weightlessly onto the table and then to the living room windowsill. It sat, looking out the picture window intently, motionless but for the twitching tip of its tail. Bird put his cup down and leaned forward in his chair.

"Mr. Hunt, Mrs. Hunt—I appreciate you talking with me," Bird said. "I know it must be hard—"

Claire Hunt interrupted. "Becca has been . . . gone . . . for three months now." She reached over and took her husband's hand, and squeezed it momentarily in a way Bird thought must have been painful to him. "We want to do whatever we can to help you arrest whoever did this, Detective."

"I'm plainclothes, not a detective," Bird said. "Can you tell me a little about her, please? Was she social? I mean, did she have a lot of friends, go out a lot?"

"She was very popular," Mrs. Hunt said, firmly. "She was always going out with girls she knew from school, to football games or movies and such. People liked Becca—loved her, you know. She was so pretty and bright. How could they not?"

"Can you give me the names of a few of them?" Bird asked. "I might need to talk with them, maybe about her job and—"

"Well"—Mrs. Hunt frowned—"I don't know how much her friends would know about her job."

The husband spoke up. "Our daughter moved away from home right after she graduated from high school," Albert Hunt told the policeman. "She lived in the city, in Lincoln Park. I don't think she saw many of her friends from here very often anymore."

Bird wrote in his notebook. "How about friends in the city, then?"

Hunt looked embarrassed. "She had two roommates when she first moved to the city, I know. They shared rent and expenses. We never met them, I'm afraid. Then she got a big promotion, a big raise, and moved into her own apartment, alone. We never really met any of her city friends."

"She was very busy," Mrs. Hunt interjected, her voice insistent as she overrode her spouse. "Especially after her promotion, her job kept her busy all the time. She had a *lot* of responsibilities to deal with there."

Bird nodded. Before he had left the TransNational offices to drive here, a far southwest suburb of mainly modest-income tract homes, he had reviewed Rebecca Hunt's personnel file carefully. There had been no major promotions, and a look at the salary for a TransNational coding clerk had failed to impress even a man accustomed to the civil service pay grade for a plainclothes policeman.

"Did she call you a lot?" he asked.

"I would call her," Mrs. Hunt corrected. "At her work, usually. Becca was very busy with her job, and that meant that she couldn't visit us as often as she would have liked to. She was very ambitious, you know. She would be working nights, weekends—all this, as well as going to . . . that place . . . before dawn." Claire Hunt's eyes closed for a moment. "I used to call her apartment first and leave a message— but after a while, it was easier simply to call her at work, when I knew she would be there."

Bird almost sighed in frustration.

"Was there anything she mentioned about her co-workers you found unusual? Anything about her work that struck you as out of the ordinary?"

"She handled insurance claims on cars that were damaged, or stolen, or destroyed," Mrs. Hunt said. There was an undertone of irritation in her voice, as if she were dealing with an incompetent waiter. "She dealt with people whose roofs had been blown off in a storm or caught fire, or had their basements flooded. There wouldn't be much to say about that, would there? We just talked, mother to daughter, like we always had."

"I don't know if this is important," Albert Hunt said, and Bird thought there were more than a few people who might have thought the half apologetic tone in his voice rang less than true. "About two years ago, I had a minor accident—not much more than a fender bender, really. It was my fault, I'm sorry to say, so I put in a claim with my insurance company and everything was settled. It was so minor that I didn't even think to mention it to Claire. She gets upset over things like that, you see."

Bird glanced at Mrs. Hunt. She was looking at her husband as if he were a distasteful task scheduled, but not yet completed. Then Bird nodded to the man—partly to encourage him to continue, and partly in sympathy.

"Well, Claire happened to call Becca one Saturday at her office," he said. "And my daughter sort of . . . made fun of the fact that I had had an accident. She told her mother that she was working on the claim right then. Joked that she was going to make it a really big settlement for the other driver."

Hunt shook his head. "Oh, Claire was very upset that I hadn't told her about it. I guess Becca teased her about that, too. Quite a bit, didn't she, Claire?"

Bird, reading between the lines, was beginning to

develop a new image of Rebecca Hunt, devoted daughter and hard-working employee.

Rebecca Hunt, he thought, *is beginning to sound like a* mean *little package.*

He tried to make light of it.

"Guess that's what happens when you insure your car where a relative works, huh?" Bird said, with a wry smile.

"That was the oddest part, you see," Albert Hunt said. "We don't insure our car through TransNational. Apparently, the other driver put in a claim to them for the accident, too. That's how Becca knew about it."

He glanced over at his wife and said, in a guileless voice, "I didn't know one could present a claim for an accident that another insurance company already paid."

And then Hunt looked directly at Bird.

Deep inside, Bird thought he saw a flash of something that should not have been in the eyes of a grieving father. It might have been a measure of satisfaction, or even glee at a payback for some carefully stored litany of slights, humiliations and other casually inflicted injuries, the nature of which Bird could only imagine.

On the ledge of the picture window, Pepper was lost in the intensity that places felines among the most relentless of predators. A few inches away, on the other side of a barrier that could be seen through but not penetrated, something was fluttering amid the foliage, as enticing as it was maddening. It was a finch, and Bird could see it hopping from branch to branch in the hedge.

Pepper was motionless in a way that, for a reason he did not quite understand, raised a chill on Bird's neck. He watched as prey and predator each eyed the other from different sides of an invisible barrier that negated the usual rules of the game.

Bird knew how both felt. His sympathies were nor-

mally with the hunter, but he was beginning to understand how the prey felt, too.

"I still don't get the insurance angle," Posson said,
her voice a cautious near whisper over the cellular
telephone connection. "Why would anybody go to so
much trouble to fake the coverage?"

"What if Levinstein insisted the art be insured?"
Bird pressed. "He probably did. But insuring the artwork would have documented its existence and placed
it in Levinstein's possession. So somebody couldn't let
that happen."

"And Levinstein's other insurance coverage was
through TransNational," Posson said. "That could
work. It let the killer bring in Rebecca Hunt. She
made sure nothing got into TransNational's databank,
and she issued the phony confirmation letter."

"Might be a stroke of luck for us," Bird said. "The
bad guy didn't just pull Hunt's name out of a hat.
Whoever it was, I'd bet our little Rebecca had worked
with them before, on other insurance scams." He
paused. "So where do we go with this now?"

Terry Posson thought for a moment, then made one
of the worst decisions of her life.

"Nothing else I *can* do," she said. "I've got to fill
Nederlander in on this."

Chapter 24

It had only been two weeks since my last visit, but in that time Sam Lichtman had traveled far along a darkening path.

Orval Kellogg had told me that Lichtman had been sent to Stateville's hospital ward a week before, and transferred into the intensive care unit two days later. "They rolled him in on a wheelchair," the guard said, as once more I went through the prison's rituals of entry. "Ain't nobody expectin' to see him come out of there 'cept in a bag."

Even prepared, the difference from my last visit was jarring.

This time, the invader inside Lichtman's brain had mutated into a far more malevolent presence, insinuating its tentacles throughout the living tissue in a manner both merciless and inexorable. It had leached his complexion to that of plumber's putty, carved away the flesh under his skin to leave him a gray, hollow-eyed wraith. Every few seconds, an involuntary shudder would ripple the left side of his face as the cancer short-circuited doomed synapses somewhere within. His once thick hair, which had thinned noticeably, was spiky and dull, disheveled from the pillow against which it pressed. Only his eyes were still Sam Lichtman's—the blue of arctic ice, afire with an almost inhuman intensity.

A clear liquid dripped steadily through a tube, ter-

minating in the back of a hand mottled with the
bruises of previous IV lines. Various other conduits
and connections led to arrays of electronic monitors,
breathing-gas manifolds, micropumps and waste-
removal filters—all the technology that makes the
modern ICU an impassively cruel place. The chain
that looped from his ankle to a ring on the bed frame
seemed an afterthought, redundant in its mission.
Lichtman looked like prey held immobile in a spider's
web carelessly spun, but nonetheless inescapable.

"Can you believe it? They won't even let me have
a smoke," Lichtman rasped, the arrogance of his smirk
an obvious effort. "Guess they're worried it might become a habit, huh?" He eyed me clinically. "*You* look
like hell, Davey boy. You give up sleeping or something?"

I said nothing. A nurse pulled aside the curtain
around Sam's bed and stepped in. She was Hispanic
and solidly plain-featured, her hair dark and pulled
back in a thick tail. She smiled fleetingly at me, and
I noticed a faint lacework of old scar tissue below the
left corner of her mouth. As the nurse checked the
various tubes and wires, she did not look at Lichtman.
But his eyes carefully, almost warily, followed her
orbit around his hospital bed. Then she left, not having said a word—realizing, perhaps, there was little
she could say that the object of her ministrations
didn't already know, much too well.

"Shit." Lichtman breathed rather than spoke the
word. His eyes found mine. "You think I'm already
dead, and this is hell?" He did not make the question
sound rhetorical.

"Sonnenberg," I said. "I busted him, he got himself
sprung, and now he's missing. A Russian woman he
was living with is dead—messy dead, Sam. Someone
enjoyed putting blood spots on the ceiling. I need to
find Sonnenberg, or what's left of him."

Somehow, my words seemed to give Lichtman a

focus, as if the act of concentrating energized a part
of him unravaged so far by his disease.

"Where?" he asked. "Where did all this go down?"

"He was hanging out with some Russians up on
Devon."

"If old Sonny has got Russians mixed up in this,
he's a bigger goddam fool than I thought he was. If
he's trying to screw them, they'll *skin* the little dickhead," Lichtman said. He stiffened suddenly, and I
saw the pain turn his face the shade of parchment.

Then it passed, and he let out the breath he had
been holding.

"Russians. I never fucked with them, they never
fucked with me. But I hear they've been getting hun-
grier out there, so maybe they invited themselves into
Sonny's deal. Could've happened."

He grinned, a sickly effort compared to his former
self. "Hell, a couple of million bucks' worth of artwork, just sitting there? Like I told you the first time,
if I had been on the outside when I heard about it, I
might have wanted a taste myself. I still can't figure
how even a fuck-up like Sonny could've blown this
one."

"Sam," I said, "I need to know who's flying top
cover for Sonnenberg. When I hauled him up to Lake
Tower, he just about came out and bragged that he
was tight with somebody up in the high branches. He
even warned me I could expect to get pissed on."

Lichtman's eyes had closed, and his mouth was a
thin smile of amusement.

"Well, nobody ever claimed that Sonny was the
sharpest pencil in the box," Lichtman said, and his
voice was less weak now. "I don't suppose he was
stupid enough to name any names?"

I took a chance. "I'm guessing Nederlander," I said.
"If the idea was to sell the artwork back to the owner,
that ties all this to insurance. We have some indica-
tions that Nederlander might have been involved in a

car insurance scam at least a couple of years back. One idea might be that he's caught a dose of ambition and decided to move up a little."

"Could be," Lichtman said. "You'd love to put Nederlander in the crapper, wouldn't you? He do something recently to smoke your ass all over again?"

"I have the tax man crawling all over me, Sam. Unreported 'bribe' income. Nederlander is probably the bastard who sicced him on me." I noted Lichtman's reaction. "It's not as funny as it sounds, trust me."

"Wow—just when you think you're all clear, somebody calls the IRS," he said, shaking his head more in amusement than sympathy. "Hey, you don't know how much I feel for ya. That's cold, man. That's downright brutal."

He chuckled, despite the pain it cost him.

"Sonny's mother used to live in the county, unincorporated burb out past O'Hare. I dunno exactly where, but I know he got his ass busted there this one time. Dumb fuck—you remember the blizzard five or six years back? The big one, three and a half feet in twelve hours? Took days to plow out the streets.

"Old Sonny, he's looking for a parking space that wasn't under a ton of snow. Gets lucky—couple of doors down from his mother's, there's this nice spot somebody dug out. Wide open, 'cept for a damn kitchen chair." He laughed. "You getting the picture here?"

I nodded; in a Chicago winter, few commodities are more valuable than a parking space painstakingly cleared of snow. By sacred tradition, the act constitutes an uncontestable claim, staked out by placement of a card table, a sawhorse, an ironing board. Or a kitchen chair.

"Sonny pulls in anyway, goes up to the old lady's place. Hour later, he looks out the window and sees some guy beating the hell out of his car with a tire iron. Broke out the windows, smashed off the door handles—even beat in the trunk and threw all the shit into the street."

Had it not been for the pain, Lichtman might have been convulsing in laughter; as it was, tears of mirth marked his cheeks.

"By the time Sonny gets down there, a Cook County deputy had already stopped. What do you know? He finds a half dozen cases of liquor, some of 'em still in the trunk and some of 'em sticking out of the damn snowbanks where the citizen had thrown 'em. Problem was, none of the bottles had a state tax sticker on 'em."

This time, the mixture of laughs and pained groans took a few minutes to subside. Finally, after a fit of coughing, Lichtman's eyes swiveled to look directly at me. "I know Sonny's old lady died a year or two back. But last I heard, he still has the place."

"What else can you give me, Sam?"

"That's all I can come up with, Davey boy. Least, for right now."

I made my voice impatient.

"Come on, Sam," I said. "How about Nederlander? You either know or you don't, and I don't have time to screw around playing games."

"I do, huh?" he retorted, and fell silent. "Man, I wish I had a smoke."

He stared at the ceiling for what seemed like a long time, looking like a man doing long division in his head.

"I'll tell you this for free," he said finally. "You've got some bad boys in this thing. Sure, maybe Nederlander's a player, okay? But, there's shit going down that's a lot bigger than he ever was."

Lichtman shifted on the bed, a white-knuckled movement that appeared to cost more in pain than it bought in relief. I half rose to help, then stopped at the warning in his cold blue eyes. His chest heaved deeply several times before he could continue.

"Tell you a little story," he said, and the smile on

his face was condescending through the residual pain. "Once upon a time, there was this fuckin' bear—a tough little turnip-eater goes by the name of Mikhail, no last name. This Mikhail, he's only been in from the old country for a little while but he's already got the local Russkies sweating bullets whenever he walks into a room. He hooks up with a local Mafiya hood, hires him to hold the pliers when he goes to sweat an old Jew name of Stan Levinstein. With me so far, Davey?"

I stared at him. "What might we call the hired muscle?"

"Let's call him 'Vladimir Kolchenk,' long as we're agreed this is a fairy tale. So Mikhail and Vlad are outside Levinstein's waiting for him to show up— when all of a sudden they see this other guy going in the place."

He shook his head, a tentative movement meant to mock.

"Terrible crime problem we got in America, ain't it? I mean, all of a sudden these two Russians are witnessing a burglary go down. Or maybe not; see, in *my* story the guy comes out again in a couple of minutes, empty-handed. Little while later, maybe, Levinstein and his wife show up and our two boys go in for their little chat. Next day, newspaper's printing two obits and a picture where the house used to be."

"Sam, are you telling me it was a hit?"

"Davey, Davey—this is just a story I'm pulling out of my ass, remember? But say, just for the sake of argument, that Levinstein was hiding something they wanted back. They'd need to use a little persuasion first, right?"

I said nothing, remembering how Katya had looked.

"So Mikhail maybe starts to work on the wife, figuring what the hell, it might make one or the other talk. Instead, Levinstein goes on the attack." He smirked. "Here's the good part, Davey—the old Jew gets his brains blown out by Kolchenk, since our boy

Mikhail was distracted by the noise the wife was making. That leaves Kathleen—who, as it turns out, knows nothin' about nothin'. Tough luck all around, wasn't it?"

"Who is this Mikhail, Sam?" I asked. "Where can I find him?"

"Can't help you on that one, man." It sounded final, but in a way as if Lichtman had reached some line he had drawn rather than some limit to his knowledge.

He studied my face and I saw him make a decision.

"But maybe I have something else for you. Little advice on your tax problem."

I frowned, taken aback.

"Past few years, I've been kind of busy trying to get back in court, you know? Had my lawyer talk to a few people in law enforcement, hint around that maybe I'd be open to a little tit-for-tat action. So, like a year or so ago, I found myself talking to the Feds. The fuckin' Eff-Bee-Eye, okay? They sent two of 'em here with some numb-nut from Justice to take notes and make sure the coffee's hot."

Sam's eye twitched in what might have been a wink.

"So I'm playing kinda coy, letting my lawyer sketch in the . . . uh, outline of what I might be willing to deal. This one FBI shithead was leaning against the wall the whole time, givin' me the smile and the hard eye, you know? So all of a sudden, he decides to get in my face. He leans up close and asks me how I'd like to have a tax rap thrown at me instead of a deal. Says it's real easy to arrange, says he'd be happy to do the honors if I wanted to be a hard guy. My fuckin' lawyer went ballistic, finally, and the discussion moved on to other areas."

Lichtman pulled a face, and again shifted uncomfortably on the hospital bed. His eyelids fluttered, and he forced them open again only with effort. The strength I had heard in his voice a few moments earlier was fading fast.

"Okay—you want to point the finger at Neder-

lander, maybe you're not all that far off target," Sam
Lichtman said. "But you're screwing around with the
Feds on this, Davey boy. Like I said, I been there.
You ask me, that tax shit is a lot more their style."

I tried hard not to look too interested. "You remember any names?" I asked, with as much nonchalance as I could muster. It was a wasted effort, for
Sam Lichtman was no longer interested in me or my
problems. His eyes were again closed, and he looked
suddenly like a very old man.

"Tax Man had some wop name," he said, his voice
once more sounding nearly drained. "Santini, Santo-
relli, I dunno. Dressed real sharp. Nice haircut."

"If he was busted when they found the liquor, it will
be on his rap sheet," I told Gil, speaking low into the
telephone in an assistant warden's office. "That will
at least give us the street where it happened. If we get
real lucky, Sonnenberg may have given his mother's
address as his residence."

Cieloczki's voice came through the receiver clear
and calm.

"Terry Posson's still across the hall in the police
office," he said. "I'll get her on it right away."

"Tell Terry I can be there in ninety minutes, maybe
a little more."

Gil's voice was firm.

"Terry can handle it," he said. "You've been on
this thing for two days without a break. I want you to
go home and get some rest. She can call Bird, take
him along."

I started to object, but Gil's voice was flat and final.
"No arguments, Davey—look, I know a guy named
Erlich, heads up Major Crimes in the sheriff's office.
Posson and Bird can work with him. Maybe Sonnen-
berg is hiding out in his mother's old place, maybe not."

"I want to be there," I said stubbornly.

"Go home. Davey, this thing is getting hotter and
hotter. Bird thinks he may have a handle on the insur-

ance angle of all this, and it could even lead back to
that car theft ring. Get some sleep. I want you to be
in a condition where you can help me make sense of
it all."

There was a pointed silence, and I understood Cieloczki had made an astute guess about my choice of
self-medication.

"I'll be fine," I said, and hated the defensive tone
in my own voice.

"Go home and go to bed," Gil repeated. "Anything
comes up that we need tonight, I have your phone
number."

I left Stateville in the gathering dusk. Sundown moves
quickly in the early springtime, feinting with an
orange-red sky that is spectacular in its brevity, then
falling back with the speed of an electric lamp suddenly switched off.

I drove north, the display a panorama over my left
shoulder. Before the dark red disk drowned itself
somewhere over the far side of the horizon, it had
flared on the windshields of the oncoming traffic and
tinged the cars in my rearview mirror with the color
of flame. By the time I reached the outskirts of Lake
Tower, the stars were bright pinpoints in the inky
blackness of the cosmos.

I pulled into the parking lot of a 7-Eleven, and
stopped near a pay phone bolted to the outside wall.

Three youths, all in the pseudo gangbanger cos-
tumes made by Hilfiger and marketed extensively to
the children of the affluent, looked at me like I was
trespassing. They smoked with an inexpert awkward-
ness they no doubt hoped passed for style, and moved
down the curb as I stepped to the telephone. One
looked back at me over his shoulder, with a deadeye
expression that may have been meant as a challenge.
None of them was more than fifteen years of age,
and their aura of nonspecific hostility made me feel
very old.

The coins rattled loudly as I thumbed them into the slot and punched in a number I had called enough to remember without effort.

The phone rang at the other end once, twice. Then a familiar voice said "Yeah?" in my ear.

I had noticed the car in my rearview mirror just after I pulled away from the prison grounds. It had kept pace on the drive north, closing up when the highway became thick with rush-hour commuters and falling back casually when the traffic thinned. The car was now parked well back from the blue-white circle carved into the dark by the streetlamp. It was too dark to see the two men in the front seats, but I could still recognize the shape of the vehicle.

"Your people still use Fords on surveillance, Ronnie?" I asked, turning my body away from the street.

There was a moment of dead air on the line.

"This who I think it is?" Ron Santori asked, careful to sound nonchalant.

"I want to know if you've got a tail on me," I said. "Two men, green Taurus, front license plate masked by a muddy smear. Which is just a little odd, since the rest of the car looks so nice and clean."

"Why would *I* have you followed?" Santori's voice sounded calm, mildly puzzled, reasonable. "I know where you've been. Hell, I called down there to get you cleared to visit our sick friend."

I shifted the phone to my other hand. "By the way, he said to say hello."

Again, a pause.

"Who did?" Santori asked, bemusement in his ·voice.

"Our friend. He said you helped him out with a tax problem last year."

"He must have me confused with somebody else," the FBI agent said. "I've never met the gentleman. Not in person."

I turned, trying to make it look casual. The car that

had followed me into Lake Tower was no longer parked at the curb. It was nowhere in sight now, a fact that did little to ease my growing awareness that I was no longer sure of what role I had been assigned to play.

"They seem to have driven away," I said. "What do you make of that?"

Santori sighed. "Maybe you're just a little over-wrought, my friend. But if you're sure you're being followed, get me a plate number and we'll do what we can about it."

"Then you're not having me tailed?" I asked again. "Not even, say, for my own good?"

"A lot of people drive a Taurus, Davey," he said, using my name for the first time. "It's a very popular car." Then he hung up.

As I pulled away from the convenience store, the three teens were standing together in their hip-hop finery under the bright sodium lights. One of them, possibly the same boy whose unspoken challenge had greeted me a few minutes earlier, watched me leave. He had the body attitude of someone nothing could really touch, someone convinced that life held no sur-prises except those for which he was already equipped.

He was wrong, and I knew it. Still, I envied him.

Once again, I left the lights off when I entered my apartment—but this time, not because I considered it soothing.

For a moment, I stood stiffly against the wall next to the door, but there was no sound except for the hum of the refrigerator's compressor. A square of white from the streetlamps outside, bisected into two distinct rectangles by the window frame through which it entered, lighted my way into the small bedroom where I spent my nights alone.

I put my hand under the folded underwear and rolled socks in the top drawer of my dresser, and felt for the towel-wrapped bundle I had put there months before. It was heavy in my hand as I lifted it out and unwrapped the contents.

The leather smelled lightly of oil, and was worn smooth at the side loops where it threaded onto my belt. I unsnapped the thumb break and slid the stainless steel of a Smith & Wesson automatic from the holster I had worn during my time on the police force. As always, the compact weapon felt solid and warm in my hand.

I ejected the empty magazine, and worked the action to lock the slide back. Then I thumbed round after round into the clip, pushing the shiny brass-and-silver hollowpoint cartridges in until the magazine was full. I pressed it into the pistol, and with my thumb released the catch that freed the slide to snap forward. The automatic, now fully loaded and with a powerful Silvertip cartridge chambered, was noticeably heavier in my hand.

On the nightstand was a bottle of vodka and a tumbler. I reached for it with my free hand.

No. Not tonight. Not until all this is finished, one way or another.

For a long while my mind would not surrender to sleep. Suspicions writhed and coiled back upon themselves. Several times I found myself checking the action of the pistol I had placed on the nightstand.

When I finally slept, I dreamed of spiderwebs and fiery skies like the reflection of cities burning in the distance. I saw Ellen as she was when I first met her, and when I tried to go to her I realized my hands and legs were shackled. In the midst of it all, I could hear the low rasp of Sam Lichtman's voice speaking the same sentence, over and over. I could not discern the words.

But in the way one possesses certainty during dreams, I knew the convict was speaking of trust and secrets and betrayal.

It might have been a nightmare; asleep or awake, I could no longer tell the difference.

Chapter 25

Despite the demands of an arson investigation, Gil
Cieloczki still had a fire department to run. It was a
fact that was brought home to him each time he returned to his office, the excitement of the chase
slapped down by a nagging sense of guilt. Fires still
ignited, alarms still rang. Firefighters still expected
paychecks and, in general, the bureaucratic beast still
demanded to be fed.

A large part of his job, Gil had told me in a rueful
voice, was to stalk the beast of management routine
that roams every organizational jungle. It was a quarry
as wily as it was prolific, and throughout our investigation it left its spoor in ever-mounting piles on his desk.

During the nine days since the fire chief had taken
over the Levinstein investigation, Jesús Martinez had
doubled up on his normal duties as line lieutenant.
From my temporary desk outside, I had watched Martinez trying gamely to fill the administrative gap left
by his boss's preoccupation with arson and murder.

But even the best efforts of Gil's right-hand subordinate only slowed the pace at which the work backed
up, taunting and daunting the fire chief whenever he
found a spare minute to stop by his own office.

It was there that I had reached him when I called
from Stateville; he was still there hours later, thanking
God for an understanding spouse at home alone.

The clock on his desk read 10:26; Kay would be

watching the late news, then tuning in to the Letter-
man show. It was a ritual they usually shared, and that
both of them had missed for much of the past month.
Outside, through his office window, the night sky twin-
kled with stars. Gil mentally sighed and pulled another
clipped sheaf of reports from the still considerable
stack of his in-basket.

Underneath was a videotape cassette.

Gil frowned, and picked it up. There was no label,
or anything else to identify its contents. He riffled
through the other papers in the box, looking for an
accompanying memorandum or note. There was nothing, and Gil's sense of puzzlement grew.

A tall, thin figure passed in the hallway outside his
open office door, then doubled back.

"Working late, Gil?" Talmadge Evans stood in the
doorway. He was in his shirtsleeves, and carried a
paper cup of coffee from the vending machine just off
the center's public lobby. "Remember, we're management. We don't get overtime for these kinds of
hours."

"A cup of coffee would help," Cieloczki jibed. "But
some penny-pinching bureaucrat on an economy drive
ordered it all locked up after five o'clock. I think it
was you."

Evans laughed, and gestured with the paper cup
he held.

"Well, I've been punished," he replied. "This is hot
and it's black, and it only cost me fifty cents. But I
can't call it coffee. Not with a straight face."

"This keeps up, I'll start carrying a thermos," Gil
said.

Evans looked at his watch. "Well, don't stay too
late," he told the firefighter. "There's better places to
spend an evening." The city manager nodded, and
turned toward his own office on the second floor. Gil
could hear his footsteps echo in the deserted hallway.
It was a lonely sound, almost heartbreaking in its soli-
tary isolation.

Gil knew a little about Talmadge Evans' personal life. The city manager's wife of twenty-seven years had died a short time after Cieloczki had come to Lake Tower. It was common knowledge around the municipal center that Evans' subsequent remarriage three years later, to a significantly younger woman from a socially prominent family, had been less than successful.

By all accounts, the city manager had buried that— and whatever other disappointments he kept locked away from gossip and innuendo—under the mountain of work that his job faithfully provided. It was a dedication, or an obsession, or simply a substitution that Gil found he both understood and dreaded.

There, but for Kay, go I, he thought to himself.

He sat still for a moment, looking at the papers on his desk. Then he abruptly picked up his phone and dialed.

Kay answered on the second ring.

"I've been thinking a little popcorn might taste pretty good," he said. "Particularly if somebody's sharing it with me."

Kay laughed.

"Okay," she said. "But I get to hold the bowl."

Gil left the municipal center by the side entrance, the one closest to the parking lot. Under his arm was the remaining contents of his in-box, scooped up in a sense of duty or guilt as he left. The hard plastic of the videocassette pressed into his arm.

As he crossed the parking lot to where he had left his car, Gil saw that he and Evans had not been alone in burning the late-night oil.

"Beautiful night, isn't it?" Robert Johns Nederlander said, his keys in his hand. He stood in the section of the lot reserved for the personal automobiles of police personnel, next to a black Lincoln Navigator; its finish flared expensively in the reflected gleam of the overhead lighting. The slot was marked

with the words RESERVED FOR DIRECTOR—PUBLIC
SAFETY.

"Beautiful car," Gil countered, in sincere admiration. It was a large and muscular machine, yet graceful
in its design.

Nederlander ran a hand over the vehicle's smooth
lines. He smiled with satisfaction.

"Yeah," he replied. "Best damn car I ever had. This
winter, all the snow and cold? I'd just drop her into
four-wheel drive and plow through without a hitch.
She's a hungry beast—hell, filling the tank sets me
back fifty bucks. But she handles great and the suspen-
sion's soft as a baby's hindside. You ought to get one
for yourself, Gil."

"Couldn't even afford the gas," Gil chided. It was
common knowledge that Nederlander was a frequent
visitor to the gasoline pumps behind the municipal
center, the ones installed to fuel vehicles assigned to
police, public works and other departments.

Nederlander looked at Gil and shook his head,
though whether in sympathy or in disgust the firefighter could not tell.

"You're a department head, and that means you're
on twenty-four-hour call," Nederlander said. "When
your phone rings in the middle of the night, you have
to use your personal vehicle, right? Why do you think
they give each of us our own fuel account code?"

"My luck, I'd be in trouble," Gil said, sorry he had
started the conversation. "It's safer for me just to eat
the cost myself, out-of-pocket."

"They don't give you points for being dumb around
this place," Nederlander retorted. "When I first
started here, it was standard practice to check out a
city car, fill it up and siphon the gas into your own
car."

"You're kidding."

"The hell I am. It was the only way to make up for
what you paid out of your own pocket. Now we get

to fill up our damn cars at the municipal center. Consider it a perk of your job."

"I'd prefer a pay raise." Cieloczki grinned. "How about it, boss?" He held up the papers he carried, the videocassette on top. "After all, I *am* taking all this work home with me."

"Talk to Evans," Nederlander responded, and his expression lost all measure of good humor. "The murder today, in Chicago. The Butenkova woman. This is going way beyond an arson case. Are you certain you feel equipped to continue supervising it?"

Cieloczki pretended not to notice the chill in Nederlander's voice.

"I think so," he said, careful to keep all challenge from his voice. "We have good cooperation from the different jurisdictions involved. And our local team is continuing to develop what we feel are some solid leads of our own."

Nederlander was silent for a moment, his eyes closely examining Gil's face. Then he nodded, and turned abruptly to his vehicle.

"Keep me informed," he said, without turning.

"I'll be sure to do that," he said. "See you, Bob. Drive carefully."

"You, too," Nederlander replied.

Later, when he reflected on the events that were already careening out of control, Gil Cieloczki would remember the comment.

It had sounded, he would tell me, very much like a warning.

April 23

Chapter 26

My eyes snapped open, and my heart was pounding. For an instant, I thought someone was with me in the dark of the room; without conscious thought, my hand groped for the pistol on the nightstand.

Then the phone rang again, and I knew what had broken into my troubled sleep was a different kind of intruder.

"I'm turning onto your street now," the voice of Ron Santori said in my ear. "Get dressed. We're going into the city."

I started to rub my eyes, and realized that I was holding the loaded automatic. The red digital numbers on the alarm clock read 12:02; I had been asleep less than an hour. I felt like hell, and half regretted my decision to give up vodka as a sleep aid.

"You there?" His voice was irritated. "Get it together, Davey. We're meeting Charlie Herndon downtown."

"Why?"

Santori laughed, once. "Apparently he stirred up a hornet's nest. He says the Russians have landed." From outside the window, I heard a car pull to a stop. "I'm parked outside. Hurry up, Davey. They're waiting for us."

I pulled on jeans and a turtleneck pullover, and dragged a comb through my hair. The face in the mir-

ror looked drawn, and there were dark hollows under
the eyes. It was a face I had to work hard to recognize.

The only addition to my outfit was a light leather
jacket I pulled from the closet. It would ward off the
chill of the evening, and had the advantage of hanging
loosely just below my hips. It also had large side pockets, into one of which I slipped my tape recorder.

I zipped the jacket up halfway, and glanced in the
mirror as I went out my door.

I looked stylish, and there was no sign of the holstered weapon I had threaded onto my belt.

It is never really night in Chicago, at least not along
the length of North Michigan Avenue that centers on
the old Water Tower. Sodium-vapor streetlamps ally
with the pearl-white necklaces of lights strung year-
round in the branches of parkway trees, joined at each
intersection with the tricolor of traffic signals. The effect is to forever banish the darkness of night to neighborhoods less favored by both fortune and fate. In the
area around the Water Tower, the attitude is one of
cheerful, arrogant invulnerability.

It has not always been that way.

The last serious attempt to level the city was the
Great Chicago Fire of 1871. As a schoolchild in Chicago, I had been taught the blaze began when Mrs.
O'Leary's cow kicked over a lantern. Today, an
increasing number of historians reject the bovine-
arsonist legend that has prevailed for more than a century in favor of alternate suspects. One of the more
intriguing of these focuses less on the cow than on
the cosmos.

A handful of revisionists now theorize the Chicago
fire was ignited by white-hot fragments of a meteor
flung from the heavens at the sinful frontier metropolis. If true, either the meteor or the Hand that threw
it was blithely nonchalant about inflicting peripheral
damage: two hundred miles to the north, in the single
largest conflagration history has ever recorded, the vir-

gin Wisconsin forests around Peshtigo also burst into flames—suspiciously or coincidentally, depending on your point of view—on the same day, at about the same hour.

Whatever the cause, the limestone Water Tower was among the handful of Chicago's structures to withstand a firestorm that reduced most of its largely wood-and-frame construction to smoking ash. When Chicago rebuilt itself—making millionaires of the well-connected businessmen who owned the limestone quarries and brickyards suddenly made essential by new building codes—the fanciful stoneworks of the Water Tower and its accompanying waterworks facility were at the center of what gradually became its showcase commercial section north of the Chicago River.

Today, luxury hotels glitter in their opulence, surrounded by famous-name shops and world-class restaurants; its ten-square-block area comprises some of the most expensive real estate in the world. Even at this hour, with the new day less than fifty minutes old, an endless procession of cars flows past sidewalks thick with pedestrian traffic both along the main drag and on the side streets that branch off *Boul Mich*.

And presiding over it all is the now antique Water Tower, a spotlighted survivor whose single stone finger still points toward the sky as if in some urgent but only vaguely remembered warning.

"Her name is Petra Natalia Valova, and she's some kind of official at the Pushkin Museum in Moscow," Ron Santori was saying, waving me ahead as we entered the Omni Hotel's impressive lobby. "Fairly high on the food chain, from what I understand. Charlie Herndon's already up there with her." We stopped in front of a bank of elevators and Santori pressed the button. "I hope nobody's declared war yet."

We walked down the hallway to a suite.

"Since Cieloczki's visit, Charlie's been impossible to live with," Santori said in a low voice. "He's been burning up the phone wires talking to his sources all over the goddam world. He's spent hours on the Internet, posting notes to news groups connected to the Holocaust, art experts, military historians—dozens of 'em. Next thing I know, we get a call from the Russian consulate that this Valova woman is in town, needs to see him on an urgent and confidential matter. Believe it or not, it's not the kind of phone call the FBI gets every day."

He knocked on a door, which immediately opened. Even silhouetted, I had no problem identifying the figure whose bulk filled the entrance to the suite. Herndon looked at both of us with ill-concealed irritation.

"This whole thing is turning into one major ratfuck," he said, then looked at me. "Don't even think of using that damn tape recorder of yours when I talk to these people. Understand me?"

"I don't even have it with me, Agent Herndon."

"Uh-huh." He did not sound convinced, but stood aside to let us enter. "Come in, then. The Russian Mata Hari is waiting for us."

Petra Natalia Valova was young to be a senior official anywhere, let alone at one of the premier art institutions in the world. I guessed her age in the mid- to late thirties. Her center-parted straight black hair fell to her shoulders. She wore a no-nonsense business outfit of black wool that looked better suited for a colder climate, its skirt tailored to the middle of her knees. Red plastic glasses of a style that had been fashionable a few years before gave her an earnest, studious appearance. If she wore makeup, it was applied artfully enough to be indiscernible.

When Santori and I entered, Valova was talking in a near whisper with a trim, balding man of indeterminate age. From their expressions, it did not seem to be a casual conversation.

"Tarinkoff, from the consulate," Herndon said to Santori. He did not whisper. "Cultural attaché, so he's probably SVR."

The man turned away from the conversation and approached with his hand outstretched. "Anatoli Tarinkoff," he said with a practiced smile, "and no, Mr. Herndon—I am not with the Foreign Intelligence Service, though I suspect this matter will not long be without their most sincere attention. Nor was I with their predecessor, the KGB. I am that most rare of all specimens, a *genuine* Russian cultural attaché." His chuckle was carefully self-deprecating, his handshake was firm, and his accent was of the American Midwest. He might have been the manager of a hardware store, greeting latecomers to a Rotary Club meeting.

"I'm disappointed," Santori said, with a smile of his own. "I missed out on the excitement of the Cold War. I was hoping to meet a real live Russian spy."

"I do not have the time for spying," Tarinkoff said pleasantly. "Chicago is a city with a passion for the arts, and as a result all of my waking hours are quite fully accounted for. In just the past week, I have met with an automotive parts corporation that wishes to sponsor a tour by the Petrograd Symphony, arranged for one of your Chicago filmmakers to enter the Moscow Cinematic Festival, and attended two exhibition openings." He smiled broadly. "It is good that I enjoy my job, is it not?"

The woman stepped to Tarinkoff's side and looked at Santori with a gaze that was steady enough so that I suspected it was forced. Without appearing to do so, I studied her. Her lips were a thin, tight line and there was a slight, almost imperceptible, tremor to her fingers that I had seen before, most recently in myself. It was not the product of a tranquil mind.

"May I introduce Dr. Petra Valova, senior curator of fine arts of the Pushkin Museum?" he said, turning to include her in the introduction. "She has come here on an urgent matter—one she believes may also be of interest to you, Mr. Herndon."

"It is a well-known fact that large parts of the Soviet Union suffered almost catastrophic devastation when

the Nazi army invaded our country in 1942," Petra
Valova said. Unlike her consular companion, no one
would mistake her for a native English speaker. She
addressed the room as if she were standing in a university lecture hall filled with undergraduates, which
seemed to amuse Santori as much as it annoyed
Herndon.

"The Nazis hated Slavic culture," the woman continued. "They bombed and shelled our cities without
restraint, and many ancient and irreplaceable objets
d'art were destroyed. It was only right that this terrible
destruction should be punished, and that lost Soviet
art treasures be replaced with those taken from the
aggressors. This became a principle of Soviet state policy, which was duly carried out when Hitler and his
followers were defeated by the Red Army.

"Unfortunately, there was a corrupt element among
the leadership who saw this as an opportunity to enrich themselves in an illegal and antisocial manner.
One of these was Viktor Abakumov." She paused
for effect.

I was seated on a low sofa, directly in her line of
sight. It was probably for that reason that she looked
at me and nodded solemnly. I felt mildly embarrassed,
as if I had skipped the assigned reading for the day.

"You have probably never heard of Viktor Abakumov," Petra Natalia Valova said, "but during the
Great Patriotic War and for a number of years afterward, he was a very powerful person in the Soviet
Union. He was head of SMERSH—the Soviet internal
counterintelligence apparatus—and later, minister of
state security. All of this is to say that, during that
unfortunate period, he was in charge of the official
use of terror and murder to eliminate traitors, political
dissidents or potential enemies of the state. There
were many abuses during this period. No one was im-
mune, and no one knew when—or for what reason—
one would be denounced and arrested.

"In Germany, even as the Red Army crushed the

Nazis in battle after battle, SMERSH remained a power unto itself," she said. "Even the great Marshal Zukov, who commanded all the Soviet forces in the western campaign, was exceptionally cautious in any matters where SMERSH was involved. For that reason, he kept a blind eye toward Abakumov and his activities. This allowed Abakumov to be very brazen.

"It was also well known that when Abakumov wanted to send items for his 'collection' out of Germany, he would often commandeer an airplane. The official requisition always stated it was for the 'transportation of arrested persons.' But the airplane was always met by armed soldiers from SMERSH; customs officials were not allowed near these transports, nor could they examine the many crates which were removed from them."

Valova laughed without mirth.

"The story is told that in May of 1945, a shipment of appropriated items was sent by a special railroad from Dresden to Moscow. On the side of each railcar, painted in white letters as tall as a man, was the name ABAKUMOV. That alone was sufficient to ensure the train arrived in Moscow untouched by either bandits, Red Army inspectors or state customs authorities.

"After the war, there were countless conspiracies by which these men attempted to remain in Stalin's favor by denouncing each other," she said. "By this time, Abakumov was head of the ministry of state security, and as a powerful man he had powerful enemies in the regime. In 1954, it was his turn to be denounced, arrested and executed. The many art treasures he had collected for his personal property were confiscated and turned over to the Pushkin Museum. Subsequently they were sent for safekeeping to a place then called Zagorsk, now renamed Sergeyev Posad. Specifically, to the Trinity-St. Sergius Monastery there."

For the first time, she shifted her gaze to Herndon, who had been standing at the decorative fireplace

against the far wall. He was tall enough to rest one
elbow on the high mantle, and irritated enough to
look bored while doing it.

"I apologize if I have taxed your patience during
this story, but it is important for you to understand.
Both as official reparations seized from German museums and as the very many 'unofficial' confiscations by
officers such as Abakumov, almost three million objects of art and other cultural properties were removed
to the Soviet Union. This occurred during a chaotic
period when a world conflict was ending. It had no
precedent in history—and regrettably, it was not always handled in the most organized manner."

She hesitated. "By this I mean that documentation
of the individual pieces remains . . . incomplete." I
saw her eyes shift quickly toward the FBI art expert
before she continued, her voice quickening in her de-
fensiveness. "With so many items, neither the Pushkin
Museum nor the other cultural facilities where these
pieces have been stored have completely catalogued
these holdings. Nor have they successfully traced prior
ownership in every case.

"For that reason, many of these items have not been
made available for display or study in many years.
This has resulted in some unfortunate misconceptions
related to my government's intentions and motivations
regarding them."

I felt rather than saw the effect the long-winded
apologia was having on Charlie Herndon. From my
initial meeting with Herndon, I had no illusions about
the art expert's tolerance for even well-phrased obfus-
cation. I could sense that the storm clouds were gathering, and I wondered how long we had before
lightning began to strike.

"During perestroika, many strides were made to
remedy this matter. And perhaps you will recall that
several years ago the government allowed many of our
national treasures from the Hermitage to be exhibited
here in the United States as a goodwill gesture. This

trend toward a more open sharing of our artistic heritage continues today under the Russian Federation.
Very recently, in this very city, we have placed on
display a collection of our Impressionist paintings—
among them, may I point out, pieces that were confiscated as reparations—that is unmatched in its compre-
hensive nature and value to art scholars."

The tempest broke: Herndon snorted, loudly and
derisively. "Ms. Valova, could you kindly cut the snow
job? You know as well as I do that the Soviets—that
is, your government, under whatever name you want
to call it today—are in possession of a helluva lot of
artwork you people looted at the end of World War
II."

Herndon walked to an empty chair near Santori,
and carefully lowered his frame into it. He made a
show of crossing his long legs, and only then did he
return his attention to the rest of the group.

"The Nazis were great art lovers, too," Herndon
said, his tone scathing. "As Ms. Valova no doubt
knows, they planned to construct a number of cultural
centers after they won the war. Like the Linz
Gallery—right, Ms. Valova? Never got built, but Hitler had already designated more than five thousand
paintings for it, had some beautiful architect's plans
drawn up. Would have been a world-class place filled
with world-class artwork the Nazis 'rescued,' too. Only
difference was who the Nazis 'rescued' the art from."

He made his voice mockingly conversational.

"There's this guy I talk with every so often—name's
Ori Soltes, he heads up the National Jewish Museum
in Washington," the FBI agent said. "His museum's
made kind of a crusade out of searching for lost artwork taken by the Nazis. Like the Linz artwork, for
instance. Ori says that they've confirmed that about
twelve hundred of the paintings earmarked for Linz
were confiscated outright from Jews who were sent to
the camps. Most of the rest, they bought at a reasonable price. Really reasonable—fire sale rates, you

might say. It was an unprecedented collection; priceless, in every way. Funny thing, though. After 1945, most of them just . . ." Herndon flicked his fingertips and his eyes opened wide in sarcastic amazement, "vanished. I guess it was pure coincidence your troops were occupying the country at the time, right?"

Herndon recrossed his long legs and leaned back in the undersized chair. His posture left no doubt of what he was feeling.

Valova eyed the FBI agent from under brows that were arched in derision.

"Your . . . passion is admirable, Mr. Herndon," she said. "But may I point out that the problem is not one encountered only in Russia. Do not your museums themselves possess so-called stolen artwork? Are not many of the sixteenth-century religious drawings of Albrecht Dürer, which the Nazis stole in 1941 from the Lybmomirski Museum in the Ukraine, still in your American museums? In your Cleveland Museum of Art, your Boston Museum of Fine Arts—even here, in your Art Institute of Chicago, no?

"Please correct if I am mistaken. At least some of these museums are contesting claims of the previous owners on the grounds of your 'statute of limitations' laws, I believe—that too much time has passed since the so-called crime occurred. The same amount of time has passed for us; where is the difference, please?"

Herndon showed no signs of being impressed by the Russian curator's arguments.

"One hell of a difference is in the sheer volume of what your people stole," he retorted. "Then there's the fact that you continue to hide most of it, and deny you know anything about it."

"That is untrue," Valova protested. "Our exhibition at the Hermitage in 1995—"

"Only included a fraction of the 'missing' artwork," Herndon interrupted rudely. "Most of it pieces your own dissidents had already leaked to the Western press. You people have never given us anything we didn't already know. But we know enough not to swallow some fairy tale about your government's good intentions."

He addressed the room again. "Let me just add something Ms. Valova neglected to mention about that monastery in Zagorsk. It's the largest single storage location in Russia for artwork they . . . uh, appropriated. It's still considered a 'secret' location—am I right, Ms. Valova? And it doesn't just hold paintings and statues they took from the Nazis, as she might like you to believe. They have items that came from French, Polish and Austrian museums and private collections."

"My point," Valova said, "is that ownership is a very complicated issue to—"

"Not always," Herndon interrupted. "For instance, some of those pieces you've stashed in Zagorsk came via guys like Eichmann, who made a little habit of expropriating anything of value from the Jews he rounded up for the death camps. I have in mind pieces like *Fisherman at Rest*—that's the famous 'lost' Donatello, right, Ms. Valova? It came from the collection of Ibrihim Fehyman, appropriated about the time he and the other Warsaw Jews were taken away to be gassed. How about *David Espies Bathsheba*, by Artemisia Gentileschi? I've heard scholars say it would be an icon of today's feminist movement—if it hadn't been 'lost' after Emil Tassilmann fled France to avoid a Nazi arrest warrant. His collection was shipped to Germany, and then reported captured by your troops. And there's *The Fire of the Soul*, painted for Pope Julius by Michelangelo. Last known owner was Jakub Weissman, beaten to death at Theresienstadt. Nobody's seen any of those pieces since the end of World War II."

He turned back to the Russian art expert. "Or have they? That's really the point you're leading up to, isn't it?"

For a moment, Petra Valova tried to match his hard-eyed glare. Then she blinked rapidly several times, and her eyes refocused on a point on the wall above and behind Herndon's head.

"In part," she said, and hesitated. I watched her compose herself with an effort that was almost physical. "In point of fact, I am authorized to tell you that the three pieces you describe are listed among those kept in Zagorsk."

Herndon straightened, and his eyes flared with a triumphant flash that was extinguished by Valova's next words.

"They, and six other pieces with a similar history, are no longer there," she said. "As best we can determine, they have been missing for at least six months."

Chapter 27

It is a fact of the human condition that as mortals we are subject to what the Greeks call hubris. Roughly translated, it means an overweening pride—a frequently fatal flaw that blinds us to our own peril. The hunter is stalked, the biter bitten. Few of us ever consider the reality that we are not in control—that someone else, a little more paranoid or maybe a little less sane, has turned the tables on us.

Case in point: Ron Santori, who took great pride in his ability to monitor events, even to the point of having microphones hidden in a barroom frequented by those he stalked. In his own hubris, Santori never considered the possibility that someone else—a former policeman, perhaps, his nerves ragged and possessed of his own sense of impending doom—might secrete a voice-activated tape recorder under the seat of Santori's vehicle, to be recovered later.

As I had, after Santori had picked me up at my apartment.

When I finally recovered the tape, much later, Santori's voice crackled in counterpoint to the sounds of predawn traffic along Michigan Avenue.

"Well," Santori said to Herndon, "you seem to have lit a fire under some major-league players. Hope you're ready for the consequences."

Even with the car seat set in its farthest back position, Santori's government-issued car was tight quarters for the oversized art expert. He grunted, studying the pages of a legal pad covered with his untidy handwriting. His knees—uncomfortably close to his chin—served as a makeshift desk.

"You saw the files," he told Santori. "You knew Levinstein had involved his pet Russians here to bring in something from the Soviet Union"—Santori decided not to correct Herndon's out-of-date geopolitics—"and it was only logical to figure he'd use his old contacts there, too. Throw in the missing artwork, and it all starts to fit together."

"You think Levinstein has—had—paintings from the Nazi loot," Santori said, eyeing the traffic, "and these Russians—they're looking for our help?"

"If you believe they told us everything," Herndon said. "I don't. Valova comes halfway around the world because I'm sending e-mails about unspecified missing paintings? Then neither she nor that slick bastard Tarinkoff asks us if *we* have them?" He shook his head skeptically. "Uh-uh. I don't trust them—any of them. I think she knows where they are, or at least thinks she knows."

"Now you're starting to sound like a fruitcake," Santori retorted. "Just like our poor paranoid pal Davey."

Herndon looked at his companion.

"And, speaking of your friend, I suppose you noticed?"

"Yeah," Santori said. "Right hip. Haven't seen him carrying before tonight." The FBI agent was silent for a moment. "He's starting to lose a little stuffing at the seams, Charlie. We're going to have to keep that in mind from now on. He called me earlier—wanted to know if we're having him tailed."

"He called you to ask *that*? Does he keep his brains in his ass?"

"Oh, he's *smart*," Santori said. "He's got some kind of guilt complex because his dad was a crook, but he's no dummy. The trouble is he's just not as smart as he thinks. He likes to freelance, to force the play. He's an impetuous sort of guy, Charlie. That's why I brought him into this. When the temperature goes up, Davey forgets about being smart and pushes too hard. That's what got him in trouble before, and it's what he'll do this time, too."

Santori's voice was philosophical. "He's so focused on Nederlander that he can't see the bigger picture. But he'll push in ways we can't. Davey will create the kind of pressure that stampedes our guy into a mistake." Santori's lip twisted wryly. "That is, if Davey doesn't do something to self-destruct first. His character fault makes him his own worst enemy."

"Bullshit, Ron," Herndon said, and the tape clearly captured the distaste in his tone. "Hell, given everything he's had piled on his head, he's reacting exactly the way I would. Or you."

Santori might have smiled; it was there and gone so quickly that Herndon could not be certain.

"Well," Santori said, without taking his eyes from the traffic, "maybe we're not as smart as we think, either."

Chapter 28

Virgil Erlich chewed ferociously at the gum he had just popped into his mouth, and remembered how good a cigarette tasted before an action began. The memory did not improve his temper.

"Do I need to remind you two whose party this is?"

"Yeah, Lieutenant, we remember," Mel said sourly. He looked at Terry, sitting beside him in the backseat of Erlich's sheriff's police vehicle, and rolled his eyes. "We're just along for the ride."

"You're along out of professional courtesy," Erlich said, and his tone brooked no discussion. "You're out of your jurisdiction. If there's a collar here, it's a *county* collar. Are we clear about this?"

He made a point of waiting until both Lake Tower officers had nodded, albeit grudgingly in Bird's case. Then the Cook County detective pulled a handheld transceiver from inside the leather jacket he wore.

He keyed the transmit button.

"Central, this is Erlich. I'm gonna be out of service for a few minutes."

When I reviewed them later, the reports made no reference to the noises of the night, the nocturnal background ambiance that is noticed mainly when its absence signals danger. Neither was there a description of what, if anything, was said as the three officers entered the building. If a suspicious vehicle had been parked along the curb, they did not notice it; if a figure watched their approach from behind a darkened window, it did not register.

From the official incident report, there was nothing unusual noted about the building: nothing to raise suspicion, no reason to hold back or call for additional support in the postmidnight darkness.

Later, I would pore over the official record again and again, reconstructing it in my mind, trying to determine if there was any intimation of the peril that awaited them inside. Had one of them, I wondered, sensed that it was all about to go wrong?

As it did, swiftly.

Erlich, with Bird and Posson in tow, slipped into the foyer of the three-flat. There, Erlich studied the lock on the inside door before producing a thin piece of flexible flatmetal. This he inserted into the jamb where the lockset met the frame, working by feel alone to finesse the slimjim between striker and bolt.

The spring-loaded bolt snapped back with a satisfying metallic snick, and Erlich turned to wink at Posson and Bird.

"Benefits of a misspent youth," he murmured, and held the door wide.

The trio eased through to the stairway passage and crept upward, stepping close where each riser met the wall to minimize unwanted noise. On the landing immediately below Sonnenberg's apartment, they eased their weapons from concealed holsters before tiptoeing up the final stairs.

It was anticlimatic. The door to Sonnenberg's place hung open, the room behind it empty and dark.

Still, they entered cautiously, moving in practiced drill through each of the three small rooms inside. In the beam of Erlich's pocket flashlight, they saw a thin patina of undisturbed dust on the lamps and tables. Despite the open door, there was no sign that the apartment had been visited in weeks.

Finally, the three of them stood again in the darkness of the front room, framed by the still ajar door.

"Well, this is a waste of time," Erlich said, lowering his pistol. "A damn wild-goose—"

There was movement from across the hallway, as the door to the other apartment abruptly opened. Then the darkness flared blindingly white, as if a photographer's strobe had been triggered.

Erlich spun and fell back against Terry, clutching at her arm and shoulder with a iron grip. It hurt, and she tried to push him away with the hand not holding her own pistol. But he clung to her with a desperate strength, and the sudden deadweight of his body dragged them both down, hard.

Terry hit the floor painfully, her head striking something solid on the way down. Her pistol bounded from her hand, clattering away in the dark. She lay flat on her back under an immovable weight, pinpoints of white-hot comets spinning crazily across her vision.

Simultaneously, another double flash and concussive explosion came from the hallway outside, countered by a volley from within.

Terry felt something hot pulse wetly against her jaw, again and again. She opened her mouth to shout, to scream at Erlich to get off her; as she did, the metallic taste of fresh copper pennies flooded her mouth.

For a single panicked moment, she knew that the torrent of blood was hers, that she was bleeding out from some horrendous pumping wound high on her neck. She tried to reach up with her left hand to find the severed artery, to somehow stopper it with her fingers. But she could not free her arm, pinned underneath Erlich's now inert body.

Then there was another gunshot flash, a double tap, and in the blue-white light of it she saw the terrible wound that had torn away the side of Erlich's throat.

She twisted frantically, trying to free herself. Then a fresh fusillade of gunshots erupted from both in front of and behind her, and the stroboscopic supernova provided an irregularly spaced, surreal illumination.

At the wall beside the door, she saw Mel Bird kneeling, his upper body bent around the jamb and both arms extended in a shooting stance. Then Bird was looking at her, his face contorted and his mouth moving as if in speech.

There were more flashes now, each stark in her vision as bolts of forked summer lightning; but she no longer heard the discharges that generated them, nor the words that her partner must have been shouting to her. The world had become a silent film, moving in a jerky, slow-motion parody of reality.

Terry saw a hand that might have been her own, the one that had held her lost pistol, push futilely at the leather-jacketed weight that held her down; it was no use. She looked up to see her partner moving to help, impossibly slow, and reached up toward him and safety.

Instead, the door frame against which Bird had been leaning erupted into splinters, exploding once, twice. The third shot was into flesh, high on Mel Bird's upper body—a shuddering impact that threw his body back into the hallway, out of Terry's sight.

But not before the shock of the bullet had flung Mel's gun arm against the wall, knocking his heavy automatic loose from his grip. The pistol careened against the plaster and landed, spinning, on the hardwood inches from Terry's outstretched arm. She stared at it for what seemed like an eternity, then strained the extra inch required for her fingertips to brush the weapon into reach.

Terry snatched up Bird's pistol in a hand whose tremors she could not control. Then there was movement, two figures silhouetted against the window behind moving forward in wary half crouches.

Terry twisted one last time, enough to center the luminous three-dot sight of Bird's pistol on the foremost of the two figures. She fired, and in the recoil felt the slide lock back on an empty magazine. For an instant the muzzle flash dazzled her vision. She could not tell if her target had fallen, or what the second figure had—

The pistol flew from her hands even before she felt the pain of the kick that smashed against her wrist.

And then a man was standing over her. Terry could not see him clearly; all she could see was the impossibly large bore of the revolver he held, arm extended downward so that the muzzle was only inches from her forehead.

"My friend seems to have been wounded," a voice from above said, cheerfully; for the first time, Terry heard a low moaning from behind him. "You shoot well. That, or you are quite lucky. Let us see."

She heard the double click as he thumbed back the hammer, an instant before he pulled the trigger.

Instead of the explosion Terry expected, there was only the snap of a firing pin on an empty chamber.

"As I thought, fortune has smiled on you," he said, and she heard the slight accent of his words. "But in the future, be advised: luck is a fickle mistress."

Before she could react, the dark figure kicked her again, this time viciously alongside her temple. Her world went black, as suddenly as a lightbulb is extinguished.

She did not see him study her, almost fondly, before he stepped nimbly over her pinned form and was away through the doorway.

I flipped through the faxed pages that had just been hand-delivered from the police department across the hall. Quickly, I scanned them.

"We've got an NCIC hit on the second guy—the one Terry shot," I said. "His name is Vladimir Kolchenk. It's the guy Sam Lichtman was talking about. He's got a rap sheet a yard long, and that's just what we know about in *this* country. There's a notation that he's suspected of involvement in overseas organized crime."

I read further; the National Crime Information Center's conclusion was clear.

"Gil, he's Russian Mafiya. We need to sweat him about all this, and about the other one. The one Sam Lichtman called Mikhail."

Cieloczki was silent for a moment, and I could hear the murmur of voices talking in the background.

"We've got all we're going to get out of Kolchenk, Davey. He died in the ambulance on the way to the hospital. Shock and loss of blood."

"Damn."

I could almost hear Cieloczki thinking before he said, "Look, we've got to find out how all this fits together. Call Santori again, tell him what we have. Let's get some federal support on this. Whatever we can pull together, let's do it now."

"I want to take this outside," I said. "Some of it, at least. All of a sudden, we're knee-deep in Russians on this case. And remember, Levinstein had a history with them on the Jewish emigration issue. There are people, experts, who might have a better handle on the Mafiya angle—give us a new direction to start looking, maybe. I could make a couple of calls."

"Make the calls," Cieloczki said, and his voice was grim. "We need answers. I want them before anybody else gets killed. What else do you suggest?"

"We need to find Sonnenberg fast," I said. "Vladmir Kolchenk and this Mikhail thought they hit a dead end on finding the paintings. But they had seen Sonny creep into the Levinstein house and come out empty-handed. By now, Mikhail knows he wasn't just some unlucky break-in artist. Sonny may be all any of us have as a lead on the missing artwork."

Chapter 29

Kay Cieloczki stood at the doorway to the converted downstairs bedroom that served as Gil's den. These days, it also served as a makeshift home office, a substitute for the downtown office her husband saw only infrequently.

It was now late morning, hours since the shootout. Gil had called from the hospital, concern for the two wounded officers weighing down his words. One man—a Cook County officer named Erlich, with whom Gil had recently met—was dead; two Lake Tower officers were wounded, one of them critically.

Gil did not know when he would be home, he told his wife. In the interim, Kay was not to worry. Right.

She needed to calm her mind—*no*, she told herself, *to* fill *it*. She walked through her home, looking for labor that would block out her concern. And so she found herself outside Gil's home office.

This was, she recognized, a once-in-a-lifetime opportunity for her.

By nature, Gil was a neat person—so well organized, in fact, that it sometimes exasperated Kay, who considered herself no slouch when it came to the neatness department. Typically, Gil would enter a room—say, the kitchen—on one errand or another. There, he would notice a spoon or bowl on a counter, and thoughtfully return it to its assigned space and designated cupboard. Or he would enter the living room, note that it was empty, and innocently press the button that turned the TV off.

Never mind that in both cases Kay—herself perfectly capable of clearing counters and powering down electronic devices—might have stepped out of the room only momentarily.

Early in their marriage, it had been a source of occasional domestic friction that startled, then puzzled, a consistently contrite Gil. Now it was usually relegated to the status of an inside joke between them, one that Kay had taught herself to accept with grace. Still, bowls she had set out moments before continued to fly back to cupboards, and television screens mysteriously were blank upon her return to whatever room her husband had passed through in her absence.

It could be, Kay occasionally admitted to herself, maddening in the extreme. It brought a kind of Odd Couple aspect to their relationship.

Ironically, Gil's deep preoccupation with the Levinstein arson was almost a relief to Kay. The demands of the case, combined with the fire department's administrative workload with which Gil routinely dealt, had an impact in the Cieloczki household. For virtually the first time since their marriage, the roles were reversed.

Kay surveyed the low coffee table next to Gil's favorite chair with some measure of satisfaction. File folders, computer printouts, stacks of loose paper covered the tabletop—left where they lay when the call summoning Gil to the hospital had come early this morning.

It's my turn to be Felix, Kay thought, and smiled to herself. *And he can find out how it feels to play Oscar.*

Kay moved toward the clutter, and almost stepped on the plastic box half hidden on the floor beneath the table. It was the case to a videotape, but there was no label or marking to identify it or the cassette inside. She frowned; *that* was unusual in the Cieloczki household, unless the tape was blank. And if it was blank, why would it be in Gil's stack of take-home work?

Kay shrugged, and put the videotape on Gil's chair. She began to straighten the table, starting with the tallest stack of folders.

Maybe, she thought to herself, *I'll pop it in the VCR later. Then I'll paste on a label—handwritten, so he may even notice somebody's picking up after him.*

It was a satisfying thought, one that almost made her chuckle out loud.

Chapter 30

"I have to see you," Ellen said to me. "I think I'm being followed."

Then she giggled, as if she had told an off-color joke.

She had called from the cell phone she had taken to carrying, telephoning the Lake County Fire Department and catching me at the desk Gil's secretary had found for me. I sat on the periphery of the fire department's cramped administrative work area, hard against a waist-high railing that marked the Lake Tower Sanitation Department's turf. I tried not to think of it as a metaphor for my current circumstances.

Around me, clerical workers whose names I did not know typed and filed and checked yellow work orders against plat maps. It was not the most private place to discuss whatever pursuit fantasies might have motivated my former spouse to call.

"Davey? Are you there?"

In the background, I could hear the ambient sounds of automotive traffic, the muted hum made by a multitude of conversations and, incongruously, the strains of what sounded like a mariachi band.

"Where are you, Ellen?"

"Where am I?" she repeated, and for an instant I thought she was asking me for the information. "Downtown, at a darling little sidewalk cantina. I don't know the name of it—oh. It's Hermosita's, just off Michigan on Erie. I took an early lunch, Davey. I can do that, you know."

"Have you been drinking?"

"I won't dignify that with an answer." Then she giggled again; this time, it sounded decidedly tipsy. "Besides, it's almost noon anyway."

"Ellen, I can't talk right—"

"Don't hang up! I'm serious, Davey—I think somebody's been watching me. I saw him when I left the house this morning, and I just saw him walk past my table."

"What does he look like? Give me a description."

There was a pause.

"He's . . . tall. Maybe your height. Dark hair, I think." Her voice brightened. "And he was wearing glasses. Or . . . sunglasses."

I had picked up a pencil, which I now placed back on the desk.

"I'll call the Chicago police; they'll send an officer to help. What's the cross-street nearest you?"

"Oh, don't do that, Davey. Could you come?"

I frowned.

"Ellen, I—"

"Please. When you get here, we can talk."

And then, before I could analyze her motives or even phrase my response, she broke the connection. I sat at my borrowed desk among people I did not know, a dead telephone in my hand and a sudden, disquieting sensation in my gut. Throughout my marriage to Ellen, I had felt it often—usually, when she was about to do something that anyone else would see as cruel.

I wanted to call it curiosity, but I was fairly certain it felt like suspicion.

Ellen was not at the restaurant called Hermosita's when I arrived from Lake Tower, almost forty minutes later.

She had not returned to work, either, as I discovered when I called there from the cantina's office. In fact, nobody at Ellen's office had seen her that day; she had called in sick before eight o'clock, telling her supervisor she intended to spend the day in bed. But when I dialed the house where she and I had once lived together, there was no answer.

She had said she was being followed, stalked; but Ellen always knew how to push my buttons, get my interest.

Of course, she might have been telling the truth, in her own way.

The telephone rang for a long time before I hung up.

Chapter 31

Chicago has always been one of the great newspaper towns, a place where the term "journalist" has never really replaced "reporter" as the preferred descriptive for the majority of the men and women who ply that trade here. It is a city whose tradition of thumb-in-the-eye competition is fiercely waged each morning between its two surviving major daily newspapers.

Not surprisingly, each claims leadership in the market they share. Impartial observers credit the *Chicago Sun-Times* with providing its largely urban readership a slightly stronger coverage of both crime and the omnipresent city hall political machinations, two staples the city delivers in ample supply. In state and national issues—two areas of substantial concern to its somewhat more affluent and far more suburban readership—the *Chicago Tribune* is given a slight edge.

But there is one area where the *Trib* is acknowledged the hands-down winner—not just locally, but arguably among its peers throughout North America. The *Chicago Tribune* still fields its own expert, expensive corps of foreign correspondents. Other newspapers may fall back on the penny-wise solution of relying on wire services or CNN to interpret the world at large—but in the words of "The Colonel," founder Robert McCormick, the *Chicago Tribune* is the world's greatest newspaper, with the accent on 'world.'

As a result, the newspaper remains home to an unmatched syndicate of experienced reporters and col-
umnists who know as much about the world stage as
anyone alive today. Many of them are legends, like
Kathy O'Banion, who had spent her career filing exclusive reports from trouble spots around the world
and who now sat at the Formica table across from me.

It was midafternoon, though no evidence of the sunlight bathing Michigan Avenue filtered down to the
plate window near our table. Fluorescent tubes and beer
company promotional fixtures provide the light in the
Billy Goat, a subterranean hangout for generations of
Chicago newspaper reporters. Until the place was turned
into a campy sort of legend by a cadre of expatriate
Second City alumni, hard-drinking newshounds had
rubbed elbows here in relative obscurity with
pressmen and typesetters and delivery truck drivers.

The phrase "cheeseboiger, cheeseboiger" altered
that dimly lighted universe forever—and although it
had made owner Sam Siannis a far more prosperous
man, long-time regulars of the tavern still pine for
Sam's heirs to return to their senses, and for Billy
Goat to return to its true roots.

There was a Cubs game on the television, a tribute
to Sam's legacy. Decades ago, he had smuggled his
trademark pet goat into the ballpark, had been sum-
marily banned by the club ownership, and in response
had called down an Olympian curse on what hence-
forth had become known as the "hapless" Cubs. Subsequent removal of the curse had not had a noticeable
effect on the team's ill fortunes, which continued un-
abated to the present.

At least, that was one explanation; on the screen, a
bobbled grounder to third made the score Houston 5,
Cubs 1. But it was still early in the season.

I sat beside Leonard G. Washburn—"Lenny" to the
police, court officials, crime-beat reporters and assorted crooks and criminals about whom he wrote,
and "Mr. Washburn" to just about everybody else.

This category included the various representatives of his publisher. These functionaries did whatever was necessary to keep rights to the latest of his true-crime books, knowing it was destined for a slot on the best-seller lists.

When I had called Washburn, I had been greeted like a long lost friend. Neither of us made any reference to how I had blown him off almost two weeks before, on the night when Washburn had waited outside my apartment.

Lenny looked around approvingly, a strong-featured black man clearly in his element.

"*Love* this place," he crooned. "It's about the only place I know where I can walk in with an accused multiple murderer, wave hello to the cops who busted him, and have the prosecutor on the case send us over a free beer. In fact, that's just what happened last week. Swear to God."

He bit into the sandwich the Greek at the grill had paper-plated and passed to him with a disdain bestowed only on favored regulars. "And the cheeseburgers are still the best in town. So, Kath—how long did you spend in Moscow this time?"

"Two months, this trip," Kathy O'Banion said, "and I've never been so happy to get out of a place in my life. Every day is a new crisis over there."

She looked at me. I saw her eyes flicker over my face, and take in the still raw scrapes on my hand. I got the distinctly uncomfortable feeling she didn't miss much. Almost in self-defense, I studied her in turn.

O'Banion had a disarming smile—an attractive woman in her mid-fifties, who at first impression could have been mistaken for a high school principal. When you looked closer, particularly at her eyes, you might imagine it was a particularly tough high school.

"Lenny says you got the smelly end of a faked-up bribery stick in Lake Tower. My guess is that makes you the subject of his next book, am I right?"

Washburn answered for me. "That may depend on

what you can tell us, Kathy. Davey's got a lot of problems"—he winked at me, taking part of the sting from the comment—"and he needs to consult a few people who are in the know. That's why I called you, love."

O'Banion opened her shoulder bag, pulled out a pack of cigarettes and lit one with what looked like a very old and battered outsized Zippo.

"I don't know why you want to know about the Russian Mafiya, but I guess I'll be reading about it on a plane soon," she said. "Lenny's books are always so good at making a long flight feel shorter. That's a compliment, kiddo."

She took a deep drag on her cigarette. "Okay. I've filed stories on this for the past four years, so I'm not exactly telling you any secrets. You tune into *Meet the Press* or *McLaughlin*, and you hear about how the Russian Mafiya poses one of the biggest threats to the Russian government, right? That's crap, children; in just about every important way, the Mafiya *is* the Russian government today."

I frowned. "Putin's a former KGB thug, but I have a hard time picturing him as a gangster."

"Look, you've heard the term 'narco-state?'" O'Banion asked. "Colombia, some of the Caribbean island countries, and probably pretty soon even Mexico—countries that are so tight with the drug cartels that their national policies genuinely reflect the interests of the bad guys. The government and the dopers are in bed together, the two of 'em.

"Well, here's the difference: Russia is in bed with *itself*. It's the first modern instance of a major nation that has become completely criminalized. They've turned capitalism into a blood sport over there. You have an oligarchy of new-money billionaires—crooks, all of 'em—pulling the strings of the government at the same time people are starving on the streets."

She peered at me intently, willing me to understand. "Look," she said, "I'm South Side Irish, and a little hanky-panky was an accepted part of doing business when I was growing up here. Hell, still is—that's Chicago, you gotta love it.

"But in Russia, everything is connected—everything! You want to start a business, make an investment, open a franchise, you'll pay extortion money up front, or more likely you'll agree to take on a 'partner.' The concept is 'either you deal with us or we deal with your replacement.' Simple, but they've found it uncommonly effective."

"Just like the Capone era," Lenny interjected, "real icepick-in-the-eye stuff."

"Right, but Capone never got this big," she said. "Think Citicorp, BankAmerica, Chase Manhattan—hell, just make a list of the ten largest financial institutions in the U.S. Now imagine if eight of them were owned by the Cosa Nostra. That's Russia today, kiddo."

"I imagine they'd loot my Christmas Club account, right?" Washburn said.

She snorted, a harsh laugh.

"Embezzlement, money laundering, any of that sort of small potatoes—that's just hit-and-run stuff. You do it if you're in a country where you know the bank regulators are going to catch on to you sooner or later," she said. "In this case, imagine GM, IBM, Exxon and the rest of the Fortune 500 being forced to come to you when they want to borrow money. Think about the leverage you have—in every aspect of the economy."

"As Marx used to say," Len observed, "capital drives the capitalist system."

"Yeah, well—that goes double for economies that are in a transition *to* a capitalist system," the reporter said. "But it's not as simple as it once was, either. Today, 'developing' countries like Russia have to cope with the realities of a global investment community. The rules are all changed."

She took a deep draw on her cigarette.

"Okay, you have the big players—the major investment funds, the international banks and brokerages in New York, London, Hong Kong and so on," she said. "Used to be, they brought a kind of stability to the whole game, long as a country stuck to what was deemed the 'proper' fiscal path."

O'Banion's face screwed up in a disdainful scowl. "Today, global investment is schizophrenic as hell. A couple of rumors, a bad headline or two—all it takes is one major investor to get cold feet and pull out its money. Everybody else follows suit, and bingo! The abrupt withdrawal of credit causes an economy to collapse."

"I remember the crisis a few years back." Washburn nodded, his expression dour. "Sent stock market into the crapper around the world. Even worse, my little mutual fund got burned bad."

"I saw you listed in that *Fortune* magazine profile of successful authors last month," Kathy said dryly. "So don't expect sympathy from me. But, yeah—that set the pattern for the Russians since then. They lurch from crisis to crisis, and the IMF or World Bank jumps on their butts." O'Banion shrugged. "A few cosmetic changes, and we send 'em just enough money to keep the Russian economy from imploding."

"And that *works*?" I asked. It sounded like a confidence game writ large, and the thought offended my policeman's sensitivities. "Enough to send them billions of dollars?"

"Now you've asked the really big question," she said. "Can the Russian government be trusted? The first time they had a chance to cheat, back in '99, they did. They tinkered with the books they used to sweet-talk the IMF, and got caught misrepresenting their cash reserves. A couple of months later, they got caught laundering money through a New York bank. All it cost them was a good tongue-lashing."

O'Banion frowned in thought. "Trust? On the surface, the IMF is saying yes. Or at least, maybe. Given the mess Russia's in, socially as well as economically, that's the only thing that's kept the rest of the Western investment community from bolting. And that would completely sink the Russian economy."

"But the Russians don't seem all that worried about bucking the United States," I said. "They've even rubbed our noses in the fact that they're selling arms and nuclear-reactor technology to—what? Places like Iran and Iraq."

"You don't understand how international power diplomacy works," she retorted. "Before the Iraq war Putin could have been photographed pushing a hand dolly to deliver a nuclear bomb to Saddam, and unless the American public found out—and got outraged about it—the international community could cover it up, in the name of maintaining 'stability.' It's an old story, my friend."

"Ah, for the good old days," Washburn said, mock nostalgia in his voice. "Thank God for Ronald Reagan. He won the Cold War. He upped the ante on the arms race so high that the other guy had to fold."

"The Soviet Union was doomed long before Reagan used Star Wars to spend them into bankruptcy," O'Banion retorted. "Back in the fifties and sixties, they weren't faking it—Soviet Communists really believed they had the philosophy that would save the world. They were like Jesuits with nuclear missiles. The whole damn country was based on that belief, and it died because its people lost the faith.

"I interviewed some of the old-timers—veterans of their 'Great Patriotic War' against the Nazis, even a few people who remember back to the twenties and thirties. They said that as far back as the late seventies, the writing was on the wall—and I don't mean the Berlin Wall. The younger people didn't believe in the Marxist philosophy. They preferred listening to Western rock music and wearing secondhand Levi's and pretending to understand *Doonesbury*—all smuggled into the country by what the Soviets liked to call the 'antisocial criminal element.' You can't maintain a system based on an ideology if nobody believes in the ideology anymore."

O'Banion wiped her fingers with a paper napkin, and carefully picked a potato chip from Washburn's paper plate. "So it turned into a free-for-all. In the late seventies and eighties, the Soviet press was full of stories about corruption and murders involving people pretty high in the Party apparatus. Even Leonid Brezhnev's son-in-law. These were the top people in the *nomenklatura*—the Soviet ruling class." She shook her head sadly, as if she were talking about a scandal in a close friend's family.

"Hell of a story," Washburn said. "But you said they also snookered the West."

"Remember when banks were sending credit cards to every college kid in America?" O'Banion asked. "Unsolicited, through the mail?"

Washburn laughed. "Got one myself. Man, I thought I had hit the jackpot."

"So what did you do?"

The writer looked rueful. "Maxed out the damn thing in less than a month. I was still in school—no job, no way to pay. Missed a couple months' installments, so they called my old man." He shook his head at the memory. "I thought he was going to *kill* me."

"But he bailed you out," she noted. "Not because he loved you, hard as that may be to believe"—she dug an elbow into Lenny's side—"but because he didn't want you to screw up his credit rating."

"So we let the same thing happen to the Russians," I said. "We let them get hooked on easy credit to an extent far beyond their ability to repay."

"Uh-huh." O'Banion nodded. "Through most of the nineties, Western investors literally poured money into Russia. Real boom times, all based on credit. Good Lord, it was our government's not-so-secret strategy: turn 'em into capitalists and tie their economic base to the West. Bingo, they'll never be able to go Communist again. And it triggered the loan default in '98 that almost brought on a worldwide financial disaster."

She drew at her cigarette, long and hard. "So that's where we are today, guys. Both the big investment funds and the IMF got burned, bad. Now with Putin and a new bunch in power—I kind of miss Yeltsin, the poor schmuck—they're still bending over backward to attract outside money. They need cash, desperately, just to stay afloat. Russia's still a helluva mess."

She eyed Washburn's remaining potato chips. Lenny grinned and pushed the plate over to her.

"I shouldn't, but I'm going to," she said, taking another chip. "So everybody is looking out for Number One in Russia. I've even seen reports that some of the elite units—airborne, even Spetsnaz units—have sold their services en masse to Mafiya factions."

"What's Spetsnaz?" Washburn asked.

"Russian Green Berets," O'Banion said. "The real hard boys. In Afghanistan, they made an art form out of torturing dissidents and rebels for information. If the stories I've heard are even partly true, they had guys who would have been right at home with the Spanish Inquisition."

O'Banion finished the chips, and dabbed at her lips with the paper napkin. "The point is that without communism, none of them have any other value system," she said. "Russia has no tradition of democracy—hell, the Enlightenment missed czarist Russia completely—and they didn't have the underpinning of Confucianism that gives most Asian countries their cultural values. No Koran, no Vedantic tradition to serve as the kind of sociomoral compass the Muslim and Hindu cultures have. Whatever cultural traditions they had came from a basic feudal system—take whatever you were strong enough to, and run a saber through the babies."

She checked her watch, and stood up to leave. "Speaking of running, I have to go," she said to Len.

"Every time they get me back in Chicago, they hardly leave me a single unscheduled minute."

Kathy O'Banion turned to me. "Remember how cagey the Russians were being before the business in Iraq?" she asked. "Sure, they 'apologized' afterward. But while they were hinting at using their U.N. veto, all along they were bargaining for the best deal they could get in a post-Iraq world. That's what Russians do, and always *have* done.

"The best advice I can give is to follow the money. In Russia today, outside investment is the key to their whole economy. To get it, they have to maintain their credibility—with the IMF, with the global investment community, with all the groups out there that can influence public policy."

"If you had to guess—" I began.

"Frankly, I think they'll blow it," she said. "I've written about the Russians for three decades. Deception is just too ingrained in their nature." She laughed in a manner more experienced than cynical. "But until then, they'll promise anything. The Russians need us to believe them. No credibility, no credit. And that means the government, the Mafiya—everybody—is in deep manure."

She held out a hand to me, and I shook it with a single, solid grasp. I was surprised to find that I loomed above her; Kathy O'Banion was probably no more than five feet tall, though throughout the conversation I had been convinced that she was a much larger figure. I wondered how many other people, including world leaders, had had the same impression.

"Anyway, it's no wonder the antisocial criminal element won so fast," she said. "There was nobody on the other team."

Lenny Washburn walked me up the metal stairway that led to the street above. On Michigan Avenue, in the growing shadow of the Wrigley Building, Len

raised his arm and a yellow taxicab swerved to the
curb.

"So," he said. "What did I tell you? You got what
you needed, right?"

"It's scary as hell, Lenny," I said. "She makes the
whole world sound like a neighborhood going bad.
But, yeah—it's helping me get a handle on what I'm
dealing with. This Mikhail; he's something out of your
worst nightmare. Even after he found out that Kathleen Levinstein knew nothing, he kept working on her
until she died."

"Where'd you come up with *that*?" Washburn
scoffed. "You're guessing now."

"No. We had the forensic pathologists take another
look at the bone we recovered from the ashes," I said.
"It was a femur—a leg bone. They found a series of
spaced, microscopic nicks on it. The marks were con-
sistent with what Mikhail did to Katya Butenkova."

"Don't forget our deal," he said, climbing alone into
the backseat. "Russian Mafioso, stolen artwork, arson
and murder. Not to mention the other stuff it's
wrapped in. I *love* it!"

I looked at him through the cab window, the skin
on my face feeling suddenly tight.

"There's at least four dead people here, Len," I
said. "There's people I know in a hospital right now,
and they're lucky to be alive. So don't love it too
damn much, okay?"

Washburn held both hands palm up. "All I meant
is, we're partners, right? It's your story, Davey—but
it's my book, hey?"

I nodded. "Soon as I know what I'm sitting on."

He winked as the cab started forward.

"You know what you're sitting on," he said, irre-
pressible as ever, unable to resist a last lame joke
thrown from the window of the departing taxi. "That's
what we're both trying to save."

Chapter 32

It was shortly after four o'clock when I returned to the Lake Tower Municipal Center. I was about to pull into a parking slot when Chaz Trombetta's car, coming from the opposite direction, slid to a stop alongside. His window was already rolled down.

"I heard about Posson and Bird," he said, without greeting. "Are they going to be okay?"

I nodded. "They were lucky. By all rights, they ought to be dead right now. They were in way over their heads."

Chaz's face was grim and tight-lipped.

"Aren't we all," he said, not as a question. "This shit has got to stop, damn it. It's time we had that talk, J. D. But not here."

I looked at him closely. There were dark circles under his eyes, and his face appeared slack and parchment-colored, as if it had been weathered outside over a hard winter. "I have a . . . workout scheduled at the health club at six," I said. "Why don't you come with me?"

"Sure," Chaz replied sarcastically. "I really want to be seen driving around with you, don't I? How about I meet you there instead. I think I remember where you park." He looked directly into my eyes. "Six o'clock. Bring your friend Ronnie. He might be interested, too."

He drove off without another word, and I went inside to make the telephone call.

*   *   *

This time I brought along a vacuum bottle, filled for
me by a teenaged clerk at a Starbucks along the way.
As I checked in at the desk, the aluminum container
tucked deep inside my bag, I felt a bit like a smuggler
passing through Turkish customs.

Ron Santori was in the health club meeting room
when I arrived. Within minutes, Chaz Trombetta
opened the door and entered. We all shook hands,
awkwardly, as if we were little more than strangers.
In the light of the situation, perhaps we were.

I handed Chaz a paper cup filled with coffee.

"Davey says you want to cooperate," Santori said.
"You know the way it works. It's probably a good
idea for you to get a lawyer."

"Yeah," Chaz said. "I have a lawyer—I think.
Whenever I try to call him, his secretary tells me he's
not available and he'll call me back. My guess is he's
trying to write a book."•

"Same thing's happening when I call somebody in
Justice," Santori sympathized. "It's that goddam Gris-
ham. Ever since he got rich and famous, every lawyer
in the country is trying to write a best-seller. Problem
is, lot of these guys can't write their own name."

"It'd surprise me if my lawyer could *spell* his own
name," Trombetta replied tightly, "but he sure knows
how to churn a case. Keeps those billings coming, you
know? They must learn it in law school."

"Well, you know what they say about lawyers,"
Santori said. "Ninety-nine percent of them give the
rest a bad name."

Chaz was too tense to respond to the joke. "Yeah.
Anyway, when we get down to the deal making, I'll
be represented by legal counsel. Meanwhile, I just
want to get out from under all this, and I want to get
started now."

Santori took a microcassette tape recorder out of
his pocket.

"Uh-uh," I said. "No recording—at least, not yet. I

told Chaz we'd agree to use him as a deep-background informant. Nothing goes on the record until he gets a deal that protects his interests."

Santori smiled. "No," he said, "my bet is that you didn't tell him anything like that. But I'll go along with it anyway, for now." He looked at Chaz. "If you're straight with me, I'll play it straight with you. So for now, it's deep background—but you don't hold anything back unless it's directly self-incriminating, understand?"

Chaz Trombetta looked briefly at me, then turned his eyes back to the FBI agent. He nodded, once.

Santori put the recorder on the table, pushing it off to the side.

"All right," he said. "So let's start with a name. Who's in charge? Who set up the system, Chaz?"

"Bob Nederlander," Chaz said, and I realized I had been holding my breath. I had long known Nederlander was dirty—but knowing it as a gut-level belief is far different from being able to prove it as fact. I also knew my former partner; if Chaz said it, incontrovertible proof existed somewhere.

"Nederlander came up with the idea of scamming insurance companies with phony car theft reports," Trombetta said. "He's been running that play for a couple of years, up until last summer or so."

I interrupted. "Old news, Chaz. Before I was tossed, we already figured Nederlander for that. Let's fast-forward a little. How'd they drag you into it, Chaz?"

Trombetta took a deep breath and blew it out in a long, sustained hiss. He sounded disgusted with himself.

"You were the object lesson, J. D.—the stick," he said. "After you were busted, Nederlander called me in for a little chat. He knew you had been feeding information to these guys"—he thrust his chin in the direction of Santori—"and he arranged it so you'd hear about those phony chop-shop guys 'bribing' the local cops. Said he figured you'd go there and do something dramatic, right in the middle of a county sting operation. He said you always did try a little too hard, J. D."

Chaz tried to smile and failed dismally. "Anyway, he told me what I could expect if I wanted to rock the boat. Remember, old buddy—at the time you were in county lockup, looking at maybe five years' hard time. I was still out here, alone. He asked me if I liked wondering which of my fellow officers would be watching my back every time I kicked in a perp's door. Then he showed me the carrot—a *lot* of carrots. Asked me if I was in or out. So I made the choice. Now I'm living with it."

"We'll want dates and times when you make your formal statement. For now, let's try some details on how it all fit together," Santori said, smoothly moving the interrogation into deeper waters. Chaz, painfully aware of how far he had already drifted, had to follow.

"They had—hell, who am I fooling? *We* had rules," Chaz said, his lips twisting bitterly. "We didn't shit where we ate, which means we mainly left Lake Tower alone when we were working our little moneymakers. We'd hit the unincorporated areas in the county, or go down into the city. About the only thing we did local was the stolen car scam."

He laughed ruefully. "It was *so* convenient to dump 'em in the Sanitary Canal. You'd drive it out, pop off the plates and dashboard VIN, and roll it in. Afterward, one of the guys would drive you back. Sometimes it wouldn't be ten minutes, and you'd be home drinking a beer and watching your own TV."

"Exactly how did that scam work, Chaz?" Santori asked, sounding sincerely interested, as if he were inquiring about the best fertilizer to use on his lawn. "For instance, the claims. Any problem with getting claims through the insurance companies?"

"When I first got into it, there was no problem with anything—they had the system down to a routine. Nederlander handled the theft reports out of his own office, and the 'victims' would just file their claims through normal channels. We'd confirm and forward a copy of the report to the carrier."

"How did Nederlander control the insurance side?" I asked.

"Word was that by then Nederlander had found somebody at the insurance company, on the inside," Trombetta said. "He made sure the claims would be called in at certain times, like real early in the morning or at particular hours over weekends. That way he could be sure of getting them into the system without a lot of questions being asked. But that was Nederlander's side of it; the rest of us weren't in on names or many of the details."

"Sure," Santori said. "But everybody knew it would look suspicious if Lake Tower suddenly turned into the car-theft capital of the Midwest. So the people who were in on it—I'd guess friends and family members at first, then other folks you figured you could trust—started making their reports to other police departments, saying the cars were boosted in those towns. Then they'd call the insurance people and make a claim. Is that about right, Chaz?"

Chaz snorted, again.

"More or less," he said. "Usually by the time they filed a report, the cars were already in the canal."

"What made it stop?" Santori asked.

Chaz twisted his mouth sourly.

"About a year ago, County got a tip to look for a body in the canal, right where we were sinking cars," he said. "Nobody exactly thought it was a coincidence, but it must have really freaked out Nederlander. A couple of the guys wanted to keep going, only find a new way to lose the cars. But after a few more months, Nederlander pulled the plug on the whole deal."

"He said he was ending the car-ring operation?"

"Temporarily—that's what he said at first. Next thing I hear, there's a new bunch of chop-shop profes-

sionals in the area, and Nederlander passes the word
they've got a free ride from us. Maybe he figured getting paid for protection was the safer way to go. Whatever, it kind of retired all of us from the faked-claim
business."

"What came next, Chaz?" I asked. "What are you
guys into now?"

"It turned into a friggin' free-for-all, that's what
happened," Chaz replied, addressing the response to
Santori. "Getting stiffed out of the car-theft scam cut
out the major source of income for everybody involved. We had gotten used to the money; some of us
had made commitments, counting on it being there."

Chaz's eyes fell, and I wondered how many nights
he had spent sleepless, thinking about the ultimate
cost—for all of his family—to landscape his yard or
put a daughter through Notre Dame.

As if he could read my thoughts, Chaz looked up
at me. He tried to hold my eyes, and failed.

"So everybody started scrambling around to find
their own little sideline to make up the difference," he
said. "Some of the guys are shaking down the betting
professionals—just the independents, of course, which
keeps it all pretty penny-ante. Others started stepping
on tavern owners just outside Lake Tower, in the unincorporated areas."

"You mean shakedowns," Santori said. "Extortion."

"Whatever." Chaz didn't rise to the bait. "Guys
who put an electronic poker terminal in back, near
the rest rooms. Or maybe they have a cigarette machine, but if you look real close you see the packs
don't always have state tax stickers on 'em. Penny-
ante crap, sure. But what the hell—we're dealing with
players here. It's kind of like collecting the local
taxes, right?"

"That's got to put you in competition with the mob
boys, doesn't it?" Santori speculated. "Wouldn't seem
the smartest business venture you people could have
taken. Not for the long run."

"Nobody's thinking about the long run these days," Chaz retorted. "For the past few months, it's been like make your money now, because it's all going down the tube. A few of my fellow law enforcement colleagues have even decided to go somewhere a little heavier."

This time, we waited him out.

"The First National Bank of Crack," Chaz said. "You know—drive down to the city for a little hunting trip. Grab one of the shitheads selling on a corner, sweat an address out of him. Then they just kick the door, flash the badge and leave with whatever cash they find. A little armed robbery, that's all it is. So what if it's out of our jurisdiction? Or if they get a wrong address every now or then."

"Serve and protect," I said, not trying to make it easier on him. "Classy bunch you're hanging with these days, Chaz."

"It gets even classier," Chaz said, and shook his head in disgust. "Now, the latest thing is fairy shaking."

He glanced over at Santori, who had sketched an expression of polite inquiry on his face. He, too, was disinclined to ease Chaz's journey.

My former partner leaned back in his chair, trying to sound jovial. "Hey, Davey—you remember a couple of years back when the department got the federal grant to buy all that electronic surveillance equipment? Well, these days it's getting put to a brand-new use. The guys sign out a video camera and stake out the Alamo, or the Tom Cat—the gay bars over in Polktown and Westphalia Springs," Chaz said, for Santori's benefit. "Or sometimes they'll pick one of the sleazier places downtown that specialize in boy-on-boy porno flicks.

"Any event, they'll check the cars parked on the street. If they see one with a child safety seat or one of those MY KID'S AN HONOR STUDENT AT— stickers, they write down the license plate and wait. Camera's rolling, pointed at the door of the bar or the theater.

If one of the creepies coming out gets in that car and drives away, they got a fairy hit.

"They use the department computer to run the guy's plate. The next day, guy gets a call at home. Depending on how he reacts, they'll let him know they have him on camera, maybe even drop him a copy," Chaz said. "The poor dumb schmuck either pays up, or everybody finds out what side of the plate he swings from. Courtesy of your local law enforcement."

He looked nauseated, like he had tasted something indescribably foul and wanted to spit.

Santori's voice was calm, encouraging, almost seductive. "And throughout all of this, you continued to work cases as a Lake Tower detective—is that correct? For instance, you worked the Levinstein homicides, didn't you?"

"I did some of the legwork on the Levinstein case," Trombetta said carefully. "One time or another, just about everybody in the detective bureau got pulled into it. It's a major case for the department."

"To your knowledge," Santori asked, equally carefully, "was that case handled in a legitimate way? For example, case supervision. It seems an awfully important investigation to assign to a relatively inexperienced investigator, doesn't it?"

Chaz blew out a deep breath.

"Nederlander set up an arrangement with Terry Posson," he said. "She got to be the lead investigator on the case, officially, but in every other way Bob Nederlander had direct control of the investigation."

"His idea," I asked, "not hers?"

Chaz nodded. "It didn't exactly thrill her, but the kid's hungry to make detective grade. The way I hear it, he sold it to her on the basis that this way, she'd get the credit when the case was solved."

Santori made a short note on his legal pad, as if Trombetta had cleared up a minor point of confusion.

"So Terry Posson got the job of lead investigator,"

he mused. "What was supposed to be in it for Nederlander? Were he and Posson . . . involved?"

Chaz laughed out loud, though not with mirth.

"I doubt it," he said. "Nederlander told a few of his people that he thought she might be a lesbian. Once he called her his 'bull-dyke girlfriend.' What I know of the bastard, that means he probably tried and she handed him his head back."

"So what was it?" Santori persisted.

"Nederlander supposedly told her he was on the hook with the affirmative action people." Chaz grinned. "Hell, that part of it is probably true. We don't have any women carrying gold shields. She'd be the first, and all she had to do was pass on the directions Nederlander gave her."

Trombetta's expression turned serious.

"Problem was, the way he was running the investigation didn't make any sense. Like, for the first month after the murders, he had Posson keep me running a canvass of gas stations and convenience stores, showing clerks a picture of Levinstein. I was supposed to ask, like, had he bought any gasoline in suspicious quantities. Dumbshit questions like that, about a guy who was dead before the fire started."

"Not real productive," Santori agreed noncommittally.

"Went that way for almost two months," Chaz said. "Oh, there was a lot of activity—hell, we questioned Levinstein's employees four or five times, asking the same routine crap each time. It made for a helluva lot of reports, but zip results."

I was watching him carefully, noting the hesitations, the inflections, and all the other signs Chaz was so clearly broadcasting.

Whether indirectly or not, he was deeply involved in a conspiracy to commit fraud, blackmail, extortion, armed robbery and more; it was not the stuff that would have sat easily on the conscience of Chaz Trombetta. He might have come to an uneasy accommodation with them. But there was still a line he had drawn, still certain crimes that he could not countenance.

I understood a few things better now. Following me to the health club, leaving a message on my car, standing in a rainstorm to pass me the results of an investigation he knew he could not pursue himself—all had been acts of contrition. They were self-inflicted penances, a collective down payment against the punishment that, as a career police officer, he had to know was inevitable.

I spoke up. "You knew Nederlander was tanking the investigation. And you wondered why."

Chaz turned his head, and his gaze was now steady.

"Yeah," he said. "Then you and Cieloczki showed up. So I figured that as long as they wanted me to check on gasoline, I might just as well see what kind of mileage Nederlander gets with that goddam battleship of his. Everybody knows he hasn't bought his own gas in twenty years, so I pulled his records for the fuel pump in back of the muni center."

"That's when you knew," I said. It was not a question, though Chaz answered it as one.

"That's when I knew," he agreed, in a quiet voice. "That's when I knew for sure."

Chapter 33

In Chicago, the consulate of the Russian Federal Republic has its address on the city's Gold Coast, on the Near North Side along Lake Michigan's shoreline. It is an area of expensive office suites, exclusive condominiums and other high-priced, high-prestige real estate. Located on an upper floor of a modern twenty-story building, several of the larger offices boast an impressive view of the lake designed to stir the stoniest bureaucratic soul.

As with the consulate itself, the view was inherited from the old Soviet Union, and as such, retains much of the unique ambiance it gained when the hammer and sickle was bolted to the front door. That is to say, most informed visitors—particularly those who are also senior Russian officials—automatically assume their conversations are being monitored and recorded by security staffers.

Their own, as well as those from their host government.

It was by the latter—an FBI microphone planted, ironically enough, in the frame of an acrylic by LeRoi Neiman and presented to Anatoli Tarinkoff by an Atlanta media tycoon—that the following conversation was recorded.

It was an odd exchange, decipherable only in the hindsight that I would later acquire.

Having for years served his government, first as a

loyal communist and later as an equally dedicated (if less experienced) capitalist, Anatoli Tarinkoff had become an accomplished master of circumspection as a method of communication. He had even come to enjoy his talent at inflicting frustration on eavesdroppers, whether foreign or domestic.

Petra Natalia Valova had not. It privately irked her to waste so much time and energy shielding herself from the formalized structure of paranoia that was so ingrained in her culture.

The curator and the attaché sat across from each other, a low coffee table between them. Tarinkoff carefully filled two tall glasses with a liquid so brown it was almost black. He wrapped a linen napkin around one glass and, with a delicacy that was almost antique, handed it to Valova.

In public, she was his superior, if only unofficially. Here, in his office as elsewhere in private, they addressed other as equals—and even that, Valova understood, was but a courtesy proffered like a small gift. She was a senior official with her country's foremost museum; still, she had the uncomfortable feeling Tarinkoff could, with a word, destroy her career, or worse. The thought did little to soothe an anxiety that was already close to consuming her.

"I hope you do not mind that we will have a late dinner this evening," he said, gracious as always. "It is only another of the interminable charity events they have in this country. I agreed to attend as a courtesy. Then, too, it is important that our country be seen in as favorable a light as possible. These small duties are vital if we are to keep Western funds flowing to Mother Russia." He smiled condescendingly. "Perhaps you will find American opera of interest."

"Perhaps," she replied, and heard her voice tremble.

To cover her feelings, she changed the subject.

"You have had word today from your . . . friends?" Valova asked, careful to sound casual.

Tarinkoff nodded. "In fact, a few minutes ago." He tapped the pocket where he carried his small cellular telephone. "They now expect to secure, in the near future, the . . . minor pieces of art that you have discussed. You will, of course, need to personally verify the authenticity of these items."

She thought for a moment. "Certainly. But I have little time before I must return to my duties in Moscow."

"Yes," he replied. "We are working on a number of different approaches to resolve this situation quickly."

She studied his face, which she had learned to read fairly well.

"But there is a problem?" she probed, and even she heard the nervousness in her words. Not for the first time, she noted the way Tarinkoff looked at her carefully—measuring her, almost—before replying.

"A small one," he acknowledged. "The American who took delivery died in an accident, relatively recently. Apparently, there was a fire in his home."

Valova turned suddenly pale. "The paintings? They escaped damage?"

Tarinkoff's voice was calm, and intended to reassure. "We have information that they were removed prior to the fire," he said.

"And?" Valova asked.

Tarinkoff shrugged. "And they will be found. I have another resource who claims to have this knowledge."

"I do not like dealing with these people," Valova said, and Tarinkoff raised his eyebrows to remind her of other ears that might also hear.

"In a matter such as this," he said, "they are an adequate resource. This way, we can ensure that their interests mirror ours." He paused, and decided to take the chance. "Or at least, guarantee they are not in conflict with what must be our primary objective."

Tarinkoff's voice took on a tone that was reasonable, almost gentle.

"Petra Natalia, you must be aware of the circumstances. These are difficult times for the Russian Federation, and we all walk a fine line, no? There are those in this country who would politicize the very . . . existence of the artwork in question. Already, the American Congress is being pressured by certain elements to require a 'more candid' discussion of this issue. Can you imagine the subsequent uproar if this issue became no longer abstract, but real?"

He caught himself; it was unwise to reveal too much to the microphones.

"So," Tarinkoff said, in a voice intended to sound lightly philosophical, "if we cannot obtain these paintings for . . . ah, our own collection—well, 'these people,' as you term them, are our best insurance that the items in question do not surface in the possession of anyone else."

Valova stared at him, heart pounding.

She realized, suddenly and fully for the first time, that she had no allies.

Across the table from her, Anatoli Tarinkoff was careful to keep his own expression impassive as he watched the parade of emotions traverse the face of his companion.

"Have no concern," he said, to any microphones as much as to his companion. "The matter is in quite capable hands. You will have your paintings to take home, as . . . souvenirs of your visit here. I, your cultural attaché, guarantee it."

Tarinkoff raised his glass as if to toast the pledge. After a moment's hesitation, Petra Natalia Valova followed suit. They drank the tea in unison.

Chapter 34

On the wall, the hands of the clock formed a steep uphill slope, a diagonal that indicated the time as a few minutes past eight. For the past half hour, I had been a trespasser on unfriendly ground, an unwelcome intruder on the side of the hallway that belonged to the Lake Tower Police Department.

I sat at the desk assigned to Terry Posson as a parade of uniformed tactical officers, plainclothes and the occasional detective stalked past, their attitudes alternating between a pointed indifference and dark, challenging glares. No one spoke, but the generalized atmosphere of unrestrained hostility communicated volumes.

It had been a long day, and not a good one. Listening to Chaz detail the cesspool into which he had fallen left me feeling drained. I wanted to leave—to go home, or at least what passed for it now. I wanted to see Ellen, if only to determine how I had offended her once again. I wanted a drink, or several.

But more than all that, I wanted to close the circle; worse, I *needed* to, desperately. I now knew that Nederlander was deeply involved in the Levinstein case. He had graduated from insurance fraud to murder, and tracing the path he had taken would draw the ring closed around him. But too many pieces were still missing, and my frustration was becoming a physical presence.

Terry was anything but a fastidious person, if her
desk was any evidence. The numbing detritus of
bureaucracy—forms, folders, reports, memoranda in a
quantity that had constituted a death sentence for entire forests—slumped in untidy heaps covering every
available surface of her workspace. A half-filled cup
of coffee sat forgotten next to the telephone, a film
of its oils shimmering on an inky surface long cold.

In total, the effect was one of an uncharted desktop
wasteland, a trackless morass that dared any outsider
to enter and promised only peril if he did. Salvation
took the form of a ringing phone somewhere on the
desk. I navigated by sound and touch until I found a
heaped-up mound of paper that was more firm than
the others.

I picked up the receiver, but before I could identify
myself the caller began to talk.

"There's procedure, Officer Posson, which you people seem to think you can bend just for fun," an angry
voice said in my ear. "Then there is the law. That's
supposed to be unbendable, from what I understand."

"I'm not—"

"Look," the voice said. "We *want* to cooperate. But
you're supposed to file a court order with us when
you want cell phone records. Seeing as how this particular phone has been reported stolen, I'll make an exception. *Another* exception, I ought to say. But can
you please follow proper procedure hereafter?"

One reason I avoided cellular phones is a simple,
though paranoid, fact: every time you use one, you
leave a trail. Calls made, calls received—the cellular
phone company charges for both, and tracks those
charges by computer. The potential for abuse, even
by authorized law enforcement officers, is immense.

Only a fool ignores the gifts that fortune drops onto
one's lap.

"What do you have?"

"You're welcome, I'm sure. The five calls you asked

us to trace—three to your Chief Nederlander, two to the City Administration Department? Apparently, the caller wasn't moving around all that much this afternoon. The calls were all made from approximately the same location, within two square blocks of our cellular repeater station at 2937 Lakeshore. That's on the west side of Lake Tower, of course."

"You're sure?"

"I'm looking at the screen right now, Officer Posson." There was a pause. "In fact, you might want to know that the party has just placed *another* call to the municipal center. Are these bomb threats?"

Before I could answer, the telephone buzzed rather than rang, signaling a call from an internal line.

"Hold on a minute, please." I pressed the button marked INTERCOM.

"Officer Posson's desk," I said.

"Davey, I need you in my office—right *now*." Gil Cieloczki's voice crackled over the wire with an electric energy. "Sonnenberg's on the line, and he wants to make a deal."

As I entered his office, Gil was holding the handset to his ear, listening intently. He pointed to a chair in front of his desk, and pressed the button that activated the speakerphone system. A low sound filled the air, somewhere between a hum and a hiss, as the circuit engaged in the middle of a sentence.

". . . don't have to trace the call. I'm on a cellular phone, but I'll tell you where I am—I'll cooperate right down the line, but I have to have some assurances from you. You help me and I—"

Sonnenberg's voice was tinny, but it was more than the mediocre quality of the amplification that made it sound different from the last time I heard him speak. The confident timbre of a man who knew the score, who had perhaps even rigged the game, was gone. I was listening to a man who had just tugged nervously on his lifeline, only to feel it pull loose and fall in coils around his ankles. I looked at Gil with an unspoken inquiry, and the firefighter nodded his head, once.

"Did you hear how Katya died?" I asked, interrupting. "Listen up, Sonny—you might find this educational. After all, you know, the guy was looking for you."

Sonnenberg had stopped speaking, and there was no sound from the telephone's amplified receiver.

"It was an unusual kind of torture," I continued conversationally. "One of the Feds told me there's a long tooth chipper of a name for it in Russian. It translates into a sort of rough slang for deboning. You know—like you'd do a piece of chicken. Katya's attacker took a knife and methodically started cutting through each of her muscles, right where they connect to the bone. The Soviets used it a lot after they invaded Afghanistan. It's slow and very painful, and somebody who knows what he's doing can make it last a long, long time. But I hear the subject almost always tells you what you want to know."

I paused, as if inviting comment. When Sonnenberg spoke again, his voice had a ragged quality, as if the air he was drawing in was scarcely sufficient to fuel speech.

"You *shit*," he said, his voice almost a whisper.

"They say the worst part—I mean, aside from the pain itself—is that you can hear the knife as it saws through your flesh," I continued. "Of course, you've got to be gagged, like Katya was, or the screams will drown it out."

I listened to him breathe heavily at the other end of the line.

"You still with me, Sonny?" I asked, mock solicitousness in my voice. "In case you didn't know, these people are back to looking for you now. That apartment where your mother lived? A couple of them were there last night, waiting for you to show up. We only got one of them. Sorry it wasn't the guy with the knife. He's still out there."

I made my voice cold. "So you keep on telling us all the things you want, okay? Because when you're done, I'm going to tell you how much I don't give a damn."

There was a silence from the speaker that stretched out for what seemed ages.

"You need me," he said finally. "You need what I know."

"Keep telling yourself that, Sonny," I said.

"The Levinstein place—I had a key," Sonnenberg said. "I got there a little after five o'clock and cut the power to the alarm system, just to be on the safe side. Then I went in through the front door—just like I was told."

"Told by who?" Gil asked.

"We'll get to that, maybe. But there wasn't anybody in the place, and there weren't any paintings either. I left the way I got in, and that's the truth."

"I'm insulted, Sonny," I said. "I had hoped you'd show enough respect to make up a better story."

"Listen, goddamit!" he said. "It's the truth. How do you think I felt when there weren't any fuckin' paintings in the damn house? I'm standing there with my butt hanging in the breeze, and nothing to show for it. So you can bet that I got the hell out of there, fast."

"When we hang up this phone," Gil said, "I'm going to get an arrest warrant issued, charging you with murder and arson."

"Bullshit," he said angrily. "I'm not buying into any murder rap. I didn't kill anybody."

"That's not the way it looks, Sonny," I said. "Here's the way I'm reading the script: sure, maybe you went in there thinking the place was empty. It wasn't, and you shot Stanley and Kathleen."

Sonnenberg tried to interrupt, but I rode roughshod over his objections.

"Stan Levinstein wasn't the kind of man who'd just let you walk out, was he? Not with something that meant so much, had so much symbolism attached to it. What did he do, Sonny—try to grab the gun? Did he *force* you to shoot him? Amazing how things can go bad so quickly, isn't it? So what can you do? What the hell—in for a dime, in for a dollar. You decide torching the place is the best way to make sure you covered your tracks. I only have one question: where are the paintings?"

Sonnenberg's voice was almost frantic.

"Listen to me, goddamit! There weren't any paintings in the place! That's what I'm trying to tell you. Somebody else must have got there first. And there wasn't nobody in the house—not when I got there and not when I left!"

I could feel Sonny try to calm himself.

"Look, the whole idea was to keep everything cool," Sonnenberg said. "I don't do the strong-arm stuff. This was a pure B and E job. We cart out the stuff, call Levinstein and he uses the insurance money to buy it back. There was a plan, man! We knew when they were home, and when they went out. Hell, we checked everything out. Ask me about it—you want to know how much the stuff was insured for?"

"Oh, we've got that pretty much locked," I told him. "There wasn't any insurance. No policy was ever issued for any art. That makes your story a lot harder for a jury to swallow, doesn't it?"

"Yeah, right." Sonnenberg's voice regained a measure of assurance, if only a shadow of its usual cockiness. "Now pull the other one. I saw the letter from the insurance company, okay? TransNational Mutual. Sound familiar? And the paintings were covered for seven and a half million bucks."

"Sonny, Sonny," I said, and put humor into it. "You poor schmuck. How hard do you think it is to take a piece of company stationery and fake up a letter of confirmation? Pretend for a minute we believe you.

The kind of paintings that were in there weren't worth any seven-point-five million. At a minimum, multiply that by ten—and then double *that*. You got caught in a big con, you dumb jerk. We tracked down a girl who was in on it. She worked at TransNational headquarters."

"Hold on," he said. When he spoke again, his voice was shaky. "This girl—she told you the letter was a fake?"

"No," Gil said. "The girl is dead. In February, somebody strangled her."

"So, you see how that looks, Sonny," I added. "Think about the timing. You've admitted doing a breaking and entering job based on what she helped convince you was in there. Let's say you're playing it straight, and you didn't find any paintings. The Levinsteins are still dead. And just a couple of weeks after the job blows up in your face, this girl gets killed, too."

We could barely hear Sonnenberg over the wire. "Holy shit," he muttered. "That son of a bitch!"

"Why so surprised, Sonny?" I said. "You had to at least suspect that somebody had pulled a fast one. But maybe you're just dumb enough to think that gives you some leverage. Maybe like you thought you were protected when the Levinstein job fell flat.

"Except that you had already shot your mouth off to Katya Butenkova, telling her that you were going to score big," I said. "You were even stupid enough to say it was an art heist, and hint that 'corrupt public officials' were involved. You just weren't quite dumb enough to name names."

I gave him a moment to react; when he didn't, I added a measure of contempt to my tone.

"Still, Katya was a lady who knew the value of the information she did have, and I guess she was already getting a little tired of you, Sonny," I said. "So even before the job went down, she tipped off the local Russian hoods. I can imagine how you must have felt when the local Russian mob shows up to put the pressure on you, looking for a taste of the profits. Here you thought you were free and clear, no connection to the Levinstein case. Then, all of a sudden, not only do these hard guys know you were involved, they want a piece of the action you don't even have. That's why you're dodging your Russian pals; that's why you took off through the window when I came to the apartment you shared with Katya."

"You're a real prick, Davey."

"Then things really spun out of control, because the Russians were talking about all this," I continued. "And inevitably, some bad people heard about it. One of them is a thug named Mikhail, who's hanging with the local Russian 'Mafiyaoso.' You heard he was trying to get a line on a screwup who botched a recent art heist."

I laughed, twisting the knife. "He has your name, Sonny. It's just a matter of time now."

I looked at Gil, and raised my eyebrows. He nodded; whether or not Sonnenberg was telling the whole truth, the priority now was to bring him in where he could, at minimum, be kept alive. He was a solid link, and the only known witness we had left.

"Tell you what, Sonny—for the sake of discussion, let's assume that we care enough about you to bring you in before your Russian friends find you," I said. "You're going to have to dig a lot deeper to make it worthwhile for us."

"I don't get what you mean."

"We could start with this one: how come all of a sudden you're calling *us*? Did something change around here, that you've got to shop the market for somebody to keep you alive?"

"Talk English, will you?"

I made my voice conversational, almost warm. "Last time we talked, you seemed pretty confident about your situation. I seem to recall you implying that you had a friend around here. How did you put it? That

my life was going to take a turn for the worse? Or
did I misconstrue your comment?"

Sonnenberg tried to sound abashed, contrite; but his
words came out too rushed.

"Look—I might have done some big talking. You
know how it is; you were coming down pretty hard
on me, and I wanted to maybe make you sweat a
little, all right?"

"Not good enough, Sonny. I'm not convinced we
need your help anymore. See, since you and I last
spoke, we've done a little homework here. And I'm
pretty sure that we can make a case that will have
both of you sharing a cell. Maybe even on death
row."

I took a chance. "You might want to start thinking
about a motion for separate trials. Judges tend to
throw the book at public officials who go this bad.
Separate yourself, you might get lucky and avoid the
hotshot down in Joliet. Though I hear a lethal injec-
tion is supposed to give you a hell of a rush, at least
before your heart stops."

Sonnenberg said nothing for a moment, and I could
imagine the wheels that were turning in his mind.
When he spoke, his voice was soft as an obscene
caller.

"If you want your big-name public official for it,"
Sonny Sonnenberg told me, "I can give him to you."

The clock on the desk read 8:38, its subdued blue
digital numerals somehow calming. Immediately upon
ending the discussion with Sonnenberg, Cieloczki had
hustled me upstairs to the executive offices. The room
resembled a beehive during the daytime, but the assorted queens, drones and workers had left hours
before.

Now Talmadge Evans presided over an empty and
quiet fiefdom.

"We're bringing Sonnenberg in," I said. "He heard

how his girlfriend died. He knows he's a marked man out there."

Evans looked surprised, then dubious. "Where is he?"

"In a dark room where people try not to meet each other's eye," I said. "He spent the day hiding at the Lace Panty."

"The *what*?"

"It's a strip club and peep show emporium, over on the West Side," I said, straightfaced. "Open twenty-four hours a day, seven days a week."

"Davey and I are going over there together," Gil said. "It's important to get Sonnenberg in custody immediately, for his own protection. The deal is he opens up completely when's he's safe."

"Should we send a police car?" Evans suggested. "Would that be faster?"

Gil answered as if he was considering the question for the first time.

"I think Davey and I should handle it," he said. "We can be there in twenty minutes. But, given the nature of the allegations, I felt that you should know the situation immediately. This is all about to become very, very complicated."

Evans glanced at the clock. "That is an understatement," he said, and his voice was low and tense.

"At least Santori will be happy," Gil said, his voice grim. "He finally has somebody who can give his Operation Centurion what it needs: an informant ready to testify that a top public official is involved in multiple homicides, arson and a variety of other assorted felonies."

"To be frank, that is part of our problem," Evans said, a dark expression on his face. "We're talking about an official of Lake Tower—the man who runs our police department. If what you believe is accurate—"

"It is," I piped up unhelpfully.

Evans' look was intended to make me reconsider further contributions to the conversation.

"*If* it is true," Evans emphasized, "then, additionally, a substantial percentage of our police force is involved in such illegal acts as armed robbery and extortion." He shook his head stonily. "This is a disaster for . . . for Lake Tower. The FBI has its agenda, but we must focus on our own priority. Santori's investigation is, and must remain, secondary."

Gil was looking steadily at the city manager. "What are you saying, Talmadge?"

Evans returned the firefighter's gaze. In the moments before he spoke, I imagined that some kind of complicated mental calculation was going on behind the intensity of his stare. It puzzled me, and was somehow troubling. Then a curtain came down behind his eyes, though whether in defeat or to conceal a hidden resolve I could not discern.

"People have already died, and there is risk that more may," Evans said, as though that wasn't what he had been thinking. "If Bob Nederlander is behind this . . . well, we have no choice but to act in a way to preserve the safety of the public. But my point is that there may be a way to act that will also preserve the image and reputation of this city."

"Are you suggesting," I asked, "that we leave Nederlander in a room with his pistol and hope he does the honorable thing?"

"I'm suggesting that we do what we can to limit the damage," Evans said with heat, "while still removing the bad apple."

"Nederlander is corrupt," I told Evans. "He's been running your police department like he's Ali Baba and they're the Forty Thieves. He's not just a 'bad apple,' Mr. Evans—he's the center of a ring of bad cops. He's been playing fast and loose with a fake stolen-car insurance scam for at least three years. We've found evidence of this insurance fraud, and Mel Bird identified a young woman we think was his accomplice inside the insurance company. We believe she also provided falsified insurance documents to Stanley Levinstein, which ties Nederlander to our double homicide."

Evans looked appalled. "You've arrested this woman? She can implicate Bob Nederlander?"

"She's dead, too, Mr. Evans. Her name was Rebecca Hunt, she was twenty-two years old, and she died in a parking garage with a nylon cord knotted around her throat. This was within days of the Levinstein murders."

"There's more, Talmadge," Cieloczki interjected. "We have strong circumstantial evidence that indicates Nederlander might be directly involved in the arson itself."

"Evidence? What kind of evidence?"

Gil looked at me.

"Davey has . . . obtained . . . records that detail Nederlander's use of the municipal gasoline pumps," he said. "Specifically, it shows that Nederlander filled his car's tank with almost thirty gallons of gasoline the morning of January 23."

Evans looked puzzled. "He put gasoline in his car. And that proves *what*? That he drives a car with a large gas tank?"

"It would have to be a hell of a gas-guzzler, Mr. Evans," I said. "You see, according to the records, he used the municipal gas pump to put in virtually the same amount—before midnight, later on the same day."

"That's the day of the Levinstein murders," Cieloczki said. "It's approximately the amount of gasoline our investigation indicates was used as an accellerant in the arson. We've verified he spent most of January 23 in his office, at least through midafternoon. That makes it hard to explain two fill-ups in one day. My guess, Talmadge, is that we've discovered why there were no gas cans found at the fire."

"All he would need was a bucket and a length of plastic tubing, if he knew how to siphon gasoline from a car tank," I said.

Gil Cieloczki looked out Evans' window at the municipal center's parking lot. He could just make out the sign that reserved a space for DIRECTOR—PUBLIC SAFETY. Tonight, no shiny black Navigator filled the parking slot.

"He knew how," the fire chief said. "He told me."

"This is just a thought," I said. "But does anybody know where Nederlander is, right now?"

Gil looked puzzled. "I haven't seen him all day."

Evans shook his head impatiently.

"Me neither," I said. "And somebody's been tracing Sonnenberg's calls today. Whoever it is may know where to look by now."

Evans looked at Gil for a long moment.

"Do whatever you must," he said. "End this disaster."

As we left to bring in Sonny Sonnenberg, I looked back over my shoulder at Talmadge Evans. He was staring out the window, his eyes unblinking and his face deeply furrowed. Slumped in his chair, he looked very old, almost ancient. I could almost hear the intensity of his thoughts.

But his features revealed nothing; at least, nothing I knew how to read.

In hindsight, perhaps Gil should have called for a patrol car to pick up Sonnenberg. At the least, he could have had one dispatched to stand by as backup outside the Lace Panty.

As it was, he did not. And so, by 9:11 P.M. when we arrived at the sprawling complex, there was no possibility of a witness—someone who might have seen what had happened, or recognized a familiar face among the patrons there.

All we had, as we fought through the crowd of firefighters and theater patrons milling around outside the

theater, was a nineteen-year-old transvestite named
William Poplouski, aka Fawn Lopez, aka Kimberly
Clark, aka Poppie Tart, aka a dozen other entries on
her computerized rap sheet.

Her face was smudged with soot and ash, and the
beaded flapper's dress she wore was burned through
to singed flesh in several places. She also had second-
degree burns on her hands and arms, which were
being dressed by paramedics from the ambulance
parked next to the fire pumper at the curb.

"I was standing at the urinal," she was telling one
of the medics. "Then this guy in a suit—big fellow,
but not fat, you know?—he comes in and tosses something over the door of one of the stalls."

She winced at the dressing the other paramedic was
placing on her burns.

"Damn, honey—this your first night? Next thing I
know, something goes 'poof,' and this little guy comes
running out of the stall, all on fire. What else could I
do? I tried to chase him down and put it out. I just
couldn't get to him fast enough."

Gil pushed his way to the tableau.

"Where's the other victim?" he asked the lead paramedic, but it was William Poplouski who answered.

"Where you think the poor fucker is?" she asked,
and a tear washed a clean streak down her cheek.
"Even when I got the fire out, I couldn't do nothing
for him."

Gil and I looked at each other, and moved through
the crowd.

Inside, the large room was dominated by a shabby,
spotlighted stage. Some of the small tables and most
of the chairs here had been overturned, as if the audience had left in a panicked rush.

Several firefighters were standing in a loose ring to
the right of the stage, staring down at the floor and
oblivious to the stench that permeated the air. As we
neared, they separated and we could see what had
focused their attention.

Tendrils of smoke still rose from a body, twisted and hideously charred. Bright shards of glass glinted under the spotlight's harsh glare like sharp-edged jewels, welded by fierce flames to what had been his head and face.

There, amid the debris of the Molotov cocktail that had burst and ignited against him, lay the lifeless remains of Paul "Sonny" Sonnenberg.

April 24

Chapter 35

The Illinois State Crime Laboratory is located at 1941 West Roosevelt Road, a modern brick building on Chicago's West Side—as the pigeon flies, only a few miles from the impressive, glass-and-steel wedding cake architecture of the James R. Thompson State of Illinois Building in Chicago's downtown. Both are relatively new buildings, though the crime lab's roof is rumored to leak significantly less.

Overall the State Crime Laboratory has benefited from its relative proximity to the State of Illinois Center. But there are also a few disadvantages, including the tendency of visiting state legislators to drop in at a moment's notice. Legislators like to know where the money is being spent, in the unlikely event a taxpayer ever has the opportunity to ask. And, being more or less human, lawmakers share the public's general fascination with seeing the latest technological marvel on which so many tax dollars have been spent.

One such technological marvel was BMRS, an acronym that stood for Ballistics Mapping and Retrieval System. Among the forensics staff, it was pronounced "bummers." This was not an affectionate nickname; BMRS was a fickle beast, as evidenced by the relative lack of hits the system had produced to date. While everybody expected that to change as more crime-scene samples were scanned into the system, BMRS had not yet engendered wild enthusiasm among the division's forensics experts.

Which was why, on this fine April morning as Ballistics Division Supervisor Darnell Whitrow stood before a visiting contingent of downstate legislators to detail the workings of BMRS, he reminded himself to refer to the system by its formal name rather than the unofficial pronunciation.

"I thought all you guys needed was a bullet," said one of the visiting lawmakers, a prosperous-looking, short man with a shiny balding head, "and you could trace it all the way back to the lead mine it came out of." His legislative district included Galena, the erstwhile hometown of U. S. Grant and, not by coincidence, once one of the premier lead-producing areas in the United States.

Darnell smiled politely.

"That's not quite the way it works," he said. "You probably know this from TV: a gun leaves distinctive markings on each bullet it fires. Basically, the rifling that's cut into the barrel of a gun presses grooves and leaves lands—the raised areas—on the surface of the projectile.

"Each bullet is just like a fingerprint—unique to the gun that fired it. Aside from some relatively minor differences related to wear inside the barrel, every bullet fired from a specific gun will all have the same markings." Darnell was into his patter now, enjoying himself.

"Traditionally, we've used what we call 'comparison microscopes' when we're trying to see if a certain gun fired the bullet. That involved optically placing two bullets side by side and examining the markings to see if we had a match."

The forensics technician made a face. "Problem is, that meant you had to have the two bullets—or, even better, a crime-scene bullet and a suspect gun. In real life, bullets can fragment or mushroom, leaving you with only a partial pattern to work with."

"I thought you test-fired the guns in the lab," one of the legislators spoke up.

"That's right—and you can get a pristine bullet from a test-firing in the lab," Darnell agreed. "Even with that, finding other crimes where the same gun had been used meant a lot of time digging through records and manually comparing any suspect bullets. Ballistics identification has always been labor-intensive—harder than actual human fingerprints to work with, from a forensics point of view."

Darnell patted the computer screen with a confidence he sincerely wished he felt. "Bummers"—*shit!* Darnell winced at his slip—"pardon me, I mean our new Ballistics Mapping and Retrieval System, changes that equation because it does most of the work electronically," he said. "Using an ultraviolet laser, it scans the surface of a bullet and creates a digital map of it. If the bullet is mushroomed, or even fragmented, the systems uses sophisticated logarithms to enhance whatever markings are discernible. Finally it files that record in an electronic database.

"Here's the payoff for Illinois law enforcement," Darnell said. "We—and all participating Illinois police departments—can access that database. When the database is completely set up, we'll be able to compare any bullet to every other bullet in the system, in seconds."

"The database is inclusive statewide? You get a bullet from, say, Peoria; you can tell if the same gun was used in a Chicago shooting?" This from a studious-looking man in a sports jacket. In one hand he carried a Palm Pilot, on which he was making notes.

Ah, a techno buff, Darnell thought to himself. *One in every crowd.* He made his face light up in an encouraging smile.

"That's it, exactly," he said. "For the first time, ballistics comparison becomes a *proactive* crime-solving tool, rather than a technique that can only react.

We've already scanned in recovered bullets from a number of crimes."

"Really?" the boyish-looking senator asked. "How far back do your records go?"

"Only for the past six months," Darnell replied apologetically. "As you can imagine, there are a lot of bullets flying around these days. We're kind of swamped trying to keep up. But over the next year, we hope to expand the ballistics files dramatically."

He hesitated, then decided to take a chance. "Maybe you'd like to see the system work?"

He turned to the attractive Asian woman who had been working at a BMRS console in a corner of the room.

"Cathy, what do you have that we can run right away?"

Cathy Li had been listening to her supervisor's practiced patter. She had heard it before. In fact, she had contributed to it, adding her comments and criticisms and suggestions—often as she lay beside Darnell in the Near North Side apartment they had shared since the previous Christmas.

She tried not to look surprised at her boyfriend-supervisor's request. A real-time demo of the system was definitely not part of the standard presentation— *and shouldn't be,* she thought, *not until the database was firmed up enough to provide a reasonable chance of a match. So now I get the opportunity to look like a boob.*

Cathy made a mental note to make Darnell pay for that transgression when the two of them were alone.

All right, Bummers—try to make me look good, okay?

She called up the most recent file, a bullet that had arrived at the lab in the morning delivery from the Cook County Sheriff's office.

"This bullet was fired at a police officer this week," she said, her hand moving over the trackpad as the digitized image rotated on the screen. "As you can see, BMRS has mapped out all the surface characteristics and generated this screen image. It's pretty precise as an image already. But let me assure you, the digitized information is even more exact. That's the data the computer is working with. It's accurate enough to be used as evidence in court, though our current practice is to confirm every BMRS match through traditional ballistics-comparison techniques."

She moved the pointer to a menu line and tapped the pad lightly twice. "We are now searching through the files to see if this mapping duplicates anything there." She looked up at the group of visitors. "It's not very likely we'll have a match," she cautioned them apologetically. "We still have a relatively small database to work with, and there's—"

"That was fast," the young senator said, impressed.

She stopped, blinking in surprise. The image had switched to a split screen mode that looked much like what you'd see in the old-fashioned comparison microscopes, except this image was much more colorful. On the left was the original green-shaded graphic of the first bullet; on the right, in shades of red and yellow marking the grooves and lands, was an image identical to it.

In capital letters, centered and flashing across both, was a single word. MATCH.

"Well, well," she muttered softly. "I'll be damned."

"I'll be damned," I said. "Tell me that again."

Gil spread his palms in a "what can I say" gesture.

"The state crime lab says that the bullet that killed Erlich in Sonnenberg's apartment came from the same gun that killed Stanley Levinstein," he repeated. "There's no mistake, Davey. After their computers picked up the match this morning, they did a test-fire of the gun. A manual comparison confirmed the match. Kolchenk's gun killed Stanley."

I sat upright in the chair, thinking furiously. "So that locks it; everything happened just as Sam Licht-

man told it. Nederlander is tied to this Russian thug,"
I said flatly. "That links him with the Russian Mafiya.
Or maybe it was some kind of contract job, with
Nederlander—"

"Davey, stop for a minute," Gil Cieloczki interrupted, and his voice was a mixture of placation and
exasperation. "Listen to yourself. This is evidence that
points *away* from Bob Nederlander. I'm not saying
there isn't a connection of some kind, somewhere—
but dammit, I'm concerned that your first inclination
is to assume as indisputable fact that there is a
connection."

I stared at Cieloczki, feeling my anger rise.

"We have Chaz's statement that Nederlander was
tanking the investigation," I said tightly. "We've established his involvement in the car insurance scam—
it's only a matter of time before we find his link to
Rebecca Hunt's murder. We have the receipts for the
gasoline he used to torch the Levinstein place. Are
you saying Nederlander isn't our primary suspect?"

"I'm saying that I won't have this investigation run
into a ditch simply because you dislike Nederlander,"
Gil said, his own tone matching mine. "Davey, every
damn thing doesn't incriminate him. If you keep acting
as if it does, trying to make everything fit a precon-
ceived notion, we are going to miss something
important."

I nodded stiffly, my lips a thin line on a face I struggled to make impassive.

"So how would you like me to proceed . . . boss?"
I asked.

Gil looked at me for a moment. Then he glanced
at his watch; it was almost noon.

"I'm going over to the hospital to see Terry and
Mel," he said. "How do I want you to proceed? I
want you to act like a trained investigator. Like a
professional."

I pivoted back to my desk, feeling a pulse pound

hot in my ears. I knew Cieloczki was right, a fact that
did little to temper my emotions.

I craved payback on Nederlander badly; I ached to
see him force-fed the same flavors of hell I had been
through. The need was a physical force in me; as I
flexed my neck I felt tendons strain and pop with the
need of it.

But I had seen other investigations derailed by that
motivation. The law needed hard-edged particulars,
cool reasoning, analytical processes. It needed facts—
incontrovertible evidence that Nederlander had led a
badge-wearing band of thieves, grifters and strong-arm
thugs into a scheme that had spread to include multiple murder.

Whatever relief my rage might provide me, it was
doing little to build a case that would stick. We
needed evidence.

And I had a good idea where we might, with luck
and a little help from the Feds, find some.

Chapter 36

"Those goddam movies have it all wrong." Chaz Trombetta grinned at me, pulling the T-shirt over his head. He wadded it into a ball and tossed it onto my coffee table. "You know—all that bullshit about some unwritten code, that no cop would ever wear a wire to catch another cop."

With thumb and forefinger, he picked gingerly at a strip of clear surgical tape under which his chest hair matted in flattened curlicues.

"Brother, is *that* a load of it," he said. "Give a guy the choice between wearing a wire and going to the slammer, there's only one question." He looked up from under the black arch of his eyebrows, waiting for me to pick up my cue.

When I didn't respond after a beat, he provided the punch line himself. " 'Where do you want me to stick the microphone, boss man?' Alimentary, my dear Watson." He looked at me, clearly peeved. "Chrissake, J. D. You're starting to turn into a real *dull* SOB."

"It'll hurt less it you don't play with it, Chaz. One fast pull, just rip it off."

"Fuckin' Santori. Bastard's giving me a little early payback."

He stared dourly down his torso. The threadlike microphone lead was taped down his chest, all the way to the tiny recorder—itself taped, snugly and intimately, where Chaz's leg joined his torso.

The arrangement minimized the chance of discovery should anyone decide a pat-down was in order. But adhesive tape pulls painfully with each movement, particularly when the wearer is possessed of the Mediterranean genes of my former partner. Earlier this morning, when he had met with Chaz to prepare the hidden wire, Santori had not thought to bring a razor to provide a smooth clearing in the jungle of follicles on Chaz's chest and lower belly. Or so the FBI agent had claimed.

But that was just physical discomfort. Worse was the strain of trying to manipulate the conversation so as to get statements that would be admissible—or even relevant—in court. Trombetta had found what countless moles and informers had always discovered: left undirected, most discussions tend to focus on irrelevant minutiae. It was seldom easy to lead the discussion to a review of the criminal activities in which the other party was engaged—at least, not without sounding both comic and suspect.

"So I says to him, 'How's the crooked-cop business going for you?' " Trombetta was saying. " 'And while you're at it, could you please speak a little more clearly into my chest?' "

I was finding it hard to match Chaz' bantering tone.

"What did you get?" I asked. "Anything we can use?"

"Mostly crap," Chaz said, and then a look of satisfaction came over his features. "And then I went up to see Dixon."

This, supplemented by the recording he had made, is the story Chaz Trombetta told me.

Chaz had, throughout the day, compiled a litany of his fellow officers' complaints—windy bitch sessions that were largely unworthy of the miniaturized computer chip on which they had been recorded.

In fact, most were just like the conversation Chaz was having now with Sergeant Dahl Dixon, seated in the windowless evidence lockup that—in casual violation of the access-limitation regulations—doubled as a lunchroom for many of the Lake Tower cops.

Dixon's voice was surprisingly high-pitched for one with a physique so wide.

"Ever wonder why I'm still a sergeant?" he asked plaintively. "I mean, hell—I've got twenty years on the job here, and Nederlander couldn't blow his nose without me. So how come I'm not a captain, or at least a goddam lieutenant?"

"Might have something to do with your record, maybe," Chaz's voice speculated. "As I recall, there was a public protest—right out there on the steps of the municipal center, wasn't it? All those citizens, upset about some bumper sticker you had. Refresh my memory: what did it say, exactly?"

"It was your basic, valid political comment." Dixon said. "And it was pretty damn funny, too. *'If I knew it was going to be such a problem, I'd have picked the goddam cotton myself.'* Ever hear of free speech?"

"Sure," Trombetta said. "It's just that not many captains, or even lieutenants, drive around with something like that on their personal car, even. Let alone on a squad car owned by the city."

Dahl Dixon shrugged. "Judgment call," he said philosophically. "Did I complain when they torched that store mannequin? The one they dressed up like a cop? No, I goddam did *not*. Not even after that sign they put around its neck. You remember what they called me?"

Chaz nodded. RACIST DIXON, the sign had said, with a swastika in the place of the x.

"Hell, they want to burn a dummy, that's their right, okay?" Dahl said, oblivious to the irony of his statement. "Free speech. But if they get it, I ought to get it, too."

"You oughta file a complaint, Dahl. You're being discriminated against."

Dixon laughed, a sour sound. "Right. Discrimination. I'm Anglo-Saxon, I'm male, I'm straight and I'm a cop. Hell, Trombo—I'm probably the last person left in America you *can* discriminate against."

Chaz grunted in what he hoped sounded like agreement, or at least appreciation. He decided to force the issue, and lowered his voice confidentially as he leaned forward.

"Dahl, what's your take on where we stand?" Chaz asked, as if he truly valued the other's observations. "Things are starting to feel real loose around here, if you get my meaning. I even heard that this Levinstein case bullshit with Cieloczki is a cover—something to keep us on the ragged edge while they're really looking at what we've been running here. Is it true? The fireman—is he getting close to chilling out Nederlander's action?"

Dixon looked at Trombetta for a moment without speaking.

"Chaz, my friend, the trick is that you gotta stay cool—cool as a cucumber, right? Look, you ain't been in as long as most of us. Trust me. Nederlander ain't gonna let anybody shut us down. Far as Cieloczki running the murder case—Nederlander's doing what needs to be done, okay?"

Chaz stitched a frustrated look on his face.

"None of us are virgins sitting here, *Sergeant* Dixon," he said. "You don't have to rub grease on it for me. But I'd feel better if I knew our fearless leader was doing more than just waiting for the roof to cave in. Think what you want about Davey—he's a damn good investigator. And Gil Cieloczki strikes me as a guy who won't just go away."

"Cieloczki gotta be one cool character, I'll agree with you there," Dixon said.

He made a show of looking around the room, as if searching for an eavesdropper.

"Look, things are in the works, okay? Week ago, I took one of the video cams out for a little exercise.

Nederlander told me to shadow Cieloczki's wife and shoot some footage. Normal shit, you know? Walking down the street, going into stores—just stuff to show we had been watching, and knew where to find her. Then I sneaked it into Cieloczki's office. Put it right on his desk."

"And?"

Dahl's lips twisted in a disgusted expression. "And Nederlander's been on my ass every other day since. Yesterday, I got fed up and told him, 'Look—I shot the tape and put it where he couldn't *not* find it. I can't help it if he's hasn't run in to you shittin' bricks over his poor, endangered wife.' "

Dahl rolled his eyes and took a bite from his meatball sandwich.

"I mean, Christ! Maybe Cieloczki's got balls of steel where his wife's concerned," he said. "Or maybe he's just tired of the old ball and chain and wouldn't mind if somebody did take her off. Fuck do I know, huh?"

Chaz frowned in shared puzzlement. "You sure he even *saw* the damn thing?"

Dahl shrugged. "I put it on his desk. It ain't there; hasn't been since the day after I did it."

"Threaten a guy's wife, you got to expect some reaction," Chaz said, hoping he was getting all this on the FBI recorder. "Especially when you're trying to shake him off a double homicide case."

"Who cares, anyway?" Dahl said, almost yawning. "Hell of a note, giving one of our cases to a goddam fireman. Nederlander wants to rattle the guy's cage, fine. But you ask me, Nederlander'd do better comin' up with something to make up for the car thing. It's starting to hit me where it hurts."

"Same here. You got anything going on I can maybe get a taste of?"

Dahl shook his head, sadly. "Nah," he said, and his face brightened with the joke. "Not a *cotton-pickin'* thing. Cotton-picking, huh? Get it?"

"Got it," Chaz replied, and summoned up a half-hearted laugh.

Cotton-pick this, *you asshole,* he thought, very aware of the recorder taped against his groin.

The quality of the videotape was poor, like much of the surveillance footage I had seen in my career. The image blurred as it moved in and out of focus, occasionally bouncing as the camera was shifted by the unseen operator. It would never win a *Palme d'Or* at Cannes. But then, it was never meant for widespread distribution. The intended audience for this movie was only one person.

Kay Cieloczki sat across from me, at an angle to the television/VCR in her living room. From the moment I arrived, as well as during the few minutes it took for us to watch the recording, she had not taken her eyes off me.

"Davey, what's this all about? Is somebody following me?"

"I don't know what to tell you, Kay," I said, trying to sound calm as well as calming. "Yes. You were followed, and somebody wants us to know that. Has Gil seen this?"

She shook her head. "I don't think so. He would have said something. I found it in the den, under a stack of things he must have brought home from the office. There was no label, no marking—I didn't know if it was a program he had taped here, or one of the training tapes Gil's people use."

She looked at me intently. "Davey, what should I do?"

I wondered if Kay sensed that I was the worst possible person to ask. I liked Kay, and respected Gil's determination and commitment. But I also understood how Gil felt about his wife. He was a firefighter, not a policeman; I had no illusions about his probable reaction. Gil had not envisioned a situation where his family would be in danger.

In all likelihood, he would pull the plug on the investigation.

I recognized how selfish I was being. I wanted Nederlander, badly; I wanted him badly enough to barter everything I possessed, and almost everything I was.

But I did not want the responsibility Kay was asking me to take.

"Kay," I said slowly, "I believe this is a real threat against you. Somebody's trying to pressure Gil by implying that you can become a target."

She nodded, a hint of impatience in the gesture. The significance of what her husband was involved in obviously had not escaped her; nor had the implications of this tape, sent anonymously to him.

"Gil would do anything to protect you," I said. There was a cautionary tone in my voice; I did not say it to provide comfort, and she knew it.

"You mean he might withdraw from this investigation," she said, and it was not a question. I nodded.

"He's told me some of what's going on, Davey," Kay said. "Maybe more than he thinks he has. I know how important all this is to everyone involved." Her eyes took on a sudden new intensity, and looked piercingly into mine. "Especially for you."

I felt a sudden sharp emotion, and recognized it as shame.

"Kay, Gil should know. Whatever . . . whatever the consequences."

There was a moment of silence that seemed to stretch forever. Then Kay's posture changed, and she shook her head.

"No, Davey," she said. "Not now. Not yet." She looked at my face, and I understood part of what Gil must have seen the first time he met her.

Before I could speak, she did.

"Try not to look so guilty," Kay said. "I'm doing this because I think it is the best thing to do."

"Kay, I don't know what kind of protection I can arrange, but I'll—"

"Finish all of this, Davey—finish it quickly," she said. "That's the best protection any of us have."

I nodded, and rose to leave. "The people who did this. We're going to get them, all of them. I promise you. And when I do, somebody is going to be very, *very* sorry."

Kay Cieloczki looked at me with eyes that saw more than I wanted to reveal.

"Davey," she said, "have they tried something like this against you?"

I shook my head. "There's nobody that I—"

I stopped short, the words stillborn in my throat.

From her seat across from me, I saw Kay's face furrow with sudden concern; her lips moved, but I no longer heard her voice.

Instead, in my mind I heard Ellen's voice, tinny over the cellular phone she had taken to carrying, making an appointment with me that I thought she had not bothered to keep.

Chapter 37

Lenny Washburn once told me that he approached the writing of his books as if they were construction projects. Assemble the needed tools. Procure the nails, lumber, the trim. Clear the time and *write* the goddam thing.

There were no flashes of deep insight, no nuances of writing style to carefully hone, no painstaking seduction of the muse. Washburn was a craftsman, not an artist. He knew this, accepted it and had even come to revel in the fact that his books were built on story, not style.

In his writing, Washburn was aggressively nonjudgmental: he laid out the facts with the precise accuracy of a master craftsman, and the facts communicated the only story they could possibly tell.

But every craftsman knows that there has to be a blueprint. All the corners must square with each other, and every structure must exist in symmetry and logic. The best craftsmen have a sixth sense that triggers alarm bells when a design—even one that, on the surface, looks rock-solid—somehow fails to make sense.

That was the problem with the story that was, by now, dominating his every waking moment.

What I had known, the facts that I had given him—to the author, they felt loose, sloppy, at best incomplete.

And that troubled Len Washburn deeply.

Which was why he was seated on a bench upwind of Buckingham Fountain, watching the less wary of the midweek tourists and midday office workers try to dodge the swirls of chilly spray shed by the choreographed, synchronized water jetting high into the air. The sun, high in a cloudless sky, warmed the back of his neck.

Had he turned his head slightly to the north, he would have been rewarded with one of the most impressive cityscapes in the world. If he had turned to the south, the broad greenbelt of Grant Park would have directed his eyes to the classical architecture of the Field Museum of Natural History, the world-famous Shedd Aquarium and the Adler Planetarium. And directly behind him, had he looked, the broad-shouldered heights of the Sears Tower soared high above the gritty hustle of the South Loop and its Sullivan-era historic buildings.

But that was the direction from which his source would approach this prearranged meeting site, and Washburn knew the strict protocols the man insisted the writer follow. He had even specified the bench on which Washburn now sat. It faced east, where the expanse of sparkling water that is Lake Michigan touched the horizon in three directions. In the foreground, a river of vehicles streamed past, their exhausts layering a shimmer over the clear April air.

His source was late. Washburn was no longer accustomed to waiting for tardy sources. In normal circumstances, he might have blown off the appointment: he had done it before with other tardy informants. But these were not normal circumstances, and this was not a normal source.

"*Mister* Washburn," a deep voice intoned from behind the writer, a mild chiding evident in its tone. "To what do I owe the pleasure of your . . . what? Should I call it a 'summons'?"

Washburn felt the bench settle heavily as his source sat beside him.

"Call it a cry for help," Len said, staring at the swaying masts of the sailboats moored in the Grant Park basin. "I need your reaction to two words: 'Operation Centurion.' And just so you understand that I'm not just on a fishing expedition, I already know it's an investigation to root out corrupt cops."

Silence, heavy as a secret sin, settled on the two men.

"Not my operation," the deep voice finally said.

"But you know whose it is. In fact, you're working with him these days, aren't you?"

Again, there was a momentary pause.

"You've been talking to some people you shouldn't." There was a measure of amusement in the words. "Or more likely, they've been talking to *you.*"

"Operation Centurion," Washburn repeated. "It's targeted on the mess in Lake Tower, isn't it? You know I wouldn't ask you if it wasn't important. Since when is Ron Santori concerned with busting dirty cops out in the suburbs? Somebody get demoted, or what?"

The bench shuddered slightly, rhythmically. Washburn was surprised; his source was quietly laughing. Then the shaking stopped, and Washburn waited with an unaccustomed patience.

"You're skating pretty close to interfering with an ongoing federal investigation. Doesn't that worry you?"

"Not much," Len shot back. "What worries me is a government agency that uses people like they were Kleenex. One that plays fast and loose with the judicial system, and suborns perjury when it's convenient. One that dicks around in a case where people are getting tortured and murdered—just to protect an 'ongoing investigation.' That kind of bullshit worries me a helluva lot. I thought it worried you."

Again, there was a pause. Then the man seated beside Len Washburn sighed deeply.

"I was around when we used to do black-bag jobs, breaking and entering, planting illegal mikes, building

files on the sex lives of political radicals," he said ruefully. "*Now* I start growing a conscience." Then he
laughed, with only a slightly bitter edginess to it.

"Look," Washburn said. "I've been researching this
almost since the start. I was in the courtroom the day
the judge dismissed charges against John Davey, and
I've been around too long not to smell a case that's
been fixed."

"You're asking me to maybe blow an important
investigation."

"I haven't asked you to do anything you didn't offer
when you first talked to me," Washburn retorted. "If
I was out to screw you, or the FBI, I've had a year
and a half to do it. I'm going to write the book on
this Lake Tower thing, and I'm going to write it
straight—but I'm convinced it's not the book I started.
Things have gone wrong, gotten out of control. And
I think you know it."

Washburn's voice rose in irritation. "I've talked to
Davey, so I know a little of what's going on now—at
least, what he *thinks* is going on. Hell, thanks to you
guys he's ready to start shooting at shadows."

"Davey. Yeah, you might say he's a little rattled. I
reached under a car seat the other day and found a
little tape recorder he had planted—he's all the way
to bugging FBI vehicles now." There was a heavy silence for a moment. "What do you think you know,
exactly?"

"I know about the Russian Mafiya going after some
kind of rare paintings. I know about the rich couple
who burned up in that house. I know Nederlander is
mixed up in it, up to his neck—and I know this is
bigger than a probe aimed at crooked cops. This Operation Centurion of yours."

Both men fell silent as a pair of young women
walked by, one of them pushing a baby stroller.

"Centurion isn't aimed at corrupt cops," the man
said, when the woman had passed beyond earshot.
"Oh, if we find a few when we turn over the rock,

fine. But Operation Centurion is designed to hunt bigger game, Mr. Washburn."

"Meaning?"

"Centurion's whole objective is to identify whatever crook is highest on the ladder. And, of course, pull him down. Hell, why do you think the bureau has spent the past two years on the damn thing?"

Len nodded, solemnly. "And of course, even a police *chief* wouldn't be high enough on the pecking order to justify that kind of investment."

It was not a question, and the writer expected no answer. For that reason, he was surprised to get one.

"Maybe not," the voice replied softly. "But the guy he's working with might be."

For the first time, Len Washburn turned to look up at the outsized man on the bench with him.

"I think maybe it's time I got all the facts, Charlie," Len Washburn said.

"Yeah," said Charlie Herndon, "I do, too."

Chapter 38

I tried to sound patient. It was, I sensed, an effort I would soon abandon.

"You want I should page him?" the police dispatcher asked, as if he had been asked to explain quantum physics. "Yo, I'll give it a shot. Wait one," he said.

I waited, listening to the slight crackle of static over the radio patch.

"They tell me Cieloczki's in the building, but I can't track down where," the dispatcher said, when he finally came back on-line. "But I know he's hot to talk with you. He wasn't happy about you deciding not to leave a number, neither."

Beside me, Chaz looked as if he was fighting down an urge to laugh out loud.

"Must be nice," the dispatcher continued, taking my silence as an invitation to converse. "Seems like everybody decided to take some time off today. First you go ten-seven, out of service, then Chaz Trombetta calls in sick after lunch. And Nederlander's been among the missing all morning. Is there, like, a holiday somebody forgot to tell the rest of us about?"

I grunted noncomittantly. "When Gil checks in, tell him I'll be back in an hour."

I imagined I could hear the dispatcher scribbling it down, probably inaccurately.

"Okay, if you say so. Any explanation I should give him?"

I pondered for a moment.

"Personal emergency. Whatever it is can wait for me to get there."

As it turned out, I could not have been more mistaken.

"I can take it through midnight," Chaz Trombetta told me. "Later, if you need me to. Hell, it's just baby-sitting, you know?"

The dashboard clock said it was quarter to two—ten hours to midnight, and a long watch by any standards. Trombetta was ready, even eager, to rack up the penance he was so certain that he deserved.

I must have looked doubtful, because Chaz underscored the offer.

"Hey, I'm serious—just gotta call Junie if it goes late." He thought for a second, then grinned. "And I think I better call her now, tell her not to let on to anybody that I'm not sick in bed at home. I can imagine what she'll do if somebody from the shop calls and tells her I checked out with stomach flu. She'll think maybe I'm stepping out on her."

We were sitting in Trombetta's car—his personal auto, not the city-issued unmarked vehicle assigned to him. When we had confirmed the threat to Kay, Chaz had wasted little time.

He immediately called in sick—his act, complete with graphic descriptions of the stomach cramps he was experiencing, was Oscar caliber. From his trunk he withdrew the tools that equipped his auto for the mission, tools selected on the basis of years spent waiting and watching from parked cars.

He pulled out a pair of binoculars, the kind with the extrawide aperture that made low-light surveillance easier. I noted the paper sack that I presumed was filled with candy bars and chewing gum, good for frequent jolts of high-energy fructose. There was also an oversized vacuum bottle for coffee, and the empty coffee can—complete with tight-fitting plastic lid—to be used as necessity required.

"It shouldn't go that long tonight," I said. "Gil's been working late hours, but he's usually home by eleven-thirty or so. I'm more worried about tomorrow, and every day after that until this thing is over."

"Yeah," he agreed. "We're staffed a bit thin for this kind of bullshit."

"I tried Santori again. His line still is there's no real threat involved. Says as long as Kay didn't want to take it any further, there's no need to tip Nederlander about how much we know." I shook my head in frustration. "Herndon wants to help, but he's locked into some kind of stakeout himself. I'd call somebody at County, except then it's certain to get back to Gil. Hell, Chaz—I should just *tell* him. If he decides to bail, that's his right."

"Sure," Chaz said. " 'Course, that kinda leaves a few other people hanging their bare tushes in the breeze. You, whenever the tax boys get the urge. Me. Maybe I'll get an adjoining cell, since I've copped to every kind of crooked-cop shit there is."

"They won't use that against you—"

"Right," Chaz said sarcastically. "You think Santori is gonna feel charitable after we've fucked up his big investigation—for the *second* time? Grow up, J. D. We do that, he's going to come down with a convenient case of amnesia. He'll forget any promises and stick it to whoever he can."

"There's no—"

"He'd do it, just to keep his own career from going down the toilet. No matter what else, Nederlander will walk. You can forget about bringing down the lowlives who killed the Levinsteins and that insurance girl. Do you get it, J. D.? Stack all that against the fact you feel guilty about keeping the investigation rolling."

He glanced at the Cieloczki house, half hidden by the parkway trees.

"From what I hear, Gil Cieloczki is an okay guy," Chaz said. "He'd *want* to do the right thing. His wife knows it, J. D. She made the decision not to put him in a position where he'd feel he had to bail. Don't *you* put him there, either."

"Yeah," I said, but my voice carried no conviction.

Chaz's words were spoken low and tight. "I'm talking from experience here," he said. "A guy thinks he's protecting his family, he'll do whatever he's got to do. Even if he knows it's not the right choice. Then it eats him up inside, every damn hour for the rest of his life. And maybe he never gets a second chance to try to make it right."

He raised his head and locked eyes with me.

"Look," he said, "let's us just handle it for a couple of days, okay? See how it plays out then, right? Posson should be out of the hospital by the end of the week. Maybe she can take a coupla days' sick leave, log a little stakeout experience off the clock. That is, if you trust her now."

"I think she's with us, solid," I replied. "Yeah. I'm sure of it. Too bad we can't use Mel, with his shoulder and all."

Chaz shook his head. "Bird hears what we're doing, he'll raise hell if you *don't* bring him in. Hate to admit it, but I kinda like the little prick."

My mind had already moved away from the long-term logistics of bird-dogging Kay Cieloczki, and back to the immediate problems it entailed.

"Well, for God's sake stay out of sight," I cautioned. "You don't want any of Nederlander's people spotting you out here." I took a deep breath, blew it out. "And that goes for Cieloczki, too. If he makes you as some kind of watcher, the whole game could go up for grabs."

My former partner looked at me from under his impressive eyebrows. "Uh-huh," he said. "You ever know anybody to spot me on a stakeout? Ever?"

He flapped his hand in an exaggerated, effeminate gesture.

"You run along now, dearie," he said. "I need anything, I'll be in touch."

At that moment, as I would find out much too late, sixty miles to the south Orval Kellogg was hanging up the telephone at the attendant's station outside Intensive Care.

"They're still tryin' to find your guy," he said, his eyes not meeting those of the man leaning against the wall nearby. "Suppose to be back in an hour, their dispatcher says."

The guard glanced into the ward, through the half-closed curtain that did not quite surround Sam Lichtman's bed twenty paces away. A form moved under the light blanket, but with only a feeble effort. "Too much longer, he'll save hisself a drive out here."

"Well—nobody should die alone," Ron Santori said, but he did not sound as if he believed his own words, or cared to conceal the fact.

Kellogg did not miss the flat, careless tone of the federal agent's comment. He studied Santori's face without appearing to.

Huh—kinda cold even for a Fed, the correctional officer thought. *'Specially after all the time them two've spent rubbin' stubs together in a locked room.*

He made a mental note to check the visitor's log—not the official register, which special visitors like Santori never signed anyway. Kellogg kept his own, unofficial visitor's book, in pencil. You could never tell when knowing the various comings and goings—*all of 'em,* he thought grimly—might turn out handy.

Over the past year, Ron Santori had spent many long hours with Lichtman. Sometimes the convict's lawyer had been present, but usually not—particularly in the past six months or so. Then this Davey guy had become a semiregular visitor, and Santori's own visits

even increased in frequency—but not once, Kellogg
had observed, had the two ever visited Lichtman at
the same time.

Orval Kellogg did not know the subject of Santori's
conversations with Sam Lichtman—secrets, he thought
dryly, and Lichtman and Santori seemed to have a lot
of those, between the two of them. Kellogg did not
like secrets, particularly when they involved one of his
prisoners. Still, FBI business was FBI business; he had
his own headaches to keep himself busy.

*See all the reasons to keep your fuckin' nose outta
it?* he told himself, sternly.

But he did resent Santori's casual arrogance. He
resented the way Santori had warned Kellogg against
mentioning his visits, specifically and categorically, to
Davey. And he particularly resented that the FBI
agent had not bothered to conceal the unspoken
threat behind the words.

And so, when Santori walked down the long
corridor—the only unlocked men's room was on the
other side of the security grate—Orval Kellogg waited
until he was out of sight. Then the corrections officer,
cursing himself silently, walked into the ward and
pushed aside the curtain at Sam Lichtman's bed.

Two eyes, sunken and narrowed with pain, blinked
death back a step or two and stared at him.

"Santori's takin' a piss down the hall," Kellogg said.
"They cain't find Davey. So if you got anything you
want me to pass 'long, now's your last chance."

"And you couldn't find her?" Father Frank Bomorito
asked, sipping at the coffee he had insisted on making
for us. We were in the kitchen of the parish rectory;
the priest had exchanged his Roman collar for a knit-
ted polo shirt that had seen better days.

"Ellen's office says she's taking a few days' personal
leave," I said. "She called them yesterday morning,
about an hour before she telephoned me from Hermosita's. I checked out our house before I came

here—*her* house, I mean. Yesterday's mail was still in the box, and there was nobody inside."

Father Frank raised his eyebrows. "You went in?"

"I still have a key."

He thought for a moment, looking as if he had something to say.

"No sign that anything was wrong," I continued. "No overturned tables or smashed lamps, nothing dramatic like that. I couldn't tell if any of her clothes were missing from her closet. It looked as if all her cosmetics were still in the bathroom."

"You're saying that you don't think she's in any danger."

"This isn't the first time she's decided to take an impromptu vacation, Father."

"I know that. But the situation is a little . . . *unusual* right now."

"Coercion only works when the threatened person knows about it," I said, not meeting his eyes. "If somebody wanted to use Ellen to leverage me, they'd have to tell me that they have her."

"Cut the crap, Davey. You're worried."

"She said she thought somebody was following her, but she didn't act like a woman being stalked. At the time, I thought it was just Ellen being Ellen. Yeah, I'd feel better now if I knew where she was."

"Why did she call you from that restaurant? Why wasn't she waiting there for you?"

"I don't know, Father," I said, suddenly angry. "Ellen plays games. Maybe she just wanted to see if I'd come. For all I know, she was at another restaurant across the street, watching poor dumb me stand there like a mope. Then she took off for a few days R and R without a second thought."

He sipped at his coffee and regarded me with serious eyes.

"How about this one: why did *you* go, Davey?"

"I guess it's our pattern," I said. "Or my pattern, at least. When we were married, I walked out a half dozen times; she threw me out at least as many. Each time, I thought it was over and that I was—'free' isn't quite the right word. Cured, maybe."

I shrugged. "But there always came a night when I'd find myself standing outside her door, like a cat scratching to be let back in. I guess some things never change."

He nodded, and there was sympathy in the gesture.

"There's a term for the kind of pattern you're describing, Davey. They're called 'toxic relationships,' and they're usually destructive to both parties."

"I know," I replied. "That doesn't make it any easier to stop."

"As a Catholic priest, I counsel people to make their marriage work, whatever it takes," Father Frank said. "I might advise you to try a lot harder—to make your *divorce* work. Don't tell the Pope."

I checked my watch and stood. "Thanks for the advice, Father. And for the coffee."

"You didn't touch the coffee."

"I don't know if I can take the advice, either," I said.

It was almost four-thirty when I walked into the office. Through the opened door, I saw Gil look up as I entered. He met me midway across the room. From the expression on the firefighter's face, my first thought was that Gil had somehow found out that I had concealed from him the videotape threat to Kay.

"Where the *hell* have you been?" he demanded, with uncharacteristic heat.

I took a chance.

"Personal business, Gil," I said, not meeting Cieloczki's eyes. "I needed some time. I'm sorry."

He studied my face for a moment.

"You know better," he said. "It doesn't happen again."

His voice was flat, stating a fact. I nodded.

"Stateville called more than two hours ago," Gil

said. "They said that Lichtman's condition was crashing, and he was asking to talk to you."

"Jesus," I breathed. "I'll get down there now, talk to him."

"The conversation will be a trifle one-sided," Gil said, and his voice was still angry. "They just called again. Sam Lichtman died thirty-four minutes ago."

Chapter 39

There were not a lot of neighborhoods in Lake Tower that one could call a slum, let alone a site known nationwide as an environmental dead zone. But there was one: the Stannard Munitions complex, an abandoned hulk of flaking masonry and ground-cast concrete that occupied ten overgrown acres on the western city limits.

At the peak of the Vietnam War, even inefficient, outdated plants like Stannard Munitions could be flogged for the last government dollar they could bring. But when Vietnam had finally bled down enough to make marginal production sites like Stannard obsolete, there was no reprieve. Less than two years after Tet showed there was no light at the end of the tunnel, Stannard also was dark and abandoned.

A commitment to cost savings by the plant's last environmental manager—who was also its first—helped ensure it would stay that way. Reflecting the unconcealed viewpoint of his management, the engineer considered out-shipping even the most toxic manufacturing byproducts as an unnecessary expense. What was not dumped outright on a far corner of the site was sealed into steel drums and stacked along a back wall.

Inevitably, they leaked.

Seven years after it closed, Stannard was placed on the waiting list for massive Superfund environmental cleanup, where today it still remained. Not surprisingly, that fact had discouraged prospective developers.

But the building, surrounded by a shiny chain-link fence the EPA had installed, had not remained entirely empty. Chain-link fencing is easy to climb and easier to cut through, even by people too dazed or too desperate to read warning signs.

That was why Donald Lundeen and Josie Clark, his partner-of-the-month, were gingerly stepping through the soggy, debris-strewn labyrinth, at about the same time Gil Cieloczki was telling me of Sam Lichtman's death. In the Lake Tower Sanitation Department, checking out the Stannard Munitions property was a regular, if distasteful and potentially dangerous, routine.

Clark wore reinforced waders. Lundeen, who had two years' more experience, preferred the heavy steel-shanked boots he had purchased—with his own funds—from a retired firefighter. They both wore Class IV full-face respirators and Tyvek coveralls, which were mandatory fashion accessories for visits to Stannard.

As always, they had spread out to a five-yard interval—the better to cover ground quickly. The two health workers were hoping to wrap up the chore before dark. Already, their room-by-room canvass of the massive building had taken almost two hours.

Neither had found anything out of the ordinary, a fact which depressed Lundeen. That was not out of the ordinary, either; everything about the Stannard property depressed him. He occasionally wondered if depression might be one side effect of the chemicals here. He doubted it; any reaction to this place other than depression was what would have been unnatural.

He could understand the broken bottles, most of them pints of inexpensive whiskeys and fortified wines. Alcoholism is a disease, he knew, and a progressively degenerative one at best. *By the time you get down to drinking this stuff,* he thought to himself, noting the off-brand labels on the broken bottles, *it's definitely any-port-in-a-storm time.*

The broken needles and smashed glass crack vials were considerably more depressing. Still, Lundeen had to admit that the concept of using whatever means possible to escape a reality that defined this place as "shelter" had an undeniable, logical appeal. In a bleak sort of way, of course.

Then there were the condoms.

Lundeen had long ago accepted that there was often a wide gulf between love and sex. As a health worker, he had often seen the much closer relationship between sex and commerce played out on the streets.

But to do it here, amid the rats and the human excrement and the lingering substances that could raise blisters—Lundeen just shook his head in near despair.

Once, a fellow health worker had suggested that perhaps the condoms had been used to transport drugs. Lundeen had, for a while, found even *that* notion almost cheering. Just about anything was better then the other images evoked by the pitiful latex spoor.

All these things were bad. But there was something worse—something that completely perplexed him, and would utterly depress him for days. It was the toys. For Lundeen, worst of all were the child's toys they would occasionally find as they picked their way through places like this.

"How," he would ask whoever was his partner on days such as these, "how can anybody take their kids into a . . . a goddam vile *hole* like that?" He would obsess on the subject, embellishing the actuality of what he had seen with mental images that bordered on the grotesque.

And Don Lundeen had an imagination that was vivid, to say the least. That was the main reason his partners seldom lasted more than one thirty-day as-

signment cycle—that, and Lundeen's habit of drifting
ever deeper into his bleak musings.

Josie Clark was now on Day 22, and no longer saw
a benefit in maintaining even the appearance of a
chummy relationship.

"Don! Yo, Lun-*deen*—hey, shake it out your ass, all
right?" Josie was standing at the far wall, leaning one
work-gloved hand against the crumbling red bricks.

At this rate, she thought sourly, *we'll have to come
back to this rat hole tomorrow.*

Josie watched her coworker trudge sadly through
the muck and assorted trash. She sighed; Don Lundeen wasn't a bad guy—he was just a walking argument for mandatory lithium therapy.

"Let's try to pick up the pace, okay?" she suggested, as mildly as she could manage. It still came
out sounding like a rebuke. Lundeen nodded, and
through the plastic faceplate she saw the expression
in his eyes. Josie Clark recognized the signs, and she
shook her head violently.

"Don, I don't want to hear it," she said. "I've been
working with you less than a month, and I'm spending
half my pay on Valium and Saint John's wort. You're
not just a depressed guy; you're a *carrier*."

They walked down a windowless corridor, and
turned a corner. This was once the assembly area of
the plant, where even a frugal management recognized
the essential value of light.

In its heyday, the place had been a beehive of activity. Vehicles pulled trains of low carts into the room.
They entered from one side filled with brass casings
packed with propellant, or steel-and-lead projectiles
filled with a smorgasbord of lethalities. The cart trains
left filled with artillery shells, ready to be loaded on
trucks for shipment. Here, rows upon rows of indus-
trial windows had once filled the high walls.

No longer. Would-be fastball pitchers, practicing
with chunks of brick, had shattered most of the lower
glass panes long years before; BB gun marksmen had

taken out the rest. An army of glaziers could work
for a week, and still not fill all the sharp-edged holes.

But at least it was bright here. The late afternoon
sunlight poured into the room, a blinding glare that
dazzled the eyes of the two workers. Josie shielded
her eyes, squinting in the unaccustomed brightness.
Don looked away, scanning the far end of the cavern-
ous room.

Which was probably why Don noticed it first.

He squinted, trying to see clearly through the glare
off his plastic faceplate.

"Josie—you see that?" From behind the respirator,
his voice came out flat and other-worldly.

It was a burned-out car. The tires had flamed and
burst, and the vehicle squatted on its rims in the center
of an irregular burn ring. Somebody had pulled it into
the building through one of the old shipping entrances,
and torched it. On the muck-covered floor, a second,
larger set of tire tracks led out the same way.

They approached the car, interested but not surprised. This was not the first burnt-out hulk they had
found in the Stannard complex. Most of them were
old beaters, or had been stripped for whatever parts
could be easily sold.

*This one looks like it was fairly new before it caught
fire,* Lundeen thought. *Not stripped—not even the tires
were pulled. That's odd.* Aside from the damage when
the tank blew, the vehicle appeared relatively intact,
though he noticed that no license plates hung on the
blackened bumpers.

Then Josie Clark stooped, and peered intently
through the cracked, soot-coated window. She stiffened, and her eyes opened wide behind her faceplate.

"Don," he heard her shout to him, "I think there's
a *guy* in there."

Lundeen stepped closer. He saw the car was a Ford,
a Taurus that might once have been painted green.
He cupped his hands against the passenger window
and pressed his face close to the heat-crazed glass.

Up until then, he sincerely believed his dreams—both asleep and awake—were already populated by the worst the Stannard had to offer.

As he looked inside at the blackened figure slumped forward stiffly against the charred steering wheel, he realized how wrong he had been.

Chapter 40

The harsh fluorescent lighting in the police department made my eyes burn, and the chronic headache it fueled pounded in my temples. I felt drained, and very close to defeat.

I was sitting at Terry's desk, again; this time, the piles of paper, files and assorted detritus seemed to me too wearying to contemplate.

Lichtman's death had not been unexpected, but he had been the one constant on which I had fallen back every time the case hit a dead end. I still had no clear picture of his motives, even now, and I held to no illusions that Lichtman was acting from pure benevolence.

But the question of how much, if anything, anyone owed Sam Lichtman was a moot point now; those ledger books had been cleared and sealed to mortal eyes forever. There would be no more answers from him.

Finish the job quickly, Kay had said. But whenever a door looked as if it might lead to an answer, someone slammed it shut. I looked again at the case files I had pulled from the safe. They provided no answers—only more questions, more blood-stained squares in a patchwork of violence that I still could not force into a coherent picture.

The missing artwork was the key, of that I was certain. Stan and Kathleen Levinstein had acquired it, and both died. Rebecca Hunt had faked insurance documentation on it, and that had ensured her death, too. Sonnenberg had tried to steal it from the Levinsteins, and for his troubles had been incinerated by a gasoline bomb. The two Russians at his apartment wanted it; one of them was now dead, along with the county cop named Erlich. The other Russian had been ready to kill Posson and Bird to find it, and had almost succeeded on both counts.

He was still out there, along with God knew how many others willing to kill and maim over a collection of damnable artwork—and I was running out of leads to follow.

I thought about calling the Travers woman again, and wondered why.

I had tried to reach her several times throughout the day, only to listen to the ringing of an unanswered telephone. The phones were either still off the hook or, like me, she had no answering machine.

I found the thought somehow intriguing. When she wasn't seducing the random artist, did she live in an enforced isolation? Was it to deny outsiders one more way to admit themselves, easily and indiscriminately, to her life? She had mentioned being estranged from her husband; was this her method of holding him away, of denying him the opportunity for either reconciliation or recrimination?

Or did she simply prefer to ignore her ringing telephone, seeing it as an uncouth electronic challenge to her own sense of privacy and of self?

I suddenly smiled, realizing just how tired I was. I had busily constructed a complex picture of Ms. Marita Travers that revealed more about myself than about a woman I had met only once. Of the mores or motivations of Marita Travers, I had no clue.

That was, however, an easy lapse to remedy. Gil was still in his office, and that meant that Chaz was still outside Kay Cieloczki's house. I had a choice: if I left now, I could take over the watchdog job for the hour or so until Gil called it a night.

Or I had time to satisfy a certain curiosity before it became yet another obsession.

I checked my watch: a few minutes past eight-thirty. It was still early, and the Travers' address was only slightly out of my way.

Chapter 41

Later, when it was all over and the paper-pushers had taken over, the bureaucrats wrote a postmortem. With twenty-twenty hindsight, one of the questions they raised involved the whereabouts of Nederlander on the final day of the Levinstein case.

How, the authors wondered—with no effort to contain their sarcasm—could a police chief simply not show up for duty one morning without raising an alarm, or at least a few eyebrows? It was a valid question, but one that overlooked the realities of Nederlander's authoritive—even dictatorial—rule.

It is a fact that he—or at least, his car—had been seen that very day, parked near the Lake Tower Municipal Center. Not just seen, but the image logged and recorded on the digital surveillance system that had been installed throughout the municipal center the year before.

One of the Big Brother cameras was mounted on an exterior corner of the building, so as to command the street outside. There, at ten frames per minute, it dutifully recorded a vehicle that had parked for hours down the street.

It was a shiny black Lincoln Navigator, and subsequent digital enhancement of the license plates showed the vehicle was registered to one Robert J. Nederlander.

He must have been watching all day, waiting for his

quarry. It was not the most exciting way to spend a day, but at least his car was large and comfortable.

Once, in the early afternoon, when he had spotted Talmadge Evans leaving the building on foot, he had left the Navigator where it was parked on the corner opposite the municipal center, and risked following on foot.

According to the surveillance camera that captured his image, Evans had walked down the street to a small coffee shop; a burly man, who is seen only from the back, left the Navigator and followed. The city manager had spent fifteen minutes there, then returned to his office. He had not reappeared the rest of the day.

Finally, shortly before eight-thirty, the recording showed Evans crossing the parking lot to his own car and pulling away.

If Evans noticed the big black vehicle, following him at a discreet distance, he gave no sign.

Chapter 42

"Mr. Davey." Marita Travers sounded as if she had expected me, though I had not called to make an appointment. "Would you care to assist us?"

Her eyes sparkled with a slightly unfocused resolve, and in the hand not braced against the open door was a tall glass only partially filled with an amber liquid. With it, she motioned me into the house, spilling only a teaspoon's worth in the effort.

I stepped around a stack of boxes, badly packed suitcases and men's clothing still on hangers that had been dropped haphazardly on top of the pile.

"Please forgive the—" She searched for the word, then dismissed it with a fluttering of fingers. "It's moving day, and Peter is helping." She turned and cupped her hand at her lips.

"Peter!" In a less elegant woman, it might have been called a bellow. "Help has arrived!"

"You're moving?"

She looked at me brightly. "Me? Oh, no. I live here."

At that moment, Peter Comstock came around a corner, bent forward from the weight of the carton he held in his hands; his face was smudged with sweat and dust. He walked to the pile near the door and dropped the box with an expensive-sounding crash.

Then he straightened, with the exaggerated care of a person who has imbibed well but not wisely.

"Peter, this is Mr. Davey," Marita said. "Mr. Davey, Peter-Comstock-the-abstractionist." She made it sound like one word. "Darling, he has offered to help you carry that big wooden . . . *thing* from the lower level."

The artist grinned. "Thank God. It's a hell of a heavy crate for one man. Especially one who hasn't slept for a week."

"Peter has completed three and a half paintings while he's visited here," Marita said. "They are manifestations of his evolution as an artist, Mr. Davey. But he is too proud to keep them, you see."

I didn't, but that did not slow the conversation.

"Peter, are you sure?" she asked. "They're yours, if you want them."

Peter nodded with grim determination, and the slight swaying of his body diluted the effect only minimally.

"I don't," he said. "It's *his* canvas—I just spread a little fresh paint on the back. Your husband can decide which side he wants to face out. Far as I'm concerned, they leave with the rest of his stuff. I put 'em back in that damn crate and screwed it shut. Except for the one you want me to finish."

"Pardon me," I asked, "but what's going on?"

"She's throwing him over for me," Comstock said, patient as if explaining to a child. "He doesn't even live here, you know. Hasn't, for months. So all the stuff he's stored in Marita's house goes to the trash."

"To storage, darling," Marita corrected him. "I don't want to be uncivil, or to . . . to anger him."

"Screw him. I don't care if he's angry or not."

Marita turned to the artist. "Peter, you should know that my husband is . . . a dangerous man. He is involved in activities that may be—that *are*—illegal."

Comstock frowned. "What kind of activities?"

"The kind that get your telephone tapped, or your car followed," she said. "The kind that causes people from the government to examine your bank account. The kind that makes those people question some of your friends, who then can't wait to ask you about it. Those kinds of activities, Peter."

She finished her drink, and carefully centered the empty glass on a lamp table. "I guess you think I should tell the police," she said to me, in a chastising voice.

"I am the police," I said. "Sort of."

"The police?" she said, and her eyes opened wide. "If you're with the police, you know about—" She stopped, as if she had said too much.

"Ms. Travers, right now I don't know about anything. Except that I want to see these paintings."

"Most of them are in a shipping crate, downstairs. But the one Peter is using is still on the dining room table."

We walked through the kitchen and into the dining room, with its dark cherry formal chairs and oval table aligned beneath an impressive brass-and-crystal chandelier.

On the table rested a large canvas mounted on a modern metal-rod stretcher—remounted, rather; a row of small rust-marked holes around the edge of the fabric indicated where mounting pins had been removed from a traditional wooden stretching frame. I picked it up and examined the whorls of paint brilliant against age-darkened canvas; it was the piece on which Comstock had been working when I visited earlier.

And then I turned the frame in my hands, and the mystery that had cost Stanley and Kathleen Levinstein their lives suddenly became clear.

The three of us walked back toward the front of the house in single file; I walked with caution, mindful of the value I held between my two hands. Whatever the thoughts of my companions, they held them quiet inside.

Marita was still in front when we reached the large foyer. She stopped short, so abruptly that Peter almost crashed into her, and I into him.

In the still open doorway, surrounded by the stacks of what he obviously recognized as his belongings, Talmadge Evans stood staring at the three of us.

"Hello, Talmadge," Marita said cordially. Ignoring me, she addressed the artist. "Peter," she said, as if the situation was the most natural thing in the world, "this is my husband."

Before anyone else could speak, Talmadge Evans lurched forward, his hands outspread. For an instant, I thought he intended to attack Marita, to seize her by the throat in fury.

But he was only stumbling forward, his arms flailing to keep his balance.

A large man had replaced Evans in the doorway. The heavy revolver he held in his hand was steady, as he stepped inside and closed the door behind him. I saw his face brighten as his eyes fastened on the painting I held.

"I think we have much to discuss," he said. "I am told, by an unimpeachable source, that you have several items here I have been employed to recover. It seems he spoke truly."

His left index finger pointed to Evans. "You. If you continue to move your hand, I will shoot you in the stomach."

He stepped forward and removed a small revolver from Talmadge Evans' belt. His lip twisted in derision as his thumb snapped open the cylinder.

"Such a useless toy!" he chided. "Fit only for children to shoot at empty soup tins."

The Russian shook the weapon, and six .22-caliber cartridges clattered on the hardwood floor. He threw the empty pistol through the arched entry into the dining room.

"Who are you?" Evans said, as though offended rather than frightened.

"Ah, forgive my poor manners," he said, but his

face betrayed no geniality. "You may call me Mikhail."

"I have a message from a mutual acquaintance," I said, looking hard at the Russian. "A police officer named Posson. You told her she was lucky."

"I remember."

"She says you can take your luck and shove it."

"How refreshingly blunt," Mikhail said. "I, too, have a message you may deliver to her. One way or another."

With characteristic thoroughness, Mikhail had brought along a roll of packing tape. The polyester filaments bonded inside the cellophane could immobilize an angry orangutan, if one used it as he had ordered me to do.

It was a small roll, barely enough to wrap each wrist with what a less self-confident man might have felt was a sufficient number of turns. Judiciously, he had told me to secure the artist first and the woman last. He kept his pistol leveled at me as he checked my handiwork.

"Like *The Three Bears*," Mikhail laughed. "If you used perhaps too much on the larger man and perhaps too little on the woman, at least the length used on the older man was just right."

He patted me down, smiling when he found my Smith & Wesson automatic. "A *real* weapon, yes? Join them, please keeping your hands on the top of your head."

Now we sat, side by side, on the ivory-colored silk sofa, against which Mikhail had also propped the painting—or rather, the two paintings, modern and antique, one on either side.

At the moment, in a decision based on more than a century of critical acclaim, the Comstock painting was turned from view. Instead, the Russian contemplated the painstakingly unique style of Cézanne's *Ville du Temps*.

"You know," Mikhail remarked, casually, "I am told that this single piece would be valued at more than thirty million U.S. dollars. That is, if one could place any figure on such a work." He shrugged. "Myself, I do not see it. It is just one more old painting—and there are so many old paintings in the world, no?"

He turned his stare to his captives.

"For example, there are eight others quite near to us at this moment, are there not? Somewhere in this very house, I have been told."

He stepped close to Talmadge Evans, who looked up at him silently through expressionless eyes.

"You, my aged gunslinger," he said, not unkindly. "Would you like to tell me? Come, grandfather—speak to me, eh? No?"

He turned to Peter.

"Perhaps you are more informative, yes?" Mikhail said, for all the world as if he were asking directions from some perversely reluctant passerby. Without waiting for an answer, he turned to Marita: "Or you, lovely lady. Do you not wish to aid me?"

"Say nothing," Talmadge Evans said calmly.

Mikhail raised his eyebrows.

"That is one option, I am sure," he said, as if he were weighing the choices available to us. "Another is for me to employ my considerable powers of persuasion on each of you, in turn. I will then compare the answers which all of you will, I assure you, provide to me."

He smiled, and gave a dismissive shrug.

"The final option is for me to burn this house to the ground—with all of you in it, of course. You see, I am no sentimentalist. These paintings you have hidden here—it is the simple knowledge that they exist that presents a danger to my employers."

He addressed Evans. "You must appreciate the irony of solving this matter by fire," Mikhail said. "It is a solution you—please do not quibble: the policeman was your underling, this I know as truth—also

employed in the home of the Jew Levinstein. Better
if they had been destroyed in that fire; I would already
be on a warm beach somewhere, spending my fee for
this assignment."

His voice took on a scolding tone. "But you see,
you cleverly convinced the Jew to turn these paintings
over to you"—he winked at Marita, a broad vaudevil-
lian gesture—"for 'safekeeping,' is that not hilarious?"

He returned his smile to Evans. "I will tell you a
secret, old one. Had not an *idiot* been with me, I
would have known your name from the start. Poor
Mr. Levinstein would have told me, assuredly. But I
was cursed with an inept assistant, and your Jew died
too soon—not as you had planned, perhaps, but dead
is dead, no? And then you had your pet policeman,
this Nederlander, burn that beautiful home to the
ground. Such a pity, no?"

Mikhail's smile disappeared, abruptly and chillingly.
"So you have the paintings, and I have *you*."

He stared at Evans with eyes that spoke of death.

When Evans replied, his voice carried no more apparent emotion than if he were rebuking some errant
subordinate for a minor lapse of judgment.

"In a few minutes—fifteen at most—two officials
from the Russian Consulate will arrive," Evans said.
"Do not act in a way which you will certainly regret."

"So? Enlighten me, please."

"I have been in discussions with one of them for
some weeks, and we have reached agreement. The
artwork will be returned to your government. Its existence will remain confidential, or at least unconfirm-
able. But if you violate this arrangement—*in any
way!*—you will answer to your government for it."

Mikhail listened, thoughtfully nodding.

"Perhaps that is another option," he said reasonably.
"My way is much more simple, and I am a simple man.
We will see—if your 'Russian officials' arrive soon."

The doorbell rang, a refined double chime. Mikhail
grinned at Evans broadly.

"Rather, I should say 'when' they arrive. Such excellent timing, yes?"

Mikhail stepped sideways to the door and squinted through the small door light. He nodded, as if in recognition.

Mikhail opened the door like a host welcoming dinner guests.

"How are you tonight, Anatoli Tarinkoff?" he said, in English. "And who is this lovely woman?"

Anatoli Tarinkoff grunted a response. His eyes swept the room, noting without reaction Mikhail's captives on the sofa, accepting as normal the fact that our hands were taped in front of us. He appeared outwardly calm at finding Mikhail here; but his companion did not. She stared at him, and then around the room, eyes wide as if her worst fears had been confirmed.

Petra Natalia Valova looked like a woman nearing the end of her rope. Her distress at our tape-wrapped tableau was apparent, and the very effort to conceal it only added to her agitation.

I was certain I knew what she was thinking. Valova clearly understood the potential consequences if it became widely known that the paintings existed; as the Pushkin's senior curator, she had been responsible for maintaining the secret. But she also considered herself responsible for their preservation—indeed, their survival. At first, perhaps, she had not grasped that the secret was as inviolate as the paintings were expendable. Now she did, and the knowledge was ravaging her.

Tarinkoff must have known, have understood all along. He had to be an agent of State Security, under deep cover; it was the only explanation for his presence here. Perhaps he, too, was pained by the thought of destroying the artwork; still, his training would make him philosophical about certain unpleasantness. But he would be worried about Valova's instability. He could well predict her reaction if the need to destroy the paintings became a reality.

But I was also certain that neither the fate of the paintings, nor that of the others in the room with him, was his most immediate concern. I watched his side-long glances at Mikhail, and observed how he studied the door and windows around the room.

To my mind, he had the look of a man faced with a worrisome dilemma, one unsure whether the greater danger existed outside or within.

I had recently felt the same anxiety, one that had increased with each mile as I neared Lake Tower. It was the belief that one set of headlights behind me had become a too familiar, troubling feature of the landscape.

At that instant, from outside came the crunching sound of tires on the gravel drive.

Chapter 43

"We are expecting more company, perhaps?" Mikhail's eyes had narrowed, and his voice—though still level and reasonable—had lost its bantering tone. At the sound of an auto crunching to a stop on the graveled drive outside, he had become unnaturally, ominously alert.

Then the door shook under three hammer strokes.

"Answer it," he said to Tarinkoff, and it was not a request. He smiled, dangerously without mirth. "If it is the police—well, you have diplomatic immunity, and I do not."

Tarinkoff moved to the door, and to me it was obvious that the art attaché was already reviewing the range of possibilities facing him.

It could be the proverbial misdirected pizza delivery. If so, it was good luck for Tarinkoff and bad luck for the hapless delivery boy. For an official of the Russian Consulate to be seen at an address that, I had no doubts, would feature prominently in the news by this time tomorrow—well, that could not be permitted. In such a case, the delivery boy would be invited inside, and Mikhail would have one more addendum to his assignment's final report.

On the other hand, if Tarinkoff had been followed, it could have been only by the FBI or some other law enforcement authority—in which case his predicament was dire. He was probably safe enough from the

Americans; Tarinkoff did have diplomatic immunity, and I thought it unlikely he would be foolish enough to provoke any hostile response before he made that fact known.

No, the real danger came from the Mafiya cowboy, who had skewed everyone's calculations merely by showing up.

I had no illusions about Mikhail's intentions, and I was certain Tarinkoff also understood. Should anything unexpected happen, Mikhail's first impulse would be to shoot anything and everybody, including any cultural attaché who might be inconveniently in the line of fire.

Tarinkoff opened the door, wide enough for him to at least attempt a rolling dive to the bushes outside if it proved necessary.

I saw his mouth light up in a smile, but I was not prepared for what he said next.

"*Mister* Santori," he said, emphasizing the civilian honorific to avoid any chance it might sound like an official title. "What brings you here?"

"What the hell is Nederlander's car doing outside?" an angry voice said, as Tarinkoff stepped aside to admit the unexpected visitor. "And exactly what are you doing here, Mr. Tarink—"

Ron Santori stopped in midword at the sight of Mikhail's gun pointed at his chest. He stood stock-still as Tarinkoff closed the door, and stiffened only slightly when the attaché patted him down and removed the pistol from his belt.

"He is alone?" Mikhail's eyes flickered to Tarinkoff only for an instant before returning to the new arrival.

"So—our little company has grown again!" Mikhail said. "Please join us out here—being most careful, of course, to keep your hands on the top of your head."

At his gesture, Santori walked slowly, carefully into the large sitting room. As he did so, he passed momentarily before a window. Its curtain was only slightly ajar; as it turned out, that was enough.

Chapter 44

Charlie Herndon moved well for a man of his size and relative age. He stayed in the dim shadows that dappled the lawn, and followed the lines of sculpted shrubbery until he half squatted against the brickwork of the house. He was not, he noted with a measure of pride, even breathing hard.

At least, he thought, *not that hard.*

Following the Russians had not been a difficult task. He had been double-parked down the street from the garage where Tarinkoff kept his consular car, a shamefully decadent Cadillac Seville. As the Russian had steered though the Gold Coast traffic, Charlie Herndon had merely stayed several cars back, counting on his peripheral vision to deal with the rest of the northbound traffic flow.

Now, what could be so important to drag you out this time of night? Herndon thought to himself. *With the lovely Dr. Valova in tow, no less.*

He kept what he hoped was the right distance behind the Seville with the consular license plates—not so close he could be tagged easily, not so far that the unpredictability of the city traffic could easily cut him off from his quarry.

Jeez, he thought, *when was the last time I did a street tail—let alone a solo job?*

It was a rhetorical question; Herndon had known the answer all too well, and decided to ignore it. At

least he was in one of the older cars in the FBI pool:
a dark blue Crown Victoria, a gas-guzzling battleship
with a seat large enough to fit his oversized frame.

He relaxed somewhat when the car he was following
turned onto Lake Shore Drive. Now he could fall back
a little more without the risk that a sudden turn could
end the chase.

"Okay, Mr. Tarinkoff," the FBI agent said aloud,
"lead on and I'll follow. I've got a full tank of gas,
and all night to waste."

In unconscious tandem, the two cars sped north-
ward.

But then things became even more interesting, as
he drew up beside another northbound auto. Something about the car, or the profile of the driver, struck
alarm bells in Herndon's head.

"What the hell?" In his surprise, he had spoken
aloud. "Santori, you son of a bitch."

Without making it obvious, he fell back. He did not
know why Ron Santori would have chosen to follow
a Russian consular car; but he did not believe in coin-
cidences, either.

Once in Lake Tower, it had taken all his remembered skills to keep both of his target vehicles in view
on the thinly trafficked streets. Finally, he had
watched with furrowed brow as the Cadillac pulled
into the circular drive of a large house alongside several other vehicles. Santori, too, had stopped, watching
the two figures enter. For several minutes, he sat at
idle, and Herndon fancied that the dark silhouette of
the other agent wavered in indecision; then Santori
followed the Russians' lead.

But when Santori had stepped inside the house,
Herndon could have sworn he saw the agent stop
short an instant before the closing door blocked his
view.

That could mean nothing, or everything.

Short of kicking in the door, there was only one
way to find out.

And so now Herndon was at a window, the glow from inside diffused by the curtain drawn across it. He cursed silently and guided himself along with one hand lightly grazing the cool brick wall.

He had better luck at the next window; a gap, no more than a half inch wide, where the curtains did not quite meet. If he stretched—*like this!*—and twisted his head like this—*dammit, that hurt!*—he could just see inside the room where—

He pulled back, quickly and silently. The trip back to his car took longer than the previous foray, because Herndon now knew the odds were much higher.

Herndon slid into the car seat, ignoring the radio microphone that hung almost out of sight below the dashboard. He trusted neither the Lake Tower airwaves nor the resources they might dispatch. Instead, he fumbled his cellular phone from his coat pocket and thumbed the buttons. A calm voice responded midway through the first ring.

"Federal Bureau of Investigation, Central Dispatch," a male voice said. "State the nature of your emergency."

"Federal Central, this is Special Agent 1488," Herndon said, speaking in a low growl. "I have a hostage situation in progress. Lake Tower, 2759 Terrace Pointe." He smiled to himself, and raised the ante. "One bureau agent and possibly two members of a foreign diplomatic mission may be among the hostages."

"Ten-four," the voice came over the airways, unflappable as always. Herndon wondered how dispatchers stayed so calm. "Hostage situation in progress. Number 2759 Terrace Pointe, Lake Tower. Stand by, 1488."

Thirty seconds later, the dispatcher again spoke.

"Agent 1488, we've scrambled the HRT alert team. Be advised their ETA at your location is twenty minutes. Do you require immediate backup from the Lake Tower police?"

"Hell, no—I mean, negative on that, Central. Do not, repeat, do *not* contact Lake Tower PD. We're running a local corruption case here, and they may be part of the problem."

There was a moment of silence as the dispatcher digested that information.

"Ten-four. Okay, we have the HRT en route by helicopter. Stand by for their arrival. Do not attempt entry or initiate action until that time. Also, Chicago SAC is being alerted as to the situation. We will patch her through to you for direct briefing."

"Yeah," Herndon replied, "1488 standing by." He made the dispatcher repeat his cell phone number and broke the connection, his lips pursed.

Twenty minutes. If this all blows up, that's twenty minutes too late. I need somebody to watch my back, now. *And I've run out of options.*

He flipped through the small spiral notebook he always carried, until he found a list of names and numbers. Gil Cieloczki's house was only minutes away, based on the address Davey had given him. Scrawled a few lines under it was the name Chaz Trombetta, and the number of a cellular phone.

Maybe you can *bend a crooked cop back,* he said to himself, punching in the numbers.

The hammering on the side door was loud and insistent—definitely not Gil, Kay Cieloczki knew, not even if he had somehow misplaced his house keys. Cautiously, she peered through the glass of the door light. Outside, a dark figure held up a policeman's badge for her to see.

Given the recent events, it could not have eased her concern.

She snapped the chain into its metal slot before opening the door the few inches it allowed.

"Yes? What is—"

The voice was low and urgent as it interrupted.

"Mrs. Cieloczki, I'm working with Davey—but

something important's come up and I have to leave. Ma'am, I need you to lock your door and not let anybody in until your husband—"

At the same instant, they both heard the movement from the darkness behind. Kay's eyes widened as the man on her porch half spun, his hand flashing under his suit coat.

"No!" she said, and there was fear in her voice. "That's my—"

"What's going on?" Gil Cieloczki demanded, staring at the large pistol that was now pointing steadily at his chest. He swallowed hard in a mouth suddenly dry. "What's this about?"

Chaz Trombetta lowered the heavy automatic, and let out the breath he had been holding. The ragged sound could have mistaken for a sigh.

"Ask me in an hour, Chief Cieloczki," he said, his voice unsteady as he looked at the man he had almost shot. "It looks like we're all about to find out."

Chapter 45

Marita Travers' house was old; in a place less patrician, the room where we had been herded would been called the basement. It showed no evidence of regular maintenance, and the stairs were warped in places. Worse, there was no handrail, which had made it a dicey trip for a person with his hands clasped on top of his head, fingers entwined firmly.

Paradoxically, it was easier for the three whose hands had been taped together in front; when they stumbled, they could brace themselves against the wall without receiving a hard poke in the back with a pistol muzzle.

Once, as we descended single file down the dark basement stairs, I had intentionally slowed to test the Russian's response. The result had been a single vicious rap of a pistol barrel against my ear, hard enough to hurt. It earned me nothing for the pain; the Russian was too professional to remain close enough for me to risk turning and grappling for the weapon.

If there was a weak link here, it was not the man with the gun.

Santori, directly in front of me, had glanced back at the sound of the pistol striking my head. His expression was surprisingly calm, almost detached.

I envied him his apparent state of mind.

Neither Gil nor Chaz knew we were here; there could be no rescue, and the odds of turning the tables on my own were slim to none. Whatever else he was, Mikhail knew his business. Trying to rush him would only get me shot, immediately. Not that I would die alone: ultimately, I was convinced, Mikhail would ensure that no secrets left this place.

For that matter, I was not even certain who was friend and who was foe. I studied the figures below me on the stairs. The three—Evans, his wife and the artist, whose wrists were taped—were presumably allies, in varying degrees; but they would be of little help. Neither Tarinkoff nor Valova were bound, but neither of them had acted in a way to indicate they were not also hostages. Their attitudes were no indication, either. Tarinkoff was almost unnaturally poised and polite, while Petra Valova looked on the verge of raving hysterics.

As for Santori—why he was here, how he even knew to come here, mystified me.

Something hard jabbed near my kidney. "Do not daydream, my friend." Mikhail's voice said from close behind. "There is much still to do."

Below, Tarinkoff groped along the wall at the base of the stairs until he found the switch. The sudden glare from naked lightbulbs that dangled from rafters was momentarily dazzling.

"That's it, in the corner," said Peter Comstock, in a voice that sounded almost abashed. He muttered something I didn't catch, and the Travers woman made a reassuring sound.

"You didn't know, Peter," Marita Travers said. "How could you have?"

"I should have," he said, his expression that of a man who wished he could kick himself, hard. "I thought they were just good reproductions. For God's sake, I took a class in art history."

The wooden box was scarred and stained, and heavier than it appeared at first glance. Petra Valova had gone to it with a possessiveness that was greedy, so much so that it was startling in its intensity.

She pulled at the top, straining. The lid didn't move, held in place by substantial-looking screws.

"We must open it," Valova said urgently. There were no tools in evidence. She turned to the gunman. "You—do you have a knife?"

"Do I, indeed," Mikhail replied. "And unless you begin to show respect, I will use it in a way that will astound you."

With his free hand, the one not holding the pistol, he reached behind and under his jacket. The sheath was concealed along his belt where it crossed the small of his back. He tugged out the blade, and slid it along the concrete floor to where the curator knelt next to the shipping crate.

"I will want that back," he said to her. "It has great sentimental value."

Valova ignored him. The screws were tight, and the pointed tip of the knife was ill-suited as a screwdriver. Abandoning the effort, she instead focused on the joint where the lid fitted tight against the crate's side. With a determined scowl, she worked at spreading the two pieces with the blade. The tempered steel flexed, dangerously close to snapping.

But a gap opened, and Valova pried at the stubborn planking until she could slip her fingers under the wooden edge. Dropping the knife, she pulled hard with both hands. The wood squealed as it released its grip on the tightly fitted sides of the packing case.

Then, so gently as to be almost reverent, Petra Valova began to remove the canvases—each still on their fitted metal stretchers—from the slotted partitions inside. Delicately, she placed them against the wall near our small group.

I was close enough to hear what Mikhail spoke to Tarinkoff, in a voice not intended to carry.

"I repeat: it would be simpler—and far more certain—to burn them. Here, in this place," he said. *With all of these inconvenient witnesses,* his eyes added wordlessly to the cultural attaché. "I was given that

option, in my orders." His eyes still locked on Valova,
Tarinkoff shook his head once, a cautionary gesture.

"This isn't necessary, Anatoli," Ron Santori said, as
quietly as the other two had been. "My government
has no desire to see your country embarrassed over
anything as . . . *irrelevant* as this. We can help; you
have my word."

Tarinkoff regarded him gravely.

"What of—" An almost imperceptible movement of
his eyes included the captives.

"We can work it out," Santori insisted. "A few details, nothing more."

"*I* can work it out," Mikhail said to Tarinkoff. "This
man is merely a detail himself."

Before Tarinkoff could speak, I did.

"So," I said, and my voice was clear and conversational, "you've decided that burning the paintings is
necessary?"

Valova's head snapped up, and she looked at the
two Russian men with an expression that was of equal
parts horror, defiance and supplication.

"No!" she said. "Anatoli, do not allow this. You
cannot listen to . . . to this *criminal*!"

The cultural attaché studied Valova with a solemn
detachment that bordered on sadness, obviously
weighing the potential for disaster.

Tarinkoff sighed, and I could read his thoughts as
clearly as if he had been speaking. Mikhail was correct: one more fire would simplify many issues. But
any threat to the paintings would provoke a response
from Valova, one that certainly would require an executive decision Tarinkoff was loath to make. Even with
the option available, Tarinkoff would not relish explaining to his superiors why nine priceless masterpieces were destroyed rather than returned; he would
like even less the prospect of rationalizing why he had
to preside over the shooting of a senior curator of the
Pushkin Museum.

Tarinkoff shook his head firmly.

"If they can be returned to Mother Russia," he said, "we will all have fewer questions to answer, in the long run. It will be safe. They will travel under diplomatic seal."

Evans looked at Tarinkoff. "And our deal?" he asked, in the mildly disapproving voice of a man who had begun to realize he was not associating with honorable folk.

Tarinkoff shrugged, half apologetically. "It would seem," he said, with a slight inclination of his head toward Mikhail, "that a renegotiation is in order."

Evans made his voice harder. "Unless you release me—and return to the terms of our agreement—my associate has instructions to release information on . . . on all of this." Evans took a shuddering breath. "There is a full record of everything that has happened—how and why Levinstein acquired the paintings, our negotiations—even photos of the paintings."

I watched Evans' face closely; under the bravado was, justifiably enough, a growing awareness that had not yet spilled over into fear. But it was coming.

I began to move, as imperceptibly as possible, to the side. In my peripheral vision, I saw the artist's eyes flicker sideways at me; then Comstock, too, moved slightly, in a way that put himself between Mikhail's gun and Marita Travers.

The Russian's attention was focused, mockingly, on Evans.

"Ah, yes—your associate." Mikhail snapped the fingers of his free hand, and spoke as if discussing a forgotten detail. "A very accommodating man. In fact, I drove here in the vehicle he . . . loaned to me."

He addressed Tarinkoff.

"I would not concern myself excessively about any *evidence*"—his voice sneered at the word—"or about any associate. Before I left him, the gentleman—a Mr. Nederlander, I am pronouncing it correctly?—was quite eager to provide me all the information I needed. How he killed the thief Sonnenberg, and the girl at the insurance company. Even what he called 'torching' the Jew's house; an apt expression, to be sure. I'm sure that he was surprised to learn I had been there earlier, that very day."

He turned toward Evans. "Did you know your Mr. Nederlander lived quite well for a humble policeman? I was quite impressed when I went to his house—and obtained the steel box he kept in his attic. The one with the Polaroid pictures, yes?"

Mikhail stared at Talmadge Evans, enjoying the look in the older man's eyes.

Then he turned to Tarinkoff and spoke in a voice that was disinterested, almost bored. "There are no longer any photographs, or any other documents that involve this matter."

Santori's voice was no longer reasonable. "Listen to me, Tarinkoff. Evans is going to jail—maybe even to death row. You want things quiet, and your government wants back its paintings. Okay. But if there's a bloodbath in this room, all bets are off. Look, we can handle all of this."

"How are you going to handle *me*, Ron?" I asked, and Tarinkoff stared at me dolefully.

"You're easy to handle, Davey," Santori said tightly. "You want to protect Ellen, don't you?"

Now it was my turn to stare.

"Oh, she's cooperated nicely so far," Santori said. "She even agreed to take a little Florida vacation, all expenses paid by Operation Centurion—right after we had her play that little phone prank on you. But you don't want to get the government annoyed, Davey. Life can get very difficult, especially when it involves a woman like your ex-wife."

If ever I felt rage—hatred, even—it was at that moment. That may explain, at least partially, what happened next.

"The Donatello! What . . . what *is* this?" Valova's voice, coming from the circle of light behind the Rus-

sian cultural attaché where she had moved to better
study the Italian master's work, was shrill with outrage. She had turned the painting facedown, and was
staring at what seemed to be the reverse side of the
canvas.

Anatoli Tarinkoff turned to look over her shoulder.

"Ah. I recognize the distinctive style of Mr. Comstock," he said, and glanced at the artist. "When the
compulsion to create possesses you, sir, it must be
quite irresistible. You appear to simply seize any available surface for your work."

Comstock said nothing; it didn't appear that he
could. The artist was fixed on the painting Valova still
held, and his face looked aghast. But close beside him,
Marita Travers answered instead.

"For an art attaché," she said, "you clearly know
nothing about artists."

It was a mild rebuke compared to the expression
on Petra Valova's face.

"You . . . you ignorant Philistine!" she almost spat
at Peter Comstock. "You dare to . . . to pollute works
of genius!" She placed the painting on the table, reverently turning it so the original work was uppermost.
Only then did she return her fury to Comstock.

"How many?" she demanded. "What other priceless masterpieces have you vandalized?"

Marita answered for him. "Peter completed three
masterpieces here," she told the Russian curator, in a
deceptively sweet voice that did not match the steely
glint in her eyes. "The painting he's doing on the big
canvas is a . . . a work in progress."

"Not the *Cézanne*!" Petra Valova almost shrieked,
and her eyes swept madly through the pieces she had
leaned against the wall, as if she could somehow have
put it there without realizing. "What have you done
with it?"

"It's upstairs," said Marita, a scornful twist to her
lips, "you hysterical little harpy."

Mikhail spoke up, amusement in his voice.

"Did I not mention this?" he said. "I *am* sorry. This man scribbled all over a number of your precious paintings." He winked at Tarinkoff, but again addressed Valova. "I believe they are hopelessly ruined, are they not? This is but one more argument for simply piling all of them together and striking a match."

I spoke to Mikhail, though my words were meant for other ears. "You'd really destroy them?" I said. "Irreplaceable masterpieces, burned to ashes. Priceless artwork, going up in flames. That would certainly be something to watch."

"Yes," Mikhail said, "perhaps I shall have that opportunity. You, I fear, will not."

I shot a quick glance at the curator. With widening eyes, Valova had taken in the scene and understood: except as it served our own interests, the paintings were meaningless to anyone else here. They would be destroyed without compunction.

If she did not act first.

But Valova was both frozen and frantic, torn between her need to stand guard over the pieces down here and an overwhelming compulsion to verify the safety of the remaining painting. She looked past Tarinkoff at the gunman, who stood watching as if deeply amused by the spectacle he had helped orchestrate.

"You!" she ordered, a slightly unbalanced czarina imperiously commanding a lowly foot soldier. "Go up there and find it! Bring it here, immediately!"

Mikhail threw his head back and laughed.

It was not quite a mistake—more a lapse, or perhaps simply a momentary oversight born of overconfidence. Whatever it was, it was possibly the only one he might make. I did not wait for him to correct it.

The instant Mikhail's eyes left the little conclave, I dipped, low and fast, and threw myself in a sideways roll toward the wall. When I came up, it was with one of the paintings in a two-handed grip. It was the Michelangelo, and I held it in front of myself like a shield. I edged sideways, toward the light switch near the base of the stairs. It seemed a very long way away.

It was less a plan than a prayer.

Mikhail pulled a mock terrified face.

"And that does . . . *what*, my deluded little friend? Am I now to cringe in horror, to drop this"—he made a slight movement with his pistol, now aimed at the midpoint of the canvas—"and surrender to you?"

Mikhail smiled, and I saw his knees flex slightly as he settled into a shooter's stance. "I think not."

To the side, there was a sudden commotion and a woman screamed something in what might have been Russian. From the opposite side, in my peripheral vision I saw the figure of the artist begin to move toward Mikhail—too slowly, too awkwardly to cover the distance in time.

The gunman seemed not to have heard or seen anything. His attention was elsewhere, as was that of his target.

Even at that distance, I could see his fingertip begin to flatten against the trigger, and involuntarily I tensed against the bullet's impact.

Outside, Charlie Herndon listened to his joints pop as he squatted behind a thick bush. He cursed, softly but with a heartfelt intensity.

The thin foliage offered no protection as such; the Kevlar vest he had taken from his car's trunk was designed for that. When the vests had been issued, the FBI quartermaster—a former Marine gunnery sergeant—had assured Herndon that it would stop a handgun bullet. "Or at least," the quartermaster had said, straightfaced, "slow it down enough so it don't go through and ruin the other side, too."

Around him, the sights and sounds of a suburban night added a surreal touch to the situation. The vibrato night songs of a million crickets reverberated through the air. Herndon could see the flitting specks of nocturnal insects in their ceaseless orbits around the streetlamp a dozen yards away. Farther down the street, only an upper window—probably a bedroom, the FBI agent guessed—glowed in an otherwise darkened house. Even here, despite what he suspected was under way inside the Travers residence, the appearance was one of domestic normalcy. The vehicles, parked in the circular drive in neat alignment with the curbing, only added to the air of genteel prosperity. Surely, it all seemed to insist, nothing untoward could happen here.

Herndon twisted his wrist, trying to read the luminous dial of his watch.

"It's ten thirty-eight," Chaz Trombetta said, in a low voice. He had arrived minutes before, materializing from the shadows so quietly that he had momentarily startled the FBI man. In his hand was the heavy .45 Army Colt nobody could convince Chaz was antique.

Gil Cieloczki too knelt alongside, not knowing exactly why he had come, but unwilling to be left out of the endgame that appeared so close. All three men stared at the Travers mansion, each of them wondering what to do next.

It had been almost fifteen minutes since they had seen any movement against the backlighted curtains of the downstairs windows. The FBI dispatcher had patched Herndon's cell phone through to the Hostage Rescue Team's helicopter.

Even now, they were still at least five minutes away.

The HRT team leader confirmed what a dour Herndon had already guessed: even when they deployed, it would take at least another five minutes before they would all be in position to do anything useful. So Herndon, Gil and Trombetta had crept noiselessly over the manicured lawn and past carefully clipped ornamental shrubbery. The front door of the house was only a few yards away.

They said to stand by, Herndon grumbled to himself

with ill humor. *So I'm goddam standing by, and some mutt inside there is the one who's really running the play.*

The thought made him bristle anew. For the third time in as many minutes, he checked the action of his side arm, and waited.

Through the cellular phone he held shoulder to ear, he had listened to the terse, cryptic reports as other elements of the FBI mobilized. Herndon had briefed his SAC on the situation, then asked for and received confirmation of his status as senior agent at the scene.

Soon there would be more than a dozen men, armed with automatic weapons and dressed in black jumpsuits, surrounding the house. They would await only the word to begin an assault. Presumably, Herndon would give that word—though at this moment he had not the slightest idea what course of action was possible, let alone advisable. And, he reminded himself, right now his strike force consisted of a possibly corrupt cop, a fireman—and one pissed-off special agent less than two years from retirement.

Still, he mused irritably, *it is good to be in charge.*

From somewhere deep inside the house, he heard a noise. It sounded like a single note struck from a muffled bass drum.

"Gunshot!" Trombetta hissed near his ear.

"Oh, shit," Herndon said, and ordered his stiffened knees to push him upright as he spoke into the phone. "Team Leader, this is Herndon. We have shots fired in the house. Repeat, there's a shooter inside. We're going in." Without waiting for a response, he stuffed the cell phone deep in his side pocket.

He started forward. "Cieloczki, stay here. Trombetta, you're watching my back," he growled, without turning his head. Chaz Trombetta, grateful but determined not to show it, just nodded grimly. He moved forward, a few steps behind the FBI man.

Gil Cieloczki watched them edge, quickly but cautiously, toward the door. He definitely did not want

to follow them; he was a firefighter, not a cop. He had
no weapons. There were any number of very good
reasons to stay where he was, not the least of which
was Herndon's direct order.

Then the other two men were on the entryway. Gil
watched Herndon rise and turn his back to the door.
His leg swung forward, and then smashed back. The
powerful mule kick shattered the doorjamb, and the
two officers pushed past, guns drawn.

Gil waited another moment. Then, muttering something that might have been either a curse or a prayer,
he rose from the lawn and followed.

It had all happened in an instant; the sound of his
single shot still echoed from the concrete walls. Petra
Natalia Valova had pushed hard past Tarinkoff and
lurched forward, her hands outstretched. *"Nyet, piris-
tán'!"* she screamed, just as the pistol fired.

And then she was flailing madly at her countryman,
a wordless wail on her lips.

"Let go, you insane cow!" Mikhail shouted—for
reasons he himself probably did not understand, in
English.

The woman fought like a wildcat, digging her fingernails into the wrist just above Mikhail's gun hand
and hanging on with both hands. She had slapped
Mikhail's pistol at the instant of its discharge, and then
it was if the demons of hell had been loosed on him.

Mikhail could not have known if his shot had struck
the painting—which was, to the Russian, merely old
paint on older cloth. More urgently, he did not know
if he had shot the lunatic who had stupidly hidden
behind it. He did not know what the others in the
room were doing, or were about to do.

All he did know was that he must remove this
shrieking madwoman from his arm.

The two figures lurched across the concrete floor,
crashing against one of the naked lightbulbs that hung
from the raftered ceiling. The light swung wildly, cre-

ating moving shadows that only added to the chaotic
confusion of the melée. Mikhail was the stronger, but
Valova's strength was fueled by a raging desperation.
She clung, limpetlike, to her adversary's gun arm.

Mikhail thrashed sideways, the movement whipping
the pistol barrel against Valova's temple. The impact
unlocked her grip slightly, enough for him to peel one
of her hands from his wrist. He was not gentle; with
an audible crack, one of the woman's fingers broke
under his grip. A sudden hard jerk freed the hand that
held his gun.

And then I crashed heavily into the pair of grappling Russians, and the force of my impact sent the
three of us scuttling across the concrete floor. As one,
we careened off a wall and spun back into the middle
of the room. I struggled to reach Mikhail's gun hand,
as the Russian struck the screaming woman with a
tight fist.

As Petra Valova was knocked free of the scrum,
Mikhail twisted the pistol toward me.

But my hand chopped hard at his arm, striking the
knot of muscle alongside his elbow. As the brachial
nerve spasmed, Mikhail's fingers opened and his gun
fell away. He half turned to retrieve it, and I lunged
onto his back. My weight dragged both of us to the
floor, the Russian on the bottom facedown.

I moved up into the chokehold, elbows gripped in
the opposing hands, clamping against the sides of Mikhail's neck. In response, the Russian dropped his chin
into his chest, using his jaw to partially block the pressure on his carotid arteries.

It was not enough. He bucked under me with the
panic of a man feeling his consciousness begin to slip,
and I knew that white-hot shooting stars were swim-
ming madly on the fringes of his vision. He had only
seconds before he would pass out.

I clung to his neck like a murderous monkey.

But with an urgent strength fueled by his own desperation, Mikhail pushed hard against the floor until

his arms levered his torso upright. From close behind, I could feel his labored breathing rasp against my ear.

With a great effort, Mikhail smashed his head back into my face, hard—once, then again. The Russian's head smashed solidly into my cheekbone, and the second blow took me alongside my jaw. The double impact sent twin thunderbolts of pain flashing across my vision. I felt the gunman slip from my grasp, and I tumbled bonelessly to the cool concrete. Above, the naked ceiling rafters spun sickeningly in and out of focus.

Mikhail came to his feet, gasping, looking right and left for his pistol.

During the few seconds it took for my vision to clear, as if from a distance, I heard the voice speak— a soft undertone, the words in an unaccented English.

"Is this what you need?"

When I could finally push my upper body from the floor, the gun was in Anatoli Tarinkoff's hand—held loosely, but not inexpertly. As Mikhail held his own hand out for the weapon, I could see that he was breathing hard. But now it was not only from his exertion. His features were those of a man trying hard to ignore the alarm that his instincts were suddenly, urgently sounding.

The light glared from above and behind them, and the two figures were almost silhouettes against it. I couldn't be certain, but I thought I could see the consulate official's lips moving. Mikhail did not respond; he just stared at his countryman, standing as still as death.

Upstairs, there was the sudden crash of glass and splintering wood. Then the sound of rushing men, moving room to room and shouting in an unmistakable drill, filled the air. Mikhail's head snapped in the direction of the stairwell door.

When he turned back, Tarinkoff's grip on his gun was no longer casual.

"Anatoli." It was Ron Santori's voice, and it came

from where the agent had flattened himself near the heavy packing crate. He slowly rose to his feet, and an unspoken communication seemed to pass between him and the art attaché.

"I am sorry, my friend," I heard Tarinkoff say with a philosophical shrug. "But we must salvage what we can. After all, I have diplomatic immunity."

He turned toward Mikhail, a movement not unlike that of a serpent coiling.

"Sadly, you do not."

And then Tarinkoff shot Mikhail once, in the forehead.

A mist of blood and pulverized bone jetted from the back of the Russian's head, iridescent in the harsh backlighting. He stood motionless for a heartbeat, and then collapsed into himself. The body that had been Mikhail twitched furiously for a moment, its heels bouncing on the concrete floor, and then was still.

The echo of the shot was still ringing in the room when Charlie Herndon kicked through the door. He was flanked by Chaz Trombetta, and both were training their weapons into the room. Behind them, I recognized Gil Cieloczki, his face tense with the moment.

Anatoli Tarinkoff raised both his arms high, the pistol dangling from one finger, hanging by its trigger guard. His face bore a casual welcoming smile that was inappropriate to the event.

"Please do not shoot," he said amiably. "There is no further danger here."

Nearby, Petra Valova half knelt before the paintings she had propped against the wall. She was staring at some indeterminate point in the distance, her eyes wild in a face battered bloody and her arms spread wide. One of her fingers dangled at an impossible angle, but she did not appear to notice her pain.

Instead, she looked like a mother desperately trying to shield her brood against a threat still unaddressed—one that only she could fully comprehend.

Then I heard a sound that must have been there all

the time. It was a woman calling for help, loudly but not hysterically. Under that sound was another, that of a man groaning in pain through clenched teeth.

On the floor, Peter Comstock was being rocked side to side by Marita Travers. Her hands, still bound with the tape, were smeared with something dark. I could barely make out the pool of blood spreading on the floor beneath them.

With the instincts of a trained paramedic, Gil pushed past Chaz and Herndon and knelt beside the two civilians. He disentangled the woman's arms and gently lowered the man to the concrete floor. An arc of black blood pulsed from a wound, rough-edged and large, in the man's temple.

As Gil began to work, his face was grim.

"Get an ambulance here, quick," Gil said, and Herndon spoke into his cellular phone in a voice low and urgent.

I sat on the floor, still half-dazed and unable to move forward. Now I knew, with a terrible certainty, where Mikhail's final bullet had gone.

April 25

Chapter 46

"So that's what this whole thing was about?" Mel Bird asked, incredulous. "A damn publicity stunt?"

He sat in a wheelchair near the edge of Terry Posson's hospital bed; his shoulder was encased in a fiberglass cast that elevated his arm to a right angle from his body. For herself, Terry had raised the bed to a half-propped position. She sat clear-eyed and upright, the thick hospital dressings looking like a lopsided gauze turban on her head. I stood with a shoulder against the wall, leaving Charlie Herndon to shift uncomfortably in the remaining chair, undersized for his bulk.

"In part," I answered. "Or you could call it an attempt to resolve a fifty-year-old crime. Levinstein wanted to put the Russians in the spotlight, with the whole world watching."

"I still don't get it," Bird said. "Okay, these were valuable paintings. But you said the Russians stole what, thousands of paintings? Millions of 'em?" He shook his head stubbornly. "They were sweating a little bad *press*, for God's sake? Why so much trouble to get back *nine* of 'em?"

"Money, pure and simple," Herndon said. He fished in his side pocket, and pulled out a page torn from a newspaper. As he passed it to Bird, I could read the headline:

RUSSIA TERMS NEW IMF LOAN ESSENTIAL; SAYS DELAY COULD IMPERIL ECONOMIC STABILITY.

"Basically, Levinstein's plan was to focus world attention on all the artwork the Russians had looted after World War II—that is, art stolen by the Nazis from Holocaust victims," Herndon said. "In '98, the Russians pledged to give it all back. But over the years they kept finding reasons to drag their feet. This left Stan Levinstein seriously pissed. The Russians claimed they didn't know what they had, or what paintings belonged to dead Jews? Okay, fine—he'd show the world the bastards weren't even trying.

"Stanley got in touch with his Mafiya contacts, outlined what he was looking for: world-famous pieces known to have been stolen from Jews who went to the death camps, specified by name and artist. Pieces the Russians had pledged to return. At first, it had to look like a straightforward snatch job, probably using some inside help. They round up the usual suspects, catch one of the people Levinstein used, sweat him big-time. Of course, the guy talks—gives them an American 'art collector' named Stan Levinstein."

"When they run Levinstein's name through their computers, all kinds of alarm bells go off," Herndon said. "Nine paintings—world-famous works that most people thought, or at least had been willing to believe, had been destroyed—are stolen *to order*. By a guy their files describe as a Jewish activist, with an ax to grind and the know-how to grind it in a very creative, very public way. Imagine a press conference where Levinstein unveils all nine pieces and tells the world how he got them."

In his voice was grudging admiration.

"Fast-forward to early this year," Herndon said. "Just when they need another massive infusion of cash, the Russian government finds out what Levinstein was doing. They were looking at a public relations disaster. So they tried to play it cagey."

Bird scanned the clipping he still held, and looked at Herndon. "No paintings, no loans? That was it?"

"More like 'no credibility, no credit,' " Herndon replied. "That's why they told Mikhail the paintings were expendable. Valuable as they were, they were nothing compared to the billions that were at stake. The last thing they could afford was to be caught in a lie—a big lie, on a subject that engendered strong emotions."

"So Levinstein had the leverage he needed," Terry said.

"Yeah, but Stanley had no desire to spend the next twenty years in federal prison for smuggling and art theft," Herndon said. "So he contacted a man he knew as a public official and a neighbor: Talmadge Evans, who brought in Nederlander. Stanley thought he was protecting himself—after all, he never intended to keep the paintings. When he laid it all out for those two, he didn't know he was giving them the chance of a lifetime."

"And it came along right when they needed it," I said. "Santori's Operation Centurion was closing in on them. Suddenly they're handed a multimillion dollar retirement opportunity—one that, if they played it right, looked untraceable."

"Until the Russians showed up, looking for the stuff," Gil said. "Must have been a shock for Evans to get a call from the Russian consulate, asking about the missing artwork."

"Tarinkoff called the bastard?" Mel's voice was frankly disbelieving. "How'd you get that?"

"Before we left the Travers place, the FBI found an excuse to confiscate Tarinkoff's cellular phone," I said. "Evans' office number was in the speed-dial memory. It was listed under the name 'R. Hood'—

Tarinkoff's idea of a joke, I guess. When we looked at the phone records, we found a half dozen calls to Evans' office since early March."

"The slick bastard says he was inquiring about a 'rumor' of missing artwork," Gil said. "A logical question from a cultural attaché, and it didn't directly implicate him. But Tarinkoff sent a strong signal that he, on behalf of his government, was ready to make a deal for the artwork. Evans considered the opportunity too good to pass up. It meant there was suddenly an immediate market for the paintings—the payoff could come in days, weeks at the most, instead of having to wait years."

"It was a smart play for Tarinkoff," I said. "Why not work all the angles? They already had the local Mafiya hoods out looking."

"As well as their psycho Mikhail," Terry said. "They had a lot of people trying to get their paintings back."

Herndon nodded. "Or to make sure they were destroyed. Valova came to the United States to keep Mikhail from doing exactly that. She was lucky; Levinstein died before Mikhail could make him talk. But the Russian kept looking. When the house burned down later the same day, Mikhail knew there had to be another person involved. So he started shadowing the investigation."

"Mikhail followed me back from Stateville Penitentiary on at least one occasion," I said, and shook my head ruefully. "I thought it was Santori's people, or somebody Nederlander had sent."

"Actually, destroying the paintings would have been the easiest solution, and maybe the smartest one," Charlie Herndon said. "She took a big risk coming over here to try to recover the paintings and get them back to Russia."

"She took a bigger risk at the Travers house," Gil observed. "Going after a psychopath with a gun. Even if he was *her* psycho, more or less."

"*She* took a risk?" Bird said, sarcastically. He shot a thumb in my direction. "How about this idiot?" He turned to me. "Something give you the idea that painting was bulletproof?"

It was my turn to look abashed.

"I just took the chance," I said. "Valova had worked herself into a frenzy. Maybe I got caught up in all the excitement, too. I would have looked pretty foolish if Ms. Valova hadn't cracked."

"Like a dead fool," Posson said, "with pieces of a multimillion-dollar painting stuck all over his body."

"I was lucky," I admitted, "but there was a lot of luck in all this, good and bad. Nederlander panicked and pulled the plug on the whole insurance scam. That forced all the dirty cops in the ring to scurry around for new income sources. Plus it forced Nederlander— as well as Evans, as it turned out—to look for a big score to retire on."

"Enter Levinstein," Bird said, "and the rest is history."

I grinned widely. "Or it will be. Len Washburn's been laughing like a bastard all day. He's promised his publisher a hell of a book out of this. Kellogg is filling him in on Sam Lichtman's deathbed statement, and providing documentation that backs it up. That should light a fire under Ron Santori's career, when the book comes out."

"Until then, Ronnie should be a happy man," Herndon said. "He's got a whole platoon of Justice Department lawyers busy. Evans is trying to make a deal; he'd like to avoid a potential death penalty. He's offering to give up a whole raft of your aldermen, building inspectors, contractors—there's even a mob tie-in he's dangling in front of the legal boys. They'll be writing up charges until next Christmas. And he's got a ton of crooked cops to cook for dessert."

"I hear the state police is patrolling Lake Tower," Mel Bird said.

Gil nodded. "Should be a lot of vacancies on the

police force when you two get out. Including on the detective division."

"What about Trombetta?" Bird asked me.

Herndon answered first. "He's down as a confidential informant—that's a step up the immunity ladder from just being a 'cooperating witness,'" the FBI agent said gruffly. "I don't know if he'll save his shield. But I don't think he's going to jail, if that's what you mean. Hell, if that bastard Tarinkoff gets a free ride, Trombetta probably deserves one, too."

"Story in the paper today said he was a hero," Bird remarked sarcastically. "Tarinkoff, I mean. They said he grabbed the gun and saved Davey's ass. But how come they didn't have anything about gazillions' worth of stolen paintings?"

"Because they didn't know," I said quietly.

"Decision from Washington," Herndon said, and his voice was curiously flat. "They decided it would be inadvisable, particularly at a time when—and I quote—'the Russian government is moving toward an equitable resolution of the trophy art issue.' Translated, Washington and Moscow made a deal."

"All that happened, they still don't have to give it all back?" Bird was incredulous. "Or even admit they have it hidden away?"

Herndon shrugged, and I looked away.

"But the pieces Levinstein got out of Russia." Terry paused and looked around the group. "What happens to those paintings now?"

All eyes turned to Herndon. The FBI agent's oversized shoulders rose in a shrug.

"That's a damn fine question," he said, in his deep voice. "You see, there's been a kind of . . . complication come up."

Chapter 47

"So who do *you* think the paintings belong to?" asked Marita Travers, her voice icy. "I assume there's some question, since you say they have not been turned over to the Russians yet."

I looked out the window, marveling at the view that was being wasted on the majority of us locked inside an FBI conference room.

Outside, it was a beautiful late April day a few minutes before noon. I could see a slice of Lake Michigan framed by the skyscrapers. A sailboat, made tiny by the distance, wove through the sparkling waters on the gulled-out wings of its sails; in aspect, it appeared like a bird sculling through a field afire.

I had gained a new appreciation for art, and for the passions it engendered.

Beside Marita sat Peter Comstock, his head swathed in a thick gauze turban that covered the groove across his forehead. The bullet had skimmed along the bone of his skull, nicking the temporal artery; an eighth of an inch difference in trajectory would have left the world one abstractionist poorer.

"That is, in a legal sense, an interesting question of international law."

The speaker was one of a well-dressed trio, all men, who sat together on the long side of the table. They were, of course, lawyers—one each representing the

Justice Department, the Treasury Department and the
State Department.

Justice continued. "The paintings in question were
stolen by the Nazis, then by the Russians, then by
this Mr. Levinstein, and finally, Ms. Travers, by your
husband and his police chief. I assume there are heirs
of the original owners somewhere. And of course, the
Russian government also wants them back."

He shook his head in what I was certain was not
sincere sorrow; for any lawyer, such a tangled web
of potential litigation was tantamount to lifetime job
security. "I suspect there will be no shortage of claims
for the courts to decide on the legal issues involved."

"With all due respect," a new voice said, "all this
is now much bigger than any questions of legality."

The speaker was a middle-aged woman who sat between Comstock and Marita Travers. She was past
fashionably thin, dressed in a tailored Gucci suit of
pearl gray; her eyes burned, twin embers behind tor-
toiseshell frames.

"Monica Troutman," she said, rising to her full five
feet of height. "Ms. Travers has retained my firm to
deal with the . . . ah, communications-related aspects
of this issue."

Santori groaned softly. "Public relations," he said,
to nobody in particular.

Troutman shrugged good-naturedly. "In the larger
sense, who *really* owns these works?" she asked theatrically. "Because of what Mr. Comstock has done, at
this moment that is a much more complicated question. As rare and unique as they previously were, they
have now become something much different. They
have changed, forever."

"Not necessarily," Treasury noted drily. "There are
restoration experts who can remove Mr. Comstock's
work without damaging the oils on the good side."

Marita Travers looked horrified, then exasperated.
"The *good* side? You still don't understand, you ba-
boon. There are—"

"Allow me, Marita."

Monica Troutman spoke, her voice calm and patient.

"This morning, gentlemen, I received a call from the Museum of Modern Art in New York. They assured me that they were prepared to do whatever is necessary—court orders, legal action, *anything*—to preserve what their staff of curators is terming 'a uniquely modern, authentic artistic vision!' Their legal counsel is already preparing the papers to block any attempt to remove or otherwise damage what they are calling '*the* definitive Peter Comstock.' "

She smiled, innocent as a hired assassin.

"Not five minutes later, I received a similar call from the Museum of Contemporary Art here in Chicago. They also swear their unyielding support—particularly since, according to the newspapers, the Art Institute here appears to be on the other side of the fence. The two institutions are notorious archrivals, it seems."

Behind his large hand, Herndon stifled a very unprofessional grin.

"Since that hour, more than a dozen major museums—here and overseas—have publicly registered either fervent support or furious outrage. Mr. Comstock is being seen as either a vandal, or as the most enlightened artistic talent to emerge in decades. The legitimacy of his . . . uh, most *recent* works is being debated in every corner of the art world!"

Peter Comstock winked at the lawyers, a serene smile on his face.

"Good God!" State exclaimed. He turned to Herndon. "You're the art expert here. Is what this man did 'art?' "

Herndon sobered, fixed him with a withering stare. "*You* try to define art. Damned if I can."

"What Mr. Comstock has done is to invent a whole new artistic concept," Troutman insisted. "He has created a work of genius—an expression that incorporates as part of its wholeness, even as part of its very being . . . *another* masterpiece! This unique work of his cannot exist without the underlying work; at the same time, it is a master work that is independent of the older vision! My God—remove his work? You might as well suggest they sandblast the Sistine Chapel!"

Treasury rolled his eyes, and looked at his companions. "This is beyond belief!"

The publicity agent grinned hugely, and began pacing. "What any of us might believe is irrelevant, sir. The whole art world is taking up sides on the issue—and they're all talking about Peter Comstock!"

The government lawyers looked at each other, then at Ron Santori.

"Okay," Santori said, "what do you want? If we can all agree to keep this out of the public eye—"

I spoke for the first time. "That might be a little difficult. You should turn on the television. Try the noon news, channel nine. I'm told it's supposed to be the lead item."

He frowned at me for a long moment. Then Ron Santori fumbled with the unfamiliar remote control until he found the correct button.

The large screen flared into life, the volume painfully loud.

"—millions in art stolen from Jews, sir," an amplified female voice blasted from the hidden speakers. "What is the response of the Russian government to accusations that—"

Santori found the mute button.

On the screen of the suddenly silent television, Anatoli Tarinkoff's lips still moved. His face appeared serious, earnest, and completely without guile. The shot widened to include an attractive young woman, pointing a microphone under the cultural attaché's lips as if it were a weapon. Her face bore the kind of studious impartiality that every television viewer knows is meant to signal extreme skepticism.

As we watched, the image on the screen abruptly jumped to an outside crowd scene, with many of the participants angrily waving placards. Prominent among the crowd was the figure of Rabbi Bernard Jerome, who was windmilling his arms as he led the crowd's chant.

Then the picture cut to a closeup of one of the signs. In large, bright red handlettering it read: RUSSIA: RETURN OUR STOLEN ART HERITAGE.

Santori pressed something on the remote, and the screen went blank.

"Why, Davey?" Santori asked, not looking at me. "I know you turned the Cézanne over to this Jerome person—the rabbi from Levinstein's synagogue. I guess you got Trombetta to smuggle it out of the Travers' house before the cavalry arrived. But to go public? Do you know the extent of things you've fucked up?"

"What do you care, Ronnie?" I countered. "Operation Centurion is a success. The artwork issue makes your case easy. There's no need to fuzzy up the motives behind all the murders; it's a straight line from Evans and Nederlander to the Levinstein killings, the Hunt murder, and everything else."

Santori looked at Herndon, who sat—massive—near the head of the conference table, then back at the ceiling.

"What could any of you possibly gain from creating an international incident?" His smile was thin and bitter. "Aside from the petty personal satisfaction of making me look like an idiot, I mean."

"You sell yourself short, Ron," I said. "That kind of satisfaction isn't petty. Not to me."

"You've opened up Pandora's box, a . . . a shitstorm," the lawyer from State breathed, appalled. "The Russians, the Secretary of State—my God, even the President. *Everybody* is going to be furious. Do you know what we could have squeezed out of the Russians? Trade agreements, or arms control?"

"And the artwork would still be locked up in a Russian monastery," I said, "probably forever."

Santori twisted his lips in scorn. "Don't try to tell me you give a damn about that. You wanted to nail Nederlander. You wanted to let everybody know you were Officer Davey, the world's most honest cop."

He slumped, his chin in his hand. "Well, I guess you finally made up for your old man's reputation. Congratulations. I hope it was worth what happens now."

I looked out the window again.

"It is," I said.

But not even I could tell if I was speaking the truth.

"So in the end, I guess Levinstein got what he wanted," Herndon said, and I could swear he sounded pleased. "About the Holocaust art, that is. If anything is going to break the Russians loose, this is it. The newspapers will be screaming about the artwork the Russians are hiding, and the entire world will call for them to return it to the rightful owners. The United Nations, the IMF—probably even the Pope."

"The Pope? Small potatoes," Troutman interjected, and there was no mistaking the pleasure in her voice, at least. "I took a meeting with a TV producer this morning. Oprah's doing a show on us, and she's got ten *times* more clout than the Pope."

She went on tiptoes and pecked my cheek. "Thanks for putting me on to this. Gotta get over to the *Trib*. They're waiting for the rest of the story." She joined the sidewalk's hurrying throng, heading north.

At the curb, I watched Comstock and Marita flag a taxi, off to celebrate in a manner befitting the triumph of art over tyranny, or at least over expediency.

And then we were alone, Herndon and I, standing in the plaza outside the Federal Building; the garish orange girders of *Flamingo* arched above our heads.

"Ronnie can carry a grudge," Herndon warned. "Don't count on him keeping his promises."

I reached into my pocket and produced the compact tape recorder that Herndon had found under Santori's car seat and returned to me the night before. I had replaced the cassette it contained with a fresh one before the meeting upstairs had begun.

Now I pressed PLAY, and Ron Santori's recorded voice spoke: ". . . old man's reputation. Congratulations. I hope it was worth what happens now."

I clicked it off and looked into Herndon's suddenly grinning face.

"Insurance," I said. "Should give Len Washburn's book a nice ending, don't you think?"

"Not to mention Ron Santori's career," Charlie Herndon said.

I swung by the church, hoping to talk to Father Frank. But the church was empty, and no one answered when I knocked at the rectory door.

I spent the rest of the day at Wrigley Field, where the home team pulled off one of its rare, improbable victories in a game where the smart money had said the underdogs had not had a prayer.

Like the strangers who sat around me, I cheered for the Cubs loudly. It was still early in the season, but who knew? The kids might just have a chance.

"A Louisiana saga propelled by dark deeds
and the politics of greed...stylishly written...
shrewdly plotted." —*Los Angeles Times*

"Dark and sometimes bitterly funny."
—*Chicago Tribune*

COLD STEEL RAIN

KENNETH ABEL

Danny Chaisson resigned from his job as assistant
district attorney three years ago to work as a bagman
for New Orleans political boss and state senator
Jimmy Boudrieux. Danny is resigned to his fate—his
old man worked for Boudrieux, too—but then he
inadvertently witnesses the murder of a gun runner by
Boudrieux's henchmen. Soon, Danny's running for
his own life...

0-451-20545-6

To Order Call: 1-800-788-6262